GW00359543

Three-times Golden Heart® learned to pack her suitcase to read. Born to a military fa United States, Puerto Rico, addition to travelling, Tina loves to cuddle with her pug, Alex, spend time with her family, and hit the trails on her horse. Learn more about Tina from her website, or 'friend' her on Facebook.

Once making her home in sunny Brazil, **Luana DaRosa** has since lived on three different continents—though her favourite romantic locations remain the tropical places of Latin America. When she's not typing away at her latest romance novel, or reading about love, Luana is either crocheting, buying yarn she doesn't need, or chasing her bunnies around the house. She lives with her partner in a cosy town in the south of England. Find her on Twitter under the handle @LuDaRosaBooks.

ER DOC'S MIRACLE TRIPLETS

TINA BECKETT

SURGEON'S BROODING BRAZILIAN RIVAL

LUANA DaROSA

MILLS & BOON

First published in Great Britain 2024
by Mills & Boon, an imprint of HarperCollins*Publishers* Ltd,
1 London Bridge Street, London, SE1 9GF

www.harpercollins.co.uk

HarperCollins*Publishers* Macken House, 39/40 Mayor Street Upper,
Dublin 1, D01 C9W8, Ireland

ER Doc's Miracle Triplets © 2024 Harlequin Enterprises ULC

Surgeon's Brooding Brazilian Rival © 2024 Harlequin Enterprises ULC

Special thanks and acknowledgement are given to
Tina Beckett and Luana DaRosa for their contributions
to the Buenos Aires Docs miniseries.

ISBN: 978-0-263-32161-6

06/24

This book contains FSC™ certified paper
and other controlled sources to ensure responsible forest management.

For more information visit www.harpercollins.co.uk/green.

Printed and Bound in the UK using 100% Renewable Electricity
at CPI Group (UK) Ltd, Croydon, CR0 4YY

ER DOC'S
MIRACLE TRIPLETS

TINA BECKETT

MILLS & BOON

To my wonderful family!

PROLOGUE

"BELLA...*QUERIDA*. I'M so sorry, but I just can't...with any of it. We agreed this would be the last time." Sebastián held a sheaf of papers in his hand.

She bowed her head and stared at the dining room table, willing herself not to cry over her latest loss. *Their* latest loss. She knew they'd agreed. Six weeks had passed since their latest attempt at IVF had ended with her spotting again. It had followed the same pattern for the last couple of years: implanting the embryos only to start bleeding a week or two later and hear she'd lost them. Their doctor had even tried a new regimen of hormones, hoping that she would be able to retain the pregnancy this time.

It was obvious she hadn't. Again. Even though she'd held on to it for weeks longer this time.

Seb wasn't telling her anything she didn't already know. And although he hadn't been cruel and mentioned that they'd both agreed that the time before this one would be the last attempt, he might as well have. Because today he seemed different. Harder, somehow. As if he'd made a decision and was walling himself off from what had happened…walling himself off from *her*. Brick by brick. Layer by layer.

"But…" She forced her teeth to bite down after that single word came out, refusing to beg him for one more attempt.

As if he knew the words were swirling in her brain, even if her lips weren't uttering them, Seb slowly shook his head, a pained tightening of his mouth the only indication of how difficult the gesture was.

She stared down at her hands, knowing he was right. But after all this time…after all of those tries, how could he just…give up?

The fact that he hadn't mentioned adoption or surrogacy like he had after the last failed treatment was telling. Her head came up to look at his face. The gorgeous face of the man she'd loved. The man she'd once burned for with the fire of a thousand *estrellas*.

Once?

No. She still loved him. Desperately. But when was the last time they'd made love deep into the night? The last time she'd reached for him without the fear of jarring something loose in her womb? Everything had become so timid and fearful and…careful. Her glance shifted back to the papers in his hands and her breath hissed out.

Divorce? Oh, *Dios*, no! She swallowed hard.

"W-what are those?"

He didn't even have to ask what she was talking about. "I've accepted a temporary assignment with Médecins sans Frontières." A muscle worked in his cheek. "You need some space, Bella. *We* need some space."

Part of her wanted to sag in relief that he didn't want to end things completely. But wasn't this the same thing? A trial run to see how he would fare without her and her relentless attempts to carry a child? He was probably wildly relieved to get away from her.

Unlike her, who needed him on so many levels. Especially right now. She wanted to shout at him that he needed to stay, needed to at least try to work things out. But she wondered if there was even anything left to work on. So she didn't say any of that. Instead, she simply asked, "When do you leave?"

"Next week."

Next week. So he'd already applied for this position some time ago. How long did it take to be accepted? Had he been busy filling out forms even as they'd implanted the embryos? The thought filled her heart with anger, and bile swept up her throat, leaving an awful taste in her mouth.

"How long will you be gone?"

Did she really want to know?

"I'm contracted for eight weeks in Angola. But it depends on the conditions I find when I arrive."

In other words, he might stay even longer. Her anger went up a notch.

Let him go. He'd already decided all of this without consulting her. Without even asking her if she wanted to go with him. In the back of her mind there was a little nudge. He *had* asked her. A few years ago, when they were still making love with a fervor that left her breathless. When trying to have a baby had actually been filled with adventure and lots of steamy experimentation. Before the desperation had set in. Before they'd turned to fertility specialists and all that it entailed. Yes, he'd asked her about Doctors without Borders, but she'd been too excited at the possibility of being a mom, so she told him to ask her again in a year or two. He never had.

And he evidently wasn't going to.

She hardened her heart against the hurt, against the feelings of abandonment. So yes, let him go. She didn't even ask him where in Angola he was headed. Maybe the separation would reset her system and she'd be able to let go of the dream of having his child once and for all. At forty-one, and after ten years of trying to beat the odds, she knew those odds were now stacked higher than ever against them. And if he decided he wanted a divorce? She wouldn't fight him. She was too tired to. Instead, she'd simply move on with her life and let her career be enough.

So she said all she could say right now. "Okay. If that's what you want."

She didn't promise she'd be here when he got back, and he didn't ask. While Seb was gone, she had a lot of thinking to do. About what she wanted to do with her life, and if he'd even fit into it after this.

Once that decision was made, there'd be no going back.

So she wished him well and headed on to work, leaving him to pack or do whatever else he needed to do. And Bella would do whatever it was that she needed to do and hope to God that she could figure out what that something was.

And soon.

CHAPTER ONE

AN AMBULANCE SCREECHED to a halt in front of Hospital General de Buenos Aires. It looked like he'd returned to Argentina and the hospital at just the right time, since there were two more parked in the huge entrance of the emergency department. The heat of summer seemed to envelop Sebastián Lopez in a thick layer that made it hard to breathe. Seb stepped up to the open ambulance to see if he could help, only to be met by Gabriel Romero, who was already leaping down and shouting orders to whoever else was inside the vehicle. "Be careful with that neck brace."

Seb peered inside and could only see yellow feathers everywhere. What the hell? It looked like some huge bird had exploded inside the roomy interior of the truck. Then he realized it was a costume. "What have you got?"

Gabriel glanced over and his eyes widened, then the paramedic clapped Seb on the back. "Well, well, well, welcome back, *porteño!* Or do you not claim Buenos Aires as your home anymore?"

Porteño was the word Argentines used when referring to people who were from the country's capital.

"Very funny." He gave his friend a mock scowl. "I take it your patient has been practicing with one of the Carnival troupes?"

"Yep. And he took one too many steps and fell backward off the stage, landing on his head. He's already got some nasty swelling on the back of his skull."

"Right. Let's get him inside."

Gabriel nodded and pulled the gurney far enough out of the vehicle that the wheels snapped down into place. Hurrying to the emergency entrance, Seb blew a feather away from his mouth as he struggled to keep the long plumes of the costume out of his face. He tried to assess the patient as they went, using his penlight to flick light at each eye. He'd only arrived back in Argentina a few hours ago, and had booked a room in a nearby hotel, not knowing what kind of reception he was going to get from Bella when she found out he was back. He wasn't holding out much hope at this point.

"Pupils are equal and reactive. That's a good…"

He glanced up to make sure he wasn't going to run into anything, and his penlight stopped midair as he spied a familiar face rushing toward them.

"What have we got?" If Bella seemed startled by the costume, she didn't show it. Nor did she show any reaction to him. Or maybe she just hadn't noticed him yet. Or worse, maybe she just didn't *want* to notice him. She hadn't contacted him once since he'd been gone over the last two months, not even to wish him a *Feliz Navidad*. He'd sent her a text and had even tried to call but had gotten no response. Seb was pretty sure that didn't bode well for the state of their relationship. He'd braced himself to receive a divorce petition when he returned. In fact, he'd delayed his flight one week rather than face that possibility, although he'd argued with himself that it was because the little clinic where he'd been working had been overrun with dengue fever cases at the time. But in his heart of hearts, he knew that wasn't why he'd delayed his return.

After all the fertility struggles, he'd decided that if he was never going to be a parent, that was okay. He definitely didn't want to go back down the road he'd been on during that particular journey. Not with her. Not with anyone.

He took a few seconds to glance at her as the paramedics filled her in on the patient. She didn't look any worse for wear. If anything, the slight gauntness she'd developed over their last year of heartache seemed to have melted away. The curves that he'd always loved seemed to have returned full force, despite the shapeless scrubs that didn't reveal much, and her face and cheeks glowed. And her ready smile…it was back.

His leaving had been a good thing for her, evidently. And even though he knew his marriage was very probably over, he was glad that she'd made peace with things in his absence. That she seemed to have rediscovered her sense of self and purpose. He just had no idea where he fit into that. Or *if* he did.

Just then the patient groaned, and Seb leaned in to reassure the man. "Take it easy. You're at the hospital. We're going to take good care of you."

When he glanced up again, Bella had gone dead still, her gaze fixed intently on him, and any color he'd seen in her face just now had disappeared without a trace. Her eyes closed for a long minute before reopening. Then it was as if a switch was flicked back on. Her body reanimated, going about her tasks with the patient as if she'd never stopped. As if his reappearance was nothing more than a minor blip on her horizon that she'd already forgotten about. Indeed, she hadn't even said so much as a hello to him.

Even Gabriel seemed a little uncomfortable at the sudden tension in the room, finishing his report and turning the patient fully over to the hospital staff. As he turned to go, he murmured to Seb, "Give her a little time."

Hadn't he already done that by going to Angola? What else did she need time for? To make the break final? To figure out how to ignore him even more than she already was?

He nodded at his friend as if he understood the words, but in reality his head was spinning with a sense of doom.

They got the patient into a room and transferred him over to a hospital bed, letting the other medical tech take the gurney back out to the emergency vehicle.

She was still avoiding eye contact. Well, to hell with this. He was not going to walk on eggshells around her or anyone. He couldn't do it. Not anymore.

He moved closer to Bella, leaning down to whisper, "We need to talk."

She finally looked at him again and gave a sharp nod. "Once he's stable."

Of course. What else would he have meant? That they just leave the patient and hammer out their personal business in the hospital corridor? No. They were both professionals. They would have to work together, no matter what happened between them.

Unless she was planning on leaving the hospital? A sharp pain went through his midsection at the thought of never seeing her again. Even when he'd been in Africa he'd never once thought of relocating there or making his assignment anything more than an emergency stopgap to assist the staff already on location, who'd been so swamped with patients that they'd struggled to keep up.

Bella was as adept at her job as ever, consulting him briefly as they decided which tests needed to be run. An MRI to rule out traumatic brain or spinal cord injury was at the top of the list.

Once they'd done their physical exam to rule out other problems they could see or feel, the imaging department whisked the patient off to have the scan done. It would take about forty-five minutes before they could get him in and get it finished, so he turned to Bella and found her watching him with wary eyes.

"Do you have time to meet in our office briefly?" he said.

As the joint leads of the ER department, they shared a place to do consults and have meetings with staff. As soon as he said the words, though, he wondered if he was crazy. He and Bella had sometimes made love in his office, whenever her sexiness had particularly gotten to him, back in the early days of their relationship. But it was the only really private place he could think of to talk to her, off the top of his head.

Except she shook her head. "Could we go to the little café around the corner instead?"

She didn't tell him why she preferred going there instead of to the office, but it probably had to do with the same reasons. But it still rankled that she didn't want to be around things that reminded her of happier days. Maybe because those days were long gone, lost in a tidal wave of failed pregnancies and flagging hope.

"Sure. That's fine."

"Let me just tell them where I'll be."

Where *she* would be. Not them. It seemed she'd already disconnected from him. But maybe it was just as well. Until they could figure out where they stood it was better not to feed the rumor mills with anything that could have people wondering what was going on.

Mainly because he wasn't sure what was going on himself.

So the coffee shop it was.

When she'd seen him with that patient, her heart had skipped a beat. Or maybe it had been five or six, because the shock had quickly given way to other feelings entirely. Hormones. Or maybe it had been that she hadn't been entirely sure he was going to come back at all. That had to be it.

Seb looked as hot standing in a mess of crazy yellow feathers as he did when he'd been emerging from a shower completely naked. The man just did it for her. He always had.

But as she'd learned over the last couple of years, those kinds of feelings weren't always enough. That in trying to drag their love through a minefield of broken dreams, it had emerged tattered and torn, looking very different than it had at the beginning of their relationship. Oh, she definitely still loved him. Still wanted him. But instead of their relationship maturing through the heartbreak they'd shared, it seemed to have crumbled under the strain.

She knew she'd pushed him hard for a baby, but if they'd given up earlier, when he'd wanted to... She had to force her hand not to travel to her growing midsection where three tiny beings were relying on her to keep them safe. That meant no major emotional upheavals. The fact that he hadn't even noticed the change in her body was telling.

Seeing Seb—telling him about the pregnancy—wasn't that going to be one of those upheavals?

It wasn't like she'd purposely kept it from him. She just hadn't wanted to tell him over the phone. Hadn't wanted him to rush home just because of the babies. And if he chose to stay in the marriage for that reason? Oh, *Dios*. She didn't think she could do it. It hit too close to home with her biological father.

He came back from the counter with his café con leche and her herbal tea, which thank God she'd been drinking for years now, so it wouldn't tip him off. Although she was going to tell him. She had to. She'd run out of reasons not to.

She took a sip and sighed as he sat down. He'd added just the right amount of sugar. And somehow the fact that he remembered that made her eyes prick. She blinked and forced back the rush of emotion. This was not how she wanted this meeting to take place. She needed to be strong. Especially now.

"How was your trip?"

"Good." He stared at her for a second or two. "Are you still in the apartment?"

Dios, had he expected her to move out in his absence? Pain slashed through her chest, and she had to force herself not to react. "Yes. I thought it was both of ours."

He sat back in his seat and dragged his fingers through his thick black hair, shoving the unruly locks back off his forehead. It was longer than it had been when he'd left and if anything, it gave him a sexy, rugged air that made her swallow.

"God, Bella, I didn't mean that. I just thought you might have preferred to…" He stopped again. "I wasn't sure if there was even an apartment to go back to anymore or if you'd sublet it to someone else."

"It's still there. *I'm* still there." How could she tell him, though, that she didn't think it was a good idea for them to live together? At least not until they'd figured things out. She didn't trust herself not to cave in and fall back into old patterns that she was no longer sure were healthy for either of them. It was time to tell him. Time to let him know he was going to be a father. "But there's something I need you to know."

Seb sat in silence, staring at her face as if he didn't want her to say another word. But she had to. He deserved to hear the words so that he could make whatever decision he felt he needed to. So she pushed forward. "I'm pregnant."

"Pregnant." A series of emotions crossed his face. Emotions that she couldn't read. Or maybe she was too afraid of trying to figure them out. "But the last attempt failed."

Even as his words faded away, an awful twist of his mouth gave evidence to what he was thinking. That the babies weren't his. She hurried to correct him. "But it didn't. I assumed when I started spotting that I'd lost the pregnancy, because it was the pattern with the other IVF attempts. And I didn't go to have it checked out right away because of all the stress. I waited until you were gone to try to sort through things."

"So you didn't lose the baby?"

His words were tentative, as if he was afraid that even saying them out loud might jinx everything. She got it. She'd felt the same way when they'd done the ultrasound on her and told her the wonderful news.

"Babies. I didn't lose the babies…plural."

He sat up in his chair. He was shocked. Obviously. But was he also happy? Dismayed? Angry? She could no longer read him the way she'd once been able to.

"You're carrying twins?"

She slowly shook her head, unable to prevent a smile from reaching her lips. "There are three of them."

"*Dios*. Triplets?" His fingers raked through his hair again, but this time there was a desperation to it that caught at her heart. "No. It's not safe."

Safe? What wasn't? "What do you mean?"

"There are risks. Big risks to carrying that many fetuses. Why didn't you tell me, Bella? Surely you could have responded to one of my texts. Before it was too late to…"

Too late to what? Reduce the number? No. That was her decision to make. "I didn't tell you because it didn't feel right doing it over the phone. And I know the risks. I've already told my doctor I'm willing to accept them."

And she was. But was he? Would he turn his back on his own children?

He wouldn't. She knew him well enough to know that. At least she hoped she did. Even if they were through as a couple, she knew Seb would still be an amazing father.

"You made a decision like that without even talking to me?"

This time she did read the dismay in his words. She understood how it probably sounded. That she'd already been cutting him out. And maybe she had been. The way he'd left for Angola had crushed her. She'd wanted to cut him out of her life forever. Had almost convinced herself to go see a lawyer. And then she'd found out she was carrying his children. It shouldn't have made a difference, but it did. In some way that she didn't quite understand.

"How is it any different than when you left for Angola, making that decision without even consulting me?"

He stared at her for a minute before responding. "You're right. I should have discussed it with you first. I'm sorry."

His admission tugged at her heart. But she needed to be careful. The hurt they'd inflicted on each other... the fire they'd walked through didn't vanish with just a few words of regret. It might be something neither of them got over. But this was about more than just the two of them now.

So what did they do? Focus on the babies. And the only way she could think of to help him understand why she was willing to carry multiple fetuses held some emotional risks of its own. But she wanted him to see the reality for himself. To see why the decision to lose one or two of them was untenable for her.

"I—I have an ultrasound scheduled later today if you want to be there. And then I meet with my doctor. You can ask her any questions you want."

There was a moment's hesitation before he said, "Of course I'll be there." He pulled in a deep breath. "I'm in a hotel room at the moment. And I'll stay there until we have time to sit down and decide what to do."

She'd expected him to say that, but still it hurt to hear it. Especially now. Especially after giving him this news. While she'd known he wouldn't sweep her off her feet as he once might have, she had thought he'd show some sign of happiness about the news that she was pregnant. No matter how he felt about her on a personal level. Although maybe he felt it now chained him to her. To the babies.

Give him time, Bella. Time to digest the news.

So maybe it was time to end this meeting and let him do just that.

"Okay. Maybe we can talk more after the ultrasound." She glanced at her watch. "But now I need to get back to the patient. He should be just about done with the MRI at this point."

"And I need to see how much paperwork has piled up in my absence."

They got to their feet, and Seb's eyes traveled over her midsection as if seeing what he'd missed before. When they reached the door to exit the café, he touched her arm, sending a shiver over her. She glanced up at him.

"I'm happy for you, Bella. Truly. I know you've wanted this for such a long time."

He was happy for her. Not for himself. Not for them as a couple.

And that made her heart hurt in a way that it hadn't over the last eight weeks. And she wasn't sure how she would ever get past it.

Seb sat in a chair in the waiting room of the small IVF clinic that was in an annex of the hospital, feeling completely disconnected from what was happening. He was numb, unsure of how to react to anything. Including the thought that he was going to be a father.

Two other couples were there, and from the little touches and knowing looks that traveled between each of them, they were very much in love. Very much wrapped up in the new adventure of expecting their little ones. And yet here he was. Alone. He'd felt pretty much that way for the last year of their marriage, though, so he should be used to it by now.

He wasn't even sure how they'd gotten to this point. When love had turned to something so unrecognizable that he was no longer sure their marriage was worth fighting for. He'd halfway hoped that she'd made the decision for him, moving out of their apartment and getting on with her life.

In fact, when Bella had first told him she was pregnant, shock had bolted through his system. He'd thought she'd lost the other pregnancy, and since he'd been out of the country…a few soul-sucking thoughts had flown through his head, such as maybe she'd found someone else while he'd been gone. Wasn't that what he'd just hoped for? That she'd get on with her life?

No. Because as soon as the thought had entered his mind, he'd dismissed it. She wouldn't have done that. Not without divorcing him first.

And even the thought of her with another man made his flesh crawl. Whether it was eight weeks from now or eight years. Yet before he'd left Angola, he'd come to accept the fact that they were probably through. That it was only a matter of time before they signed documents cementing that fact.

They said that time healed all wounds, and maybe that was true. But it was tricky when it came to the healing that a couple needed to do to stay together. It seemed, if anything, they'd grown even further apart since he'd been gone. And that was on him. He'd been the one to walk away.

When he'd caught sight of her in that hospital corridor, though, he couldn't deny the rush of relief that had slid through him that she was still there, looking as beautiful as ever. She hadn't disappeared from his life. At least not physically. But emotionally?

The tinkle of a small bell over the door drove him from his thoughts, and his head turned toward the entrance. Bella. Again, that weird sense of relief swamped him, and it took him a minute to stand up to let her know where he was sitting. It was a signal that had been ingrained in his system, since she tended to run late. The fact that he did it now, when there was no longer any need, made him uneasy. It should be easier to let go—to walk away from something that didn't work—shouldn't it?

Their lives had been consumed by one goal for so long that they hadn't spent the time that was desperately needed to nurture their relationship. And it was damned obvious now that that had been a mistake. A mistake that might just have cost them everything.

"Sorry," she muttered. "I had a patient and couldn't get away."

He glanced down at her middle and saw what he'd missed earlier. The signs of pregnancy were more evident than he'd realized, or maybe the scrubs had just been better at concealing it. Or maybe it was just because he knew the truth. Surely if Gabriel had known, he would have said something to him earlier. And her blouse did a pretty good job of flowing over the swell of her midsection. He forced his eyes back up to her face.

"You're not late. As a matter of fact, you're five minutes early."

"Huh." She said it as if surprised by that information, even glancing down to look at the watch strapped to her wrist. "Well, that's got to be a first."

So much had changed. She had changed. But then again, so had he.

One couple came out—the man dropping a kiss on his partner's head—while another one was called back.

How the hell did he handle being a father when he wasn't even sure he and Bella had a future together? He had no idea. But he'd better figure something out. And soon.

Fifteen minutes of agonizing silence went by before they were called back to the exam room. Liz Everly, their IVF specialist and ob-gyn who'd walked them through the other heartbreaking attempts, was there with a ready smile. She held her hand out to him. "Nice to see you again, Seb. I'm so happy for you both."

He must have mumbled something that made sense

because the woman didn't stare at him like he had two heads before she said, "Are you ready to see your babies?"

He swallowed the words he wanted to ask about the likelihood of her carrying this pregnancy to term when so many others had been lost. He wasn't sure he even wanted to see them for fear of that happening. But he'd told Bella he'd be at this appointment, and Seb tried to always keep his word. Even if he might not be able to keep the vows he'd made at their wedding.

One step at a time. You can do this.

But could he? Right now, he wasn't sure.

Liz didn't make her put on a gown. Instead she had Bella hop up on the exam table and lift her top and slide the zipper on her jeans down. Smooth skin came into view. Skin that he'd once loved to kiss. Skin that still made him weak at the knees. Only now that her stomach was exposed to his view, he saw he was right. What used to be a concave surface now sported a definite curve. And her breasts were even fuller than they'd been before he'd left for Africa.

He averted his glance. Everything had become so clinical that they'd both come to view sex as a means to an end. And to look at her now without that hanging over their heads?

It was dangerous. He'd come back from his medical mission with the idea that if she asked him to help her get pregnant again, he was going to suggest a trial separation to see if their goals in life were even compatible anymore. At forty-four, he'd made peace with the fact that he wasn't going to be a father. And yet here he was—about to see babies he hadn't even known existed before today.

She should have told him. A flicker of anger went through him. If he'd known earlier, he could have prepared himself, maybe even wrapped his head around the fact that she was expecting not one but three babies.

Liz squirted a puddle of gel onto Bella's stomach and then picked up the ultrasound wand, running it through the lubricant before getting down to business. There was silence in the room while she searched for the fetuses, and then suddenly a conglomeration of disjointed sounds filled the air. Sounds reminiscent of several metronomes that had all been started at different times. And yet when you tried to separate each out, there was a rhythm to them that was familiar. Comforting, even. A dub-dub, dub-dub that he recognized. But they were so fast.

"Is that...?" His head came up to look at the doctor.

"Yes. Those are their heartbeats. Now let's see if they'll cooperate and let us get a good look at them." She swept the wand around some more, staring at the monitor as a series of shapes moved across the screen.

Then she stopped. "There. There are two of them. The third one must be hiding behind the others."

"I don't see anything." Then he sorted out the shapes and saw them. Realized exactly what he was looking at. A sense of wonder filled his chest, and he felt his own heartbeat increase. *"Dios..."*

His hand automatically started to reach for Bella's

before he stopped short. Her silence while he'd been away had made it pretty clear that she hadn't wanted to talk to him. Didn't want to work on their relationship. Maybe she hadn't wanted to tell him about the babies at all. And hell, he could see why. He'd up and left her at a very hard time, right as they'd both thought she was losing the pregnancy. But she'd been ready to ask for another try. He'd seen it in her eyes. And he just hadn't had it in him to cope with any more heartache.

And the heartache of never being with her again?

Not things he should be thinking about at this moment. Especially since Liz was changing the parameters and moving the wand, trying to get a look at the other baby. "Come out, come out, wherever you are." She frowned. "He's pretty well wedged behind the others, but right now I don't see any cause for alarm."

She clicked a couple of areas on the screen, marking measurements of the babies who were out in front. Then she told Bella she could sit up and fasten her clothes before the doctor turned and faced them. Her expression was serious.

Bella's eyes widened. "Is something wrong?"

Even as she asked, Seb felt a surge of panic of his own.

"Not that I can see at the moment. I don't want to dampen the happiness or excitement of seeing your little guys, but I do want to talk to both of you for a minute. Bella, we've already discussed the fact that carrying three babies is tricky, and with your age…"

"I know we have." Bella's voice was soft with a trace

of fear. It echoed his own dismay at hearing the words he knew to be true voiced out loud. It was part of the reason he had been done trying. He hadn't wanted to put Bella's life and health on the line in pursuit of something that might never happen. And now that it had, he was quickly realizing just how risky this venture might be.

"I'm going to transfer your care to Dr. Lucas, whose office isn't too far from here. She specializes in high-risk pregnancies."

And there it was. Three words that scared the hell out of him. High. Risk. Pregnancy. But it wasn't just about the babies' lives, anymore, it was about hers as well.

"Are you sure you can't be the one to follow the pregnancy? If I promise to be careful?"

Liz reached out and grabbed hold of her hand, the way Seb had wanted to earlier. "I can't. You need specialized care and constant monitoring. I can't give that to you. But what I can give you is some advice." Her look included Seb this time. "I don't know what is going on between you two, but I felt the tension the second I came into the room. Seb, if you can't be there for Bella, then you need to take a couple of steps back and let her find people who can support her. Physically *and* emotionally."

His wife's teeth bit down on her lip, and she started to say something, but he stepped in. "It's nothing we can't work out. I'll be there for Bella. Every step of the way." Surely he could do this. At least for the time it took for the babies to be born. He would do whatever it took.

"I'm glad to hear it," Liz said. "You'd be surprised at how many men can't deal with the pressure of finally succeeding with IVF and choose to withdraw emotionally."

Like he'd done when he'd chosen to apply for the position in Africa? Guilt twisted his insides. She was sixteen weeks pregnant, and he'd missed half of it already. But he wasn't going to miss another day of his children's lives.

"You can be sure of one thing. I will protect these babies with my life."

Bella turned to look at him, and there was some strange emotion in her face. And finally she did what he hadn't been able to a few minutes ago: she reached out to squeeze his hand. But she let go again just as quickly. The brief contact sent his world spinning into orbit, and he'd had to clench his teeth to keep his hand from closing around hers to prevent her from pulling away.

And when she pulled away from him for good? Another thing he shouldn't be thinking about right now.

Liz smiled. "Good to hear. Well, I'll let you two get on with your day." She handed Bella a printout of the ultrasound. "And I'll make a note for Dr. Lucas to try and coax that third baby out in the open so we can get a good look at him. I might not be your primary obstetrician anymore, but I'm still your friend. I'll be following your story closely. Call me if either of you have any concerns, okay?"

"I will, Liz. And thank you so much. For everything."

"You are more than welcome. And congratulations again."

With that, the doctor left the room, leaving him alone with Bella.

Before he could talk himself out of it, he said, "I think I should stay in the apartment with you rather than a hotel. I know we haven't decided what to do about our marriage, but Liz made it pretty obvious that you are going to need a lot of support and I meant what I said. I want to be there for our babies—for you— every step of the way. At least until they're born."

The strange look from earlier came over her face again. "I don't want you to feel obligated to live with me just because of the babies, Seb—"

"These are my children, too. I don't want to take any chances."

There was a pause before she responded. "Okay. Like you said, just until they're born. We do have a guest room."

In his rush to support her, he hadn't thought about where he would actually sleep. And he should have been the one to suggest the guest room. But maybe part of him hadn't wanted to make that break. Not quite yet. All of those decisions could wait until the babies were born. Anything to prevent turmoil in her life. In the babies' lives.

"Yes, we do. I'll move my things home from the hotel as soon as we leave here."

"Okay. And Seb, thanks. For everything. I truly mean it."

Although he'd used the word *home* when talking about the apartment, he was no longer sure it held any meaning as far as he was concerned. But for now he would stay there. And do his damnedest not to remember how good things used to be between them in the early days of their marriage. Because those days were long gone, and he wasn't sure there was anything he could do about that. Or if he even wanted to.

CHAPTER TWO

SEB HAD BEEN true to his word and had moved his effects from the hotel last night. And this morning he'd started moving the things he hadn't taken to Angola out of their bedroom while she'd sat in the kitchen and tried to banish her hurt. A hurt that grew with every sound that came from the room down the hall.

She'd been the one to suggest he move into the guest room, but she'd been thinking more about his suitcases from the trip than anything else. But Seb had been pretty quick to move things to the next level by removing all of his possessions from the bedroom they'd used to share. And he'd also made it more than plain that he was mainly there to support the babies. To do that, he had to support her. Talk about emotional turmoil. The very thing that Liz had wanted her to avoid. But the realization that her husband seemed to be more concerned with his future children than he was with her was…gutting. Her mom had probably felt the same way when Bella's biological dad hadn't proposed to her after he'd found out she was pregnant.

Except Seb had proposed all those years ago and hadn't needed a pregnancy to do it. But would he have stayed with her now if the doctor hadn't mentioned her needing help?

Her heart said maybe not. He'd been the one to walk away by taking the Doctors Without Borders gig, even though he had tried to contact her a couple of times during his absence. But there'd been radio silence for the last month. Almost the whole time she'd been trying to process being a mom to triplets.

Again, not his fault.

But at least he hadn't rejected the babies. Then again, her father hadn't rejected her, even though he'd never married her mom. He'd been a great dad, and he'd always said he cared about her mother and had supported her however he could while she was pregnant; he just evidently hadn't loved her enough to take their relationship to the next level. Her mom had ended up marrying someone else when Bella was a year old, who'd also been a great father figure.

She knew this situation was nothing like the one she'd grown up with. But things between her and Seb had definitely changed over the last year, and while, like her dad, he probably still cared about her, it seemed he didn't care enough to sit down and try to work things out. As evidenced by his quick willingness to leave for Africa…and now to move into the guest room.

The sounds of things being shifted from one room to the other stopped and a minute later, Seb appeared in the doorway. "I got most of it over there. I'll probably just box up what I don't need right now and put it into storage."

Another nail pierced her heart. It was all she could do to nod in agreement. Saying anything in her emotional state right now might make things worse. Or lead to her venting all the pain his absence had engendered over the last couple of months. So instead she said, "It's fine. I need to be at work in an hour, so I'll go get ready if that's okay."

Seb nodded. "I have the day off, so I'll see you when you get home. Unless you want me to drive you to work."

"No." The word came out quickly. Too quickly. She covered by adding, "I think the closer I stick to my normal routine, the better."

They used to drive to work together regularly. Until about a year before he'd left for Africa. Even then the cracks in their relationship had been making themselves known. At the time, they'd blamed it on differing shifts and one or the other of them having to stay longer at the hospital than expected. But looking back, she could see that it was more than that. It had been the beginning of what was probably the end of their relationship.

The triplets were just delaying the inevitable. At least for the next few months.

She couldn't stop herself from grieving what they'd lost. Never in her wildest dreams had she thought they would come to the point where they lived in the same house but might as well have been a thousand miles apart.

Like they had been literally, not even two days ago.

Nothing had changed. Except for the ache of seeing him and knowing she couldn't ask him to hold her— to promise her that everything was going to be okay. Because she wasn't sure it would be, no matter what he said.

And if by some horrible chance she lost the pregnancy? Would he just walk away from her?

Who could blame him? She could look back and see how relentless she'd been in her quest for a baby, even after she realized he was emotionally done with trying. She'd always assumed that once the IVF worked, it would repair whatever had come between them. Instead those cracks had turned into crevasses with her standing on one side and Seb on the other. And he seemed to have no interest in building any bridges.

But then again, she wasn't sure she was interested in that either.

When she got up to walk to the bedroom to get ready for work, he stepped in front of her, making her look up at him. His eyes were soft, and it ignited a flare of hope inside her. "Promise me you'll call if you need anything."

Hope fizzled as quickly as it had come, and pain washed up her gullet. Bella had to swallow the vile-tasting emotion before it robbed her of the ability to think. Because she knew he was talking about the pregnancy and not her as a person. But she managed a smile and glanced up at him and said she would. Then she waited for him to step out of the way and let her by.

He did, but it took a few seconds as he looked at her face as if trying to read something in her expression.

Dios, *please don't let him see the fear and frustration.*

Then he frowned and turned away, walking in the direction of the guest room. She sagged in relief. Or maybe it was in defeat. Right now she couldn't tell one from the other. She only knew that it was going to be a long five months. If they even made it that long under the same roof.

And after the babies were born?

She didn't know. She just didn't know. And that was the hardest thing of all.

Seb heard her moving around the apartment before six in the morning, just as he had for the last few days. She would leave for the hospital soon. Although he hadn't asked for them to have different shifts, it seemed that's how things were lining up right now. Or maybe Bella had asked not to work with him. But that didn't sound like her. She was an incredibly private person. Which was borne out in the fact that no one had yet said anything to him about the babies. He would have expected some congratulations by now. But hell, he was glad for that fact, at least. When he did see her, it seemed she was dressing in a way to deliberately conceal the pregnancy, even though to him it was now pretty obvious. And she was beautiful.

But it was getting more and more uncomfortable knowing she was just two doors down from where he was sleeping. He thought part of that was from only catching glimpses of her now and then. By the time he got home at midnight, she was already in bed asleep.

So far they hadn't hammered out anything firm about her appointments or the delivery, and those were things that should be talked about. Sooner rather than later.

So, finding some jogging pants, he yanked them up his hips and went out into the dark hallway. Why hadn't she turned on any lights? Or was she already gone?

When he turned into the dining room, he crashed against something hard enough to make it tip. Only when he grabbed at it to keep it from falling, it gave a quiet cry and he realized it wasn't some*thing*, but some*one*. Bella.

With one arm around her, he felt the wall for the light switch he knew was there and pushed it, sending light streaming through the room. He blinked, trying to let his eyes adjust to the sudden brightness.

He glanced down at her to find her fully dressed for the day and pressed tightly against him, a sensation that was so painfully familiar that he had to swallow. Her palms were pressed flat against the bare skin of his chest, and her head was tilted back, her pink lips slightly parted. She looked so much like the girl he'd married ten years ago that in his sleepy state he was having trouble remembering that they weren't that happy couple anymore. Before he could stop himself, he reached up to touch her cheek, his other arm bringing her belly against him.

As if she'd been jolted back to reality, she pushed against him and he released her immediately. "Sorry."

"It's okay. I was trying not to wake you."

"You didn't. I've been awake for a while."

They stood there for a minute or two before he remembered why he'd come out here in the first place. "You don't have to tiptoe around in the mornings, you know."

"You worked late last night, and I was hoping to let you sleep as long as possible."

So different from the days when she hadn't worried about that but had instead woken him up with tiny kisses that had driven him wild with need. The days when they'd made love with a passion that ignited instantly when they'd worked different shifts in the past, coming together whenever they could to stay connected.

There was no longer any need for that, it would seem. In fact, it was as if she was tiptoeing around to avoid seeing him, if anything.

"What time do you work until today?" Was she going to keep the grueling pace of the ER all the way up until she delivered? Liz had emphasized that her pregnancy was high risk. Surely she wouldn't agree with Bella working almost twelve hours a day.

"Five thirty. You?"

"I'm actually taking another day off." He hadn't been planning on that until this very moment. But they'd talked so little since he'd been back that he felt like it was time to get on the same page as far as the pregnancy went.

"You are?" The way she said it showed her surprise. Even though this was the time when new residents had begun working in different areas of the hospital, including in the ER, Seb had never taken personal days. But he knew he wasn't leaving the hospital short. At least not today. He was going to pretend this wasn't a spur-of-the-moment thing.

"I am. I kind of wanted to sit down and talk about how the next several months are going to go. Have you made an appointment with the specialist yet?"

She blinked a couple of times. "I…um, have. Her office called the other day."

He tensed. She hadn't told him. Or even left him a note to let him know about it. He wanted to be involved, but the question was, was she really going to let him be? "And?"

"I was going to check with you first and see when a good time would be."

A few of his muscles relaxed. Maybe she wasn't going to shut him out completely. "Thank you. Can we meet somewhere after you get off and sit down and talk about that and a few other things? If you're not too tired, that is."

"You know I won't be." This time she said it with a smile.

Bella was the opposite of him in that being in the ER seemed to energize her. She got off duty fully wired and needing time to unwind before she could sleep.

And one of the best ways she'd found to do that was to make love. Was she trying to remind him of that fact?

Despite everything, his body immediately reacted to the memory, and he had to grit his teeth and will away the rigidity of the very muscles that would give him away.

He drew a deep careful breath. "Where do you want to meet? Or do you want me to pick you up from the hospital after your shift?"

"No, I think it would be easier for me just to drive to wherever you're thinking. That way I won't have to go back and pick my car up."

That made sense, but he couldn't help but feel that the major reason for the suggestion was to avoid being in close proximity with him as much as possible. Which he got. Even if he didn't completely agree.

How were they going to work things out if they were never together?

They wouldn't. And maybe that was the point she was trying to make. That she didn't want to work anything out with him.

"That's fine." Before he had a chance to think about it he said, "Why don't we meet at the Bosques de Palermo? In the rose garden?"

The famous Buenos Aires park had always been one of their favorite places to walk. In the early days of their romance, they would rent a paddleboat and go out to the middle of the lake and just sit and talk for hours. In between make-out sessions that got hot enough to make them hurry to get somewhere more private. Maybe suggesting that place wasn't the best idea, but to go back and offer up a place with fewer memories was going to sound strange.

When he glanced at her, her teeth were digging into her lip and he thought she might refuse to meet him there. Then she said, "Sure. That sounds okay. It'll take me about twenty minutes to get there, so how about six o'clock, in case I get caught up at the hospital for a little longer."

"Six sounds good." He allowed himself a slight smile. "And thanks for agreeing."

"Of course. We do need to discuss a few things."

His smile disappeared. It might as well have been some kind of business meeting where they hashed out the points of some contract. Well, that's what they'd be doing, wasn't it? Discussing what she expected out of him during this pregnancy.

And afterward?

Well, that was a discussion for another day. And he could tell she was getting antsy...anxious to be on her way. Away from him. "I'll see you there, then."

"Yes. See you." With that, she slid the strap of her small purse over her shoulder and started to turn toward the front door. But not before her eyes slid across his midsection. Only when she was gone and he glanced down did he realize that she'd been looking at his bare chest. The chest she'd rested against just a few minutes ago. And his smile returned. Maybe she wasn't as oblivious to him as she'd seemed. He quickly quashed that idea. It was more likely that she'd felt awkward at his state of undress with his jogging gear slung low on his hips.

Well, at least he'd gotten her to agree to a meeting. Because living like this for the next several months was going to be torture, and it was the exact opposite of what he was supposed to be doing when he'd promised Liz he'd support her during the pregnancy.

So the sooner they figured out what she needed from him, the better he would feel about everything.

At least that was what he hoped. With that, he retrieved his cell phone and called the hospital to request the day off.

The rest of the day passed without incident, but Seb wished he hadn't completely skipped working today. It had left him with too much time to think. And right now thinking was dangerous. As he leaned against one of the pillars of the huge rose arbor, the scents of the flowers surrounding him and offering up a little bit of protection from the scorching sun, he wondered if they should have just met at the apartment instead. Or at least someplace that offered a cool interior. Today was steamy, but at least there were plenty of shady spots in the park like this arbor.

Still, he wondered how much exertion was safe. Then he made a face. The Emergency Department offered her plenty of that on a daily basis.

A few minutes went by, and then he saw her walking toward him. She was now wearing a loose gauzy skirt and a white top with thin straps that bared her shoulders. She'd been wearing scrubs earlier, so she must have changed at the hospital. With her hair pulled high off her neck in a sleek ponytail that bounced with every step she took, she looked cool and collected and…beautiful. Then again, she'd been just as beautiful in her hospital garb. He moved toward her and leaned down to graze his left cheek against her hers in the traditional Argentine greeting rather than kissing her mouth. Even so, she flinched at the light contact.

"Sorry, I'm late," she said.

He glanced at his watch and smiled. "I don't think one minute past six constitutes being late. Hard day?"

"Actually? Not really. Just a lot of colds and sniffles. One chest pain case that wound up being indigestion."

Seb remembered the days of the pandemic when a simple cough could signal serious illness. He prayed they would never see something like that again in his lifetime. "You're being careful, I hope."

Her brows shot up. "Of course. Just like I always am."

"Sorry. Habit."

The days of being allowed to worry about her were evidently over. Except some things you couldn't turn off like a switch.

Like his reaction to her this morning?

He pushed that back just as she dismissed his apology murmuring, "Don't worry about it. Do you want to talk here or somewhere different?"

"Do you feel like walking?"

"Yes." She glanced at him, maybe seeing something

in his face, because she went on, "I'm fine. Really. How about the bridge?" She motioned to her right where a large white Grecian-style bridge spanned a narrow area of the lake. From there it was possible to look out over the different zones in the park.

"Sounds good."

He fell into step beside her as they talked about some changes that had happened in the hospital since he'd been gone. They were looking to add a new doctor to the neonatal unit, and she'd heard they had a line on a doctor from Uruguay who was moving to the area with her daughter in the next couple of weeks. "I can't remember her name at the moment, but I've heard only good things about her."

Going up the wide steps that led to the bridge, he started to put his palm on the small of her back like he would have done when things were normal between them, before deciding it wasn't a good idea. "Are they going to interview her for the position?"

"I think so? But I haven't asked specifically." Her hand went to her belly. "It'll be good to have a fully staffed unit when the babies arrive."

They got to the top of the bridge and strolled a few yards before stopping and leaning their arms on the railing. From here it was possible to see the swans cruising down the water, their white plumage shining bright in the sunlight. Off to their right was one of the park's paddleboats. The couple inside was sitting close, then the woman leaned down to scoop up some water and splash it toward her companion. Laughter ensued.

When he glanced at Bella, he saw that she was watching them, too, before pulling in an audible breath and blowing it back out.

"So," she said. "What are some good days to meet with the specialist?"

"I'm on three days at the end of this week and off two, yesterday and today being those two."

"It'll probably be next week before we can get in. What's your schedule like then?"

He pulled his phone out to check his calendar. "I'm off the following Thursday and Friday."

"I can make next Friday work. Shall I call her and see if she has an opening on that day?"

"Yes. Probably the sooner we get in the better at this point."

She nodded. "I agree."

He somehow expected her to call once she got back to the apartment, but instead she retrieved her own phone and made a call. "Hi. This is Isabella Lopez. Dr. Everly referred me to your office."

Bella waited a few seconds, and then he could hear another woman talking. "Oh, yes, Dr. Lopez, she called the office and asked us to get you in as soon as we can. Does this week work?"

Without looking at him, she replied, "Not really. Would you by chance have anything on Friday of next week?"

Seb frowned. If Liz wanted them to get in as soon as possible, wouldn't it be better to go this week? He could certainly ask for more time off. He motioned for her only to have her cover the mouthpiece of the phone and say, "It's okay. Let's just stick with what we talked about."

All he could do was nod. Was this how it was going to be the whole time? He realized they had indeed talked about making the appointment for next week, and she had put the phone on speaker so that he could hear both sides of the conversation, but somehow he felt like he was being shut out. Already.

"Would three o'clock work?"

Bella glanced at him as if seeking his opinion, so he nodded his head and entered the time on his calendar.

The call ended a moment later, and she sighed. "And here we go."

The words were soft, and he wasn't sure if she was talking about the appointment or about their journey through it. Suddenly, she glanced up at him. "Can we rent a boat? I might not get too many more chances before my belly is too big for my legs to paddle. And it looks so cool out there on the lake."

He blinked, unsure if he'd heard correctly. She actually wanted to go out on a boat? With him?

As if sensing his hesitation, she shook her head. "Never mind. I know it's hot and you don't have to—"

"Let's do it." The words came out of their own volition. But he wasn't sorry he'd said them. Maybe this would put them back on a path of being a little more like the friends they'd once been than the strangers they now were.

"Are you sure?"

"I am, as long as you don't think it will tire you too much."

"The exercise will be good for me. I have a feeling I'll need every ounce of strength I can muster for what's coming."

"Okay. But just this once, until we can ask the doctor if it's advisable for the babies."

Something in her face fell, and he hoped he hadn't brought back sad memories of the previous failed attempts at getting pregnant. He hadn't meant to do that, or to alarm her, but he did want her to have the best possible chance of carrying these little ones through to delivery, which would undoubtedly be by cesarean section. He couldn't imagine a doctor who would let her deliver vaginally. Not with her history. Because if something happened to these babies...

It wouldn't. And thinking such thoughts would do neither of them any good.

"We'll take it easy. I promise, Seb."

The words stung, bringing up its own memories of times when he'd been hesitant to make love to her, yet she'd urged him with her hands to come to her with promises that they'd be careful. And while he knew that they had indeed always been careful, with Seb holding himself back and taking care with every gentle thrust, he'd always felt the weight of guilt whenever she'd started bleeding a week or two afterward.

But not this time. Maybe it was good that they were no longer a normal, happy couple. Because he'd have a hell of a time not giving in to her if she asked him for sex.

That was one thing at least that they didn't have to worry about. Sex.

Even as he thought it, he had to work hard to banish the images that flashed in his mind's eye.

"Let's go. I think they'll be closing up for the night pretty soon."

Crossing the bridge and walking the short distance to the boat rental area, Seb asked for one of the paddle-boats and paid for it, then held it while Bella gingerly got on. Then he pushed the vessel offshore and leaped onto the edge of it, hearing her laugh as the boat tipped dangerously under his weight. Hell, the last thing he wanted to do was dump her into the water by accident. Although he could remember a time when he'd done it on purpose. They'd gotten reprimanded by the person on duty that day, but it hadn't mattered. They were young and in love. Right now, Seb felt anything but young. But he was pretty sure he was still in love, although he wasn't going to unpack that too much, since it really wouldn't make much of a difference. Bella was no longer in love with him from the evidence he'd seen. The only reason she was letting him be around her was so that the babies could have a father, which he should probably be grateful for. At least it would give him a few months to get used to the idea of being a father, even if he was no longer a husband in any real sense of the word.

Climbing into his seat, he glanced at her. "Where to?"

"Can we go under the bridge and stop for a few minutes? It's shady there, and we can talk a little more."

Maybe that's why she'd wanted to rent a boat. They were a lot less likely to have people listening to their conversation than if they were sitting on a bench somewhere. Not that anyone here knew them. "Sure. Let's go."

It was as if nothing had changed for a few moments. They'd ridden in these boats countless times over the course of their marriage. They matched each other's pace and steered the vessel with little effort, working as the team they used to be. Before all of the heartache. It made his chest tighten. Why couldn't they have worked so seamlessly together in the harder areas of their relationship? Because relationships were messy even on a good day. Add in IVF and all the stress that went along with it, and it was a recipe for disaster. As they'd both found out.

She bumped her belly with her knee once and laughed. "Yep. I definitely won't be able to do this in a few more weeks. But it feels good to be out here now."

Within two minutes, they'd reached the bridge, and they slowed to a crawl. It was impossible to stay stopped in one place because of the natural current caused by the shifting winds. But they were able to keep to the shady side by correcting course when they reached the edge of the shadows. "Do you still feel okay?"

"I do. I'm fine. Really."

He nodded. "And you trust this specialist?"

"I don't know her personally, but she and Liz are friends, and Liz says she's one of the best in Argentina. And I trust her to tell me the truth. So to answer your question, yes, I trust her. I have to."

He'd trusted Bella to tell him the truth at one time, too. But he saw how much that had changed when he'd first heard she was pregnant and his immediate thought had been that she'd been with someone else—a thought that would never have entered his head a year ago. Two years ago. So much had changed since then. And not in a good way. Yet she'd never given him any reason to doubt her.

But surely, the same way that they'd so easily changed the boat's direction, they could find some kind of way to stay amicable. To make this whole process as painless as possible. Because he was pretty sure at some point they'd be discussing custody agreements, child support and divorce.

"What kind of instructions were you given? Surely while I was gone, they must have told you what to do—what not to do."

"I'm supposed to walk. A lot. Both for exercise and to keep my joints supple. I'm sure paddle boating would be considered good for both of those reasons."

So was that the reason she'd suggested it? Because it had been recommended? In some small part of himself, he'd hoped maybe it was because this lake held good memories for her. That maybe she wanted to try to get back to where they used to be emotionally. But so far, the conversation was as generic as ever.

"And as far as working goes? How long are you allowed to continue?"

She shrugged. "I think that's probably something I need to ask the specialist. Liz didn't have a whole lot of advice as far as that went."

The swans that had been swimming upstream of them circled back toward them, probably looking for a handout. When they drew even with the boat, she said, "Sorry, *amigos*. We have nothing for you. Not even a cracker." She smiled. "Although a month ago, I was downing them by the box."

"You were sick?"

She glanced at him. "It was normal morning sickness. At the time, though, I thought I'd lost the babies and that it was due to stress and because you'd lef—"

Because he'd left. She didn't need to finish the word for him to know that's what she was talking about. Guilt rose ever higher.

"And when did you find out it wasn't?"

"When I called Liz a couple of weeks later, she told me I needed to come in. That if I'd really lost them, I needed to have a D&C. But when they gave me an ultrasound, they heard what she thought was a baby's heartbeat. Then two. Then three. We were all flabbergasted. And…" She paused, swiping at her eyes. "And so, so happy! Liz and I both fell apart and hugged each other, screaming and crying."

Seb had missed out on all of it. His guilt changed to hurt. "I would have come home if you'd told me, Bella."

There was a long, pained pause. "You'd left. And I

didn't want to call you back when it was always your dream to be a part of Doctors Without Borders. You evidently stayed extra time, too. So I knew I'd done the right thing in waiting until you came back to tell you."

He had stayed extra time. But only a few days' worth. He knew by leaving Argentina in such a hurry, he'd hurt her badly. But he felt like he'd seen the writing on the wall. That she was going to keep pressing for them to try again, even after he'd told her he couldn't. He hadn't wanted to ask her for a divorce, but it had been swirling around in his head for a month or two.

And by being too cowardly to stick around and hash things out, he'd evidently missed some pretty spectacular moments.

But he was here now. Right? And divorce was now the furthest thing from his thoughts.

Even if he couldn't turn things around in their relationship, maybe he could regain her trust. Help her to know he would never knowingly turn his back on his children. So how could he make her believe that?

By being here now? By being the support he'd promised both her and Liz that he would be?

"I'm sorry, Bella. Sorry for leaving like I did. I could say that they were eager to have me on the field, and I wouldn't be lying. But I thought if I stayed in Buenos Aires any longer, it would make it harder on both you and me. I truly believed we needed a break from each other. I still believe that, even though I want to be here for you now—to help however I can."

"That doesn't make sense. How can we take a break and yet not take a break?"

"I think by doing it the way we already are. Having different bedrooms. Different shifts. Different—"

"Did you ask for us to have separate shifts?"

"No, but I don't necessarily think it's a bad thing. It might be easier for both of us that way. It gives us each time to process things."

"But in that case, we really shouldn't be going on extracurricular trips together like this one, should we?"

"I don't think we should avoid each other completely. And every once in a while we do need to talk. To meet for appointments. I think meeting off hospital grounds will help us cope at work when we do have shifts that overlap."

"Whatever is best for the job, right?" Her voice had a tone of bitterness to it.

"That's not what I'm saying. Do you want to work with me every shift? Never be able to get away from me?"

"Well…no, I guess not."

The jab those words gave him was quick and almost painless. Until he realized they were lodged under his skin like a fishhook, and there wasn't much he could do to get them out…or ameliorate the sting.

He cleared his throat. "So, is this better than the alternative?"

She glanced around, and they watched the swans who were gliding away, heading toward a group of people on the shore. "Honestly, it is, Seb. Thanks for suggesting it. I think I needed something like this to help me unwind."

"Then we should do it more often?" So much for all of that stuff he'd just spouted about not spending a lot of time together.

"Yes. We should." She laid her hand on her stomach. "At least until I can no longer fit in the boat." She gave him a rueful grin.

"Then we'll find another activity to take its place."

Too late he realized how she could take those words. Especially when her cheeks turned pink. Or was that from the warmth of the day? Either way, it was probably better to call a halt to this outing before she really did become overheated. Or before he did.

As if she knew what he'd been about to say, she beat him to the punch. "Are you ready to go in? I think the vendor is motioning all the boats to move toward shore."

He thought she was just saying that until his glance turned toward the rental place and he saw that the man was indeed waving at them. Actually, it looked like they were the only ones still out on the lake.

So it was time to end this field trip. He had to agree with her. It had been nice. Maybe a little too nice. But in the face of the alternative, he would take it and run with it. For as long as she would let him. Even though it might be harder when it all came to an end.

CHAPTER THREE

THE APARTMENT WAS quiet when Bella left a few days later. This pattern of getting up early and being super quiet so she could leave before he woke up was starting to wear on her, even though he'd told her not to bother. But it was easier this way. Especially after their little trip to the Bosques de Palermo. It had been so reminiscent of the old days that when she spotted him leaning against that arbor looking like a Greek statue that had come to life, she'd had to restrain her quivering mouth. Her emotions had come roaring back from the abyss and were crying out for her to go to him and put her arms around him. To lean her head against his chest and breathe in his scent. But she couldn't. And the urge to turn around and run had never been so strong. Besides, there was nowhere to go. Even if they eventually divorced, she was still going to have to see him every day—work with him on some of the same cases.

Unless she moved to another city. But even then, it wouldn't be an answer. She didn't intend to keep the babies from him—even if she could, she didn't want to—and so she would still have to see that rugged, beautiful face of his fairly often. Maybe she shouldn't have sent plea after plea up to *Dios* for the in vitro to work this time. But even the thought of something happening to the babies at this late stage filled her with fear.

No. She was going to have to be around him. And honestly, the more little side trips they took and the more he was involved in this part of the pregnancy, the better. She'd get used to it, right? Being near him without him being a part of her life anymore? Even the thought of it made her heart cramp. He'd talked about them needing their space. And in some ways she agreed with him.

She just wasn't sure she would ever become immune to him, no matter how much space there was between them.

Realizing she'd been sitting there deep in thought for the last fifteen minutes, she started the car and shifted it into reverse before she remembered that she'd set her lanyard on the kitchen counter when she went to drink a second glass of milk.

Maldición! She couldn't go through her day without it. She needed it for a lot of tasks at the hospital including the computer system and the medicine cabinets. She was going to have to go back into the apartment just as quietly as she'd left it. Sighing and hoping the rest of her day didn't follow this negative trajectory, she turned off the car and pocketed the keys. Going back up the elevator, she unlocked the door and opened it. But expecting to be met with a dark space, she was shocked when she opened the door to find the lights glaring, blinding her for an instant. She was pretty sure she hadn't switched anything on, which meant…

Seb was awake somewhere in the apartment. She blinked a couple of times before her eyes adjusted. She tried to creep toward the kitchen, hoping to retrieve the lanyard before he appeared from the guest room. Quietly picking her way toward the kitchen, she stopped midstride with the light from hallway flicked on. Her eyes shot toward the space and realized Seb was coming out of the bathroom. And he was naked, water streaming down and following the contours of his body. And those contours were heavenly. Just like a Greek statue.

She swallowed hard, freezing in place.

He hadn't seen her yet, his hands sliding through his hair and ruffling it, sending water droplets flying in all directions.

At one time, this would have driven her wild, but in a completely different way than it was right now. She would have been irritated that he was dripping water all over their expensive hardwood floors. Seb, however, would just smile that secretive smile of his and it would change everything in a flash.

She winced, realizing she'd made some kind of squeaked sound that caused Seb's head to turn her way. Her eyes widened in horror.

So much for collecting her keys and getting back out before he got up.

Her nipples tightened as she stood there and stared, a wave of need going through her that was more powerful than anything she'd felt in a long time. She forced herself to stay right where she was, telling herself if she walked toward him things were going to get messier than they already were. Not to mention he could very well reject her.

But hell, while she could stand there rooted in place, she couldn't make her eyes follow suit, and they were busy sliding over every wet inch of his body. Until she reached…

And like a master puppeteer pulling a string, it started to rise.

That made her move. Fast. But not toward him. She crossed the hallway and ducked through the door into the kitchen. "Sorry," she called. "I forgot my lanyard."

When she turned back toward the door, her errant key card in her hand, there he was. Again.

"Sorry," he murmured with a wry smile, still naked. "I forgot my towel."

She blinked, keeping her eyes averted this time.

Was he trying to torment her? He walked past her and into the laundry room, coming back a few seconds later with a towel slung around his narrow hips. But there was still a telltale sign of his reaction to her stares that she could see even through the terry cloth fabric.

She hauled her lanyard around her neck, gripping it tight when she found herself hoping the edge of that towel would come untucked. How long had it been since she'd been able to look at him for pure enjoyment's sake?

A long time. But he was no longer hers to do that

with, and if he'd accidentally come into the bathroom and stared at her like that, she probably would have yelled for him to get the hell out of there. But he hadn't.

And from what she'd just seen...

The man wasn't totally immune to her. She didn't know yet how she felt about that.

If anything, it was going to make it harder to make rational decisions. To not let her emotions get all caught up in the memories—in the sights and scents—of what they'd once meant to each other.

But she had to figure it out somehow, or she was going to be doomed to fall back in love with him.

And that would be a disaster, right?

He'd made it pretty clear that he was here only to support her because she was carrying his children, not because he wanted to go back to being married in the real sense of the word.

And her reaction to him? Hormones. It had to be. Hadn't she read that women started feeling all kinds of crazy things as they went into their second trimester? And coming up on seventeen weeks, she was definitely there.

"There are towels in the linen closet. You didn't have to go all the way to the laundry room for one."

His smile widened in a wicked way she remembered so well before he said, "I know."

That made her run for the hills before she could cut apart and analyze exactly what he meant by that. Because she was afraid if she didn't get out now, she might not leave at all.

* * *

Seb hadn't meant to make her uncomfortable. But hell if she hadn't stared at him like she'd never seen him before. And it had been enough to make him want what he couldn't have. But, damn it, to parade himself naked in front of her like that? It reeked of desperation, and he'd sworn to himself multiple times, as he lay there at night unable to sleep because he knew she was just a few steps away, that he wasn't here for sex or intimacy or anything that went along with it. He was here because her doctor thought she needed the extra support. Plus he hadn't found another place to live. Not yet. But maybe it was time to start doing that.

Their current apartment only had two bedrooms, and the guest room was pretty small, as his shin could attest after being knocked against the wooden footboard of the bed a couple of times now. And with triplets? It would seem even smaller. But right now there was literally not another bedroom he could sleep in besides the one he was in. And to get three cribs in that tiny space in addition to the bed that was already in there? It was probably impossible without somehow stacking them bunk bed–style against the wall—not the best idea.

The thought of leaving this place and going their separate ways, though? That was a hard pill to swallow. But it was bound to happen in a few quick weeks. Her pregnancy suddenly seemed far too short. For him, at least. He doubted any other human being on the planet had ever thought that, but right now, the birth of their babies probably spelled the end of their relationship, and that was a kick in the gut.

To deal with it, he got dressed and decided that rather than fixing breakfast in the large kitchen, he would go out to a nearby café and get something. He could get to work early today and do some paperwork in their office. With that, he closed and locked the apartment and headed to the hospital.

Even hours after he arrived, however, the memory of her parted lips as she'd stared at him plagued him, making it almost impossible to concentrate. But he needed to. And in actuality, just because she'd had a physical reaction to him didn't mean they would reconcile. For the very same reason that him having his own very visible reaction to her didn't change the fact that things were still not good between them. And they might never be again.

Oh, they were on the surface, in how they were civil to each other. But underneath it was a whole different ball game. She had to be angry with him because of the last time they were together when he'd refused to try IVF again. And the fact that she was carrying this pregnancy was proof that she might have been right, and him saying no might have deprived her of ever having biological children.

He'd been wrong. Only at the time, he'd been convinced he was doing the right thing. Not just for him, but for her. To save her from the heartbreak she'd experienced time after time during her fertility treatments.

Did that mean that what might seem like the right

decision at any given moment would later on turn out to be the wrong one?

Like his vague hope that they might work things out? Ten years from now, would he laugh at how wrong he'd been and how ludicrous the idea of them still being together was?

Damn. Coming in to work had not helped at all. Just the opposite, in fact, because Seb knew that Bella was out there somewhere, probably run off her feet while he sat in a nice cool…calm…office.

Calm? Maybe in the physical sense. But his brain was running at top speed trying to figure out a solution that would work for both of them and coming up with absolutely…nothing.

Tossing his pen onto his desk, he stood and stretched his back. He might as well just head out to the floor. Maybe physical work would keep his thoughts at bay, or at least give him something else to concentrate on. If they were working on different patients they would barely see each other. Which was what they both wanted.

They were both head of the department, and by him leaving for Africa, she'd had to shoulder a lot of the day-to-day running of the ER, something he hadn't really thought about when he'd left.

He wasn't due in for his shift for another four hours, so his sudden appearance made heads turn, although it really shouldn't. Seb had been known to work long hours. But the one person he didn't see was Bella.

And he wasn't going to ask.

He headed to the desk to see which patient was next, only to run into Gabriel, who looked like he was signing paperwork for one of his runs. The EMT turned and smiled.

"Hi, *porteño*. Long time no see."

Seb laughed. "Yes, it's been almost a week. We need to go out for a *cerveza* and catch up." Then he got serious. "How's life been treating you?"

"I can't complain." He grinned. "Well, I could, but it wouldn't do any good. You?"

He wasn't quite sure how to answer that, only to have Gabriel save him by holding up a hand. "Never mind. I probably don't want to know."

"Even *I* probably don't want to know."

Bella appeared. And to his relief she didn't look run off her feet. She looked as fresh as she had back at the apartment. "Don't want to know what? Something about the patient you brought in?"

For once, Gabriel looked uneasy, shifting from foot to foot. "No. Just stuff about Seb's trip."

Bella's head tilted as if she wasn't sure if she should believe him. But if she was going to ask, she didn't get a chance because Gabriel said something about his partner waiting for him in the truck and needing to get back to it.

He threw a parting shot back at Seb, though. "And, *porteño*, I'm holding you to that *cerveza*. Let's make it sooner rather than later, okay?"

His wife's quizzical look wasn't lost on Seb, but she

didn't ask this time. Maybe, like him, she wasn't sure she wanted to know.

Then she said, "Did you tell him?"

"Tell him what?"

"About the pregnancy."

Shock held him still for a minute. "He doesn't know?" He'd thought as much, but had wondered if he was right. She was in her second trimester and was definitely starting to show. He was really surprised his friend hadn't guessed.

"I—I haven't told anyone. I thought if I did that it might…"

Her words trailed off, and suddenly he knew why she'd kept it a secret. A thread of anger replaced what had happened this morning. "You thought it might get back to me while I was in Africa, is that it?"

"I didn't want you to hear about it that way."

"Are you sure? Because it's starting to feel like you didn't want me to hear about it at all." He sucked in a deep breath. "What if I'd delayed coming back even longer, Belle? What if it had been four or five more months? Would you have let me know about it then? Or would I have come back to find out that I had three children I didn't even know about? Do you know what I thought when I came back and you finally told me?"

"I can probably guess."

"Hell, I thought you'd miscarried when I left. So when you told me you were pregnant, my first thought was that you'd been with someone else."

Her face went deadly pale, and she glanced around. "Not here!"

He realized his voice had risen enough with that last sentence that a couple of nurses were looking at them. "Let's go around the corner."

He stalked toward a hallway that contained linens and supplies and tended to be quieter than some of the main areas.

When she stopped in front of him, her face was stricken. "You seriously thought I would cheat on you?"

Maldición! He shouldn't have said anything, but especially not that. He shouldn't have let his anger and resentment cause him to lash out at her. Especially not in her state. Remembering what Liz had said about keeping her stress as low as possible, he touched her arm. "It was only for a split second, then I realized you wouldn't have. Just like I wouldn't have. But our relationship was such a damn mess and I was hurt— I felt you'd kept something important from me. That you would have kept the babies from me altogether if you could figure out how to."

"No, I would never do that to you. You have to believe me. I just didn't want you to hear about it by phone or text. Or worse, by the hospital's rumor mill. When you were later coming back than you said you'd be, I decided I'd tell you if there was another delay." Her teeth came down on her lower lip. "I'm sorry I pressed you so hard for so long to keep trying."

He slid his arm around her waist and gave her a light

squeeze. "The only important thing right now are the babies, okay? Let's concentrate on them."

She stiffened for a second, then pulled away, her eyes avoiding his. "Yes. You're right. They're the only things that are important. And we might as well start letting people know that they exist, because it's going to come out soon enough." She touched her belly. "But as for us, let's stick to discussing them rather than personal stuff between us from now on."

In other words, the subject of where they stood as a couple was off the table. Maybe because she'd already come to a conclusion where that was concerned, and from her words the news wasn't what he wanted to hear. But even if he didn't want to hear it, he needed to respect what she was saying and try to remember that this was no longer about them. They were only together because of the babies. And the sooner he got that through his thick skull, the sooner he could figure out where to go and what to do after the babies were born and his "services" were no longer needed.

A nurse appeared around the corner. "Hey, guys? We could use your help."

He'd forgotten for a second that Bella was supposed to be on duty. "What's up?"

"We've got three patients who've all overdosed on something. We need some extra hands."

They rushed back down the hallway, all thoughts of relationships and talking forgotten as they came on a frenetic scene. One patient was on the floor of the waiting room seizing while a nurse and one of their interns leaned over him trying to get his vitals. Another guy was unresponsive on the ground nearby. A third guy, who'd evidently driven his car partway through the doors of the emergency room, cracking the glass of one of them, had exited his car and was drunkenly ambling toward them. Bloody foam dribbled from the sides of his mouth, and his teeth gnashed in a way that Seb had only seen in horror movies. A woman was crying inside the car. Bella started to hurry toward the man, who was slowly moving in their direction but Seb grabbed her arm, a sudden fear going through him. "Can you go talk to the person in the car? See if she knows what they took? I'm going to get security down here before someone gets hurt."

Bella's brows drew together for a second. "I can handle myself, Seb. I don't need you to step in and—"

"It's not a matter of handling yourself. We don't know what he took and if fentanyl is involved…"

"Oh, God." As if realizing the ramifications of being exposed to some of the crazy drugs people took nowadays, she headed toward the car instead.

As if already alerted, two security officers came down, already gloved and masked, while Seb hurried to do the same. Together, they managed to get the guy on a gurney and strapped down so he couldn't hurt anyone.

His pupils were pinpoints, and when Seb checked with the doctors treating the other patients, they reported the same thing.

Bella came back. "They all injected heroin. The girl

didn't take any, but she said there've been reports of it being laced with something. Other people have gotten sick as well."

Sure enough, Seb found tracks on the man's arms. "Let's get some naloxone down here."

Unfortunately, as in large cities all over the world, illegal drugs were a problem that seemed never-ending. Even as he thought it, the police were taking the woman out of the car and putting handcuffs on her. Those drugs affected everyone around the users, including people who hadn't taken it. He had no idea if she was a girlfriend or someone's sister or friend, but she'd just witnessed the horrors that went along with overdoses. Hopefully it would be enough to scare her into wanting nothing to do with it or with those who were unwilling to get help with their addictions.

They dosed the seizing patient with the reversal agent first to see if it had any effect. It did, almost immediately. They followed with the other two patients and waited until it took effect. By then there were four more police officers in the ER, waiting on reports.

Bella went over and talked to them, letting them know everything that they knew so far. Seb had no doubt that once the crisis was over and the patients were stable, each of them was going to pay a hard price for what they'd done.

They'd almost paid with their lives, had been very lucky that the man who'd gotten out of the drivers' seat hadn't crashed into something and killed them all. And Bella walking toward that man had made his stomach twist in a way that had made him act without thinking. He was pretty sure he was going to pay for that later himself.

The police accompanied the patients to the rooms, handcuffs at the ready. Seb gave instructions on watching them to make sure the Narcan kept them stable enough to release into police custody.

As soon as things were under control, everyone breathed a sigh of relief. A tow truck came out and pulled the car from the entryway, and maintenance people came to see about getting the cracked window replaced.

And when he turned around, he knew for certain he was in big trouble.

Bella was standing there, arms crossed. "Listen. I know you were worried, but you do need to know that I would not have put myself in danger. I wasn't going to try to tackle him to the ground or anything."

"I know. It's just that in your condition—"

"Exactly what condition is that?" Her voice was tight with anger.

Seb was confused. He was pretty sure she knew what he was referring to. "Do you think Liz would want you trying to control a man hyped up on *Dios* knows what? A man who's also three times your size?"

"I told you I wasn't going to try to tackle him or restrain him on my own. But you have to trust me to do my job. To know when to step in and when to step back and let security take the lead. We've been trained in this. Hell, Seb, we've trained med students for years on crisis intervention."

He was right; he was going to pay. But looking at it from her side, she was the one who was actually right. "I know that. I was just worried about..." He shrugged. "I was worried about the babies."

"Maybe you should let me worry about them, since I'm the one carrying them."

Continuing this conversation wasn't going to do either one of them any good and was just going to create the very thing Liz said she was supposed to avoid: stress. Time to wave the white flag.

"You're right. I overstepped, and I'm sorry. It won't happen again."

She gave a curt nod. "Make sure it doesn't. Now I'm going to go and make sure the patients—all of them— are ready to be released."

With that, she stalked off. Away from the conversation. And away from him.

The only important things were the babies.

Seb's words, as well as his actions during the interactions with their overdose patients, had put a face on what she feared most. That their relationship was dead, and the only thing left from it were the tiny beings they had created together. Actually, they hadn't even done that. Their babies hadn't been the product of them coming together in love, they'd been created in a test tube and then inserted inside her. They'd each just contributed their genetic material. And it seemed that Seb wasn't willing to contribute anything more.

Not fair, Bella. He'd made it clear that he wanted to have a role in raising his children. And he'd honestly been worried about her putting herself in harm's way. So it was obvious he wasn't leaving her completely alone. She'd see him periodically. And he'd worry about the kids. It would be a heaven and a hell of her own making.

She'd never asked her mother point-blank if she'd been in love with her biological father. If it had devastated her to find out that he hadn't wanted to be with her in a more permanent way. And it was something she would never ask.

Her mom had gotten through that pain somehow, and so would Bella.

The same way she'd gotten through two months of Seb's absence. That had been unbearably hard. Especially when she'd found out she was carrying triplets. The fantasy of him coming home and sweeping her off her feet and professing his continued undying love had come and gone. He'd done neither of those things. Any feelings he'd had for her had probably been crushed by her desperate search for the holy grail of having a baby. She'd seen it in his face during their last discussion before he'd left for Africa.

Unfortunately for her, she didn't have to worry about falling back in love with him. She already knew she was still crazy about him. But she was also coming to realize that wasn't enough. Love couldn't be one-sided and survive. If he stayed in the relationship just because of the babies, she would soon grow to resent him. And he would resent her if she pressed him for more. So it was better to let him go now.

He'd still been in the ER when she finished with their patients. She walked past him, telling him she needed to get something. And she had. She'd needed to pull her dignity back around her like a cloak and use it to hold back any of the softer feelings she had toward him. How pitiful would it be if he realized she still loved him?

She wouldn't be able to bear it. So he couldn't know. And while she'd told him there was no longer a reason to keep the pregnancy a secret, that didn't hold true for her feelings. They needed to stay tucked deep inside her where he would never guess they existed. She leaned against a wall and tried to catch her breath.

Finally regaining her composure, she headed back out onto the floor. Where she would probably see Seb again. But when she emerged, the ER was oddly quiet. There were no pressing emergencies. She glanced at her watch. It was noon. Maybe potential patients were eating their lunch before heading in. But whatever it was, she was going to embrace it, just liked she hoped she could embrace her new reality: that of a single mother. At least once the babies were born, their time would be divvied up between two separate households. Because there was no way she and Seb were going to live in the same house once the triplets came. She wouldn't be able to bear it, and she doubted Seb would want that either. He was probably anxious to get on with the next phase of his life. The one where his children were the only important things and where Bella was relegated to the past.

It was how it needed to be. But that didn't mean it was how she wanted it to be.

She knew you didn't always get what you wanted. So she would get the next best thing. Lunch. And she'd do her best to convince herself that it was the only thing she wanted.

CHAPTER FOUR

THE FRIDAY OF their appointment came, and a strange sense of quiet resignation seemed to have arisen between them. He convinced himself that it was better than the uneasy truce they'd had, where one careless word could send them back to their own corners to wait for the next verbal skirmish. The week had been hard. Seb had met Gabriel for beers just like he'd promised and had told him about the triplets and that despite the joy he felt about them, he wasn't sure he and Bella would stay together after they were born. The fact that that his friend wasn't as surprised about that as he was about the babies said it all. He doubted that Gabriel would be an isolated case. Did everyone in the hospital know how bad it had gotten between them?

He was getting ready to meet Bella for her appointment with the specialist when he was stopped in the hallway by a colleague. "Hey, congratulations, Seb! I heard about the babies. How great that you and Isabella were able to work out your differences. It gives the rest of us married people who are having some issues hope."

Damn. So he was right. People did know about their

problems. Had their situation looked that hopeless? And what was he even supposed to say to that? His private life was really no one's business, but he also didn't want to lie and say that things were great when they were anything but. But he could try to work out a canned response later on. So for now he just stuck to saying, "Thanks," and left it at that.

Especially since Bella came around the corner, obviously looking for him. Fortunately the other doctor didn't stick around and chitchat some more; he simply smiled and continued on his way.

"Are you ready?" she asked.

"Yep. Let's take my car."

She hitched her purse further up her shoulder. But unlike when they'd driven separately to the park, this time she didn't argue. "Sounds good. You know where it is?"

"I do. I pulled it up on my phone. It's about a fifteen-minute drive, and it's near the Rio de la Plata."

The rich sediment at the bottom of the famous river was often churned up as the water flowed into the Atlantic Ocean, giving portions of it a brown appearance. But its biodiversity was impressive, and it played an important part in the area's ecosystem.

"Liz said it's a really nice clinic, and of course the babies will still be delivered at our facility, since it's also one of the hospital's clinics."

They got into Seb's vehicle, and he carefully backed out of the hospital parking lot, which tended to be tricky with his larger SUV.

"Wouldn't it be easier to have a car the size of mine?"

He threw her a glance. "You used to love this vehicle. And I'm not sure three car seats will even fit in yours."

"I do still love this car. And you're right. I just…" She shrugged. "I'm just realizing how many things are going to change once these kiddos are born."

Including their living situation. She hadn't spelled it out, but then again, she didn't need to. He glanced at her. "Things can't always stay the way they were."

There was silence in the car for a few awkward minutes before she murmured, "No, I guess they can't. Life moves forward, even when it's not what we planned for."

The roads were crowded, even though it wasn't rush hour yet. But then Buenos Aires was a huge tourist destination. So the traffic wasn't solely due to the city's residents, but also rental cars and buses and the ubiquitous motorcycles that tended to dart in and out of traffic whenever they felt like it. Despite the fast pace of the cars around him, Seb was painfully aware that he was carrying precious cargo. Not just the babies, but Bella as well. He was not going to take any risks that he didn't have to take.

Like leaving the country and letting her face things alone?

"I think your phone is telling you to turn left at the next corner."

"Thanks." He'd been so busy concentrating on the cars around him that he'd almost missed the GPS's instructions.

He put on his signal and edged over just in time to

make the turn. He only realized how hard he was gripping the steering wheel when Bella's knee bumped his. "Do you want me to help navigate?"

It was something they'd once done, with her looking at the phone's digital map and letting him know if there was a turn coming up and how far away it was.

"That would be great. Thanks." It would be a lot like old times. Happier times.

He gave a mental sigh and listened as she gave instructions that were off in the distance, even as the computerized voice let them know when they were close to the turn. Within ten minutes they'd arrived at their destination: a large white house that had evidently been converted into a specialized maternity center that contained state-of-the-art equipment.

Finding a parking space near the back, they got out, and Seb was struck by the pristine landscaping that the clinic had done. A small area of green grass was flanked by a walkway from the parking area and another path that led the way to the front door. Two potted bougainvillea stood on either side of the entryway, their crimson blooms striking against the building's whitewashed facade. There was patio on one side, over which stretched a pergola that provided some relief from the summer heat.

Entering the lobby, they found a sign directing them to check in at one of the windows to the left. They went over and waited behind another couple. The woman was obviously getting close to term and was telling her partner that she'd be glad when she could see her feet again. Out of the corner of his eye he watched as Bella's head bent as if looking at her own feet.

She was gorgeous, and he had no doubt she'd be just as gorgeous when she, too, had trouble seeing past her stomach.

He let her do the talking when they got to the window. And when they looked past her to him, she introduced him as her husband.

It made something in his chest tighten. How many more of those introductions would he get? He knew the day would come when the prefix "ex" would be placed in front of that word. When he would no longer be her husband, but just someone from her past. Someone she hadn't wanted to stay connected to any longer.

But for right now, the word was still valid. And he was glad. More glad than he probably should be.

"If you'll just have a seat, we'll call you both back in a few minutes."

Bella thanked them, and he let her lead them to a seating area of her choosing. He had to smile when she picked a row in the back. She never had liked sitting up front, even in medical school. She preferred to sit back and observe, claiming she could pay just as much attention back there as she could up front—where she felt conspicuous.

They'd just barely settled into their seats when a door at the front of the room opened up and her name was called. "Yikes," she whispered. "I hope Liz didn't try to get us special treatment."

He understood her reservations, but triplets were

probably something they didn't deal with on a daily basis. They went through to the back and were ushered to a door on the right side of a long hallway. Once inside, a nurse came in and took her weight and blood pressure and had her lie down on the table so they could get a measurement of her belly.

"Everything looks good. Dr. Lucas will be with you in just a few minutes to do a more in-depth exam."

True to her word, there was soon a knock at the door, and an older lady came into the room. She had long wavy gray hair that she wore loose around her shoulders. "You must be Mr. and Mrs. Lopez. I'm Jessica Lucas." She settled on a stool and turned to face them. "So you're expecting triplets through IVF treatments. Were three embryos implanted?"

Bella nodded her head. "Yes. Dr. Everly knew I'd lost several pregnancies, and she hoped at least one would take this time. Instead they all did."

"And you chose not to undergo a reduction procedure?"

Seb tensed. He'd wondered about the exact same thing.

"No. I thought this might be my only chance to have children, so I'm opting to carry them all to term. Or at least I hope to."

"I understand. It will make it a little trickier for us, but we've delivered several other triplets, and Dr. Everly has a good track record for healthy embryos." She smiled and reached over to pat Bella's hand. Then she looked at both of them. "Do you have names picked out yet?"

"N-no." Bella's voice was soft. "I haven't even gotten that far yet. Maybe I'm afraid that I'll jinx things. I just worry that…"

"Hey. Let me do the worrying, okay? If there's cause for concern, I promise I'll tell you, okay?"

Bella visibly relaxed. "Thanks, Dr. Lucas."

"Call me Jessica, please."

Dr. Lucas stood, swooshing her thick strands of hair behind her shoulders in a gesture that made him smile. She would fit in with the counterculture movement that had started in El Bolsón over on the southwestern side of Argentina. He'd taken a trip over there in his teens and had been fascinated by the village, where self-sufficiency was the name of the game and where freedom of expression was valued above most other things.

"Let's get this show on the road. I know you just had an ultrasound last week—I have those scans from Dr. Everly, but I want to do our own as a baseline, although we're a little late to the game. She also said she had a hard time seeing one of the triplets. If you'll hop up on the table and pull up your shirt and slide the waistband of your skirt low on your hips, we'll get things started."

Seb stood to help her onto the table, also lending a hand and tugging the gauzy skirt low on her hips. He had done it so many times in the past and had never thought twice about it, but now there was an intimacy to the act that made him hyperaware of her. His fingers lingered for a second on softness of her skin. Her belly seemed even more rounded this week than it had been last week. Her breasts were also fuller. He'd never gotten to see any of these changes in their previous attempts, as the pregnancies hadn't held long enough to make a difference in her appearance.

It suddenly made things seem very real to him. So real that yet again he was incredibly uneasy that something might happen. That they might lose the babies that had been growing inside of her for seventeen weeks.

"Damn machine. I can never get it to… There!"

Bella's eyes met his, and her lips twitched, then as if she couldn't contain herself, she giggled. He smiled back at her in return, lifting his brows the way he used to, letting her know that he knew exactly what she was thinking.

He did?

Hell, he hadn't felt that way in a very long time. And he needed to be careful now. He couldn't let one light moment fool him into thinking things between them were better. They weren't. The fact that he'd abandoned her to go to Africa was starting to weigh even heavier on his mind. He should have been here for her. Should have seen her through whatever was coming. But he'd been afraid if he had that he might end up making a decision that he hadn't quite been ready to make.

That he still didn't want to make. Even though he knew it was probably coming anyway. They were still staring at each other. Still smiling.

He heard the sound of something being rolled toward them, and he broke eye contact so he could move away and let the specialist put the machine where she wanted it. "Why don't you go to the other side of the bed, where you can see the screen. Oh, and let me know when you come up with names, so we can label them. For now we'll just assign letters to them."

Seb did as she asked and walked around the head of the bed and wound up on Bella's right side. She reached for his hand, and he took it as Jessica put the transponder on her belly and started moving it around, staring at the screen.

Again, it was something they'd done time and time again, held hands as they awaited the specialist's verdict. It was like muscle memory. Something that had been engraved into their DNA. Kind of like when he automatically felt for her in the middle of the night only to find the bed empty of anyone but him. Only the bed he now slept in was no longer "their" bed. It was for some nameless, faceless guest. Yet he'd now become that amorphous person. Just some temporary human who would pass through her life periodically.

Like when he came to pick up the kids on agreed custody days? His fingers tightened on hers as if already unwilling to let her go.

His attention jerked back to the screen, his mind on high alert, when Jessica made a slight hmphing noise.

"What is it?" Bella's voice was shaky.

He threaded his fingers through hers, laying his other hand over them for added support.

"Nothing. I'm just trying to coax that third little guy

out from behind his or her sibling. I can see the baby's little bottom—" she pointed to the screen "—but his chest and head are tucked behind the other baby." She made another noise. "It's okay. We have time." The words were soft, as if she were talking to herself.

Time for what?

Just like last week, he heard the heartbeats and this time, he could make out the babies' forms without any help from the doctor. He watched as Jessica labeled the babies with A, B and C and put little symbols at the head and bottom of each of them, except for baby C, who was still not cooperating.

"Can you tell the gender of them yet?" Bella's question came out of nowhere.

Jessica stopped and looked at her. "I'd have a more accurate guess for you next week or the week after that. I would like you to come back in. Hopefully by then we'll get Baby Lopez number three to come out and wave at us. Right now, besides being behind baby B, he or she is facing towards the back, which also makes it a little more challenging to see any parts."

Bella wanted to know the gender of the babies ahead of time? It was something else they hadn't really talked about, having never gotten that far in the process. And honestly, he was good either way, although having an A, B and C stuck on that screen bothered him in a way he didn't understand. Maybe they should start playing the name game.

Or would Bella prefer to do that on her own? He

was hyperaware of her hand tucked in his. Of her palm brushing across the skin of his.

Hell, he hoped not. When he said he wanted to be a part of their children's lives, he meant it. He was interested in every aspect of it. Surely they could work together on that, the same way his work colleagues collaborated to make decisions about the ER. The way he and Bella would have to cochair the department until one or both of them left.

Like Dr. Everly had done, Jessica printed off a copy of the ultrasound. "As far as due dates go, I really don't want to put a specific time to it, since we probably won't be able to let you go to full term. It's a balancing act of giving those babies all the time we can to develop and gain weight, while not compromising your health or theirs. Does that make sense?"

"It does. I'm assuming I'll have to have a cesarean?"

"It's what I prefer for higher-order multiples. Especially given your age and the fertility issues you've had in the past." She leaned over and nudged Bella's shoulder with her own. "And believe me, when I say the word *age* I don't mean anything bad by it. You're still young and vibrant. As long as you try to stay in shape and not gain weight too rapidly, we should be good to go."

"I'll do my best. We were already talking about going to the Bosques de Palermo on a regular basis to get some exercise." She glanced up at Seb and he nod-

ded back. "I really want these babies. I won't do anything to jeopardize the pregnancy."

Okay, just when he'd started thinking she wasn't
planning on shutting him out entirely, since she was
including him when she talked about going to the park,
she switched gears and went back to speaking in terms
of herself.

That was another thing they probably needed to hash
out. Was he allowed to give input when he felt she was
working too hard? When he felt she was doing something that put her or the babies at risk? Like with their
overdose patient?

Jessica looked from one to the other. "Let's go at
this like a team, shall we? You and Sebastián work together, and if either of you have any questions about
whether something is safe or not, you come to me and
ask." She smiled. "And don't worry. Sex is definitely
not off the table. At least not for now. But when we
get down to the end, we'll have to start putting limits
on some things like nipple stimulation and so forth."

What the hell? Nipple stimulation?

The specialist was nothing if not forthright. But then
again, the woman had no idea that for all intents and
purposes he and Bella were separated and that sex was
not only *not* on the table, but not on any other piece of
furniture either.

He didn't even want it to be unless it meant something. Not like during their later attempts at pregnancy,
when it had lost some of that meaning. Seb had never

been one to just sleep with someone in order to gain a physical release. He wanted an emotional connection with his partner. And right now, he and Bella didn't have that.

He let go of her hand on the pretext of doing something with his sock. He couldn't blame Dr. Lucas for assuming they were a loving couple. Sitting here together, holding hands, they were certainly the picture of one. But unless Bella disabused her of the notion, he wasn't going to say anything. He was pretty sure the specialist would look askance at that. It might even add some points to whatever mental risk chart she used to assess patients. Seb didn't want to do anything that would hurt Bella's chances at having three healthy babies. He'd move out of the apartment before he let that happen.

"Do you have any other questions? About intimacy or anything else?"

"No. None."

Bella's quick answer made it pretty clear that she didn't want to go into any details about that aspect of their life. Not that they really had one anymore.

"Fair enough. If you do have something you want to know, feel free to call the office and leave me a message. I always try to get back to my patients by the end of the day." She handed Seb the printed image of their babies and wiped the transponder down with alcohol before tucking it back in its holder, switching off the machine. Then she stood up. "Well, it's been nice finally getting to meet you both. I want to see you pretty soon. Honestly, I'd like to try to get a look at that third fetus, just to make sure everything is okay with him or her. So in another week or two? Does that work for you?"

Seb looked at Bella. "It does for me, how about you?" He added, "As far as your work schedule goes, that is." To make it clear that that was all that mattered.

She nodded. "We'll figure it out. I'd also like to know if they're boys or girls, if it's okay with you."

"It is." He glanced at the doctor. "We'll work on names, although I can't make any promises that we'll come to any hard and fast decisions by then."

"No hard and fast decisions needed. There is no need to stress about things like that. Just have fun with it. And each other." She gave a meaningful wink then said, "I'll see you soon."

Just have fun with it and each other.

Her meaning couldn't have been any more plain. He gave an internal eye roll. Little did the woman know that this whole process had been stressful. And if it was for him, then it had to be doubly hard for Bella, who was actually carrying their babies.

It was up to him to make sure he didn't add to that stress. No matter how hard that might prove to be. Maybe it was time to do something about that.

"Do you have time for some coffee or some lunch?"

Bella smiled. "I don't drink coffee anymore, remember? But I am starving, actually. Can we stop somewhere for a quick bite?"

"Yep. I know just the place."

* * *

The place turned out to be one of their old haunts. An Italian eatery that boasted wonderful food and quick service. They used to come here all the time in happier days. They went through the doors and one of the waiters hurried by only to retrace his steps. "Signor and Signora Lopez. Welcome back. It has been too long."

Bella smiled. "Yes, it has, Matteo." It had been more than a year since they'd eaten here. It was funny how little by little things had changed, going almost unnoticed at first, until it was impossible to ignore that their relationship was in trouble. It still was. But it was nice to visit a little bit of the past. A place where she'd felt safe and loved. She was suddenly glad Seb had brought her here.

Without realizing it, her hand went under her belly as if reassuring herself that the babies were still there—just as safe and loved. Then she realized the waiter was staring at her, obviously wanting to ask, but probably wondering if it would appear rude to.

"Yes. We're expecting."

He clapped Seb on the back. "*Congratulazioni!* Come with me. I will get you a table in a nice little corner. Very *romantica*."

"Oh, but…" But the waiter was already walking away, glancing back to make sure they were following him. She looked at Seb to see laughter in his eyes. She swatted at his arm. "Not funny."

She followed the waiter, and sure enough they were seated in a quiet corner. But maybe that was better.

Nothing they said could be overheard. Especially if things turned heated or seemed out of place for a couple who were expecting a child and were supposed to be in love. She suddenly wanted a drink.

"Ugh, I wish I could at least have a glass of wine. They have a Chianti that I love."

"I seem to remember a time when two glasses would make you slightly tipsy."

She laughed. "I remember that too. Except I seem to remember that I wasn't always *too* tipsy."

There was a marked pause. "No. You weren't." The words were soft, and she realized he remembered those times as well. It was before they'd started trying to have kids. They'd go home and make love, except she always fell asleep right afterwards. Seb used to tell her he loved her little snuffling snores that happened when she'd had a little too much to drink.

Matteo came to take their drink and lunch order, already seeming to know that she would need something sparkling rather than alcoholic, while Seb chose to have a house ale. "I'll be back with your drinks and have your food out quickly."

They thanked him.

"I'd forgotten how nice this place was."

"Me, too." There was a short pause. "So, names. Do you have any ideas, yet?"

"No. I haven't really given it much thought. Until now. But I guess we should start looking. How about you?"

He shook his head. "No. Not at all."

"Okay, so that's something we should get together and talk about. I think I have a book somewhere."

She knew right where that book was but didn't want it to bring back any bad memories. Not when things seemed to be going better than they had in a while. So she quickly changed the subject. "What was the name of the other waiter that took our order quite often?"

"Mmm…" He seemed to think for a minute. "I think it starts with a *P*?"

"Paolo?"

"Yes, that was it. He used to flirt with you."

"He did not." She stared at him.

Seb leaned forward, his dark eyes on hers. "Yes. He most definitely did. But I can't blame him."

"I don't remember that at all. I just remember him being nice."

"Matteo is nice. Paolo…well, he was nice in a different way." He grinned. "I'm glad you didn't notice."

A small shiver went through her. "Why is that?"

His fingers touched hers for a second. "Because then I might have had to put a stop to it."

"As if I couldn't do it myself?" She tried to sound indignant, but there was something funny swirling around in her stomach. A weird yearning or something that was like…happiness. An emotion that used to come so easily for them.

"You could definitely do it yourself. But you didn't know what he was doing. So…" He lifted a shoulder in a shrug. "While he flirted, I had the pleasure of knowing that I was the one you'd be going home with."

She swallowed. She had no idea Seb had thoughts like that. But there was something sexy about it. About the pride in his voice when he said that.

"I never wanted to go home with anyone else." She couldn't have stopped the words if she'd tried. Because they were true.

"I'm glad." His fingers came up to cup her cheek, and a shivery longing came over her. His glance fell to her lips, and the world seemed to tilt on its axis.

He was going to kiss her.

His hand moved to her nape, and he slowly drew her forward, her lips parting even as he leaned closer. The lines of his cheeks stood out in sharp relief in the dim light of the lamp on the wall, and she reveled in the fact that this beautiful man had once loved her deeply. Surely she could enjoy this one little moment.

Her eyelids fluttered closed as his warm breath grazed her mouth.

Suddenly a loud crashing sound reverberated through the space, followed by cursing in two different languages. Angry voices grew in volume.

They sprang apart, and Bella saw that across the restaurant a waiter had dropped a whole tray of food, causing a huge uproar.

The mood was lost, and they sat there looking at each other awkwardly for a long moment before they sat back in their seats. Matteo appeared with their drinks a second later.

Well, Seb wasn't indifferent to her, that was for sure.

It was what she'd wanted, wasn't it?

Except that in the sheltered light of an Italian restaurant, things could appear very soft and diaphanous. Very *romantica*, as Matteo had put it. But in the harsh reality of the world outside of this space?

Things didn't always last. If Bella didn't want her heart broken all over again, she needed to be careful. Very very careful. Because she'd witnessed firsthand how things could change, going from wonderful to unbearably sad in a matter of months. And she wasn't sure she could risk going back to visit the sexy, loving moments, knowing they could quickly morph into something they might both come to regret.

CHAPTER FIVE

THE SLIGHT CREAK of the door behind her made her stiffen with the pen and notebook still in hand. It was still fairly early in the morning, and she'd come out onto their balcony while the air was still and cool. She realized today that she didn't come out here nearly as much as she should. Or as much as she used to. There was something particularly quiet and peaceful about the city in the morning. A week had passed since their time at the restaurant, and she was still shaken by how close she'd been to giving in to her feelings.

Sitting on a rattan settee with her feet tucked under her, she'd been perusing a book of baby names and jotting down the ones that struck her as possibilities.

Bella glanced to the side and saw Seb standing in the open doorway, his tall frame taking up most of the space.

"Everything okay?" he asked.

She nodded. "Just following doctors' orders." She held the book up so that he could see the title.

"Baby names. I guess you are. I didn't even realize you had that."

She licked her lips, not sure how to tell him that

she'd bought the book six or seven cycles ago, when her hopes for a successful treatment had still been fresh. "I've had it for a while."

He didn't say anything to that; instead, he just moved further out onto the balcony and sat on a chair across from her. "Do you have any ideas about what you want to call them?"

"Yes, and I'd like to get your opinion. Can you scoot your chair around here?"

He pulled his chair next to the settee while she moved so that she was sitting fairly close to him. It would have been easier for him to just join her on it, and in the old days he wouldn't have hesitated, but since the restaurant it was like they both wanted a separation between them that was both physical and emotional.

Putting the notebook on her lap, she turned it so that he could see it. She'd put two columns on it, one for boys and one for girls. She'd starred the ones that were her current favorites. "Do you want to look at the book itself?"

He gave a crooked smile that made her chest hurt. "It looks like you have almost a whole book's worth of names already written down."

The way he smiled had always made her slightly woozy, and she'd once considered herself the luckiest woman in the world to be married to someone like him. Suddenly aware of her ratty old nightshirt and the hair she hadn't brushed, she put a hand up to run her fingers through the tangled locks. "That might be a slight exaggeration."

He made a sound. "Very slight."

She couldn't hold back her laugh. This *was* like old times. Times when she hadn't felt self-conscious about the way she looked in the mornings. Times when they'd been in sync about everything down to the stuff that other people would find unimportant. But to her it had always just showed how compatible they were.

And their lovemaking. *Dios.* Even without the wine, it had always sent her into the stratosphere no matter how long they'd been married. Sometimes gentle, sometimes frantic, no two times were alike. At least that's the way it had been up until the last couple of years, when things had become robotic and awkward. Just going through the motions to get to where they wanted her to be: pregnant.

Now here she was. They'd reached their goal. But for what? The success wasn't quite as sweet as she'd imagined it to be. Maybe that's because she'd never imagined their relationship getting to the place it was now. And it made her incredibly sad.

He reached over and pointed to one of the names on the list. "Luis. That's my dad's name."

"I know. I chose it because of that."

Seb leaned back and seemed to stare through the wrought iron railing of the balcony not saying anything for a minute or two, but she knew he was touched. Last year Seb's dad had been diagnosed with leukemia. It was in remission currently, but there was no telling how long that would last or if it would come back with a vengeance. It reminded her that she doubted if his parents knew about the pregnancy, although she'd already told her mom and stepdad. Her mom hadn't been super happy about Seb's absence, and Bella had found herself coming to his defense saying he'd already had the trip planned—even though that was one of the things that had hurt her the most.

"Have you told your mom and dad yet?"

He looked at her. "No. I wasn't sure how to explain why we waited so long to let them know."

It hadn't been Seb who'd waited so long, it had been her. Her fear of telling Seb after he'd seemed so adamant about not trying again. Her fear that he'd already decided their marriage was over and that to tell him now would just cement that decision or worse, that he'd stay with her only because of the babies—something that seemingly had come true. The way he'd almost recoiled when the doctor had mentioned sex had taken her aback, although she'd had much the same reaction to Dr. Lucas's blunt words.

Even hearing the comment about stimulation had made her nipples react. She evidently didn't need him to touch her for that to happen.

"Do you want to invite them over to dinner to tell them?"

He shook his head. "I don't want you having to fix a meal, and we both know that my culinary skills are pretty rudimentary."

"Your mom loves to cook. I'm sure the mere mention of getting together for dinner will send her into planning mode."

The fact that Helena loved entertaining had always taken a huge load off her, and Bella loved them both dearly. The thought of them not being in her life anymore made her sad. Even though they would always be the triplets' grandparents, once she and Seb were divorced things would inevitably change between them. She'd no longer be invited to family meals or to go on family trips together.

Why was she so certain they would divorce?

Because the thought of him staying in a loveless marriage just for the sake of the children was unbearable. He deserved to fall in love again and find happiness, even if it wasn't with her—something that seemed just as unbearable as him staying married to her.

There was no winning, it seemed.

"Do you want me to call her?"

"Would you? My parents already know." Bella's biological dad had passed away five years ago in a traffic accident, just at the start of their fertility journey. But it was just as well. It would be hard to see him and think that her life was going down the same path that his once had.

Seb didn't say anything about her parents already knowing, but his mouth tightened. She couldn't blame him. He'd had a right to be the first one to hear the news and instead, she'd told her mom and dad while keeping the babies' own father in dark.

She reached out and touched his hand. "I'm sorry, Seb. Truly. Looking back, I realize I should have returned your call. I was scared about how you would react since you were so certain that we shouldn't try again."

"When I came home and you finally did tell me, I thought you'd kept it a secret because you'd found someone else. You have no idea how that made me feel."

The fact that he was bringing this up again spoke to how deeply that had affected him. But her pain over the fact that he'd thought she'd been unfaithful was just as sharp. They'd hurt each other without even trying. It made her wary of sharing things with him, of thinking too much about the what-ifs or the realities of their situation.

"You're right, I don't. At the time it felt like the right thing to do, but I can see now that it wasn't. All I can do is say how sorry I am."

"It's over and done now." He squeezed her hand and let it go. "So what other names do we have here?"

She glanced down at the paper again and pointed. "My dad's name is here too, of course." Her stepdad's, that was. He'd been there every step of the way for her; his love for a child who wasn't his flesh and blood was strong and undeniable.

"So, Sergio and Luis. Those should definitely stay. And if we have two girls and one boy?"

"We could still use both names. One for the first name and one for the middle name."

That made him smile again, and she did her best not to stare. Again. But it was hard. She'd always loved looking at his face. She knew it so well that she dreamed about him in living color. And some of those dreams were X-rated. It sometimes made it hard to face him in the morning, because the stuff he'd done to her in her sleep made her blush. She knew most of that was hormones; she'd read in one of her pregnancy books that the second trimester brought renewed interest in sex, and it hadn't been kidding. She wanted it. Wanted him, despite the fact that they were still not in a good place.

But maybe they could be… After all, being at the restaurant with him last week had made her take another look at things like that.

Seriously? If he was only here for the babies, how could they have a normal relationship knowing that he had very little interest in her as a person, just about what was growing inside of her? Sex wasn't always about love, wasn't that what people said?

She glanced at him, but his eyes were on the list she'd made. "I like Lorenzo and Gilberto as well," he said.

"Lorenzo is also one of my favorites."

"Okay, I'm good with Luis, Sergio and Lorenzo for boys' names, then. How about you?"

"Yes. That works." She liked the idea of having two names that represented their fathers.

She pointed at two names from the girls' side as well. "I have Helena and Rute after our moms. We could do the same if we only have one girl and call her Helena Rute Lopez."

Bella was proud of herself. She hadn't even hesitated at saying Lopez and knew if they did divorce, she wouldn't go back to her maiden name. No matter what the future held, she'd loved her life with him and wasn't anxious to remove all traces of their past, although she completely understood why many women did.

She still loved Seb. She probably always would. What she didn't love was the thought of living the rest of her life with him, if he no longer felt the same way about her. And she doubted he did. That last scene before he'd left for Angola had caused a breach in their relationship that she wasn't sure could ever be healed. She had learned a lesson from it, though. She would never plead with him for anything again. After he'd left, she'd sat there feeling humiliated and broken. A lot of that had to do with her and not Seb. And a month after he'd left, her sadness had turned to an anger so palpable that she'd been surprised it hadn't hurt her pregnancy. Shock, sadness, disbelief, bargaining, anger, resignation. Weren't those all stages of grief? She'd hit every one of those milestones during his absence, and now she was in a no-man's-land of resignation.

"What other girls' names are your favorites?"

His question made her shake off her melancholic thoughts. She was pregnant with babies she thought she'd never have. She needed to be grateful rather than wallowing in self-pity.

Yes, from now on she was going to think about her children and not about what might have been with Seb. Wouldn't it have been worse to lose the babies *and* him?

Yes, it would. So she looked down at the list and

rattled off a few names and listened to him counter them, adding Sara to the mix when he said it was one of his favorites.

After about a half hour of lighthearted negotiating and some laughter that she took joy in, they had their short list of names. "So I guess we wait until the next appointment with Jessica when hopefully she will be able to tell us the gender of all of them. Including the shy one."

"The shy one. It'll be interesting to see if that carries over after he's born. Hopefully he or she will feel like coming out to play, at least for the ultrasound. Then we can present the list to my parents."

"Let me know when they want to get together. I work days this week and nights next, so if we can schedule it in in the next few days, maybe at the very end of the week, that would probably be ideal."

"Okay, I'll work on it." He slid his palm behind her neck, easing her close enough to give her a quick kiss on the forehead.

A thousand emotions went through her at his touch, the worst of which was hope. It was just muscle memory. Things he'd done hundreds of times in the past— a habit built over ten years of marriage. It had to be. But it made her want to cry.

When he pulled away, he looked just as shell-shocked as she felt. He stood with a quick "see you sometime tonight" and left the room without another word.

She sat there for a long time, the list and book forgotten as she tried to relegate things like kisses on the forehead to the past. Because it was unlikely that it would happen again. It was also unlikely that she'd invite it to happen again, since it would just bring up painful feelings. Like longing and hope for the future. She needed to reserve those emotions for her babies. Because to do anything else would only be inviting disaster. And it could very well send her into a pit of despair all over again.

Seb had gone out on that balcony not realizing that Bella was even out there. But once he'd opened the door, it had been too late to withdraw without coming up with a plausible explanation. One he didn't have on hand.

When she'd looked up at him, her cheeks had been flushed with healthy color and the light that poured into the space had made her hair gleam in a way that seemed almost otherworldly. Pregnancy agreed with her. The book and her list had been in her lap, and her hand and arm had been draped protectively over the slight curve of her belly. It could have competed with a painting in any museum and probably would have come out the winner.

She was beautiful and...happy. And none of that had anything to do with him. In fact, she'd seemed to dim when he entered her orbit. The babies were enough for her, and he needed to accept that fact, as hard as it was.

Hell, if she lost them now she'd be devastated. So would he, but she seemed to be pinning all of her hopes and dreams on these tiny creatures and he couldn't blame her. She'd wanted motherhood for as long as he could remember.

All he could do was help make sure that her dreams came true, and that meant protecting her as much as possible…easing the way as much as he could.

He'd caught sight of her at work when he arrived at the hospital an hour early for his shift, and unlike normal days when Bella seemed to thrive on the unpredictable nature of the ER, she seemed tired. More tired than normal. It was enough that he walked over to her to ask if she was okay.

Before he could open his mouth, though, someone tapped him on the back, and when he turned, he saw one of the other ER residents standing there looking at them with a beaming smile. "I just heard. I'm so happy for you both. Congratulations!"

Bella raised her head and gave the man a tired smile. "Thank you. We appreciate it."

"Yes," Seb agreed. "We do."

With that, he stepped in between the other doctor and Bella, hoping the man got the hint and went on his way, although the move probably came across as rude. It worked, though. The doctor threw them another smile and continued down the hallway.

"Has that been happening all day?"

"Yep. I let it be known to a couple of friends that I was pregnant, since we agreed not to keep it a secret any longer. Well, the news seems to have spread like wildfire, although it was going to be obvious pretty soon. My clothes are getting tighter by the day."

"I'm sorry. I don't know how to make it better."

Her brows went up. "The clothes part? I don't think there's much hope of that."

His gaze swept over her, and his lips twitched. "No, I meant all the congratulations that will probably come our way."

"Me either. They're going to assume it means we're back together." She gave a tired laugh. "I don't think we ever told people we were separated in the first place, although it was probably pretty obvious that something was wrong by the end."

He really didn't want to get into a discussion about the state of their relationship here in the hallway of the hospital. Actually, he didn't want to get into that discussion anywhere. Not when he hadn't quite figured things out himself yet. Part of him was dreading the babies' births because it meant that they would probably go their separate ways, dividing one household into two.

Stop going down that road.

Instead, he said, "Why don't I go ahead and start my shift now. You look run off your feet. You can go home and relax."

"That bad, huh?" She smiled, though, and this time it seemed genuine. "It doesn't matter. I'm actually going to take you up on your offer if you're serious. I am pretty tired. It's been hectic today and with all of the well-wishers…"

"Let me fend them off for a while. I'm sure in a day or two, everyone will get it out of their system, and it will become old news."

At least until they broke up for real.

"Thanks. Do you mind if I head to the office and unwind a little?"

Even though the office had both of their names on the door and they were both head of the department, Seb normally did the day-to-day paperwork for the ER and used the space a lot more than she did. "Of course not. Why don't you stretch out on the couch for a bit?"

He wasn't even going to picture that, because it would lead to other thoughts that were best left for another time. Actually they were best relegated to the past, where they belonged.

The urge to kiss her on the forehead, like he had on the balcony, came and went. He'd made that mistake this morning, and it had not been a smart move. The taste of her skin was something he would never get out of his system. And kissing her had just reminded him of too many things that would likely never happen again. Like sleeping tangled so tightly together that he was never sure where he ended and she began. Worse was how uncomfortable she'd looked when he'd pulled away this morning. It had been a mistake, and it seemed they both knew exactly how much of one. So no more kissing.

He only hoped he could remember how *not* to do that. How *not* to do a lot of things. So he just said, "Go get some rest. I'll check on you in a little while."

"If your shift is anything like mine, you won't have time to. Don't worry, I'll set my alarm. Unlike you, I don't keep a second set of clothes here at the hospital."

Many doctors did, but Bella only kept a second set of scrubs in case of contamination. She'd always insisted she was going home to change and that she wasn't going to spend the nights at the hospital like Seb had on numerous occasions. It was one of the few things they'd really disagreed on and looking back at it, he saw just how many moments he'd missed with her by not coming home. How many opportunities to hold her had come and gone. Now he would never get them back again.

He rubbed at a phantom pain in his chest that just wouldn't leave. "Just for the record, you're right not to."

"I am?" She blinked a couple of times as if unsure why he was suddenly saying that. But he wasn't going to admit to her that she'd been right all along. About more than just that.

The realization that it was too little, too late and would change nothing did not ease that gnawing ache.

He caught sight of another staff member hurrying toward them and he said, "Go. Save yourself. While you still can."

She glanced in the direction he was looking and laughed. "You don't have to tell me twice." With that, she spun around and headed in the direction of their office while he did his best to smile and accept the person's happy thoughts on his and Bella's news. Only this person spelled out that he was simply happy to see them together.

It went on like that for the rest of the evening— varying messages with the same theme. And when he'd taken his break at midnight and went to check on Bella, the office was empty. She must have gone home like she said she would. He was glad. She'd sleep better in her own bed.

In *their* own bed. Heaven knew he wasn't getting much rest in the guest room, and it had nothing to do with the comfort of the mattress. It had to do with knowing she was just out of reach in the bedroom down the hall.

Sighing, he noted the indent of her body was still on the couch, and a knitted throw—a gift from his mom—was lying loosely folded on the cushion rather than draped over the back of it like it normally was. Unable to resist, he lay down where she'd been and closed his eyes. He should at least call Bella to let her know where he was, but then again, he'd often ended up sleeping in his office, and he didn't want to wake her if she was already at home asleep.

Sucking down a deep breath, he allowed himself to settle more deeply into the quiet of the night. Into the quiet of not having to run from emergency to emergency with barely time to breathe. And after a few minutes, he let his muscles relax one by one, his last thought being that he needed to call his mom in the morning.

His mom answered on the second ring. "Hi, Seb. This is early for you, isn't it?"

"A little." No need to tell the truth that he'd spent most of last night being hounded by person after person all ecstatic that he and Bella were not only pregnant, but evidently back together. He couldn't blame them, and he probably would have done the same if he'd been in their position. A few more months of this, though, and things were going to be a mess to straighten out. "But I have a question for you. Do you and Dad have time for us to come over for a visit?"

"Of course, you don't even have to ask. Can we do a meal? Bella looked a little wan the last time I saw her at the hospital."

"You came to see her?"

"We did, about a month ago. You were in Africa, and I wanted to make sure she had everything she needed. She was busy and didn't have a lot of time for chitchat. We agreed to meet for coffee, but we could never work out a good time."

Maybe because Bella didn't want to explain why she wasn't drinking coffee at the moment, even though she loved it. Her mom knew that she'd abstained from it while trying to get pregnant, but with Seb in Africa there would have been no reason for her not to drink it. He couldn't blame her for wanting to avoid that conversation, especially knowing that she hadn't even told Seb that he was going to be a father.

"Well, we have the time now. Would sometime at the end of this week work?"

"Absolutely. How about Friday?"

They had an appointment that morning with the specialist, but they were free that evening, since both of them were off. "Perfect. Want us to bring anything?"

"How about a bottle of wine?" There was a pause before her mom added, "If you guys are trying to get pregnant again, I'll understand if you'd rather not do that."

But this was one explanation he didn't want to attempt. Not without Bella at his side. "Nope, we're not currently trying. So wine it is." It wasn't a complete lie.

"Is there anything special you want?"

He'd never thought to ask Bella if there was anything in particular that she was avoiding. He knew there were certain foods she shouldn't eat during her pregnancy, so to be safe, he simply said, "Make your roast chicken dish. You know it's always been one of Bella's favorite things."

As well as nipple stimulation…

Damn! Why had that thought come to mind?

"Great. I'm happy you guys can come. Do you realize I haven't even seen you since you got back?"

He did realize it. But it was also something he'd been kind of avoiding, not wanting to go into any deep discussions on the state of his marriage. His mom had always been especially intuitive about those kinds of things. She would have probably read him like a book. So yes. Better to face his parents together. "Dad still doing okay?"

"He is. His last checkup still showed no signs of any abnormal cells in his blood."

Seb gave a sigh of relief and counted his blessings. He might wish some things in his life were different, but not this. He was hopeful his dad would have many, many more years of health.

"Give him a hug for me, and we'll see you guys on Friday."

"See you then, Sebito."

The diminutive of his name made him smile as it always did. He was head and shoulders taller than his mom, but she still called him "Little Seb." Yes, he was blessed in so many ways. So maybe he should start focusing on that and not on all the ways he wished things were different. Because they weren't. And hoping for the impossible would do no one any good.

One thing he and Bella did need to talk about was how to approach Friday's dinner. They'd always been a fairly demonstrative couple, and his mom would notice if there were no longer any little touches to the hand and arm, no upturned lips waiting for him to drop a kiss on them. And if his mom noticed, there was no way she would let it go by without saying something or asking him what was wrong.

So did they tell her the truth, that he was only living with Bella to help her with the pregnancy and delivery? Or did they put on the performance of a lifetime and hope that somehow his mom bought it? At least until after the babies were born and they could figure out exactly how to break his mother's heart.

CHAPTER SIX

THEIR SHIFTS JUST so happened to align a few days later. He'd had to go to a meeting at another hospital for a day and in the scramble to cover everything, he hadn't thought about the fact that Bella would be working at the same time he was.

Trying to stagger their shifts probably wasn't one of his smartest moves, because they still saw each other at home.

But at almost eighteen and a half weeks pregnant now, the changes in her were becoming more and more obvious. And not just her growing abdomen.

It wasn't anything she did or said so much as a paleness that seemed to hover over her whenever there was a case that required her to exert herself. He made a mental note to ask the specialist about it and see if Bella maybe needed to start cutting back on her hours. She wasn't carrying just one baby—she was carrying three. Surely that was three times the strain on her system?

They still hadn't discussed this upcoming Friday night and how she wanted to play it. But he would have to broach that subject soon as well.

Thankfully it looked like most of the people he knew

or were acquainted with had gotten the congratulations thing out of their system.

"Dr. Lopez to the ER. Dr. Sebastián Lopez, please come to the emergency department."

His heart stopped for a second. Bella? Had something happened? He'd just sat down to do some paperwork when the call came in, and he jumped out of his seat and sprinted down the hallway to find Bella crouched on top of a moving gurney administering CPR to a patient. What the hell? What did she think she was doing?

He caught up with the group and said, "Switch with me."

Bella glanced up with a frown and motioned him away, not losing a beat. He followed them, noting she was practically panting with the next set of chest compressions. He didn't want to overstep, but it was obvious she couldn't keep this up for much longer. He was just about to insist when she looked at him.

"Okay," she said, "Switch."

She scrambled down from the gurney, and Seb leaned in and took over compressions with Bella squeezing the Ambu bag, still slightly out of breath as she rattled off the symptoms. "Thirty-two-year-old man suffering electrocution while trying to illegally hook into the city's power grid. Immediate cardiac arrest and serious electric burns to both hands."

The burns were the least of the man's worries. At this point they'd be lucky to even get his heart started again. "Defibrillated?" He had to say the word between compressions.

"Twice en route. They got a rhythm twice as well, but he arrested again within a minute each time."

The fact that they'd even gotten something gave Seb enough hope to continue lifesaving measures. If his heart had sustained irreparable damage, it was doubtful they'd get him back at all.

They got him into one of the rooms and evidently the trauma department had already been assembled because Sofia Martinez—one of the group's surgeons—was waiting there with her team. One of those doctors stepped up to take over compressions.

Sofia glanced at them. "A cardiac specialist is on his way down. How long has he been in arrest?"

"Twenty-five minutes." Bella repeated what she'd been told as she hooked up the leads for the heart monitor. "They got him back twice for short stretches only to have him relapse. Let's get a central line in and administer one milligram epinephrine."

It's what he would have suggested as well, and he noted Sofia was also nodding.

A nurse got the line in and another prepared and injected the requested dosage, even as external CPR continued. Everyone's eyes were on the monitor next to the bed.

What was barely a squiggle suddenly came alive with blips and sharp peaks within a minute of the epi being delivered. "Cease CPR," said Sophia.

The person administering compressions stopped,

and the rhythm persisted. Everyone held their breath waiting to see if it would stop again. But it didn't. And while the tracing didn't look exactly normal, it didn't look nearly as hopeless as it had a minute or two earlier.

Just then, Dr. Gilead pushed into the room, eyes immediately going to the monitor. "You got him back."

"Yes," Sofia said. "For now."

The cardiac specialist's lips were tight as he perused the scene. "Let's try to keep that momentum going. The patient was electrocuted, is that correct?"

Bella spoke up. "Yes. Catastrophic burns to his hands, but he was blown off the transformer pretty quickly, so it looks like exposure was limited although it was from a higher voltage."

Dr. Gilead glanced at the man's limbs and gave a soft whistle. "I want to get an echo to look for damage to the heart. It might be beating at the moment, but if it's sustained the same amount of damage as those hands... Well, I'd rather know it now than put hours into him if there's no chance whatsoever for survival."

"Agreed," said Sofia.

Although it sounded heartless on the surface, Dr. Gilead and Sofia knew what they were talking about. The didn't want a patient to suffer needlessly if there was no hope. None of them did.

Now that the case had been handed off from the ER team to the trauma and cardiology units, there was really no reason for Seb or Bella to stick around. But Seb was curious about the case and wanted to know the outcome. From the way Bella was hanging at the back of the room, she felt the same way.

Dr. Gilead again looked at the man's hands as the echocardiogram equipment was being set up and shook his head. "Let's just hope that what's on the inside doesn't look as bad as the outside."

No one was even talking about the mangled condition of the man's hands. If he made it, it was doubtful they could save them. The current had ripped through one hand and out the other with the exit burn looking even more horrific than the entry wound. Seb couldn't even tell where his fingers were supposed to be on that one.

Fifteen minutes later, they had their answer. The heart looked intact and his values were now almost within normal limits, although Dr. Gilead said there were a few troubling PVCs happening every few minutes. They would need to wait and see if they progressed to another series of arrhythmias or if they righted themselves.

"Let's get him up to ICU. Does anyone know if his family has been notified?"

Bella again spoke up. "His wife is out in the waiting room. She's the one who called for the EMTs after the accident. She started CPR."

"He was lucky she knew how, or he probably wouldn't be here right now. Can either you or Seb go out and update her while we work to get him stable? Once that happens I'll give her another update."

Bella nodded. "Not a problem."

Seb frowned. She was looking more and more exhausted by the minute. Friday morning they had their next appointment with Jessica so she could try to get a look at baby number three and to see if she could determine the gender of all three babies, and while he wouldn't override Bella, he would like to ask the specialist how much she could expect her body to do. And for how long.

Because right now she looked like she was at her limit, much as she had the other day when he'd offered to finish her shift. Surely she could see that it wasn't healthy for her or the babies to continue to push herself like this?

Once they got in the hallway, he said, "I can go talk with his wife."

She glanced at him with a frown. "I'm quite capable of talking with family members."

Did she think he was questioning her ability to do her job? That hadn't been his intention, but then again a lot of what he did nowadays seemed to be wrong, and he wasn't sure how to correct course, or if he should even try.

"I know you can. I just meant that you look exhausted."

"So do you. But that doesn't mean you shouldn't still be here working."

He touched her arm. "Hey, stop for a minute, please."

She did as he asked and turned to look at him. "What?"

"I'm not criticizing you. I'm just worried, Bella.

Worried you won't know when to stop. Worried you'll push yourself too hard."

Her eyes shut for a long minute, and she lifted her hands and used her fingertips to rub slow circles on her temple area. She had a headache. She got them periodically, and he used to be the one who did this for her.

Without asking, he went behind her and pushed her hands out of the way and used his own fingers to apply slow, steady pressure to the sides of her face, moving from her temples to her cheeks and back up again.

"Mmm...feels good."

Someone went by them and smiled at them. Seb ignored them. It didn't matter what people thought or didn't think. What did matter was that Bella was in obvious distress.

She let him continue for a few more minutes before drawing in a deep breath and then blowing it out. "Thank you. We'd better go, though."

Coming back to stand in front of her, he used his fingertips to tip her chin up. "When we're done with the family, I want you to do something for me, okay?"

Her eyes flew open and met his. He couldn't stop his own smile. "It's nothing like that. I just want to take your blood pressure and make sure it's normal."

She bit her lip. "I didn't even think about that. I have had a low-grade headache most of the day, but just assumed I slept wrong."

The fact that she wasn't putting up a fight or telling him he was being ridiculous concerned him even more. There was a bigger risk of preeclampsia in women carrying multiples, although it was still a little early in the pregnancy.

"So you'll let me?"

"Yes. I think it's just tiredness, but if it'll make you feel better, I'll go along with it."

"Just humor me, okay? I'm sure it's nothing, but I'd rather not take a chance, and I know Jessica would agree with me."

"I know she would, too."

A few minutes after they'd spoken with their patient's wife and grown son, they found themselves in an exam room. Seb wrapped the cuff around Bella's upper arm and pumped the pressure up until he could get a reading. Letting the air slowly hiss out, he watched the numbers until they reached the bottom. "One-thirty over eighty. Not terrible, but a little higher than yours normally runs."

"And you would know that how?"

His brows lifted. "I know."

Her eyes left his and stared at the wall. "The ER has been short-staffed the last couple of days and…" She shrugged.

"Why didn't you say anything?" In the same way that he did much of the ER's paperwork, Bella was more people-oriented and kept her finger on the pulse of the department's workforce. "You cannot take everything on yourself. Especially not right now."

"I know. It's just who I am. It's hard to turn it off and walk away."

Her words couldn't have described their situation

any better. It was hard to just turn off his feelings and walk away from what they'd once meant to each other. "I get it. More than you know."

When her glance came up and met his, she sighed and shook her head. "What happened to us, Seb?"

He brushed her hair back from the sides of her face, his fingers cupping her cheeks. "I don't know, Bell. I wish to hell I did."

They stayed like that for what seemed like an eternity, with her sitting on the exam table and him standing next to her. The blood pressure cuff was still around her arm, but that wasn't what caught his attention. It was the way she was looking at him. Like she was feeling sad and hopeless—like she'd lost her way in this world. Maybe because since they'd met they'd always made this journey through life together. And now neither one of them knew quite which way to turn.

His thumbs stroked along the sides of her face, and she closed her eyes, the sounds of her breathing soft in the room. She was just so damned gorgeous.

Before he could stop himself, he leaned down to give her a soft kiss on the lips, more as a way to reassure her than anything. At least that's what he told himself.

But when she sighed again and didn't pull away, he allowed himself to stay, the pressure of his mouth increasing slightly, his fingers sliding into the hair at her nape. He massaged her scalp, even as he let his lips slide away and then come back for another taste.

Then when her hands slid up to his shoulders he

pressed closer, turning her to face him, reveling in the feel of her mouth opening to his.

It was like he'd never kissed this woman before in his life. He was aware of everything about her. The way she smelled of soap and clean air, despite the fact that she'd been working around hospital antiseptic most of the day. The way her mouth clung so sweetly to his in a way that he had trouble remembering it ever doing before.

He kissed along her cheek and moved to her ear, "Bella, *Dios*, I—"

Just then the sound of the door opening, made him jerk back so fast that he heard the Velcro on the pressure cuff rip apart. He turned toward the door to see one of the nurses retreating with an apologetic smile on her face.

Damn. He had no doubt that news would soon be all over the hospital that she'd seen the husband-and-wife team making out in an exam room.

When his glance returned to Bella, he saw that she'd hopped down the from the table. "What were we thinking?"

He didn't know what she was thinking, but he knew exactly what he'd been thinking. That he'd been caught up in the moment and in the memories of what they'd once been. Of what they'd once meant to each other. Except that was a fantasy. A fantasy that hadn't had its roots in reality for a very long time.

"I'm sorry, Bella. I was worried and wanted to reassure you. Obviously, I forgot myself."

Instead of saying she'd been caught up in the moment as well, she pulled the pressure cuff the rest of the way off with a sharp sound and tossed it onto the table. "It can't happen again, Seb. It just…can't. I can't go through this again. It hurts too much. Okay?"

He nodded, a lump in his throat growing until it was hard to breathe. Only then did he realize the depths of the pain he'd put her through. How she must have felt abandoned by him not only physically, but emotionally. And in reality he had done both. In trying to protect himself—and her, he'd told himself—he'd allowed his actions to devastate the woman he'd once loved with all of his heart. The woman he'd sworn never to hurt.

Only now it looked like he'd just done it all over again.

"It won't happen again."

He watched silently as she ran her hands through her hair and took several deep breaths. "I'm going to head home. It's been a long day, and here I am taking it out on you. I'm sorry."

"You're not. You have nothing to be sorry for. This was on me. All of it."

"It's okay." She put her hand on the doorknob. "I'll feel better after a good night's sleep. We both will. See you in the morning?"

"Sure."

With that, she left the room. Seb stood there for a long moment and looked at the door that was now shut tight and thought how appropriate that seemed. Just when he'd been starting to think that maybe there was still a spark between them, he realized he was standing over a pile of cold, dead ashes instead.

And as hard as it was to face, he needed to acknowledge that Bella did not want him. Not right now, and if he took her words at face value—and there was no reason not to—she didn't want him ever again. Not in that way. As the father of her children, yes. As a support system during the pregnancy, yes. But as a husband, lover and friend…no.

God, as a doctor, he'd had to give plenty of families pretty hopeless news about their loved ones before. But the one thing he'd never had to do was give equally hopeless news to himself. About someone he loved. About someone he would probably always love.

That was the biggest kick to the gut he'd ever had to face.

This time, Bella was earlier to arrive at the maternity clinic than Seb. She'd barely seen him the rest of the week. That was probably his doing. She knew she'd overreacted to that kiss, but she'd been really tired and emotionally vulnerable. When he'd stood in that hallway massaging her temples exactly like he'd done in times past, she'd closed her eyes, lost in a special kind of bliss that had hung on through him taking her blood pressure, to him brushing her cheeks with that sweet gentle touch of his that had made her senses ignite with a desperate need. A need that made her weak in the knees. And when he'd actually leaned down to kiss her… She'd been lost. Not in the past, but in hopes of the present. It was as if everything that they'd once meant to each other had rushed forward to that very moment. She'd been drowning in him. Drowning in the force of her need for him. If they hadn't been interrupted, he could have made love to her in that very room. And, *Dios*, what a mistake that would have been.

One that would have been hard to find her way back from.

Maybe he wasn't even coming today. The thought should have filled her with relief, but instead it spurred a dread so great that she almost couldn't catch her breath. It was as if a huge band was tightening around her chest and constricting her lungs.

Then the bell over the door sounded, and her head whipped around to see who it was.

Seb. He'd come after all.

Afraid he'd see everything written on her face, she gave a quick wave and then bowed her head to stare sightlessly at her notebook of names. Tonight they still had to face his parents for dinner and pretend everything was okay when it wasn't. When it hadn't been for a long time.

He sat down next to her. "Hey."

She couldn't help her smile as she returned the greeting. It was another old habit of theirs, and one that was evidently just as hard to break just like so many other things. Like her reactions to his touch.

There were several other people in the waiting room, so she kept her voice low. "I'm really sorry about the other night. I know I overreacted and—"

"No, you were right. It's okay. Let's just forget it and move on."

Forget it and move on? Could they really do that?

Maybe he could, but Bella had a harder time with having hope waved in front of her heart only to have it yanked away again with a taunting *na-na-na-na-boo-boo.*

Even though he hadn't said the words in a malicious way, it still sliced her open all over again. And honestly, it wasn't fair of her to cast him as the villain when she'd been the one to tell him not to kiss her again.

She decided to change the subject, keeping her head close to his. "What do you want to do about your parents?"

"I think we should cancel."

This time she looked at his face. "Seb, why?"

"I really don't want to explain what's going on with us right now, because I don't really have a good handle on where we're going to end up, and if she senses something's wrong, she's going to ask. She's not afraid of confrontation, and she does it well. You know that as well as I do."

He was right. She did. But only because she was forthright and didn't like to play games. Like the one she and Seb were playing right now? Playing house, when neither one of them wanted to be there.

Well, she did. A little too much. And that's what had scared her about that kiss. Because she wanted it to be real. She wanted it to be about her and not just about the babies, and she was terrified that that's all it would ever be at this point.

Muscle memory was evidently a powerful thing. How long before those neural pathways could be re-routed to a healthier place?

"We need to tell her about the babies, Seb. The longer we wait, the more betrayed she's going to feel, especially if she finds out the people at the hospital knew before she did."

He paused. "You're absolutely right. The longer we wait, the more betrayed she's going to feel."

Like he'd felt, when she'd kept the truth from him?

"We don't have to tell her we're not together anymore in the sense of husband and wife. Can't that wait until later? Until after the babies are born?"

They were called back before Seb had a chance to answer. Her nerves were a mess, and when they took her blood pressure, they found it was still a little elevated. But this time there was a good reason for it. She was afraid he was thinking about moving out before the babies were even born. Maybe that was the smarter path...the rerouting neural synapses path, but right now she couldn't face walking around that apartment by herself. It would remind her how horrible it had been to live there alone when Seb had gone to Africa. How the hallways had seemed to echo with memories that couldn't be erased.

She could probably face that after the babies were born. She could sell the place, or just hand it over to Seb and find another apartment for herself and the babies. But would it be any better? Would she still long for his presence in her life?

Was this how her mom had felt looking at the prospect of being a single mom? Of being the one to put her child to bed night after night without the support of someone who loved her? At least until she married the man who Bella thought of as her dad.

She smiled at Jessica as she came into the room. "Okay, we're at almost nineteen weeks, it looks like."

Today her hair was caught up in a clip that did nothing to blot out the picture that this was a woman who was not only a free spirit but also at peace with the world.

Bella felt anything but peaceful.

She found herself letting Seb do most of the talking; she was just not in a place where she could chitchat, although she did manage to tell Jessica the names they'd chosen. She couldn't stop thinking about his parents. Seb's dad had had leukemia; did she really want to break the news to him that she and Seb were probably going to split up?

She didn't. But she also didn't know how they were going to keep it from them. Maybe Seb could talk to his mom privately and let her know that things weren't good in their relationship but ask her to keep it from her husband for now.

That seemed just as bad as pretending to be a happy couple when they weren't.

Bella got onto the table and lay back, preparing for the ultrasound. This time, Seb didn't help her adjust her clothes, and she found she missed the easy way he'd done that last time.

Muscle memory. It'll fade with time.

And even though he moved to stand beside her, he made no attempt to hold her hand as Jessica waved her magic wand over Bella's abdomen as if casting a spell on the babies inside of it.

Baby C, please come out this time.

She studied the images trying to see what Jessica did, although she wasn't an ob-gyn.

"Do you want to know the gender?"

"Can you tell?" Seb asked the question.

"I'm pretty sure. Baby C is cooperating a little more this morning and doesn't have his butt to us."

Bella looked up at Seb. "I want to know. You?"

"Yes. I do as well."

Jessica turned back to the screen. "Okay…so, names. We have Sergio, Lorenzo and Luis picked out for the boys, right?"

"Yes. Wait. Does that mean they're boys? All three of them?"

Jessica laughed. "That's what I'm saying, although ultrasounds aren't a perfect science. Any specific baby you want to assign those names to?"

"Oh, Seb. We have baby boys." Bella's eyes filled with tears and she couldn't stop herself from holding out her hand, praying Seb would take it. He did, giving it a light squeeze, but he didn't let it go, like she'd halfway expected him to. And although his grip wasn't as tight as it had been the last time they'd been in this room, it didn't feel totally apathetic either. But when she looked up at him, she saw she wasn't the only one who was moved with emotion. Seb's jaw was tight as if fighting his own feelings.

They stared at the screen. The babies were in much the same order as they were the last time, except Baby C had separated himself a little more. She still couldn't see his chest or head, but he was there.

She wanted Seb to name them. She squeezed his hand. "You decide."

"Let's do them in the order you said earlier, Jessica. Sergio, Lorenzo and little Luis. Does that work?"

"It does." Bella looked closer and saw he was right. "Is it my imagination or is Luis smaller than the other two? Or is it just because there's not as much of him visible?"

Jessica was concentrating on something and didn't say anything for a minute before turning her attention back to them. "Yes, he does appear to be smaller, but he might still catch up. Or he might stay little. I actually would like you to come back again in a week or two. Something is bothering me."

"About the babies?" Fear threatened to clog her throat.

"No, just about the fact that I still can't see Luiz completely. Especially on multiples, I really want to look for congenital problems so we're ready for them when it comes time to deliver them. I'm not expecting to find anything, but I'd like to be able to mark that off my punch list."

Bella felt better. She often had a punch list of her own when patients came in, sorting through various diagnoses and marking some as possibilities and ruling others out completely.

"Do the other two look okay?" Seb asked.

"Yes, from what I can tell, Sergio and Lorenzo are perfect. And what I can see of Luis is good as well—half of his spine and abdomen are visible and look okay, but just to put all of our minds at ease, I'd like to get a peek at the rest of him."

"That makes sense to me," Bella said, glancing up at Seb again. "Are you available again next week?"

"Yes. Whatever we can do to make sure everything is okay with them." He glanced at the screen. "Can you write their names on the sonogram for me?"

It might seem like a funny request, but she understood why he'd made it. He was already visualizing them as little people, just as she was. It made them all the more real. Bella pictured Seb talking to the triplets through her belly, and her jaw tightened. Would he do that? Did she even want him to do that? The intimacy of him murmuring to his babies was something she'd once dreamed of.

She did want him to. Whether or not they ever got back together, it would mean the world to their kids that he'd interacted with them when they'd still been inside of her. Her own father hadn't, her mom had told her. She hadn't wanted him to, since they weren't together. And maybe that had been the right decision for her mother, but Bella didn't think it was the right decision for her. She and Seb had been very much in love when they'd gotten married. And she wanted him to know his children as intimately as she was coming to know them. That meant she wanted him at every screening, at every sonogram, at every doctor's appointment, or at least as many as he could manage.

She certainly wouldn't stop him from doing any of those things. If he wanted to be there for the birth, if he wanted to coach her through it, she would welcome it. All of it. She might be afraid for him to kiss her, but she yearned for his participation in the babies' birth stories.

Jessica was busy replacing the letters for each baby with his name. Once she was done, she printed off a copy and handed it to her. Bella couldn't contain her smile.

"Sergio, Lorenzo and Luis, welcome to our family."

She only realized she'd said the words aloud when Seb leaned down to softly kiss her bare belly. It was a mere touch, and then it was gone, but it sent a shock wave through her that went straight down to her toes. It also sent a streak of joy tearing through her heart. They might not make it through this as a couple, but she had no doubt that these babies would be ridiculously loved. By both of them.

She reached up and touched his face. "Thanks for being here for this. For all of it."

"You're welcome."

Armed with their paper and released by Jessica to

go back into the world with a good report so far on the babies' health, they walked out of the clinic.

"We can make a copy of this for your folks, if you want."

"That's kind of why I wanted her to put their names on it." He stopped her before they reached the parking lot. "My parents obviously don't know we're having problems, and the last thing I want to do is pretend to be a happy couple tonight if you're not up to it, but I do want to have our stories straight before we get there."

She thought for a minute. "I don't want to hurt your parents. And I also don't want to lie to them. But the truth is, even we don't know where we'll be in a year. In two years. So why don't we just approach it that way? We're certainly civil to each other, and we've proven we can hold hands without any animosity toward one another, so why don't we do that? We'll hold hands and smile at each other. The stuff we did in that exam room a few minutes ago. I think your mom will be so ecstatic over the news she's finally going to have grandchildren that I don't think she'll be looking for signs of a ruined marriage."

"Is that what we have? A ruined marriage?"

"I honestly don't know, Seb. But I don't think that's something we have to sort out at this exact moment. Maybe it's like Luis. We can't see all that's there or not there right now. We just have to wait for things to reveal themselves and then go from there."

He smiled at her and this time, it was a genuine smile

that reached his eyes and every other part of his face. "Wise words from a wise woman."

He put his hand on her stomach. "Did you hear that, boys?" Then he looked at her. "And thanks for being willing to go with me to break the news to my parents."

"I'm happy to." Right now, it was the truth. She felt happy and if not exactly hopeful, she didn't feel as hopeless as she had when that kiss had ended in the exam room.

Maybe she was carving some new neural pathways after all. And not all of them were doom and gloom. For her sake and the sake of the babies, those were the ones she was going to start nurturing in the hope that something good could still come from all the heartache of the past.

CHAPTER SEVEN

INSTEAD OF GOING back to the apartment, they'd gone to the park instead and moseyed their way through it, taking Jessica's admonition to heart about getting out in the fresh air and walking. They'd talked about his parents and even about Seb's time in Africa. She'd been moved to tears over his recounting of a couple of the stories about the conditions some of the people faced. Conditions that were faced in almost every country of the world, including Argentina. Hunger, fear, disease. They were things that spoke of the human condition.

Just like Mario, their electrocution patient who was still in ICU, but whose heart was still beating, whose brain was still functioning, even if his hands never would again. They'd both had to be amputated to save his life. His wife was just so grateful that he was alive that it didn't matter that he'd no longer be able to do a lot of things. But he'd still be able to make a living as a shop owner in a poor neighborhood. At least with some help. And he could help educate others about the dangers of trying to hook into the city's power grid without being detected. Sometimes it worked…but when it didn't, people lost their lives.

They didn't rent a paddleboat this time; instead they stuck to the shady paths and wandered with no definite direction in mind. The day wasn't quite as hot as it had been yesterday, and the park was magical. The sounds of the water, the happiness of kids running along the paths, the birds that sang in the trees. Seb didn't reach for her hand, but he felt connected to her in a way he hadn't in a long time. Maybe it was due to naming the babies, but he had a feeling it was more than that.

And when Bella asked to rest on a bench for a while, he sat next to her. Not talking, just sitting there and letting time tick by. For once it didn't seem to be rushing at a frenetic pace waiting for him to catch up with it. It was just crawling leisurely by and, for once, Seb was happy to just be there in the moment. Especially since he didn't know how many more of them he would get.

The doctor was right. They needed to come here more often and just enjoy each other's company. If not as lovers, then maybe they could manage it as friends.

"Are we ready for tonight?" she said.

"I'm not sure I'm ever fully ready for a night with my parents."

She smiled. "It won't be that bad. I love your mom and dad."

"I love them, too. My mom can just be a bit *exigente* sometimes."

"I think all parents can be that way. She just wants to see you happy."

He didn't exactly have a response for that comment, so he sat back and watched a bird hop by looking for small bits of food. "If we can get through tonight, we should be good."

Did he really believe that? His parents would be crushed when he and Bella eventually separated. But then again, they couldn't stay together just for that reason. Or for the babies. Fate had a way of making you resent not having the life you envisioned. Or being stuck in a life you don't exactly want.

With him and Bella, though, it was tricky. Because he was pretty sure neither of them knew which category they fell into. She—and her doctor—wanted him there to help her during the pregnancy, but he was pretty sure for Bella, it didn't go beyond that, if her words after that kiss were anything to go by. And he couldn't blame her. How did you tell someone you were done without telling them you're done? You do exactly what Seb did and leave for months. He'd come back to Argentina expecting to call it quits, only to find he wasn't as sure as he'd thought he was. But it seemed Bella believed in the mantra that actions speak louder than words. And his actions had done their job and more.

Trying to shake off his morose thoughts, he glanced over at her to find her hands were both on her belly and there was a strange look on her face. "What is it?"

"I think I felt them. There was some quivery little sensation a minute ago. It's gone now, but... After the ultrasound and the names, it just feels so real all of a sudden."

"It is real, Bella." This was all happening so fast. In

less than three weeks since he'd come home, he'd found out Bella was expecting, he'd been to three doctor's appointments, had picked out baby names, and had heard and seen his babies via ultrasound. If he remembered his medical training correctly, then by week twenty he'd be able to feel the baby's kicks, too, by putting his hands on Bella's stomach. No wonder he felt like his world was spinning.

"I know, but…" She glanced his way. "I'm glad you're here for it."

"I'm glad I am, too." Her words made his gut tighten, but he had to remember that what she said and what he heard were probably two different things. She was glad he was here for the pregnancy. But was she glad he was here for her personally? If he'd come home and she hadn't been pregnant, would she have kicked him to the curb? He wouldn't have blamed her if she had.

He told himself it could be worse. She could have been pregnant and still kicked him to the curb, and he would have deserved it. Instead, here she was sharing the experience with him.

He decided to ask a question that had been circling in his head for a while. "Do you want me there with you for the actual birth?"

She blinked. "Do you want to be there for the birth?"

He smiled. "We could go back and forth answering your question with a question forever. The truth is, I want to be there, but only if you want me there. Only if it helps you get through the experience. I don't want to do anything that makes the process harder for you than it needs to be."

"I want you there."

"Then I'll be there." And since he'd already voiced the first question, he decided to ask the second one he'd been fretting over. "How late in the pregnancy are you planning to work?"

"Until I'm told not to by my doctor." She twisted her hands together. "I know you're worried, but right now I can't just sit at home. I'll drive myself crazy by overthinking things too much."

He tried to put himself in her shoes. He would probably do the same thing. Sit there and stew about things that he could do nothing about. He did enough of that as it was. But he had a thought.

"What if you still went to work, but you did more paperwork for the department and I spent more time on the floor?"

"You mean reverse our usual roles?" She shook her head. "It would never work. Mainly because I don't like paperwork."

Okay, so much for that idea. "How about this, then. How about if I ask for our schedules to line up and when you get tired, you can go to the office. The upshot is, I'll spend more time in the ER doing actually emergency care than I've been doing."

"But the paperwork needs to get done, too."

"And it will get done. By me, or I can ask the hospital administrator for a medical student who's looking for some hospital experience to be assigned to the ER.

They could get some actual floor time while coming on board to learn the paperwork side of things."

"That sounds doable. But if they say no, then I don't want you killing yourself trying to get the other stuff done after your shift ends."

"I won't. But in the same vein, I don't want you running yourself to exhaustion trying to take up the slack for everyone else. When you're short-staffed it needs to be a shared load, agreed?"

"Agreed."

"That means actually picking up your phone and calling me and telling me to get my backside on the floor."

She laughed. "You want me to say it exactly like that? Because people might wonder what I am trying to get you to do."

Suddenly an image that had nothing to do with him going to the ER flickered across his mental movie screen.

"Okay, well maybe just say, 'I need you on the floor.'" As soon as he said the words he realized it wasn't any better. If anything, it was worse.

"Yeah... I don't think I'm going to be calling our office anytime soon."

But at least she was smiling.

"Just call and say you're tired. I'll get the message."

She glanced at her watch, a smile still on her face. "Speaking of tired. We have a little bit of a hike to get back to the parking lot, and I probably should get home so I can change before we head over to your folks' house."

"Are you sure you want to do this?"

She reached over and grabbed his hand. "Seb. We've been over this several times. Yes, we should go. And yes, I'll be okay. You have to trust me on this one."

"Okay." With that they got up and started the long walk back to the park's entrance. He smiled. He could say, for once, that today was a good day.

Bella positively glowed, and he'd never been more proud of her than he was at that moment. She'd dressed in a loose summer dress that didn't immediately reveal her condition, and she looked cool and beautiful as she kissed his mom and dad with genuine affection and handed over the bottle of wine they'd brought. "It's so good to see you again. Thanks for having us."

"Anytime, Bella. I'm sorry we didn't get together more while Seb was away. I dropped the ball on that," his mom said apologetically.

"No. You didn't. You did try, but I was either working or at my mom's house helping her with something so if anything, it was more my fault."

"Well, Seb is back and you're here now, and that's all that matters." She turned and gave Seb a kiss as well. "Now come and sit down and tell us everything about your trip. I'm just putting dinner on the table."

They sat down to eat, and he told some of the same stories from Angola that he'd shared with Bella. But as much as he'd enjoyed talking about it earlier, telling them to his parents raised feelings of guilt all over again. Not just for leaving Bella, but leaving his parents, especially his dad. What if something had happened to him when he'd been so far away? He finally stopped mid-sentence and decided to just rip off the Band-Aid.

"Mom and Dad, we have some news we want to share with you." He stopped again as a wave of emotion washed up his throat and threatened to choke him.

Bella came to the rescue, covering his hand with hers. "We should have told you sooner, but it was something Seb and I wanted to do together, after he came home from his assignment overseas."

"What is it, dear?"

Bella smiled. "Actually...we're expecting. I'm pregnant."

He still hadn't figured out exactly how he was going to explain the delay in sharing the news, but Bella had come up with the perfect answer.

And from his mom's shriek, it had been exactly the right one. "You're pregnant?" She came around the table and hugged Bella and then returned to her seat and embraced her husband for a long moment. When she turned back to them, her eyes were glistening with tears. "We're going to be grandparents?"

Seb nodded. "You are."

Reaching into her tote bag, Bella pulled out the sonogram with the boys' names on it and handed it to them.

His mom looked up. "Wait. What's this? Three

names? Are you trying to choose one?" Her eyes widened. "One of these is your father's name."

Seb smiled. "I know that, and no, we don't need to choose one. We've already chosen them."

"You mean…"

"Yes, we're having triplets."

"*Dios mio.* Are you telling me the truth?" This time she looked at Bella, maybe thinking she was going to say it was all one big joke. Except it wasn't.

"I swear we are. We are having three boys. Depending on how many embryos are implanted, some of them take and some don't. My doctor implanted three, but because of how carefully she chose them, they all took. And I opted to carry all three."

"You both must be over the moon. I know I am. After all this time." She glanced at her husband. "It's unbelievable. When are they due?"

Seb responded. "We don't exactly know. Because of the risks, our doctor has said she would feel better doing a cesarean, so it's doubtful that they'll go all the way to nine months. They'll probably take them out a few weeks early."

"Yes, whatever is safer for Bella and the babies." She clapped her hands together. "You've both made me happier than you can imagine. All I ever wanted was for my only child to be happy and to make me a grandmother."

Little did she know that she'd almost gotten neither of those things. If the pregnancy hadn't taken and he'd stuck to his guns, she wouldn't be a grandmother at all.

And her only child would probably be in the middle of a divorce right now and not happy at all. Seb might have asked Bella a couple of hard questions at the park, but he hadn't asked her the hardest one of all: What did she intend to do about their marriage after the babies were born?

Seb forced a smile. "I'm glad you're so happy."

"We must go shopping for clothes for you and the babies and…"

This time his dad stopped her. "Take a few breaths, dear. I can't keep up with you, and I'm not even pregnant."

"Dad's right," Seb said. "Bella has been feeling a little tired recently, and so I'm trying to get her to agree to slow down the pace."

"How far along are you?"

"Getting close to nineteen weeks," Bella said.

Here was the moment of truth. Either his mom would be upset that she was so late to the game, or she would accept it and move on. He hoped for the latter.

"Yes, I remember I felt really good in my second trimester, but I still tired out pretty easily."

Thanks, Mom. He sent the words up into the universe.

Thankfully she didn't ask very many more questions, she just rattled off sentence after sentence in a long stream-of-consciousness monologue that made him both cringe and smile. She really was one of a kind. Yet today had gone so much better than it could have. Seb tended to lean toward worst-case scenario, and it was always a relief when it didn't come to pass.

When he was finally able to get a word in edge-wise, he looked at his dad. "What have you been up to lately?"

"Well, I actually retired last week."

"What?"

His mom had the grace to look embarrassed. "That's right. I got so caught up in the news about the babies, I forgot to share some news of our own. We're going to start doing some traveling. You're not the only one with itchy feet."

That took him aback. She'd never once mentioned wanting to travel. He glanced quickly at his dad, who caught the look.

"Don't worry. I'm fine. I've been wanting to go to Scotland for a while, and I finally talked your mom into it. I figured I had one shot at this, and I'd better make it something she's interested in doing as well."

"But with the babies on the way maybe we should rethink…" His mom started to say something before letting the sentence fade away.

Seb broke in. "The babies won't be here for a while, and even after they arrive you don't have to sit at home just because of them. We'll make sure you have plenty of opportunities to be with them."

Too late he realized he'd spoken for Bella, too, in his sentence, but when he looked over at him she smiled and gave his hand a squeeze. "Yes, we will. My grand-parents meant an awful lot to me, and I want our babies to get to spend time with theirs on both sides as well. My mom and dad are over the moon, too."

His mom's forehead furrowed just a tiny bit, and he knew something about what Bella had said had caught her attention. But the expression cleared so quickly he wasn't sure he'd even seen it. "Well, I made *flan de naranja* for dessert."

His mom's baked orange flan was delicious and was another one of Bella's favorite dishes. He had no doubt she'd made it just for her.

"Yum, thank you so much."

"You're welcome. And there's no alcohol in it. Seb didn't say anything, but he hesitated for a minute over the wine, so I wondered if you were still trying to get pregnant. But I had no idea you'd succeeded." She reached over the table and took one of Bella's hands. "I'm so glad, Bella. You two have been trying for so long."

Bella was very still, and he wondered if she was thinking the same thing that he was. If this attempt hadn't worked, Seb's adamant refusal to try again would have kept her from ever having children.

Not for the first time, he wondered if he'd been wrong in deciding something for the both of them. And in reality, she could have divorced him and tried again with donor sperm. But the guilt about leaving wasn't just about that. It was about making a unilateral decision for someone else. He wasn't sure he'd been right at all when he looked at it like that. And yet there was no way for him to have known that there was a possibility of coming out on the other side with a viable pregnancy. Not after all their other failures.

When there was continued silence, he said, "But this time it did. So we're very happy about that."

"Yes, we are."

Soon the talk changed from pregnancy to his parents' travel plans, which they talked about over dessert. There was plenty of laughter as his dad's dry sense of humor finally had a chance to come out and play. He joked that he was kilt shopping and wanted to know who wanted to go with him.

Seb rolled his eyes. "And on that note, I think we're going to take off." Although Bella was still laughing and actively involved in the conversation, it had been a long day for her, and he was sure she had to be running out of steam. He knew he was.

Not to mention his parents lived on the outskirts of Buenos Aires, so they still had almost an hour-long drive back to their apartment.

They stood up and embraced his folks once again and took the proffered tubs of leftovers that his mom insisted they have.

So with arms full, they headed back to their car.

Once everything was loaded, he opened Bella's door for her and then got in on his side of the vehicle. She turned to him with a smile. "Well, that went better than I thought it would."

"Thanks to you. That was quick thinking about mentioning us wanting to tell them together."

"It was the truth, actually. Why do you think I

avoided meeting her for coffee? I didn't want to have to go back and explain why I hadn't told her about the pregnancy over a coffee date."

He touched her face, again marveling how soft her skin was. "Thank you so much for being willing to come with me and take them on."

"It wasn't a problem at all. And I'm really glad your dad is going to take some time and do the things he's wanted to do."

"Me, too. I was halfway worried that his cancer might have come back, but I don't think that's what was behind the travel bug. I truly think he just wants to do some of the things he never got to do while working."

"Your mom was happy about the babies, I think."

"Happy? I think that's an understatement."

He started the car and headed back to the city, glancing over at her a couple of times and finding her dozing in her seat. She'd seemed genuinely at ease tonight. Putting on some soft music to drown out some of the noise of horns honking and general traffic sounds, he hoped she could sleep the rest of the way home. She needed it.

But what did he need?

Her. He needed her, like he always had. He just hadn't been able to see through the grief and the mire that made up their attempts at getting pregnant. If the initial fertility treatment had worked, would they have found themselves in the situation they were now in?

There was no way to know. No way to go back and see how that particular future would have unrolled. If he could travel back in time, would he have wanted to stop their attempts sooner? Probably. The last couple of cycles, he'd only done it for Bella in hopes that something would take. But it never had. At least not until he'd been ready to give up completely.

Coming out on this side of things and knowing it was probably partly due to the fact that the last embryo transfer had worked, he only knew that he didn't want to lose her. Not now. Not after all these years of being together.

He was surprised when he turned down their road, realizing he'd driven most of the way on autopilot.

The way he'd been going through the last couple of years of his marriage?

Maybe it was time to change that. Maybe he wasn't as powerless as he'd thought he was. He could woo her and see where that got him. And if she had the same reaction that she'd had to that kiss? Well, then he'd have his answer. But if he just let her go without even trying to see if she still had any feelings for him, he would always wonder, and it would plague him for years to come.

He turned off the car and went around to the other side, opening the door and reaching over to undo her seat belt just as she stirred. She gazed up at him with glazed eyes.

"You fell asleep," he murmured. Ignoring the box of food on the back seat, he started to swing her up into his arms only to have her stop him.

"It's okay. I can walk. Plus there's all the stuff in the back seat to bring."

"Are you sure? I can come back and get it."

"I'm fine, really." She swung her legs out of the car and stood, yawning, but looking better than she had in a week. Which was surprising since she'd looked so exhausted at work the last couple of days. But maybe seeing his parents and getting the news off her chest had helped her. It certainly had him.

It could be that's where all these thoughts of trying to reconcile were coming from. They'd had a good time tonight at the park and at his parents. Couldn't they build on that?

He reached into the back seat and took out the boxes that held their food and walked with her to the elevator.

"Today was fun, wasn't it?"

"I was actually just thinking that, too."

She looked up at him in surprise. "You were?"

"Yep." He didn't want to share any more for fear of scaring her off, but decided to try to play it cool. "I think the doctor was right about getting out in the fresh air and enjoying some outings."

"I think we said the same thing on the paddleboat that first time."

"So we did."

He pushed the button in the elevator, and the car started its ascent. "Do you remember that time when that swan chased us halfway us up the bank of the lake and followed us onto the path?"

She laughed. "Yes, you'd tossed it part of a sandwich

and it decided it wanted more. Except we didn't have any more, and the thing was mad."

"It actually ripped a hole in my shirt."

She bumped against his shoulder the way that she used to. "I remember. I also remember it was a new one and you were pretty ticked off."

"I remember. I also remember what happened later. When we reached the car."

"So do I. We didn't actually make it home. We had to stop halfway and park in a secluded spot."

"If we hadn't I would have crashed the car into a tree or something."

"You were so cute." The door to the elevator opened. "And it was so hot to watch you squirm."

They'd taken the long way home down back roads, and Bella had licked and bitten at his neck as they drove, putting his hormones on high alert. Things had taken another turn when she'd slid his shirt up enough that she could splay her hand out over his abs. "What do you want, Seb?" she'd asked him.

"You, I want you."

They'd found a place behind a stand of trees and had consummated their love for each other. Even now he could feel her around him, taste her lips.

They got off the elevator and made it as far as the door. "Everything about that day was steamy, and not just because it was a hot day weather-wise."

"It was, wasn't it?" Bella leaned her back against the door to look up at him from under her eyelashes. "We were so carefree back then. We had so much fun. The park today reminded me of that day."

Seb had his keys in his hand, but he wasn't looking at the door. His attention was wholly fastened on the woman who was bringing up memories that he'd almost forgotten. Or maybe he'd forced himself to forget them. Although he had no idea how. Because right now he wanted her with a force that was almost overpowering. He wanted to relive a few of those steamy moments from the past.

"Bella…"

She reached up and cupped her face. "It's okay, Seb. We're not in a car right now. There's no danger of crashing into anything but each other." She slid her hand under his shirt, pressing her palm to his skin very much like she'd done back then.

And he came undone. His free arm went around her back and hauled her up against him for a moment, only to realize he needed it to unlock the door. When he finally got it open, he almost fell inside with her. With that he slammed the door, put the tubs of food on the nearby hall table, and put his mouth to hers.

CHAPTER EIGHT

BELLA WASN'T SURE why she'd brought up any of those memories, but the second his mouth came down on hers, she fell down a rabbit hole and found herself in another world. One she'd almost convinced herself hadn't ever really existed.

But there was nothing else like Seb's kiss. Even in those horrible days of IVF attempts, his lips against hers had always had the power to make her forget what they were hoping for. Then things had become overly cautious. And safe. It was like something, some special element, had been taken away from their relationship.

But she didn't have to be safe right now. At least not in the ways she was thinking.

She needed him. Right now. However she could get him. After all, Dr. Lucas had reassured them that sex was still on the table for now.

Reaching down, she unzipped his pants, freeing him.

"Wait, Bella, wait."

But she didn't want to wait. There was no need for condoms anymore. No need for anything "safe." She knew she needed to be careful of the pregnancy, but maybe one of their biggest failures back then had been in not experimenting with other ways to keep the mystery and passion alive.

And right now, she needed something that had some risk to it—not physical risk, because she'd never harm her babies, but emotional. Spinning him so that she again had her back to the door, she walked him over to the couch and pushed him down onto it, standing over him for a minute. She wasn't the only one who needed something, judging from the look of him.

And she'd always liked looking at him.

The day he'd come out of the shower, she hadn't been able to take her eyes off him. She'd wanted to touch him so very badly—and now she could.

She took a step closer and knelt in front of him, sliding her fingertips over his warm, firm flesh and relishing every time it jumped under her touch. "I'm so tired of playing it safe, Seb."

He chuckled. "One thing you've never been good at, if I remember right."

"Oh, really? I can be plenty safe." With that, she leaned over and kissed the flesh she'd been caressing.

She heard the hiss of air that said she'd shocked him with her sudden touch. But he didn't stop her as she tasted and nibbled her way over his skin. And when she finally enveloped him, she felt his hand on the back of her head. Not pushing or urging, but just threading itself through the strands of her hair as she picked up the pace.

"Bella… *Dios*…it's too much."

He hauled her off him and lifted her onto the couch

so that she was straddling him. Her skirt was bunched between strong hands and pulled up until the backs of her bare thighs were against his jeans. He again buried his hand in her hair and kissed her, holding her tight against his mouth while his tongue thrust deep. This time it was Bella who squirmed, needing him so badly. But before she could lift herself up onto him, he stood, taking her with him, one hand sliding under her butt as he walked toward the bedroom they'd once shared.

God, she couldn't wait to share it with him again. For tonight at least. She would worry about tomorrow when it came.

The curve of her belly was pressed tight against his flat abs as she leaned down to kiss him again, her hair falling around them, making her wonder how he could even see. But evidently he could since he walked without hesitation to her bed, laying her oh so carefully on top of the covers. Something about that tickled at the back of her brain, but right now, she didn't care. She was frantic. Frantic to be with him. Frantic to touch him. Frantic for him to push her off that very sexy cliff the way he always used to.

Her skirt was still at the top of her thighs and with a secret smile, his palms slid up her skin and reached her panties, fingers hooking over the elastic waistband and pulling them down. When they were off her legs, he tossed them to the side.

"Take off your shirt," she whispered.

He seemed to hesitate for a split second before he

hauled it over his head and tossed it in the direction of her undergarment. "Your turn."

Leaning over her, he slid her shirt up her belly and somehow got it over her head. The bra came next. He covered her breasts with his hands and gently squeezed. But it was too little. She ached to feel his mouth on them pulling hard. Ached to feel him inside of her.

He kissed her again, moving his body so that he was lying beside her but not on top of her, his hand skimming down her chest, over her belly and then lower, until he touched her gently. The unexpected contact made her arch up, seeking him. Still kissing her, he obliged, using his fingers to touch her, caress her, the sensation so painfully familiar that she gasped, her fingers reaching for the back of his head to pull him closer, to kiss him deeper, even as he slid two fingers inside of her, mimicking what she wanted so badly. She used her feet to push up into him, lost in a sensation she hadn't felt in so very long. His thumb continued to stroke her, varying his pace so that she was never sure when to meet him. She strained wanting more, wanting *him*, not just his hand. But things in her head began to get cloudy as the sensations continued to take over, rational thought sliding to the back of the line as she continued to revel in kisses that drugged her, making her forget anything except what was happening. Her hand slid sideways seeking something, but she wasn't quite sure at this point if she had the willpower to try to find it. To give to him what he was giving her.

Then his pace quickened slightly although his strokes

didn't go any deeper than they already were. When he lifted his head and looked down at her, her breath came in gasps as her hips frantically sought something that wasn't there. But release was coming whether she got what she wanted or not, so she pushed up one more time as she finally gave in and let the waves of pleasure sweep over her, calling out his name as he leaned down to kiss her again. He continued kissing her as she slowly came down from the mountaintop, her brain cells engaging one by one. When she could finally think, she frowned and went to reach for him, but he murmured for her to wait a few minutes.

Wait? For what?

She blinked. Maybe he wasn't done with her. Maybe he was just giving her a few minutes to catch her breath. Okay, that made more sense. They'd done that in the past.

He lay down beside her and she curled around him, waiting. But a sense of lethargy was stealing over her, weighty and snug, like a heavy blanket. He'd told her to wait for a few minutes. That she could do. Then they would go another round. And this time, she would do for him what he'd just done for her…and more.

In just a few minutes.

She snuggled closer and felt him stroke her hair, her temples, his index finger trailing down the bridge of her nose. His touch brought with it a sense of comfort. Of relaxation.

Sighing as he continued to skim his fingers over her, she let her eyes close for a second, opening them with a jerk. Then they slid shut again, and she gave in to the steady, slow motions as Seb seemed to hypnotize her and send her off to another place. One where everything was okay with the world.

Bella woke with a start to find the sun was shining through the blinds on her window. She was on her bed, but she was sideways somehow, and the light comforter had been pulled up from the bottom of the bed and covered her.

She moved and realized she was mostly naked, except for her skirt.

Last night came back to her in a rush and she was horrified. She'd fallen asleep on Seb before he'd gotten any satisfaction of his own. *Dios!* How could she have been so selfish? He'd given her everything and gotten nothing in return.

She turned to find him to make that right, except he wasn't in the bed. Her eyes swept the space, including the open door to the en suite. He wasn't in the room. At all. So where was he?

Looking at her watch, another wave of horror went through her. She'd somehow overslept and was now late for work. Seb would have to take a rain check on whatever he'd been planning for himself.

Except something tickled the back of her brain again, like it had last night. Surely he'd wanted to get something out of what they'd done together. What sort of person wouldn't?

So why hadn't he woken her up or stuck around until

this morning? Maybe he had, and she'd simply slept on through the night. He'd talked about them starting to work the same shifts, so maybe he'd gone on into the hospital.

She jerked upright in the bed; the remembered pleasure from last night washed over her again, making her close her eyes. She'd thought this part of her life with Seb was gone for good. So for him to want to...

Wait. She'd started it, hadn't she? With her talk about the past and leaning against the door trying to look seductive. Had she really done that?

She had. And she'd been the one to unzip him and take him in her hands. To kiss him.

But he'd reciprocated, right? He had to have wanted it, too, or he would have pulled away...wouldn't he?

Right now things were so jumbled inside of her that she wasn't sure what was what. So she was going to get up and see if Seb was still here. If not, she was going to get dressed and head into work and try to figure out what exactly had happened last night. Maybe she even owed him an apology for falling asleep on him.

She wandered out into the main part of the apartment, not even bothering to get dressed, because the second she had opened the door she'd sensed he wasn't in the apartment.

So she went back into her bedroom and took a quick shower, trying to wash away all of the little prickles of unease that were beginning to cascade over her. Something just didn't feel right about last night. But the only way to know for sure was to find him and look into his face. If what she saw didn't satisfy her, she needed to ask him outright. No more guessing about what he thought or didn't think. No more guessing about where their relationship stood. Or didn't stand. Last night he'd finally given her hope that they might get past this.

So why hadn't he stayed to talk to her? Or at least left a note telling her where he'd gone and why?

Maybe he was angry with her about last night.

No, he hadn't seemed that way. He'd looked almost... at peace. She'd seen none of the desperation on his face that she'd felt for release. Had he climaxed while he was pleasuring her? She didn't think so. He'd seemed almost singular in his actions as if he knew exactly what he was doing. And why.

Then she'd just fallen asleep! She was pretty sure he hadn't planned for that.

Taking more care with her hair and makeup than she had in a while, she draped her lanyard over her neck and went into the kitchen to get a glass of milk. A bouquet of flowers sat in a vase of water on the bar. Her favorites. White daisies and pink roses. There was no note propped up, but it had to be from Seb, unless it was from his parents. No, they wouldn't know what flowers she liked best.

She leaned down to smell the sweet fragrance of the roses, allowing herself a slight smile. He wasn't mad at her, that much was certain. Maybe they could try again tonight, and this time she would be more insistent about his needs being met.

Feeling a little lighter, she flounced out the door in

a fresh skirt and blouse and feeling on top of the world for the first time in a long time.

When she got to the hospital, she didn't see Seb on the floor, and so she went to the office to see if he was there. It was empty. Going over to the desk, she spotted a note he'd scribbled with the word *Jessica* on it along with a phone number. She frowned before realizing it was Dr. Lucas, the at-risk pregnancy specialist. He must have had a question about something, or maybe he was simply seeing when their next appointment was.

She shrugged and started to go out of the office when there was a knock on the door. "Come in."

A woman stood in the doorway. "Dr. Lopez?"

She got this a lot. "I'm Dr. Lopez, but I'm Isabella Lopez. Are you looking for me or my husband?"

She smiled. "I didn't realize there were two of you. I just came up to introduce myself."

The woman spoke Spanish, but it was accented. She was obviously not Argentine. It suddenly dawned on her who this might be. She'd forgotten her name when she'd talked to Seb about her earlier, but had looked it up later. "Are you Dr. Gonzalez, by any chance?"

She was supposed to meet with the other doctor at some point, but the administration hadn't nailed down a date for her, unless she'd missed a memo. What she really wanted to do was find Seb, but maybe it was better to let herself digest what had happened last night and think it over rather than rushing to him and blurting out everything she was thinking.

"I am. But please call me Emilia. Do you have a minute to talk?"

"Absolutely, come on in."

Emilia came the rest of the way into the office, and Bella motioned to the couch on the other side of the room. "Do you want some coffee? Water?"

"No. I'm okay." She perched on the front of the sofa and waited for Bella to sit in one of the chairs across from her.

"You're a neonatal specialist, right? And you're from Uruguay?"

"I am," Emilia confirmed.

Bella tilted her head. "Do you have family in Argentina?"

"Not yet, but I will pretty soon. My daughter is getting ready to attend university, and she's gotten a scholarship to attend one here in Buenos Aires. As a mom, it's hard to just let her go off to another country on her own, so when I heard about the position opening here at the hospital, I jumped at it."

"How wonderful." Bella was happy for her, and since there was no mention of a father being in the picture, she assumed Emilia was going it on her own. She understood that all too well. If things didn't go well with Seb, she might very well be taking a similar path. "I get it. I'm actually pregnant with triplets right now."

"Wow, how far along?"

"Nineteen weeks."

The woman looked like she wanted to ask something

else, but didn't, so Bella added a little more. "I've had several rounds of IVF, and it finally took after years of trying."

"I bet you and your husband are ecstatic."

This comment wasn't as easy to reply to. "I'd like to hope we both are."

"I'm happy for you." Emilia smiled. "I won't hold you up much longer. From your perspective, is there anything special I should know about the hospital?"

She thought for a minute. "It's a great place to work. And it's a popular medical center, so sometimes our schedules are pretty hectic. The neonatal unit is top-notch, so you'll get a lot of patients and doctors coming to you for advice."

"Which is great. I'd rather stay busy. It gives me less time to think."

About her daughter growing up and leaving the nest? That had to be it.

"It's really nice to meet you. If you ever have any questions, please don't hesitate to reach out to me or any of the other doctors. We're a pretty close-knit bunch."

"Thanks, and if you ever have any questions about your babies, please come find me."

"I absolutely will. Thank you." It was good to know that there'd be someone else at the hospital that she could reach out to if she had any concerns.

With that, Emilia stood up. "Well, like I said, I won't keep you. I just wanted to meet you since the ER probably sees a lot of our patients before we do."

"Do you already have the job?"

"It's looking promising, so I'm hopeful."

"Good luck, and I'm serious about being available to answer any questions." Bella smiled and walked her to the door. "And if you find yourself with some spare time, let me know and we can go out for coffee...well, herbal tea in my case. But at least I can still enjoy the scent of coffee."

"I will. Thanks for letting me stop by."

"Any time." With that, the other woman stepped out of the office and headed for the elevator.

Bella liked her and made a mental note to seek her out and maybe take her to see some of the sights of the city.

As she started to shut the door, something stopped it from moving. Thinking it was the other doctor coming back to ask her something, she smiled and said, "Did you forget something?" as she opened the door.

Except it wasn't Emilia, it was Seb.

"Who were you talking to?"

"The neonatology candidate I told you about stopped by to introduce herself to us. But you weren't here." She frowned. "You weren't at home, either. I looked for you."

He shifted from one foot to the other. "Sorry. You were sleeping so soundly, I didn't want to wake you."

"I noticed. You should have, though. I didn't want last night to be all about me. I hope you know that. I can't believe I fell asleep on you. All I can say is that I'm very sorry."

"Don't be. I was fine."

"Fine?" How could he be fine if he hadn't... "I don't understand."

Before he could answer, she glanced back at the desk and saw the slip of paper there. "Did you need to ask Jessica Lucas something? I saw her number on your desk."

This time he looked even more uncomfortable. She remembered asking for more last night, using her hips to try to get it, but he'd never penetrated her fully, even manually. "Did it have to do with last night?"

He gave a half shrug. "I wanted to make sure the babies couldn't be hurt by what we did."

The babies. He was concerned about the babies. Suddenly it all made sense. Even the fact that he'd been careful about handling her breasts, too. She remembered the doctor talking about not engaging in nipple stimulation, but that was toward the end of pregnancy.

Her eyes closed. "Jessica said that sex wasn't off the table. Not at this point."

"I know. But I just wanted to be sure."

"So why didn't you ask *me*? Do you think I would do something if it risked this pregnancy?" She suddenly felt like a fool. She'd practically begged him for more and had tried to reach out for him only to have him pull away. Just like he had when she'd thought the IVF had failed again.

Had he even wanted her at all last night? Or had he simply given in to what she wanted because she was the babies' mother?

She felt an initial rush of humiliation until she remembered he'd definitely been aroused. She was sure of it. But he hadn't acted on that arousal. She should have realized. Something hadn't felt right at the time, but as usual she'd pushed until she got her way and now... And now she was faced with the realization that he probably wouldn't have started anything with her on his own. He'd certainly made it plain enough when he'd said about waiting a little while. He knew her well enough to know that she often fell asleep in his arms after reaching her release. And he'd purposely coaxed her into heading in that direction. She squirmed, humiliation washing over her again.

"Don't bother calling Jessica and asking. There's no need, because I don't see this happening again in the foreseeable future."

"Bella..."

She held up a hand. "No, please don't. I think you were right all along. You said we needed some time apart before you left for Africa. *When I thought I was losing the pregnancy.*"

She knew the bitterness in her voice was coming through loud and clear, but she couldn't seem to stanch the flow. It was like he'd nicked an emotional artery, and now every single hurt that she'd felt over the last couple of years was pouring out.

"You'll be happy to know I finally agree with you. We need some time. *I* need some time. You've offered to do my shift for me, so today, have at it. I'm going to go back to the apartment and figure out where *I* need to go from here."

Before he had a chance to say anything else, she whirled around and left the office, not even saying goodbye. Because when she did say it, it was going to be for good.

Except she knew in her heart of hearts that there was nothing good about a final goodbye. There was only pain and heartbreak. But right now, she couldn't see any way around that. For either of them.

CHAPTER NINE

BELLA GOT HOME and threw herself on the bed, sobbing until she had no more tears inside of her to cry. She pulled the comforter around her, chilled and sad, thinking that nothing seemed to make sense. In all the time that he'd been in the apartment, it felt as though everything had been about the babies or the pregnancy.

It hurt like hell that he'd thought she would do something so unconsidered, so rash, to harm them. She was very aware that they were his children, too.

So why did she have to beg for everything? She'd begged last night in much the same way she'd begged him to be willing to try again before he'd left for Africa. It was so hard to believe that had been only a few short months ago.

Did she want Seb to go? To end their marriage?

Another sob escaped her throat, and she had to steel herself not to fall apart all over again. She didn't want him to leave. But he couldn't stay, either. Not with the way things were between them right now. She did not want someone in her life who was only there for the children. It would be too hard. Because she wanted

Seb, and for her that part had nothing to do with the kids, even if it might have seemed like it at the time.

So what did she do? Talk to him again? Every time she tried to do that, things went sideways.

Maybe. Maybe like she'd begged him to do all those months ago, she should ask for another chance. Not for the babies, but for their relationship.

She just wasn't sure she had the courage to. Not anymore.

But lying here on the bed feeling sorry for herself was helping nothing, either.

She cranked herself upright and took stock of the situation, going into the kitchen for another glass of milk.

She'd cried so hard that she felt completely empty, her stomach muscles sore. The flowers were still on the bar, seeming to mock her tears. She understood his need to keep the peace, and maybe he'd felt guilty over last night.

Calling Jessica may have been his way of making sure he hadn't done anything wrong. Except he had. He hadn't talked to her. He'd shut down the way he'd done before.

Except this time, hadn't she pushed him away, telling him that last night was never happening again?

She had. And he'd barely gotten a word in edgewise. She'd given him no chance to explain himself other than telling her the truth…that he was worried about hurting the babies. But maybe it went beyond that. Maybe calling Jessica was his way of making sure they actually *could* do more.

Maybe his "let's wait a little while" hadn't been an outright rejection, but a plea for some time to figure all this out.

But what was done was done. There was no going back on the way she'd slammed out of his office, was there? Yet if she didn't at least try, she might as well kiss any hope of repairing their relationship goodbye.

She would never know exactly how he felt, unless she sat down and talked to him rationally, not letting her hurt from the past come back and poison what they could have in the present...or the future. Looking at it from his perspective, maybe it had seemed the same way. That things had gotten turned around and she only wanted him as a provider of genetic material.

It was time to go back to him and find out what he wanted out of their marriage or at least know for sure if, as far as he was concerned, they were through. She would only know if she went and talked to him. Then, if there was even the smallest scrap of hope, they could go and meet with Jessica Lucas together and let her put Seb's mind at ease.

She went to the sink and rinsed out her glass, putting it on the rack beside the sink. She was tired and didn't really want to go all the way back to the hospital. But she didn't want to do this over the phone.

That sounded so familiar. She hadn't wanted to tell him about the babies over the phone, either.

So all she could do was drive back over there and find him and hopefully they could get away from the rush of the ER for a few minutes to have this out once and for all.

She turned to find her purse when a sharp pain went through her abdomen. She went still for a minute and held her breath, waiting to see if it happened again.

Okay, it had to just be a fluke. But when she went to take another step it hit again, and this time she felt moisture in her panties.

Dios. No. Please no. She held her hand over her midsection as she went into the bathroom, already knowing what she was going to find. Pulling her undergarment down, she looked and sure enough she was spotting. Just like she had earlier in her pregnancy. No. *No, no, no.* She wrapped her arms around her belly, trying to shield her babies from the unthinkable. Finally she forced herself to move. She needed to get help. Right now.

Her heart skipped a beat as she found an absorbent pad to put on. Surely the universe couldn't be that cruel. She was probably going to lose her marriage. Was some higher power really going to take her babies as well?

She hurried to the kitchen and got her phone out of her purse and pushed Seb's number, listening as it rang.

"Come on, Seb, answer, please!"

It went to voicemail. She didn't leave a message, simply tried the number again. They'd always had a system. If she called two times in a row, it was an emergency and he'd know to either pick up or call her right back.

The second call went to voicemail as well. She stared at the phone, willing him to return the call. Nothing happened.

She couldn't wait. He might be caught up in an emergency at work. Who knew how long it would take. So she called emergency services. Thank God they answered on the second ring. "What's your emergency?"

"I'm nearly five months pregnant with triplets and am having some spotting and pain." Her voice caught and she had to fight to get the rest of the words out. "Could you please send someone? And hurry!"

The dispatcher told her to go and lie down on her couch and that someone was on their way.

She went and unlocked her door, and when she went to turn away, another pain struck. Putting her hand to the spot, she somehow made it over to the couch and lay down. The relief was immediate. The pain disappeared. At least for now. She tried dialing Seb's number again, but there was still no response. She then tried calling the desk to the ER and without saying what was wrong asked if anyone had seen Seb.

"No, Bella, not in the last half hour or so. He's not down here on the floor."

"Okay, thanks."

She hung up. So he wasn't in the middle of an emergency. Where was he, and why wasn't he picking up? It wasn't like Seb, even if he was angry, to not answer her call.

She couldn't worry about that right now. She needed to worry about her babies. The pain had subsided, but she didn't dare get up and go look to see if there was any more spotting, so she did as the dispatcher had instructed and stayed on the couch.

The fifteen minutes until a knock sounded at the door seemed to take forever. "Come in," she called.

When the door opened and she saw Gabriel and his partner, an immediate sense of relief went through her. He and Seb were friends. He came over to the couch and knelt down beside it, putting his medical case on the floor. "What's going on, Bella?"

"I—I can't find Seb and…" She started to cry, and the pain immediately came back. She quickly stopped and took deep careful breaths. "I'm having pain in my abdomen and some spotting."

"How far along are you again?"

"Almost five months."

He nodded, but the concern on his face was obvious. "I'm going to get some vitals, and them I'm going to transfer you to the hospital."

"Okay. I've tried calling Seb several times, but there's been no answer."

"I'm sure he'll call you back any minute." Her sobs had subsided, but the tears hadn't and were now flowing in a silent stream down her face. Tears for herself. For Seb. And for their three precious babies.

Seb stood at the Greek bridge at the Bosques de Palermo and looked out over the water that he and Bella had been on two and a half weeks ago. There were several paddleboats in the water, and the sight made his chest ache. He should have been honest and told Bella that he'd wanted to call Jessica before actually having sex with her. But she'd been so frantic that he'd given in to her, being as gentle as he could. He knew if he'd given her what she wanted that he would have had a hard time holding himself back.

He'd called the doctor that morning as soon as he got into the office and she came right on the line and assured him it was fine, reiterating what she'd said at the appointment. They could have sex normally without fear at this point.

Then Bella had come into the office and had been so angry with him. He wasn't sure where all of it stemmed from, but he was pretty sure some of it was because he'd taken matters into his own hands rather than talking to her about it. Hadn't he tried to?

Maybe, but he hadn't told her he loved her since he'd gotten back from Africa. Because he was afraid she'd reject him. That she'd wanted him there only for the babies. But on the other hand, could it be that she was afraid of the very same thing? Of not being loved for herself apart from the babies?

How could she even doubt his love?

But if he didn't actually say the words, how was she ever going to know for sure? How would he know for sure? And he couldn't stay in the house if they didn't figure out a plan on where to go from here. She'd said they needed time apart. He'd thought the same thing at a certain point, but now he was more sure than ever that for both their sakes, they needed to know what the end goal for their relationship was. Stay together? Or separate for good?

Pushing away from the handrail of the bridge, he reached in his back pocket for his phone to let her know he was headed back to the apartment only to find it wasn't there. Had he left it in the car?

Sometimes he tossed it on the console while he was driving so it didn't bother him while sitting in the seat. Hurrying back the way he'd come, he cursed the fact that the park suddenly seemed huge, the entrance so far away. Even sprinting part of the way, it still took him ten minutes to get back to the parking area. Once inside the car, he looked for his phone again and couldn't find it. He must have left it in his office. But the last thing he wanted to do was go all the way back there to get it. Besides, he wanted to talk to Bella in person and figure this out once and for all.

Starting the car, he headed back to the apartment.

When he arrived, he was glad to see that Bella's car was there, which meant she was there, too. Taking the elevator up, he got off and opened his front door, calling out for her. But there was no answer.

He called again. Nothing. Fear washed over him in a wave. Her vehicle was in the lot, so where was she? He searched the apartment and then looked in the bathroom. There was the strip from a woman's sanitary product in the trash can.

He went very still, staring at the item, a sense of panic coming over him. Had something gone wrong? And he'd left all over again, just like he had when he'd gone to Africa. He should have at least texted where he would be, in case she needed him.

He went to grab his keys off the table in the foyer and found a note.

Headed to the ER with Bella. She's spotting and having some pain. If you get this, meet us there. Gabriel.

He wasted no time, jumping back in his car and racing to the hospital. Although he knew it was due to the stress of not being able to get to her right away, the volume of traffic seemed so much heavier right now, the people in front of him so much slower than normal. But he finally arrived and parked in the closest spot he could find and rushed to the entrance.

He knew he had to look like a madman as he stood there desperately scouring the waiting area. One of the nurses came over to him and murmured, "She's in exam room one. They're waiting for Liz to finish up with an emergency C-section, and then she'll come in and check her over."

"Has anyone called Dr. Lucas yet?"

"Yes. She's also with a patient." The nurse touched his arm. "Just go be with her. That's the best thing you can do right now."

He nodded and headed back to where the exam rooms were, finding the right room and knocking before slipping inside.

Bella's head turned and when she saw him, she fell apart, sobbing into her hands. "Oh, Seb, I'm so sorry."

He didn't hesitate; he hopped onto the exam table

next to her and wrapped his arms around her. "Hey. You have nothing to be sorry about."

"Maybe you were right about everything. Maybe we shouldn't have…"

"No. *You* were right. I called Jessica before you got to the office and she assured me that there wasn't much we could do to harm them."

"Then why is this happening to us again?" She buried her head in his chest. "Why now?"

"I don't know, honey. But I'm here. And babies or no babies, I'm going to stay right here beside you."

"But you made it pretty clear that you were only worried about them."

Her words were so muffled he wasn't sure what he was hearing at first. Then when her meaning broke through… God, how could she ever truly think that? "That's not true, Bella, and I'm sorry if I made you feel that way. What I'm terrified of is losing you. Of something going wrong. Of doing something that hurt not just the babies but you."

She leaned back to look up at him, her nose and eyes red from crying. "But you kept talking about them. Saying I needed to be careful. That we needed to be careful."

"Because you didn't seem to want me for anything but as support during your pregnancy, so that's what I became, even though it drove me crazy not to tell you I still loved you. That I never stopped loving you, even during that awful time before I left for Africa."

He tipped her face up. "I love these babies, but it's

you I want. You I need. The babies are just a bonus package. I'm here for the duration, as long as it's what you want."

She closed her eyes for a second. "It is. I love you, too. And I'm sorry for putting you through all of those treatments. I know it wasn't what you wanted."

Is that what she really thought? If so, he had done a very poor job of showing her what was really important to him. "I hated seeing your devastation every time something went wrong. But I'm here to tell you, if you want ten children, I'll do everything in my power to see that you get them. But as far as what I need, it's you. It's always been you, Bella. I'm lost without you."

Liz swept into the room and took in the scene. "The front desk filled me in, but why don't you tell me what's going on."

Seb listened as Bella recounted that they'd made love yesterday. Then how today she and Seb had had a fight and she'd gone home and cried. She'd gotten up in an attempt to pull herself together and felt a sudden pain that made her double over. She'd then felt something wet in her panties and found that she'd spotted.

Seb took her hand and gave it a slight squeeze.

"When you say you spotted, was it a lot of blood or only a little?" Liz asked.

"Not a lot. It was more like mucus with a pink tinge. Not quite as much as what happened when the IVF treatments failed, but I was so afraid…"

"Are you still in pain?"

"When I twist to the right, it hurts. Yes."

"But no squeezing or cramping?"

"I don't think so."

"Let's take a look and see what's going on." Liz wheeled the ultrasound machine from its spot near the wall and brought it over to the bed. "Seb, can you help her get ready while I set up?"

He nodded. "Lie back, honey."

Bella did what he asked and he helped her slide her skirt down over her hips and unbuttoned her blouse. "Where did it hurt?"

She pointed to a spot on her right side, just below her rib cage. When he lightly pushed on the area, she tensed.

He caught Liz's eye. "I think it might be muscular, but I'll feel better once you see that the babies are all right."

Squeezing his wife's hand again, he leaned down and kissed her cheek.

She wrapped her arms around his neck and held him. "No matter what happens, I want you to know I love you. I want to make this marriage work."

A huge wave of emotion crashed through him, and he closed his eyes and let himself be held tight. "Yes. We're going to make this work. No matter what happens." The moment seemed sacred, as if they were renewing their vows to each other.

"Are you ready?" Liz's voice reminded them that she was there, that there were still vital things that needed to be done.

Bella sucked down an audible breath before letting go of Seb and nodding.

She lay back on the bed, and Seb went to stand with her, holding her hand in his like they had the last time at Jessica Lucas's office. But this time was different. Because this time there was understanding between them in a way that there hadn't been for far too long.

Liz slid the wand back and forth over Bella's belly, looking for the babies. And when a sound filled the room—that strange cacophony of heartbeats that were not in sync with anything but each other, Seb's eyes burned. But not with sadness—it was a happiness that transcended anything he could understand.

"Do you hear that, Bell?"

She nodded, not saying anything, but her look said it all. She was incredibly relieved. "Are they all there?"

"I have Baby A, Baby B and Baby C, who is still neatly tucked behind Baby B, but not as much as he was."

Seb didn't correct her or tell her again which name went with which baby, because in the end it didn't matter. "They're all okay?"

"They seem to be. I don't see anything that could be cause for alarm at the moment. No problems with the placentas or babies, that I can tell."

"Why was I spotting, then?"

"It's not uncommon to spot. During the second trimester your cervix has a rich blood supply. Even an internal exam can cause some light spotting. It's benign in a lot of cases. As far as the pain goes, I'll send Jessica a note and let her know what happened, but I think Seb was right about it being muscular. I'm not seeing any evidence of uterine contractions, so I'm going to chalk that up to a strained muscle."

"I don't want you working today. Either of you." She glanced at him. "Go home and pamper her, Seb. Jessica will probably give you a call sometime today to check on you. I will as well. If you spot again or if the flow turns heavier, come back in immediately. Okay?"

"We will."

"Here's some tissues to clean your belly up." Liz gave her a quick hug. "You know you can call me anytime, right?"

"I do, thank you so much."

The ob-gyn shook hands with Seb. "You guys take as long as you need in here."

"Thanks again."

As soon as Liz left the room, Seb took the box of tissues and gently cleared away the lubricant from Bella's abdomen. Then he helped her readjust her clothing. "Can I lie beside you for a few minutes?"

She nodded, and Seb climbed into the bed with her and tucked his arm beneath her shoulders. "What are you thinking?"

She turned sideways on the bed and snuggled into him. "I'm thinking that I can't believe how lucky I am. And how stupid."

"Stupid?"

"To have let things between us get as bad as they were. I should have told you sooner that I still loved you, but I was afraid I'd killed whatever you'd felt toward me."

He kissed her forehead. "I was afraid of the same thing." He needed to clear the air about one item. "I shouldn't have gone to Africa. Looking back, I realize how utterly selfish it was of me."

She lifted her head to look at him. "No, you did what you needed to do. And honestly, I think I needed to get an up-close-and-personal look at what I stood to lose. Because when I saw you standing there in a mass of feathers the day you returned to Buenos Aires, I suddenly realized I didn't want to lose you. It was one of the scariest days of my life, because I thought I already had."

Bella dropped a kiss on his chin. "I hope you're happy as the father of three, because I won't be trying for anymore."

"Are you sure? We could adopt."

"We could. Or we could volunteer for some programs for disadvantaged kids."

He stroked the side of her face. "As long as we do it together, I'm open to almost anything."

Her mouth twisted sideways. "Not anything, as we saw last night."

"Last night I was worried. And I'm still worried. I want to talk to Jessica again before going any further than we did in bed yesterday, in light of what happened today. I think I may have caused your spotting."

"You heard Liz. It's nothing. Just extra blood vessels. Besides, we don't have to do a repeat of last night. I'm anxious to finish what I started."

"What do you mean?"

"I mean you interrupted me at the best part when we first got inside the apartment."

He grinned before shaking his head. "As sexy as that sounds, do you mind if we just curl up and watch some TV? I just want to be near you. I just want to sit on the couch and not have a cloud hanging over my head. Just enjoy being *us* again…being together. Do you think we could manage that?"

"I think we could manage that." She leaned forward and kissed him on the mouth. "I am so very lucky, Seb. And I promise I won't take it for granted again. Ever."

"I won't either. I love you, Bell."

"Love you, too."

He sat up, pulling her with him. "So, are we ready to get out of here and go home?"

"Yes. Let's go home."

He stopped. "Wait. I need to do something first."

"What's that?"

"I need to find out where the hell I left my cell phone. I'm never going to be without it for the rest of the pregnancy. I almost died when I saw the note Gabriel left, couldn't get here fast enough."

"Is it in our office?"

"I'm pretty sure it is. I left from there and went straight to the park to think. And then I stopped home to tell you what I'd realized—that I love you, babies or no babies. And I mean that."

"Same here. I love you, too, babies or no babies. But I sure am glad we have them."

He slid off the table. "So am I. So let's never fight again."

"I can't promise that, because remember what used to happen when we would fight?"

He smiled. "Makeup sex?"

She laughed. "Makeup sex. Wasn't it the best?"

"*Mi amor*, everything with you is the best."

"Let's find that phone and get home. Oh, and you will be moving back into our room, right?"

"Yes. Starting tonight and every night thereafter."

She wrapped her arms around him and reached up to receive his kiss. "Tonight and every night thereafter."

EPILOGUE

Three years later

BELLA SAT ON the huge picnic blanket and watched as their three boys wrestled with their dad on a grassy stretch of the Bosques de Palermo. This place had been "the destination" ever since the triplets were born. They'd gone from being wheeled in huge ungainly strollers to now, when the little guys could manage it on their sturdy little legs. They'd yet to do the paddle-boats with them, for safety reasons, but every once in a while, she and Seb would hire a sitter and come out here by themselves and rent one.

Then they would make out under the bridge, not caring who saw them.

Seb had still wanted to be cautious about having sex while she was pregnant, but she'd made him promise that once the boys were born they could be as adventurous as they wanted to be in that area. And he had *not* disappointed. The man not only had ideas, but he had *ideas*. Their sex life was rich and full and wonderful. As was every other part of their life.

And as much as she was embarrassed to admit it,

lying together on the couch after they'd put the trio to bed and quietly watching a movie had become the highlight of her nights. Seb said it was his as well.

They'd had to sell their apartment and buy something bigger, as they soon outgrew the two-bedroom place, but their new apartment was in the same complex and so it had been an easy move. And it held none of the painful memories of loss that their old place had.

So many things at the hospital had changed, but some others hadn't. She and Seb still led the emergency department, but her hours had been shortened by a quarter so that she could be home for the boys when they finished preschool. And she'd politicked for Mario Soldado, the patient whose hands had had to be amputated due to electrical burns, to lead talks on the very real dangers of electrocution and ways to avoid it.

She'd heard inklings of new and rekindled romances, but Bella was too busy with her own romance with Seb to listen to the rumors that always circulated around the hospital. She just wished everyone the same happiness that she and Seb had found together.

"Okay, guys, are you ready to eat?"

Four male faces turned her way, and her eyes went down the line, loving each and every member of her family from Luis, who was still the littlest of the triplets, but who was catching up with his brothers, to her hunky husband, who would always be her hero. They'd even talked about going on a Doctors without Borders assignment together when the kids were a little older.

There was no reason not to anymore. She wanted to be wherever Seb was.

She passed out plates of cold chicken, fruit and a fluffy chocolate mousse to everyone and watched them eat with gusto. The boys got chocolate everywhere, but that was one of the parts of being a mom that she loved the most. Watching their enjoyment each and every day.

Seb's dad was still cancer-free and had loved their trip to Scotland. So had Helena. They planned one day to all go together.

Bella had no idea what the future held for any of them, but as long as they were together, how could it be anything but good? Just like their joint prayer before bedtime that had ended with what had become the motto for their life: tonight and every night thereafter.

* * * * *

SURGEON'S BROODING BRAZILIAN RIVAL

LUANA DaROSA

MILLS & BOON

For my sister Lorena, *beschti schwöstr für ewig*.

CHAPTER ONE

THE SOUND OF water pouring out of the tap and skin rubbing against skin filled the scrub room. Carlos looked up from the sink, his eyes scanning the operating room through the window. The members of staff stood by their assigned places, waiting for their patient to be brought in. A patient that should have already been here five minutes ago when the ER had paged him to let him know an emergency surgery was coming up.

His eyes narrowed on the clock on the other side of the OR, and his lips pressed into a thin line as he watched the seconds tick by. He released the foot pedal, and the flow of water stopped. When he turned around, the OR nurse was already waiting with a towel for him to dry his arms before helping him into the gown and gloves.

'Where is our patient?' Carlos asked as he stepped through the doors.

'I'll call them to find out,' one nurse said, and Carlos nodded as she approached the phone hanging on the wall next to the monitoring equipment. As he waited, he let his eyes wander around the room, giving each staff member a once-over. The surgeon assisting him was missing, too. They were most likely with the patient transport after having done the initial consult.

He'd arrived at Hospital General de Buenos Aires almost a week ago. *This* was the first time the staff hadn't impressed him with the level of service and dedication they put forward. Sebastián Lopez, the joint head of emergency medicine at the hospital with his wife, Isabella, had approached him at a conference where Carlos had been one of the keynote speakers.

Though they had mainly spoken about Carlos's specific method of triaging during a multidiscipline surgery, he'd got the feeling from the other man that there had been more to the conversation. That 'more' turned out to be a job offer to come to Buenos Aires and teach the trauma surgeons there how to run a service the way Carlos Cabrera would.

This was definitely not how Carlos Cabrera ran his trauma surgery. In his world, early was on time, and on time was already being late. Which made this patient transport *very* late. In his discipline of medicine, every second counted, and he'd witnessed enough cases where those few extra seconds had decided between life and death.

For a member of *his* team to be late in delivering a patient was unacceptable. The ER was right underneath the trauma surgery ORs. He knew exactly how long it took for a patient to be transported upstairs because on his first day he'd timed it himself, so he knew what to expect from the people on the team.

Carlos rolled his jaw, forcing the tight muscles to relax when the doors finally opened and the gurney with the patient rolled into the OR.

'Get into gear, everyone. Time's wasting,' Carlos said, turning towards the anaesthetist with an impatient nod.

'There was a—' a female voice said behind him, but he cut her off without turning around.

'I'm not interested in excuses, only that we start this surgery with no further delay. Are you my missing surgeon?' He watched the anaesthetist remove the IV drip from the patient's arm and insert the cannula to push the anaesthetic through.

'I'm *a* trauma surgeon at this hospital, but I'm certainly not *your* surgeon.' Carlos furrowed his brow and looked over his shoulder as the woman spoke in clipped words. What was that supposed to mean? But all he caught was a wisp of brown hair that vanished behind the door to the scrub room.

His eyes shot to the window where the woman appeared a heartbeat later, her lips moving in a silent litany as she stuck her hands under the tap. Their gazes collided when she looked up, and a strange sensation of familiarity washed over him as he beheld the honey-brown eyes. Sebastián had introduced Carlos to all the surgeons on staff when he had arrived earlier in the week, including her.

Her smile had been wide as she greeted him, her grip strong when she shook his hand, and the scent of apricot had lingered in his nose long after he'd turned to other staff members to greet them. It was that scent that came rushing into his conscious mind now, setting his focus off-kilter.

Carlos's hand had lingered on hers for a fraction of a second, enough time for a spark to travel up his arm and spread an unfamiliar heat through his chest. It was the echo of that heat rising inside of him again that kept his eyes glued to her face, watching her through the glass.

'The patient had a tracheotomy performed. I'll connect the tube to the ventilator, and we'll have to switch to manual aspiration once you're ready to pull it out,' the anaesthetist said behind him, forcing Carlos out of his head and back into the OR.

'A tracheotomy?' He spun around to face the patient, stepping closer and bending down to inspect the tube sticking out of his patient's throat.

The briefing he'd received just ten minutes ago didn't include any information about a blocked airway that required this form of intubation. A part of him wanted to turn around again and face the woman—Dr Martinez, Sebastián's voice echoed in his head—to ask her what had happened. But the loud beeping of a monitor drew his attention back to the critical condition of his patient.

'His blood pressure is dropping. We need to get him open now and take care of the internal bleeding.' Pushing the swirl of thoughts away, Carlos stepped towards the patient and reached his hand out to receive the scalpel the OR nurse already held in her hand.

'This is not good,' Carlos mumbled to himself as he opened the patient up and beheld the extent of the injury.

Though he had worked in trauma surgery from the moment he had started his internship in Rio de Janeiro many years ago, seeing some of the devastation the human body could withstand didn't get any less humbling—especially when he was the one knitting people back together.

'I need an extra pair of hands,' he said, and as he was about to look up to search for Dr Martinez, two slender gloved hands appeared in his field of vision.

'I'm here,' she said, not offering any other comment about her lateness. Not that it mattered. He had meant it when he said he wasn't interested in what had taken her so long. They could have that argument later.

'Nice of you to join us, Martinez,' he said, unable to help himself with the jab. In all his years working at the largest emergency rooms all across South America, he hadn't let a single co-surgeon down, and it was that kind of dedication he expected from everyone else.

Her eyes shot up at him and narrowed into slits, and for a distracting second, he wondered what her lips looked like underneath her mask. Were they drawn into a tight line, hiding their fullness from view?

'Blood is pooling around the liver, and there's a discolouration of his kidney. Something to look at once we get the bleeding under control.' Carlos focused his mind on the surgery at hand, a frown tugging at the corners of his lips as he realised how easily Dr Martinez held his attention.

What was it about her that drew him in without his permission? He hadn't even spent any time with her outside of their brief introduction.

'Suction or sponges?' Martinez asked, her hand already outstretched to grasp whatever he said.

'I'll take suction while you pack the liver and stop more blood from pooling,' he replied, and took the aspirator from the nurse.

The sputtering of the suction drowned out the beeping of the monitor, and Carlos listened to the anaesthetist keeping him appraised of the vital signs of the patient.

'The ER said he was in an accident on a construction site. Do you know what happened?' He didn't look up as he asked the question, his hand steady as he cleared the surgical field of the excess blood. 'Hand me the stapler, please,' he said as he handed the suction tube off.

'You're going to staple the laceration shut?' That question was the first thing Dr Martinez had said since she had begun packing the liver and its surroundings with surgical sponges to soak up as much blood as possible. With her efforts on these fronts and him suctioning the rest away, he could now see where the organ had torn on impact.

'Staples are quicker than sutures and just as effective,' he countered, then placed the medical stapler onto the cut and set the first staple. 'There will be some scarring, but considering the situation he's in, it will be the least of his problems.'

Carlos didn't wait for Dr Martinez to object any further and stapled the rest of the wound with sure, swift hands.

'He got crushed underneath a steel beam,' she said when he had finished closing the cut on the liver, and it took Carlos a second to remember the context. He'd asked what had happened.

'The bruising on the kidney worries me. Not enough to put in a drain, though… He's hanging on right now, but the thread is thin. There will be follow-up surgeries in the next few days.' Carlos paused, assessing the patient before going over to the monitor with the vital signs on it. The patient's blood pressure had evened out, showing Carlos they had stopped the source of the internal bleeding.

'With an injury like this, he could suffer from crush syndrome. If he's stable enough to be transported, we should put him on fluids and monitor his kidney function every hour,' Dr Martinez said, to which Carlos nodded.

'Very well, Martinez. Let's close him up.'

* * *

The rest of the surgery went by without another hitch, and Sofia was grateful for that. Her hands were steady, but her breath quickened and came out in short, quick bursts.

I'm not interested in any excuses.

His words echoed in her head throughout the surgery, sending waves of hot and cold through her. The last time she'd received such a dressing down had been during her internship years ago from a particularly difficult senior surgeon. Carlos Cabrera was apparently trying to rival him as the most unpleasant surgeon she'd ever had the misfortune to work with.

Dr Morales had never passed up an opportunity to criticise her in front of her peers, taking any excuse to reprimand her. What exactly made her that special to the old surgeon, she never knew. But because of his scathing words, Sofia got into the habit of triple-checking every single step inside and outside of the OR. The rule book had become her best friend because her only defence had been to explain her actions in the context of medical studies and guides.

Unlike the grumpy surgeon from her internship, at least Carlos was easy on the eyes when he gave her grief. His cheekbones were set high, the gentle slope downward giving his face a regal quality that was both alluring and infuriatingly superior. Along with the perfectly groomed hair and brown eyes that seemed to note everything around them, he resembled an actor playing a surgeon. The impression had been so stark, Sofia couldn't help but stare, inexplicably drawn to him.

Sebastián himself had told her he and the chief of surgery had worked together to bring Carlos here. They wanted the entire surgical and emergency medicine team to learn from him.

And the worst part about the surgery today was that she actually *had* learned something. Staples weren't a new invention, and she had used them plenty of times when working in the emergency room to quickly patch up surface wounds. But for repairing damage she found internally, Sofia always took the time to do the sutures, sometimes even feeling hurried during high-pressure situations.

Staples were a quick and easy solution, the downside of them being excessive scarring that could lead to further complications. But in a discipline like trauma surgery, the quick fix was most often also the right fix.

The heart rate monitor beeped, drawing Sofia's thoughts back into the OR as Alejandra, the junior surgeon next to her, shuffled her feet. Alejandra's surgical gown rustled as she bent over the patient to look at his throat.

'Are we leaving the tracheotomy like this?' Alejandra asked.

'Yes,' Carlos replied just as Sofia had finished taking a breath to answer the question herself. 'In the state he's in, he'll need to remain intubated and on ventilation. There will be a follow-up surgery tomorrow where the cardiovascular team will decide what to do.'

Alejandra nodded, and Sofia bit back a sharp retort and forced her hand to relax. As he spoke, her grip around the retractor had tightened.

Why was she so bothered by this guy? He wasn't *that* special. Although she couldn't deny the admiration she felt—much like the look she saw on Alejandra's face. She recognised his potential to teach her much, and her skin flushed every time she looked at him, reminded of the expertise he brought to the table.

When he was working opposite her in the OR, it was far too easy to get lost in his lilting baritone voice as he narrated the surgery while her eyes tracked his every more.

Now as he patted the film dressing on the incision wound onto the patient's skin. His fingers moved with an unexpected delicacy, contrasting with his stern demeanour. The soft touch evoked an unbidden thought in the back of her mind as Sofia wondered what his hands would feel like without the gloves. Would they feel rough as each of his calluses scraped against her skin?

'You ready for the tape, Martinez?' His deep voice dragged her out of the fantasy playing in her head, and Sofia repressed a shudder. Carlos touching her was not only inappropriate, it was also *not* how she felt about him. Wherever that thought had come from, it needed to go straight back there and never return.

'Yes, of course,' she said, swallowing the *sorry* that was forming on her tongue. She might have been more apologetic to other colleagues, but if Carlos wanted to be abrasive, then he could take it as well.

Pulling the tape to the appropriate size, she held it out to Alejandra, who cut it. Then she angled the piece of tape to align with where Carlos's hand was holding down the dressing. She placed it at the far end, patting it so it would stick, and then slowly ran her hand up the dressing, flattening the tape until her hand connected with Carlos's, which was still holding the film in place.

The spark created by that small touch travelled down her arm in an electric wave, singeing everything in its wake. The sensation took her by surprise, her lips parting as a soft, unbidden gasp emerged.

An instant later, his eyes shot up to hers, narrowed into slits as he levelled a stare at her. Dear God, had he heard her even over the low whirring of the ventilator and the constant beeping from the vital monitors? The last thing she needed was Carlos Cabrera thinking she had a thing for him.

'You're assigned to my operating room for today?' Carlos asked as he turned away to let the nurse assist him with his gown. Sofia noted the terse undertone in his voice. He had *definitely* caught her gasp.

'I am. Is that going to be a problem?' she asked curtly, even though she knew she shouldn't, and turned as well to get help with her own surgical gown.

After the public dressing down he'd given her about being late, she didn't care. What would have the other option been? Not performing a tracheotomy on the patient? She would have been on time, but there wouldn't have been a need for surgery at all.

When Carlos didn't answer, she whirled around to look at him and caught a glimpse of an amused expression before the shutters fell down, leaving her with nothing but the mask of cool professionalism she already knew he usually wore.

'Just don't be late again and we won't have any problems,' he said before turning towards the anaesthetist, trying to get his attention.

As he turned away, a sinking feeling settled in her stomach. An entire afternoon with him? She sighed, mentally bracing herself. He'd better not make any other big deals about her conduct. Sofia was not about to withhold any life-saving measures just because he liked to keep to the schedule. Surgery was unpredictable, and she'd thought a renowned surgeon like Carlos would have understood that better.

CHAPTER TWO

THE REST OF her afternoon went by uneventfully, and Sofia had avoided any further accidental contact or any meaningful conversation with Carlos. Something that she was now, one day later, making an ironclad rule. She would listen to him whenever he conducted the staff training to learn whatever she could without getting too close.

Sofia also didn't have any issues performing surgeries with him—quite the opposite. Despite his abrasiveness, their rhythm in the OR matched each other's, like the same people had taught them how to operate, and despite her discontent with him, she had to admit that they worked well as a surgical unit.

Though she didn't want to give him too much credit for that. With the amount of praise he received from the medical community, he should be able to work with anyone and adapt to their style. Was that what had happened with them? He'd picked up on her personal style and modelled his own after it?

The thought of Carlos observing her so closely brought a flush to her cheeks, and a warm surge rose from her neck to her forehead. What else had he seen while he had his eye on her? Had he noticed how much attention she'd paid him? How impressed she had been with his skill despite not wanting to? She had promised herself she would not fall for this squeaky-clean façade Carlos Cabrera was putting on. Okay, maybe he was handsome and talented and hard-working, but that didn't mean he deserved the special treatment everyone was giving him—including Sebastián.

Sofia's eyes narrowed as the head of emergency medicine walked towards the nurses' station where she was finishing up her patient notes from a surgery earlier. The hum of the ER was a familiar backdrop as she worked, undisturbed by the rattling of stretchers transporting patients and the beeping of pagers.

'Hablando del Rey de Roma...' she said, raising her voice above the noise drifting towards them from the trauma bays as he came towards her with an unmistakable swagger in his step. 'What has you so bouncy this morning?'

Sebastián laughed at that, coming to a halt next to her and leaning his elbow on the counter. 'Love, my friend. It's the best thing out there to elevate your mood. You should try it.'

Sofia snorted at that, but the breath caught in her throat as the unbidden image of Carlos flashed through her mind again, his fingers sure and nimble as he'd stapled shut the wound on their shared patient. Whatever qualms she had, she couldn't deny his skills as a surgeon.

Sebastián noticed the hesitation she tried to mask as a cough and tilted his head to the side in a silent question. A question Sofia had no intention of answering. Love might have worked for her chief, but it definitely wasn't for her. Surgery was a very competitive field, trauma surgery even more so.

Sofia sighed. 'You know how it is out there. No one understands what it's like to be in a relationship with a surgeon until I've cancelled five dates in a row. They somehow seem to think my day ends at 5:00 p.m., regardless of whether I'm elbow-deep in someone's chest cavity.'

Every single boyfriend of hers had claimed to understand that her job needed to come first—until they didn't, leaving her to pick up the pieces. Again.

Sebastián raised his hands in front of him. 'I know you struggled, especially with that one guy. David?'

'Daniel,' Sofia said, the name twisting something deep inside her gut.

Once she had thought she'd found someone who understood that work would always be her first responsibility. But Daniel had turned out to be the worst of all of them. The other men in her life had at least had the decency to tell her that things hadn't been working out for them. Daniel had cheated on her, then blamed her dedication to work for his missteps. The words still burned a hole in her heart whenever she recalled them.

'Daniel, right...' Sebastián shook his head, no doubt recalling the mess Daniel had left behind when they'd broken up. Though it reminded her of the one good thing that had come out of the mess of their relationship. She and Isabella had grown much closer as the other woman had helped her put the pieces of her life back together.

'How is Isabella doing?' Sofia asked, pushing away the storm of emotions bubbling up within her whenever she thought about her ex and focusing on her friendship with the husband-and-wife team leading the OR.

'She's good. So are the triplets. Her doctors have asked her to take it easy, but you know how she is.

Even when she's not at the hospital, I find her at home repainting the nursery for the seventh time or cleaning out the garage.'

He rolled his eyes in exasperation, but she could see the playfulness behind his words—along with the genuine worry that his wife was overdoing it.

Sebastián and Isabella Lopez had taken charge of the ER in the Hospital General de Buenos Aires many years ago and transformed it from an underperforming emergency room to the renowned trauma centre it was now. Though Sofia hadn't been there then—she'd only started working here three years ago—she'd heard enough from other staff about the transformation of the hospital.

'That sounds like Bella,' she said with a chuckle, and a familiar warmth spread through her chest at the thought of the other woman. 'You know she won't slow down until she's too pregnant to move.'

Sebastián sighed, shaking his head. 'I've been keeping her busy with administrative things to do around the hospital. But I'm actually running out of things to distract her with.' He paused, then mumbled more to himself than Sofia, 'Maybe I should send her to Cabrera. They can document his trainings together.'

The mention of Carlos changed the comfortable warmth inside her to a searing heat, the biting flames emerging at the mention of his name. Flames of annoyance, Sofia told herself as her spine stiffened.

'I meant to talk to you about him and why the hell senior leadership thought he was a necessary addition to the team,' she said, releasing those feelings in a channelled burst towards the person who was partially responsible for Carlos Cabrera being here.

Sebastián's eyebrows rose all the way to his hairline.

'You don't like him?' His tone had a fragile edge to it, as if her words had genuinely saddened him.

'Oh, God, are you under his spell, too? What is wrong with everyone?' Sofia raised her hands in disbelief when Sebastián's face remained puzzled. 'He's a decent surgeon, but there isn't much more to him. What's with the obsession?'

'Is…there a problem I should know about?' She noticed a slight shift in his tone, one she recognised as his 'boss' voice, and she shook her head. Though Sofia had a few choice words to say about Carlos, she knew she wasn't in the right frame of mind to let it out constructively. Sebastián wasn't technically leading the surgical department, but she spent so much time in the ER that they had become close enough to share their opinions with each other. He had even helped her out with proposals for senior leadership, including himself.

'I just think he's a bit…arrogant,' she said, which was part of the truth she wanted to tell Sebastián—when the time was right.

Sebastián chuckled at that. 'I see the professional rivalry is already in full swing. Don't get too wrapped up in this, Sofia. He's here on a one-month contract, and then he'll be off to the next place.'

Her ears perked up at that. 'You don't want him here permanently?'

'Oh, no, believe me, I do. *He* doesn't want a full-time position here. Cabrera hasn't stayed at a place for more than six months for the last five years, and neither I nor the chief of surgery could change his mind.'

Sofia furrowed her brow at that. 'He's been travelling around to different hospitals for the last five years. Why?'

'No idea, but we can ask him together,' Sebastián said as he pointed with his chin to a spot behind her.

Her head whipped around, her eyes widening as she saw the subject of their conversation walk towards them. His head was tilted downwards, and the line between his eyebrows was getting progressively deeper at whatever he was looking at on his phone. He hadn't seen her, had he?

Sofia hesitated as different paths opened up in her mind. The last thing she wanted was to give him the satisfaction of running away from him, dodging wayward stretchers and scurrying colleagues in the process. But she was in no mood for being in his presence any longer than she needed to—and that included unscheduled run-ins in the ER. Everything about him was too much. His attitude, the skill he wasn't shy of flaunting, his subtle scent of pine that kept drifting up her nose whenever she crossed paths with him and brought a tingling sensation to her fingertips whenever she closed her eyes...

'I should go,' she said when the spark she had just been thinking about travelled down her arms again, and didn't give the Sebastián the time to say anything in return before speed-walking to the next door in sight and vanishing behind it.

'Cabrera.' Carlos looked up and glimpsed the grey scrubs the trauma team wore vanishing behind the door to a supply closet. It slammed shut just as he stopped in front of Sebastián Lopez, who had been the one to call his name.

'Lopez, good to see you,' he said to the head of the ER. He wasn't necessarily sure what they had to talk about, but his professional courtesy didn't let him walk past one of his superiors—especially not when he'd called on him by name. 'What can I do for you?'

Something flickered over the expression of the other man, a feeling he couldn't quite pin down. Annoyance? Carlos raised his eyes to the door that had just slammed shut a few seconds ago, and Sebastián followed his gaze with a sigh. He opened his mouth to say something when the pager hanging from his waistband went off. He glanced at it, then frowned and stood up straight.

'The chief of medicine is asking for me. Listen…' Sebastián shot another glance at the door and then shrugged. 'Don't worry, there was bound to be friction, but she'll come around. Just keep on teaching everyone like we discussed, and eventually she'll get there.'

'She…? What are you talking about? Who?' His words floated into the empty space in front of him. Sebastián had already walked away.

What the hell was wrong with this hospital? It had been three days since he'd started here, and he already had a notebook full of suggestions of things that needed to change in both the trauma department and the ER for them to be more efficient. One of these changes, Carlos guessed, wouldn't make him the most popular surgeon in the department. Not that he cared much. His placement at different hospitals was fleeting for various reasons. Sticking around for too long meant getting attached to people. His days of being attached to anyone had ended five years ago—when his wife died in a car accident.

That night was the reason he was here, the reason he'd never settled down in one place for longer than a few months.

'Did you hear about Dr Martinez? Apparently, the…'

Carlos caught the snippet of discussion as two doctors walked past him, heads turned to each other. His gaze followed them, and he had no doubt they were gossiping about what had happened between them in the OR. Throughout the day, he had heard different retellings of the story—and the embellishments as it had passed from one staff member to the other were concerning.

How could they take their work seriously when they were so busy talking about their colleagues? People's personal lives had no place in the hospital. He would never dream of bringing up Rosa…

Carlos pushed the thought of his wife away and straightened his spine. His primary concern right now was Sofia Martinez. Because clearly she was letting some personal issue impede their working relationship. He couldn't have one surgeon avoiding him, potentially causing more distracting rumours to fly around the hospital. No, he'd correct whatever misconception she had about him right now.

He took a deep breath as his hand landed on the door handle, a flutter in his chest giving him pause. In the last three hospitals he'd been at, he had always met people who were unhappy about the changes he'd recommended. Even though Sofia was behaving this way, she didn't strike him as someone to reject an opportunity to learn. When they had performed their surgery together, he'd even sensed something akin to closeness, recognising how their styles in surgery complimented each other.

Before he could overanalyse their compatibility in the OR, Carlos pushed the door open and slipped in through a slim crack before closing it again—coming face-to-face with Sofia Martinez, who stood only two handbreadths away from him.

The awareness of her proximity to him flared into life in the pit of his stomach, shooting hot tendrils of fire across his body. Overwhelmed by the sensation, he took a step back and started when his back collided with the door he'd just come through.

Carlos stood so close he could count the golden flecks in her brown eyes. They formed tiny constellations he was sure he would love to memorise if he just got enough chances to look at her uninterrupted.

The thoughts kept bubbling up inside of him unbidden and resisting his efforts to pull himself back into the moment. Seconds ticked on in which they were just staring at each other, waiting for the other one to break the stare.

'Did you need something, Dr Cabrera? Maybe some directions?' Sofia finally asked, pulling him out of his stupor. Ice coated her words, but he could have sworn that there was a slight tremble in her voice.

The speech he had prepared before opening the door was gone. So were any clever retorts he might have had. Hell, he could barely remember what had possessed him to come in here. Maybe he did really need some directions...

'Why are you running away from me?' He shot the question at her with no additional filtering, his mind too preoccupied with her sudden proximity to care about delicacy.

The sooner they sorted this out, the faster he could leave.

Sofia's eyes rounded, and he glimpsed a sliver of white around the dark brown. She blinked several times, her long lashes sweeping over her cheeks with each bat and drawing all of his attention towards them. That was until her lower lip vanished between her teeth for a fraction of a second, but long enough for Carlos to notice.

'I'm not running away from you,' she said, and at least she had the decency to blush at the obvious lie they both knew she had just uttered. A blush that tinted her cheeks in a warm, sun-kissed apricot.

His fingers contracted into a fist at his side as the urge to brush over her skin tingled in his fingertips. What was wrong with him?

'If you're not avoiding me, what's the reason you're in here?' he asked after clearing his throat to get rid of any residual huskiness.

'I…' Her quick glance up and down the shelves revealed her intention as she started speaking. Her hand shot up, looking to grab anything that she could plausibly need in this moment, and Carlos almost felt bad for her when she dropped it with a sigh.

'Fine… Even if I was hiding in here from you, what's it to you? You're not *interested* in hearing my excuses, are you?' she said, and squared her shoulders as she looked back at him.

It was Carlos's turn to blink. Had he been too abrasive with her? He knew people perceived him as direct, but that was one quality that had earned him the success in his field he enjoyed now. There was no room for waiting or hesitation in trauma surgery. He strived to embody those principles—and he expected the staff he worked with to do the same.

But he was here to teach, and he could see now that he'd fallen short of that. Otherwise, Sofia would know why he'd said what he had.

'The patient's airway became blocked during transport. You had to stop to perform an emergency tracheotomy,' he said.

In the silence between them, he could hear the sharp intake of breath at his words. Had she thought him unkind for no good reason other than being in a hurry to get the patient ready for surgery?

'That's right,' she said, pushing out her chin in a silent challenge that Carlos wanted to meet—and forced himself not to. This wasn't the first time an antagonistic employee who viewed him as an intruder had confronted him. Meeting them with the same intensity had never ended well.

Something about Sofia made him want to throw things back at her because he knew she could take it, and he wanted to see how far they could push each other. Strictly professionally, of course.

'And you think that when our patient is flatlining and about to bleed out, it's the right time to listen to the reasons you were late?' Despite trying his best, he couldn't keep the edge out of his words completely. It was a sharpness he had honed over the last five years, a weapon he wielded so no one would ever dare to get too close to him. If they all perceived him as an unpleasant and elitist surgeon, it would be easier to leave at the end of the assignment—because when Rosa had died all these years ago, his capability of forming connections to people on any emotional level went with her.

Sofia stared at him, her big eyes unblinking, and he could almost see the wheels turning inside her head.

'There is a time and place for explanations,' he said when she remained quiet, only the clenching muscle in her jaw showing any kind of outward reaction. 'When a patient lands in our OR, the only things we should be interested in are the facts that will help us perform the surgery better. We can discuss anything else in the patient notes.'

The woman still stared at him, though her eyes had narrowed further, and he would have laughed at her unwillingness to give him even a little bit of acknowledgement. Stubbornness was a trait he knew all too well. It was another reason he had made it so far as a surgeon.

'Explanations, yes, I agree,' Sofia finally said, her voice a low rumble that vibrated through the air between them. Had her voice been this deep a few moments ago? Or were his ears playing tricks on him?

Carlos didn't get the chance to contemplate it further as she continued, 'But you specifically said excuses. I never intended to give you any excuses because I don't need to justify my lateness when it hinges on getting the patient to you alive. I'm all for you being here and helping the trauma team reach the next level. But remember that the words you use do matter, Dr Cabrera.'

'Carlos.' His name flew out of his mouth before he could reconsider it, the offer to call him by his first name floating between them like an untethered ghost.

Why had he just volunteered that? He didn't want to be close to Sofia or anyone else at this place. No, the same rules applied as always. Carlos would do his best to equip the staff with all of his teachings and processes before moving on to the next place.

Yet here he was, offering his first name to this strangely disarming woman standing in front of him with crossed arms and a defiant sparkle in her golden-brown eyes.

'Carlos,' she echoed when the silence between them extended, as if she needed to try it on for size, and his name from her lips shot a flash of heat through his body that settled in the pit of his stomach with an uncomfortable pinch.

His breath was audible in the confines of the small supply closet, and he regretted following her into this tiny space to begin with. She was too close to him, noticed each reaction as her intelligent eyes raked over him, and now he could no longer control the steadiness of his breathing.

'I agree that the words I use do matter, and I will take that feedback on board. I might have come here to teach you all, but that doesn't mean I'm above learning new things myself. I appreciate your openness,' he said, in part because he genuinely meant it, but also to end this conversation and finally get back into the ER where the air wasn't as hot and filled with electric sparks that were threatening to burst into flames all over his skin. 'Rules and norms are important to me. If you feel like I'm not embodying them, I would like to know.'

Carlos braced himself for another barbed retort, but her lips parted in a genuine smile. He didn't know how to react as more heat surged through his veins, forcing him to expel another ragged breath.

'That might be the first thing we have in common. Sebastián has, on more than one occasion, described me as "aggressively by the book". He makes it sound like I need to loosen up, but I don't see any reasons to change,' she said, the smile tugging on her lips reaching her eyes and giving them a soft sparkle.

'You won't catch me trying to change that about you. If anything, that's something I encourage in the staff I teach. We need to think on our feet and have enough agency to go with whatever is needed in the moment.

But to do that, we need to know all of our internal processes inside and out, and adhere to certain standards.' Speaking about that set his frayed nerves at ease, letting him sink into a topic he had a full mastery of and knew how to navigate.

'So, what made you fall in love with rules and regulations?' she asked as she leaned against the wall in a gesture far too casual for his liking.

'Excuse me?' Half of his effort went into remembering that they were still in a professional setting, with the faint buzzing and humming from the ER filtering through the door. Carlos couldn't remember a single instance in his career when he had spent a prolonged time in a supply closet. The poor ventilation in here was evident from the flush creeping up his neck. The lack of oxygen was clearly heating him up.

'I've found that with people like us, there is one defining event in their lives that…well, that made us who we are,' she continued, and he scanned her face for the same flush rising in him. All he found was perfect caramel skin. 'Mine was in elementary school. We only had one ball to play with, so every day, a different group got to play with it. Some kids banded together to rig the system. Massive nerd that I am, I came up with a fair schedule for the ball. My teacher was very impressed with the effort. Implementing that timetable is still one of my career highlights.'

The tension rippling through his body ebbed as he considered her words, and he raised one eyebrow. 'Did you just make a joke?'

Sofia frowned. 'Joke? I'm dead serious. To this day, the school still uses the schedule for playtime.'

'I see…' The chuckle bubbled up in Carlos's chest

without him being able to stop it, and grew louder when Sofia joined in. 'Rules have led to tremendous successes in your life. I can see why they are important to you.'

That was about as much he wanted to know about Sofia Martinez. While he understood the argument that getting to know a person well improved collaboration, he wouldn't be a long-term addition to the team. Familiarity would only chain him down.

Judging by how her gaze narrowed on him, Carlos got the sense that she had picked up on his deflection tactic. 'What about you? What event made Carlos Cabrera fall in love with rules?'

Carlos didn't know what compelled him to answer truthfully when he had been so close to escaping. Something about Sofia, a quality she possessed, was strangely disarming. Maybe because they had found the one thing they could agree on in an otherwise contentious relationship?

'I lost someone important to me,' he said, and the regret rushing into his system was instantaneous and gut-wrenching.

Her features softened, and the familiar gleam of sympathy entered her eyes. An understandable reaction, but one Carlos hated seeing. He didn't deserve anyone's pity, not when he had been the one driving the car on the night of the accident that had killed his wife.

'Oh, I'm sorry...' Sofia breathed out, her voice trailing off when he shook his head.

Before he could say anything else he might regret, Carlos reached behind him, grasping the door handle while still facing her. 'Glad we cleared this up, Martinez,' he said, then turned to leave. Her sharp intake of breath stopped him.

Her eyes were wide when he shot her a glance over his shoulder, and he didn't miss how they darted down his body, as if taking in his entire frame. Her lips parted, and there was another rushed exhale he couldn't quite place. 'If I'm to call you Carlos, it's only right if you call me Sofia.'

Something about her tone told him that this concession cost her as much as his had him—though the reasons for it were much different. He wanted to ask what they were, but quickly squashed that impulse. Knowing what made her tick wasn't essential for him to do his job, and he already knew way too much about her.

'All right… Sofia,' he said, and caught himself savouring her name on his tongue. The awareness of his attraction to her, of her closeness to him, lanced through him and morphed into a flash of panic that had him throwing the door open and leaving the supply closet—before he could do anything he would regret.

CHAPTER THREE

THE ENCOUNTER WITH Carlos in the supply closet lingered in Sofia's mind—no matter how hard she tried to forget. One of the main reasons for her repeated failures was the man himself. There wasn't a single day when she wouldn't see him, and the flashes of heat that caused erupted through her without her bidding.

Sofia shook her head, angry at herself and reminding herself that she should be irritated with Carlos as well. The reason she was seeing him everywhere she went had to do with the fact that this man didn't understand boundaries.

'We can give these antibiotics alongside his regular insulin shots?' The familiar voice of Mariana Flores, the charge nurse of the emergency room, pierced through the heavy fog of her thoughts, and Sofia blinked once.

'Sorry what?' She looked down and read the text on the tablet Mariana held towards her, scanning the medication order for her post-op patient. 'This is fine. There shouldn't be any interference.'

The nurse flashed her a smile. 'Where did your mind wander off to?'

'Nowhere good,' she mumbled as a reply, then hesitated before tapping on the tablet and bringing up the OR schedule of the trauma department. She told herself that she wasn't checking what surgery was happening in OR Two and that she needed to know occupancy in case an emergency came in.

But she wasn't fooling herself, or the woman standing on the other side of the counter. 'Checking in on Cabrera? I didn't take you for someone who fancies him,' she said with a chuckle that sent a flush crawling up Sofia's neck.

'I don't fancy him. Quite the opposite. I'm checking on him so I can avoid him. This guy has absolutely no respect for how we run our trauma rooms here. Every time I turn around, he's already in the ambulance bay, stealing yet another one of my patients. He's such a pain to work with.'

Carlos had been here one week already, and rather than teaching her the things she needed to learn, he was turning her routine upside down with his constant interference. Sometimes he even had the audacity to suggest that she assist on a surgery she had every right to be the leading surgeon on. Those were the actions of a man who was completely full of himself.

'That's not what I hear from everyone else,' Mariana said, a grin on her lips. 'Yesterday someone brought him a casserole after he mentioned he doesn't have enough time to cook.'

'I know, and don't you think that's super-weird? Especially since he gives away half of the gifts he receives. He got a plate of *alfajores*, and he looked me dead in the eye as he tried to palm them off on me.'

She had pinned him with a withering look, unsure if he was genuinely interested in giving her cookies or if this was some weird mind-game he was playing with her. Someone who so blatantly stole her surgeries wouldn't shy away from other methods of throwing her off.

'But you like *alfajores*.'

'That's not the point, Mariana. Stealing people's surgeries and passing along gifts he was given is rude. Why won't anyone acknowledge that?' She curled her hand into a fist, tapping it against the counter separating her from the nurse.

Mariana lifted her hands in front of her. 'Hey, don't drag me into this mess of unresolved feelings you have for Cabrera.'

Sofia snorted at that, hoping she'd put enough derision into the sound to get her point across. Her heart had jumped into her mouth at Mariana's words, recalling the moment they had shared in the supply closet. His proximity had flooded her with awareness, the scent of spicy pine still lingering around her whenever she closed her eyes. The tension between them had reached a new level.

But then he had opened up and let her glimpse beyond the mask he wore at work every day. Something had unravelled from him, a thin, gossamer thread that connected them—because they had found common ground.

Had she imagined the electricity crackling between them? She didn't usually daydream about colleagues. Her job was way too important to her for some fanciful crushes on *gringo* doctors who came to work at the Hospital General. Especially after the last man she'd opened up to had repaid her trust by betraying her so deeply, she still kept a close guard on her feelings.

Yet somehow Carlos kept sneaking back into her thoughts. Ugh, Sofia needed to get him out of her head. How had he even become so stuck in there in the first place?

'Let me go to the ER before he can magically appear there and mess with my head some more,' she muttered, more to herself than to Mariana. Then she turned away from the nurse and trotted back to the ER. She could catch up with her patient charts while she waited for the next emergency to come through the doors—and hopefully beat Carlos to it.

As she pushed the doors to the emergency room open, she ran into a tall wall of lean muscle. The scent of woodsy spice filled her nose, a delicious—and familiar—aroma. Her head whipped upwards as she collided with Carlos Cabrera.

'How on earth are you already down here? Is it your mission to make me go nuts? Is that why we hired you?' He was supposed to be in surgery. She had just checked that two minutes ago.

He tilted his head to the side, and the inquisitive look on his face was so flattering to his features that Sofia wanted to both shove him and kiss him just to wipe that expression away. The second thought was one that concerned her. Why was she even thinking about Carlos in such a context when she had nothing but contempt for him? One tiny slice of vulnerability shared in a supply closet couldn't be enough to change her mind about him.

'What are you talking about?' he asked, and Sofia had to take several breaths to banish the fantasy of their lips connecting. Where had that come from?

'I was upstairs and saw your name on the board. But since you are standing here, right when I'm trying to get back to work, I have to assume you are some kind of *demonio* sent to torment me.'

'A demon? Really, Sofia?' The smirk pulling at the corners of his lips transformed his already handsome face into something from another planet. Her name from his lips sent a bolt of lightning down her spine.

Her mouth went dry as she tried her best to stay present in this conversation. It was probably all part of the *demonio*'s plan—setting her off-kilter. Though she still didn't know why he was going to so much trouble when he wasn't going to stick around. Who was he trying so hard for that he would steal her patients right from under her nose?

'I can't explain it in any other way,' she said after a few beats of silence.

'And what exactly is *it*?' His voice was almost a drawl, hitting her low in the stomach, where the electricity of his scent was already pooling and making it hard to form any cohesive thoughts.

What was wrong with her? Sure, it had been a while since she'd broken things off with Daniel, but was she really so starved for physical closeness that the first handsome doctor to stumble into her path had her brain all scrambled? Was that what was happening here?

'You've been stealing *my* patients and doing *my* surgeries. Even when I'm supposed to be by myself. I thought you came here to train us,' she said, crossing her arms in front of her to give her hands something to hold on to. Because her fingertips were tingling with the strange need to reach out and feel that smirk under her fingers. 'You should be in OR Two, taking care of the trauma case that came in an hour ago.'

His smile dimmed at that. The contrast between his smirking expression and this stern one was so stark that regret flooded her veins, even though she didn't know why he'd stopped smiling—or if it was because of her.

'The patient didn't make it. By the time we got to the

operating room, he had already flatlined,' he said, with the cool detachment of someone who had delivered such a message countless times—both to colleagues and the affected family members.

'Oh...' she breathed out, suddenly feeling foolish for her rant and calling him a demon.

Sofia didn't know how she would have reacted were she on the receiving end of her speech, but the contemplative look on his face wasn't what she had expected—and the shiver running down her spine as his dark eyes raked over her was an unpleasant side effect of their whole interaction. Why was he looking at her like that?

And what was going on with her that she even cared? She was no better than any of the other staff members fawning over Carlos whenever they saw him. Something about him was impossible to resist, a form of silent charm that he deployed at will to enchant the people around him.

They remained locked in silence, and just like in the supply closet, the air between them filled with an electric current connecting their bodies. That was until he said, 'As for the stealing of patients and surgeries, I'm simply admitting the patients that come in through the ER. If you feel you are missing out on surgeries, I suggest you get to the patients before I do.'

The tension between them collapsed. Sofia's eyes widened at his words and at the nonchalance in his voice. 'Are you implying I'm not present enough in the emergency room when cases come in?' she said, keeping her voice as calm and quiet as she could.

This guy knew exactly how to get under her skin, and by the grin spreading over his lips, she could guess that he got great satisfaction out of that. 'I'm not implying anything. Surgery is competitive, and I can't wait around for you to take the patients on when they're coming into the ER. You know our certification as a trauma centre is at risk if the wait times for surgeries get too high. I can't let that happen on my watch,' he said, as if she was a year one intern who had just begun her first day in the emergency room.

'Oh, no, Carlos. You're not putting this on me. You're the one who seems to live at the hospital. How else are you *always* here, even when I'm scheduled as the trauma surgeon on call for a shift? With how much time you spend here, I feel sorry for whoever waits for you to come home. Are you married?' The last question came out before she could consider whether she *really* wanted to know. Except she wanted to know. The sheer chemistry brewing between them demanded an answer—though she didn't plan on doing anything with that information. Even if he was single, she wasn't interested in any kind of relationship. Not when she was still picking up the pieces of herself from the last one.

A shadow fluttered over his expression, a spark of hurt entering his eyes for but a second before it disappeared along with the smirk—leaving nothing but a stony expression behind. The shake of his head was a short one as he said, 'No, I'm not.'

Sofia sensed there was more to the story than that short answer let on, and she clamped down on the urge to pry for more information. The sentence *So you're available for some fun?* formed in her head without her bidding, and those words cascaded through her in hot and cold waves. Was that what was happening to her? Did she yearn for some closeness with a man with no strings or promises attached to it? It had been a while since she'd just enjoyed herself without any worries, and even though she hated to admit it, Carlos was definitely her type. With his cut jawline and high cheekbones, Sofia believed he would be many people's type, and he could have anyone he wanted.

Except when she'd asked him about being married, he'd looked almost pained for a split second. Was the person he lost maybe his wife? Sofia wasn't sure it was any of her business to even ask.

'Ambulance inbound. Still awaiting details from the paramedics on the patient. Trauma surgery support requested at the ambulance bay.' The announcement snapped both of them out of their thoughts, their heads whirling around to the door leading to the ambulances. Then Carlos looked over at her, the smirk she had seen before back on his lips.

'I had a good time doing surgery with you the other day, so let's work on this one together,' he said before rushing off, forcing Sofia to follow.

That announcement had come just at the right time. Carlos hurried down the corridor leading to the access way, where the ambulance services came in with patients. Rushing down here gave him enough time to put his head on straight again after Sofia had knocked him sideways more than once during their exchange—along with the unbidden heat that her proximity sparked.

Are you married?

It was because of questions like that one that he never stayed in one place long enough to get to know anyone. How could he possibly admit to his marriage when he had failed the one person he'd promised to protect for the rest of his life?

He couldn't escape his guilt over the car accident, and the part he'd played in it, so he remained untethered from any form of emotional closeness. Carlos was content in his solitude, regretting forever how his marriage had ended too soon.

Those were the things he reminded himself of as he approached the doors to the ambulance bay with Sofia on his heels.

The effect she had on him was concerning, and the fierceness of the attraction snapping into place between them shook him to his core. How could he feel attracted to the one person in the hospital who was openly hostile towards him? There was no way the feeling wasn't one-sided, which brought the entire thing to a new level of inappropriate. Not only were they colleagues, but he was also leaving before they would even have the chance to explore anything.

Not that he had anything to explore. Carlos was here to work and nothing else. Affairs and no-strings-attached arrangements were for people whose hearts weren't as broken as his. Though neither of those things involved emotional attachment, they still required a clear head and conscience. He didn't have either. So whatever tendrils of attraction were floating around between them were best forgotten. He knew that would be the best for everyone involved. Yet his heart still slammed against his chest as if it was trying to escape when Sofia stepped up next to him.

Her scent was intoxicating, and it wasn't for the first time this week that he wondered if she wore perfume or if she would still smell like that as he peeled each layer of clothing off her body.

'Any more details about the incoming case?' Sofia asked as an intern stepped through the doors.

'This is an overflow coming in from Centro Médico Evita Perón. They don't have any more trauma bays open after an MVA involving several vehicles,' the intern said, reading the notes off her phone.

A cold shower trickled down Carlos's spine, a reaction familiar to him, yet he still hated it. He forced a deep breath down his nose, clamping down on the trauma reaction bubbling up in his veins. The intern had said there was a car crash, not that their case was part of one. They might have moved an unrelated case here because there was no space left in the trauma bays at the other hospital because of the MVA.

Though it had been five years since he'd been in his accident, there were still moments that brought back the memories in a vivid flash. Another reason for him to never open up to anyone around him. How could he be a trauma surgeon when he struggled to operate on car crash victims? Both medication and therapy had helped him cope, but grounding techniques could only get him so far in the chaotic environment of the OR.

'Carlos.' Hearing his name snapped him out of his dark thoughts, and he turned his head. Sofia gave him a sidelong glance with a fine line between her brows. There was a touch of softness he hadn't seen in her before as she asked, 'You okay?'

Damn, had he been that obvious about the turmoil going on inside of him? He forced his usual mask of aloofness back onto his face, staring ahead as the ambulance approached with its sirens echoing off the walls. The part of him that wanted to remain distant from everyone at the hospital wanted to ignore the question, but there was another part that appreciated the attention, even if he didn't deserve it.

'I'm...' He hesitated, searching for the right words to say. Foreboding mounted in him as he watched the vehicle approach, but he couldn't say anything. 'I didn't sleep well,' he said, settling on a plausible lie for whatever Sofia had seen in him. Then he stepped forward as the ambulance came to a halt in front of them.

The doors burst open as the paramedic stepped out of the back, dragging a stretcher with the unconscious patient. His other hand was holding an Ambu bag and squeezing it in calm intervals. As he approached, the intern stepped forward and took over delivering oxygen to the unconscious patient.

'What do you have for us, Gabriel?' Sofia asked as she grabbed the handles of the stretcher.

'We have a female patient in her thirties, involved in a high-speed MVA. She suffered significant trauma to the chest with decreased breath sounds on the left side. Potential pneumothorax,' the paramedic rattled off, keeping pace with Carlos and Sofia as they pushed the stretcher up the corridor. 'We've had to put her on supplemental oxygen and administered fluids and painkillers as per protocol.'

The edges of his vision darkened as he looked down at the patient, feeling the weight of old memories crashing down on him and constricting his chest. Breathing became harder with each step, and Carlos fought to keep the rising panic at bay. This was *not* her, and unlike with Rosa, he had a chance to help this woman come away with her life intact.

He caught another glance from Sofia, and her expression conveyed the same question she'd asked him just a few moments ago. But then her focus shifted onto the paramedic. 'What's her blood pressure?'

'Last measure was one-ten over seventy, with an elevated heart rate and a pulse ox of ninety percent,' Gabriel replied, his eyes darting between Sofia and Carlos as he gave the update.

'Lower oxygen saturation could mean you're right about the punctured lung. We should get an emergency X-ray to figure out our next steps.' Sofia looked at him. Not for confirmation. He knew that well enough after the conversation they'd had earlier today.

No, for some reason, she was checking in with him, as if she could sense the overwhelming sensations creeping in on him. Could she? His reputation as a knowledgeable surgeon who could work under pressure was the reason he could get a job wherever he wanted. Part of it was keeping a tight grip on any PTSD symptoms. So far, not a single person he'd worked with had mentioned anything.

Yet Sofia was looking at him as if she could read every single thought and see the tension in him.

So he nodded in response, and they continued to push the gurney forward. Carlos stepped up to the sink as they entered the trauma room with the patient, cleaning his sweat-slick palms before pulling on the gloves. 'I'll get the portable X-ray ready,' he said as he turned around, avoiding looking too closely at the patient. He only needed a minute to step away and collect himself.

'Set up the supplementary oxygen so she's ready for the X-ray,' Sofia said, then rattled off more instructions to the people in the trauma bay.

The confrontation with her earlier had triggered long-dormant tendrils of attraction that he didn't want to feel or even consider. Mixing that with the trauma trigger of the accident had created an explosive cocktail of stress-induced reactions inside of him. This was the worst possible moment for any of this.

'We're good to go on the X-rays,' he said, clenching his jaw when his voice came out brittle. His mind raced, wondering if he should extract himself from this situation. Sofia had it in hand, and even though they had their disagreements on methods, he trusted in her excellence as a doctor.

'Oxygen is flowing. Everyone step outside for the X-ray.' Sofia waved at the intern assisting them. They all walked out of the room to avoid unnecessary exposure to radiation. After they heard the whirring of the machine followed by a buzz, they all streamed back into the room. The images would only take a few seconds to appear on the screens, but there wasn't a second to lose in stabilising the patient while they waited.

Sofia and the intern approached the patient, both looking at him for instructions. They were expecting him to run this trauma room. Carlos took a deep breath while trying his hardest to keep his mind on assessing the situation as a doctor. But when he saw the blood of an open cut clinging to the dark brown skin, the black hair half-down from the bun it had been in—a hairstyle he used to see every morning after waking up—his breath faltered.

'Her pulse is rising. She's in distress,' the intern said as she took her stethoscope out and placed it on the patient's chest. 'Reduced breath sounds on the right side.'

'Carlos?' Sofia said his name, a soft sound laced with concern, but he could hardly hear it over the rush of his own blood through his ears. Darkness crept in on him, blurring his vision, and each breath was harder than the next. The beeping of the monitor drilled into his ears, the fluorescent light suddenly glaring, forcing him to avert his eyes.

In this state, he couldn't work on any patients. He needed to get out of here.

'I'm…needed elsewhere. Run the trauma room, Martinez. I'll send someone to assist,' he said, hoping his voice didn't sound as choked as he felt. Then he turned around without another word as more visions of the past threatened to overwhelm him.

'Good job, everyone,' Sofia said as they wheeled the patient out of the trauma room and to the intensive care unit.

The car crash had broken several of her ribs. One of them had punctured her left lung, just as the delivering paramedic, Gabriel, had suspected. The pneumothorax was small, thankfully, and could be treated with the right pain management and bed rest. After stabilising the patient's breathing, they had stitched up the cuts and checked for other injuries. As far as car crash victims were concerned, she was one of the luckier ones, having escaped any devastating injuries.

Now that she was done with the patient, she could turn her mind to the thing that she'd stowed away in a separate compartment of her brain so she could put all of her attention on her work. She quickly went by the nurses' station to see if there were any more incoming cases and was glad when the nurse shook her head. She had some time to spare just when she needed it—or rather, when Carlos needed it.

Considering the calm and experience he'd brought

into every single surgery they'd worked on together, his behaviour in the trauma room was highly unusual. He'd completely frozen when he'd seen the patient. Was she someone he knew? Panic had radiated out from him, enough for Sofia to pick up on it, and just as she had been about to ask him what was wrong, he had excused himself.

Sofia walked up and down the different beds and treatment rooms to see if he had simply stepped away to look after another incoming case. But he wasn't there, and when she called the charge nurse to ask if he was in surgery, the woman said she hadn't seen him since he went down to the emergency room. So he was still here somewhere...

She paused when her eyes fell onto the closed door of the supply closet where they'd had their rather intense exchange last week. The hair along her arms rose as she stared at the door, a strange sensation coming over her. Would he have sought refuge in the space they had shared? Or was she spinning up some strange connection to him to justify the intensity of her own reaction to him?

It wouldn't hurt to check either way. Worst-case scenario, she was making things up in her head. But if he was there and in need of help... The look on his face had been unlike any she'd ever seen on him. No swagger, none of the bravado of a surgeon who knew he was the top-ranking one in his field. Just something pure and naked, something he usually allowed no one to see.

Shaking off the memory, she stepped to the door and pushed the handle down, sticking her head through the crack. Carlos stood behind the door, his back facing her, and she could tell he was breathing in quick bursts by the way his shoulders rose and fell. She stepped into the closet, closing the door behind her and twisting the lock.

The lights were off, the only source of light whatever crept through the gaps around the edges of the door. Sofia scanned the shelves stuffed with medical equipment needed to run an efficient ER, giving her eyes time to adjust to the dimness.

'Carlos, it's me,' she said when he didn't react to her intrusion, stepping closer to his side.

She frowned as she looked at him. Even with limited light, she could see that the colour had drained from his face, leaving a dull, pale imitation of his warm-toned skin. His eyes were staring ahead almost sightlessly. Slipping her hand around his arm, she pressed her index and middle fingers onto the inside of his wrist, counting the beats of his heart. Her frown deepened, and her hand lingered on his arm, his skin cold to her touch.

'I think you're having a panic attack,' she said softly, her hand tightening on his arm in an effort to get him to acknowledge her.

Panic attacks were far too common among trauma surgeons. With the pressure they were under to assess patients efficiently and accurately, as a professional group, they rarely took enough time to look after themselves. How could they make that a priority when their days were often twelve hours long, depending on what surgeries they were pulled into? Many colleagues developed PTSD due to witnessing severe injuries and low survival rates, even in top trauma departments.

'We need to slow down your breathing. The hyperventilation is only worsening the other symptoms.' A chill ran down her spine when Carlos turned his face to finally look at her, his expression stricken. Acting on instinct alone, she reached for his other hand and lifted them both up to place them on her chest.

'You know how to do deep breathing. I watched you do it earlier when you sensed the panic attack coming,' she said. Then she took a deep breath of her own and guided him to follow her example.

Carlos did, taking stuttering breaths in and out. He slowed down somewhat, but not enough to take him out of the state of panic and ground him. Sofia rifled through her brain, thinking of other grounding techniques she'd learned during her training. With the amount of experience Carlos had as a medical professional, he probably had his own set of exercises he liked to go through.

'How can I help you? Would it help to talk me through your triggers, or do you prefer to be grounded with distraction?' Sofia clamped down on her own panic as she asked those questions. Considering how private Carlos had been from the moment he had arrived at the hospital a week ago, he probably didn't want her witnessing his vulnerable moment. They were already on shaky ground with each other, and this interaction wouldn't improve that.

But he needed help, and as much as they grated on each other, Sofia couldn't just walk away and leave him alone.

She breathed out a sigh when his fingers tightened around hers, and his eyes came into focus. The intensity of his stare took her by surprise, cascading a heat down her spine that was becoming way too familiar.

'Pressure,' Carlos said, his voice low and thick, the struggle to verbalise this one word evident.

Sofia opened her mouth to ask what he meant by

that, when the pieces clicked into place. His technique to combat rising panic was deep pressure. She glanced around, her eyes running over the shelves in search of something that would help her apply some full-body pressure to him. The hospital had weighted blankets for that purpose, but they weren't in the emergency room.

No, she would have to do it herself. 'Okay,' she said with a nod, more for herself than him, and let go of his hands. 'I can do that.'

She swallowed the sudden lump in her throat at the thought of being so close to Carlos when she had struggled to keep her composure around him ever since their last encounter in this closet. This wasn't about her or the flashes of attraction she was trying so hard to combat. If this was any other colleague, she wouldn't hesitate to wrap them into a hug if it would help.

Carlos was just another colleague. That's what Sofia told herself as she stepped closer to him and wrapped her arms around his torso, squeezing as she held him close to her.

Tiny fires erupted underneath her skin all across her body, but she ignored them along with the swooping sensation that his broad chest pressed against hers caused in her stomach. His arms remained at his sides, his muscles rigid, but as she kept her grip on him tight, his breathing gradually eased into a slower rhythm, his chest rising and falling in a more measured way.

Her warmth seemed to seep into him, his skin becoming warmer where she was in contact with it. 'Try to relax one more muscle with each breath,' she said next to his ear, and couldn't help but sigh when she felt him follow her instructions.

His legs relaxed first, bringing his entire body closer

to her as the tension left him. His arms and torso followed, becoming soft under her, and then finally his
head slumped forwards, coming to rest on her shoulder
with a drawn-out exhale.

Sofia kept her hold on him and continued to take deep
breaths of her own, setting a pace Carlos could follow.
He did, his breath soon syncing with hers as they stood
in the dimly lit supply closet, absorbing the quiet energy around them.

She didn't know how long they stood there with her
holding him close to her or at what point she'd got lost in
this simple touch. A rush of awareness flooded through
her when Carlos's hands came to rest on her waist, drawing her closer into his front. His head still rested on her
shoulder, his nose nuzzling into a sensitive spot on her
neck. He breathed deeply and steadily now, each exhale
sending a skitter of electricity down her spine as it blew
against her skin.

His hands wandered up her back, his face moving
closer, and she leaned into his touch as warmth pooled
in her stomach and shot spears of delicious heat through
her body.

'Gracias,' he whispered, and his lips grazed the shell
of her ear in a whisper of a touch.

Sofia's breath caught in her throat, and an involuntary moan escaped her lips. The sound was loud in the
confines of the supply closet. It ripped through the air
that had, until this moment, only been filled with their
quiet breaths.

Carlos lifted his head, and she took a sharp inhale
when their gazes collided. His face was close enough
to hers that if she stood on her toes, she could slide her
mouth right over his. The glint in his eyes was primal

and mirrored the erupting sparks of attraction ricocheting inside her.

Were they really going to…?

'Carlos… I didn't mean to…' Sofia forced the words out of her mouth, her throat thick from the tension between them. She wasn't sure she wanted this. But, more importantly, she didn't know if *he* wanted it, or if they were acting on some impulse that sprung out of their forced proximity.

Carlos took a deep breath, his chest trembling underneath her hands. He blinked twice, and each time the passion faded more—until only confusion remained.

The fire shooting higher within her banked when she beheld the shock spreading over his face. A second later, his hands dropped from her body, and he took a step back, almost colliding with a shelf.

Tension snapped into place between them, accentuated by the silence that spread. Sofia struggled to find the right words to say. The situation had morphed from one thing to the other without her understanding when it had happened—and by the look on Carlos's face, neither had he.

She opened her mouth, needing to say something to cut the tension, but then snapped it shut again when Carlos shook his head.

'You…' he started, but then paused and tilted his head upwards, exposing the column of his throat to her. Sofia stared at it, the urge to lean forward and taste it thundering through her.

As if he had sensed her stare, his eyes came back down to hers. He ran his hand through his short hair, expelling a heavy sigh. 'I'm not… This isn't what… Damn.'

Carlos swore as he shook his head again. Then he

turned the lock, ripping the door open and leaving in a hurried step before Sofia had the chance to process what he'd tried to say, and leaving her to puzzle over what had just happened on her own.

CHAPTER FOUR

THE WEEK WENT by without Sofia seeing much of Carlos. After their second encounter in the supply closet, it seemed as if he was now avoiding her. She would have laughed at how they had switched places if she wasn't overwhelmed and confused about what had happened—or why he was avoiding her.

Was he ashamed that he'd had a panic attack? She didn't think his confidence was so fragile. Especially since he was a physician who had admitted on his first day to the assembled staff how hard the trauma department could be on one's psyche. He'd cited this as one reason the hospital's leadership had hired him to work here. More efficient workflows would mean less stress and more freedom to focus on the things that truly mattered.

'Did you see how Adriana got rejected by that new surgeon guy? She had…' The fragment of conversation drifted towards her, and Sofia forced her feet to keep moving, her eyes trained to the front as she walked towards the doors of the hospital at the end of her shift.

'That new surgeon guy' could only be one person—the same one that had been haunting her thoughts ever since their…thing in the supply closet.

In her head, Sofia was calling it an almost-kiss,

though she wasn't sure she should say that out loud, even to Carlos. But she'd had a strong desire to close the gap between them by leaning in. Had wanted it *badly*. It had been easy to ignore her body's reaction to his when his abrasiveness kept her at arm's length.

Until the moment in the supply closet when she had glimpsed what Carlos kept under tight wraps. What she had witnessed had been a rare moment of vulnerability for him, and going by how he'd stormed off afterwards, he hadn't wanted anyone to see him like that. And he had definitely not wanted her to know that the electric current zapping between them wasn't one-sided.

After he had calmed down and grounded himself, his touch had gone from desperate to tender. The ghost of his touch on her back still lingered on her skin every time she closed her eyes, and with it came a rush of desire that sent tiny prickles across her body.

It was because of this reaction that she wanted to talk to Carlos. Sofia could admit that he was unbelievably fine. She wouldn't have been surprised to hear that he had walked off a 'Hot Docs' calendar shoot before coming here. Like all the other women and men in this hospital, she had eyes and could appreciate an attractive man when she saw one.

What had startled her during their encounter had been the heat radiating from *him*. How *he* had touched *her*. Carlos had hovered over her mouth, as if daring her to close the gap between them to claim a kiss she knew in her bones would be mind-blowing. And then the defences had come shooting back up, shaking them both out of their desire-induced stupor, and he had run away—leaving Sofia wondering if what she had sensed building between them was genuine or another of his trauma reactions.

'What's got you so down?' a familiar voice asked as she stepped outside the doors of the hospital on her way home.

Gabriel Romero stood a few paces to the side of the entrance, leaning against the wall of the building. She walked up to him with a smile she hoped didn't look as tired as it felt.

'Hey, Gabe, haven't seen your face since last week.' Gabriel had been the one to deliver the trauma patient from the car crash that had somehow triggered Carlos. Since Sofia spent a lot of her time waiting for ambulances to arrive with patients needing immediate assessment from the trauma team, she'd become familiar with all the paramedics servicing the hospital. She and Gabriel had hit it off well, and they enjoyed a chat whenever they met outside of any emergency situations.

'I keep hoping to see you, *amiga*, but whenever I come in with a case, I see the new guy with a bunch of junior doctors at his side.' Gabriel paused, flashing her a grin before he said, 'He seems to be popular.'

Sofia would have rolled her eyes at that comment two weeks ago, but now heat rushed to her cheeks, and she failed at producing a convincing snort of derision. 'He keeps beating me to any arrivals at the hospital. If I didn't know it better, I would think he's getting some insider information,' she said, deflecting from her own feelings.

Gabriel raised his hands in defence. 'You know I would never double-cross you like that, Fia.'

'Yeah, right,' she grumbled, but the smile she flashed

him this time was genuine. 'I know he's doing it to teach the junior staff, but I can't help feeling a bit…set aside.'

His expression sobered as he listened to her, nodding in acknowledgement. 'It's difficult when someone comes into a pre-established dynamic. But he's not being a jerk about it, is he?'

She shook her head. 'No, he's fine. I'm just…' Sofia paused, unsure if she should talk about what had happened between her and Carlos. But she'd been carrying it around for an entire week with nobody to talk to about it. She'd usually go and talk to Bella, but with her friend's reduced hours now that she was twenty-two weeks pregnant with triplets, she barely got to see the woman any more.

'I don't know what happened when you brought in that patient, but something triggered him that day. He had a panic attack, and I had to talk him down. Since then he's been avoiding me, and I…just don't know what to think of that.' The words were pouring out of her mouth before she could decide whether she should share so much with anyone, but Gabriel was her friend and she could trust him, even if their conversations mostly happened between patients.

'That's a tough spot to be in. We're all exposed to some triggering stuff. Maybe he hasn't had a trigger response in a long time and took it hard?' Gabriel mused, his index finger tapping against his chin.

'Yeah, maybe…' Sofia just thought of that, but if they were correct, then it was even more important for them to talk about it. What if being in a new environment was the triggering part? No one would think any less of him, but they needed to know in case anything happened…

'For what it's worth, I've never seen Cabrera misstep in the cases I brought in, and I'm sure someone of his calibre wouldn't put the hospital at risk like that,' the paramedic said, shrugging his shoulders. 'Though his aloofness is surprising. I would have thought by now *someone* would have cracked his shell open. Newbies rarely stay this closed off with how social the hospital is.'

Sofia huffed at that. 'You're telling me. I just overheard two people talking about him rejecting someone. Maybe because he's leaving at the end of the month, he doesn't think it's worth it...'

'Sounds about right. Even some of the ambulance workers have been trying to get his attention, but he seems very...single-minded.'

Heat prickled in the back of her neck, trickling down over her spine until it pooled in the pit of her stomach. She had experienced his single-mindedness first hand, though being the object of it had been mostly unnerving. *Mostly* because there was a distinct aftertaste of exhilaration flooding through her system every time she thought about their moment.

'Papá!' The shout of a child ripped her out of her thoughts, and as she turned, a young boy hurled himself into Gabriel's arms.

'Hello, *mijo*. You remember Fia?'

Sofia smiled at the boy, raising her hand in a small wave. '*Ola*, Javi. I was wondering why your dad was just standing around here when he could make himself useful.'

The boy laughed at that, just like she had hoped he would. Then Sofia raised her hand at both of them in a small wave. 'I'll get out of your hair. Thanks for listening, Gabe.'

The paramedic nodded with a small smile. 'To be continued.'

Though she had left the hospital almost an hour ago, Sofia wasn't in any hurry to go back home. Her brief conversation with Gabriel had brought up the scene from the other day, and she strolled aimlessly through Buenos Aires as she thought of what to do about the tension between her and Carlos.

As she walked down the winding streets of the inner city, her eyes snagged on something interesting now and then. A cute dress in a store window or some tasty-looking baked goods, making her stop and stare. Nothing was captivating enough to hold her attention for long, her mind drawn back to Carlos and his odd behaviour towards her. That was until she almost walked into a group of young women standing in front of the large window of a store.

Curious what would draw such a crowd, she looked up at the sign above the window. It read Academia Ritmo de Capoeira. Sofia blinked at the sign and then looked at the assembled women.

Capoeira? She tried forming the word with her mouth, the syllables not quite fitting together and leaving her with a foreign sound in her ear. With the words in front of it saying rhythm academy, it could be some kind of dance? That still didn't explain why such a dance studio would draw the attention of an entire group of women.

Sofia stepped closer, looking in between the heads of the other women, and saw what had grabbed their attention. Through the window, she could see a space that looked more like a gym than a dance studio. Mats covered the entire floor, and a row of shoes was lined up on each side, all different sizes, colours and makes.

A group of people stood in a circle, most of them clapping in a rhythm only they could hear. And in the middle of the circle stood two men facing each other, engaged in something Sofia couldn't put into words. It wasn't quite a dance, at least not one she knew of, but rather an exchange of fluid motions and movements that were somehow connecting the participants, even though neither was touching the other.

The man on the left wore loose-fitting white trousers and a tank top. His hair was more grey than brown, and deep wrinkles surrounded his eyes. Yet despite those indications of age, he moved with a graceful fluidity as he dropped low to evade the incoming leg of the other man—his opponent?

She tracked the leg as the other man dragged it back, her eyes slowly raking further up and taking in that picture of stunning, mouth-watering masculinity. His trousers were the same as the older man's, giving them both an ethereal touch as they moved about the circle. But unlike his opponent, the man on the right had opted to forgo his shirt for the practice, leaving everyone— including herself—to admire the rippling muscles underneath dark brown skin as he flowed back and forth.

Sweat pearled over his skin, and Sofia followed a trail of it over his pecs down his abdomen until the drop disappeared into the trail of hair leading from his navel down to the waistband of his trousers.

'Ay, Dios mío, qué guapo,' one of the women in front of her sighed, and Sofia felt herself nod in agreement,

her body reacting to sensations that her mind was still catching up to.

He *was* absolutely stunning, and it was no surprise he'd drawn a crowd to watch him dance. Or was it a fight? Sofia still couldn't tell. Whatever it was, the control the man exerted over his body was unearthly, each strike and step a coordination of muscle and strength without sacrificing grace. Her mouth dried thinking how this fluidity of motion would feel in other circumstances, some that required even fewer clothes...

If only he would turn his head so she could see his face. Both men were moving around the circle, but not enough for the younger man to completely face her. Not until a third person entered the ring of people, gently tapping the man on the shoulder. Sofia—and the women in front of her—gasped when he did a cartwheel that ended in a back-flip that landed close to the circle, his full front turned towards the window.

Sofia's hand shot up to her mouth in shock as she looked at his face and recognised who she'd been thirsting over. Not an anonymous man doing some sort of fighting dance, but Carlos Cabrera.

He casually looked over the crowd of people assembled in front of the window, his smile indulgent as the women clapped, and Sofia's heart stopped in the exact moment their eyes locked. His smile froze, eyes widening in recognition. They remained in place like that, neither of them moving.

A knot tightened in Sofia's stomach, an omen of the storm that was about to come. She'd already felt increasingly creepy by trying to talk to him at the hospital. Now he had caught her ogling him during his time off. Would he even believe her that she had just come here by chance? Was it too late to pretend she hadn't recognised him?

Her fight-or-flight instincts were warring inside of her, with the latter winning after a short battle—making her turn on her heel and walk down the road.

'I have to go,' Carlos said, following the instinct to go after Sofia as she hurried away.

He gently pushed through the circle and slipped into his sandals while grabbing the loose tank top lying on top of them. Disappointed chatter reached his ears when he stepped outside and pulled his shirt over his head, but he didn't pay it any mind. Sofia was only a few metres ahead of him, and even though he'd been avoiding her the last few days, he didn't stop to think as he went after her.

Coming out of his panic attack with Sofia's arms around him had been like waking up from a nightmare in the middle of the night only to realise that he had never been in any danger because his person was sleeping right next to him, her presence a protective charm.

Only Rosa wasn't here, and it was someone else's touch, someone else's face, that had brought him back to himself. Sofia.

That thought had been haunting him, driving him to avoid her as he tried to sort through the onslaught of emotions rising inside of him. Carlos could no longer deny how attracted he was to her. From the spark in her honey-golden eyes to the messy bun on top of her head, everything about her filled him with a yearning to see this well-composed woman come unravelled under his touch.

'Sofia, wait!' he called after her as she kept on walking. Despite the hesitation that had him avoiding her the last few days, he was unable to stop his pursuit of her. The look on her face had kicked something loose inside of him. An idea that had been growing ever since that moment in the supply closet.

Was his attraction to Sofia the first sign that he was ready for something new? Not a relationship. That would always be out of the question. But maybe some no-strings-attached fun while he was still in town?

Maybe closeness without any commitment was a new way of keeping his struggles inside. The high-pressure situations at work were all about releasing adrenaline to keep him going, but he could get the same effect with endorphins, couldn't he?

Carlos closed the gap between them just as she turned down a side alley. 'Don't you want to talk?' he called after her when she wouldn't stop.

He lengthened his stride, almost colliding with her when she stopped, turned slowly, and faced him. Her composure was taut, like a tightly wound string ready to snap. '*Now* you want to talk? After I've tried to pin you down for a solid week?'

Her voice shook—though with what emotion he couldn't tell. The volume at which she spoke was as usual, but something elusive weaved itself through her tone.

Despite the flame billowing alive in his chest at her proximity to him, his walls came up around him in an automated defence. 'You never needed some time to process after having a panic attack in front of a colleague?'

Her expression softened at his words, and almost instantly Carlos wished for the quiet tension back. The last thing he needed from her was pity—or her behaviour towards him changing because she thought him fragile. That wasn't what he had come here for.

'You're not the first person to get triggered by something at work. Medical professionals are one of the most likely groups of people to suffer from PTSD symptoms,' she said, and now he wanted the edge in her voice to return. He knew how to deal with someone being annoyed with him. Sympathy tasted like bitter ash in his mouth. They wouldn't be so kind to him if they knew it had been his fault that his wife had died.

The memory of Sofia's body pressed against his in the closet surfaced in his mind as her scent drifted towards him. He held on to that image and let it remind him why he had gone after her. Not to discuss what had already happened, but to see if that mutual attraction could lead to something fun—something distracting. Because the sooner she forgot having seen him so vulnerable, the better. And his instincts were telling him that he had an easy way to replace the image she had of him with a new one. He only had to allow himself to sink deeper into the attraction brewing between them. Use it to keep her thinking about him in a different light.

'I saw you looking at me through the window back there,' he said, deliberately dropping his voice low so it would rumble through the space between them. His tone was suggestive, and he hoped she would be outraged enough to take the bait and forget about the conversation she had started. Whatever it took to get her off the topic of his panic attack—of how she had seen him at his lowest. Maybe that was the best use of the attraction between them. There wasn't a long-term plan here, not with him leaving again so soon. But when she looked at him, Carlos wanted her to see one specific thing—and his trauma reaction to a patient wasn't it.

Sofia's eyes rounded, her lips parting without a sound escaping her throat. His gaze dipped to her throat, and a smirk spread over his lips as he watched it bob.

'I was looking through the window to see what the crowd was staring at. I certainly wasn't looking *at* you. You just happened to be there,' she replied. 'I'm glad you found your shirt again.' The last words came out in a breathy tone, and she pressed her lips together.

He'd caught her off guard. Perfect. 'So you noticed I wasn't wearing one before. Did you enjoy what you saw?'

Carlos hadn't been so brazen with a woman since he'd met his late wife. Something deep inside of him unfurled as a warm caramel glow bloomed on her cheeks, the blush deepening her skin tone. There was no way she'd admit it, but the reaction told him enough. The feeling of attraction was *definitely* mutual.

'I did. The exercise was fascinating, and I've never seen anything like it before,' she replied, pushing her chin forward as she decided to purposefully misinterpret his question.

'It's called capoeira—a discipline of martial arts that combines fighting moves with music and acrobatics,' he said, daring to take a step closer into her space.

Sofia squared her shoulders as she tilted her head up to maintain eye contact, but she didn't step back. He could see the thoughts swirling behind her eyes as she calculated how good an idea it was to give in to the attraction zapping between them in electric jolts.

He was asking himself the same question, but desire had overwritten any of his objections at this point.

What was the harm in giving in a little bit if he would be leaving Argentina at the end of the month?

'Have you been practicing for long?' she asked, and the fire in his veins flared at the strain in her voice. She was trying so hard to resist this moment brewing between them.

'Almost all my life.' Carlos took another step, now close enough to her that the memories of their embrace became a tangible sensation on his skin. 'I can tell you more about it over dinner. Maybe go to my place after to show you some moves…'

He wasn't sure she would accept his invitation straight away. But he wasn't trying to get her to say yes right now. Carlos was merely planting a seed—a possibility of what they could do together if they were on the same page.

So he wasn't quite prepared when Sofia bit her lower lip and asked, 'Where do want to take me?'

CHAPTER FIVE

SOFIA PATTED DOWN the fabric of her dress as she stood in front of the doors of the restaurant. The horizon had turned a dark shade of red, mixing with purple as the sun disappeared over the smooth edges of buildings dotting the skyline. Her hands had been fiddling with the flared skirt of her dress, arranging and rearranging how the folds fell while trying to get out of her head and back into the moment.

Now, several hours after Carlos had invited her to dinner with him, she was questioning the desire that had led her to say yes. Over the last week, Carlos had become the symbol for a type of adventure that had been missing from her life. One where she forgot about being cautious and letting herself live a little. Sofia *wanted* to indulge in some no-strings-attached closeness, had realised she'd wanted that ever since the tension between her and Carlos had snapped into place.

When he had brazenly invited her to his place, she knew he was interested, too. She just needed to be brave enough to seize the opportunity.

She'd finally got him to acknowledge what had happened in the supply closet, though the conversation had not turned out the way she had expected—considering she now stood in front of a restaurant with butterflies rioting in her stomach. Instead of talking about his struggles, they had somehow ended up in a flirtatious exchange that still made her blush now. Over the last few hours, she had contemplated declining the invitation to dinner. Whatever brazen energy she had channelled had seeped out of her body. Yet there was a part of her that desperately wanted to see where this would go, even though Sofia knew it couldn't go very far. Not with him leaving and with her own lack of interest in anything emotional.

But in the short two-week span that she had now known Carlos, she had seen so many different sides of him, and what she *really* wanted was to uncover the next one. To see what else lay beneath the handsome, talented surgeon.

Sofia snapped out of her thoughts when a group of people brushed past her to enter the restaurant. Taking that as a sign from the universe wanting her to proceed, she stepped through the doors, and they swung shut behind her. The noise of the busy high street of Buenos Aires was shut out by the thick glass, the sound replaced by the murmurs of conversation and clinking of glasses and plates.

The interior of the restaurant was dimly lit, making it hard to recognise individual faces. Her eyes drifted over groups of people, not catching on to any familiar features until her eyes collided with a dark stare at the back of her room. He kept his gaze on hers for a second. Then his lids dipped low as his eyes raked over her. Awareness sprang alive within her even from this distance. The fit of the dress suddenly felt particularly snug, with the dark red fabric clinging to her torso like a second skin and only flaring out at the hips into a playful skirt.

Even from here she could see Carlos's jaw tighten as his eyes came back up. Sofia had picked out that dress for a specific purpose—to show off her body in ways she hadn't for quite some time. She had *wanted* that reaction from him, yet her heart still leapt into her throat.

Nodding at the waiter approaching her, Sofia pointed towards the table with a smile and then walked over to where Carlos was waiting. He stood up to greet her, his tall frame towering over her a considerable way. Sofia suppressed a shiver when he lay a hand on her waist and pulled her closer to brush a kiss onto her cheek.

'You look stunning, but I have a feeling you already know that,' he whispered against her ear.

A semi-circular cushioned bench wound itself around the round table, creating a more intimate setting than the traditional table and chair setups she saw throughout the restaurant. Along with the mellow scent of spices in the air and the dim lights, she wondered if anyone would even notice them…and if Carlos had picked this spot for exactly that reason.

'Thank you,' she said with a smile, watching him as he slid onto the cushioned bench. 'So do you.'

That felt like an understatement. He had changed out of the loose-fitting linen trousers and put on dark chinos instead, along with a dark purple button-up shirt. The upper two buttons were undone, giving her a hint of the dark brown skin that lay underneath. Not that she needed any hints when she'd seen him shirtless earlier today.

'Have you been here before?' she asked as she slid onto the bench on the other side of the table.

'No, but the *mestre* of the capoeira group I joined

here recommended it to me,' he replied while handing her the drink menu lying flat on the table.

'Your...*maestro*?' Sofia reached for the word that sounded the most like the one he'd said, tilting her head to the side to emphasise her confusion.

'Yes, the leader of the capoeira group. He's lived in the city all his life, and he's been kind enough to suggest things I might like to do.'

The waiter stopped by their table, and they placed their order for drinks. With the drinks menu out of her hands, Sofia picked up the one for food, scanning each page. 'So, how did this recommendation come up? Did you ask for the best Asian fusion restaurant?'

The slow smile he gave her sent a spark flying down her spine. 'I asked him where he would take a beautiful woman to impress her,' he replied, his voice low and smoky.

Heat crawled up her neck and onto her face. This sort of flirting was outside of her comfort zone, because what was the point if it didn't lead to a relationship? Had she ever flirted with someone without having that particular goal in mind? The thought was sobering. Maybe Carlos was exactly the right antidote she needed to let loose without consequences.

She just needed to be brave enough to let herself go there.

And maybe the right way to do that was to be honest. He was here for a very specific reason as well, and what was the harm in telling him something about herself when he would be gone in a fortnight? She would never find out who he really was if she didn't give anything of herself.

'I've not been on a date in a long time. And definitely not on one that wasn't about romantic advances,' she said, her eyes darting back and forth from Carlos to the menu.

If her words set anything inside of him off, he didn't show it. No, he seemed comfortable in his own skin as he leaned back, his arm draped over the back of the bench and his head tilted towards her. His hand was close enough to her shoulder that she sensed a phantom touch if she focused enough on it.

Something Carlos seemed to notice as well. His fingers curled back towards his hands, then flattened out again in a repetitive motion. As if he wanted to touch her, but each time convinced himself he'd better not.

'Are you nervous?' he finally asked, his fingers once again stretching out and stopping just before they reached her shoulder.

She paused at the question, shrugging. 'I want to say no, but that's not entirely accurate. So let's say a little? I don't know what to expect, and I'm rarely in a position where I don't…know things.'

Carlos smiled at that, the lines around his eyes softening. 'I noticed. In all the short-term assignments I've accepted in recent years, I've never had quite such a vocal critique,' he said, though his tone was friendly rather than cold, as she would have expected.

Despite that, she couldn't fight the blush from deepening on her cheeks. 'I…' Her voice trailed off, and Carlos shook his head with a laugh.

'I'm not being unkind, but rather…appreciative. When you become a figure of authority in your field, people tend to take your words as the unmovable truth. Having people challenge me helps me to keep my skills sharp. Though I have to admit I can be a bit…short when challenged.' He cleared his throat as he reached for the glass in front of him to take a sip. 'It's something I'm working on.'

The earnestness of his words was so disarming and genuine that it washed away some of the nerves. Sofia may have never gone down the road of a one-night stand, but what if she didn't treat it as such and just saw what happened between them? Questions about his panic attack bubbled up inside her chest, but she swallowed them one after another. He had acknowledged what had happened earlier without going into any more details. Was she really entitled to them? Even though concern was her main motivator for asking, she couldn't push him to share more. Maybe if she let him see a piece of her, he would feel comfortable enough to share pieces of himself in return.

'I may have been a bit overprotective myself. I've spent all my senior career at Hospital General, so new things can be scary. But I'm…keen to learn from you.' In more than one way, she thought, though she didn't dare to say that out loud.

The aura around Sofia changed as their conversation went on. Shoulders that had been drawn up high slumped down, the tight smile relaxing into something small and genuine as they worked through their animosity anecdote by anecdote. As they reached the end of their main course, they'd arrived at their first surgery together, when Sofia had turned up late.

'I just can't believe you would yell at me like that in front of *my* staff,' Sofia said, with no sharpness to her words. 'And I also can't believe I apparently find that hot.'

He laughed. 'I meant it when I apologised to you. That you seem to find my lack of decorum hot says more about you than me.' They had reached a point where they could admit their shortcomings to each other, and Carlos was aware that, on his part, some of it had to do with the swirling tension of attraction between them. He *wanted* this evening to end at his place, couldn't fight the heat spreading below his skin and pooling in his stomach.

'I can't really explain any of…this.' Sofia pointed between them with a raised eyebrow, her lips curving into a smile that he wanted to kiss right off her face. The urge to touch her was a steady beat inside of him, and he knew he would succumb to it soon. Especially since she'd been getting closer to him throughout their dinner, the distance between them growing ever smaller.

'Then again, I'm not one to be casual,' she added, stopping his thoughts in their tracks.

Neither was he, though the reply wouldn't cross his lips. From the moment he'd asked her to dinner, a part of him had worried about the conversation becoming too personal. Though she might be the first person since Rosa to inspire attraction within him, he wasn't in a place where he could share those thoughts. He doubted that he would ever reach that kind of closure.

But despite knowing that, he couldn't stop himself from feeling the draw towards her.

His hand unfurled, his fingers winding through her hair until he made contact with the back of her neck. Cradling her head, he leaned into her space as he asked, 'What was your last relationship like if it wasn't casual?'

The spark in her eyes dimmed, and something inside him twisted. There was a hint of pain that might be too personal for the thing they wanted to start between them, but he wanted to know where it came from anyway.

'I've had bad luck finding the right person who fits into my life,' she said, her voice quieter than usual. 'With the work we do, it's not easy to find someone who will understand that sometimes I can't just leave work at the hospital. My relationships ended because they couldn't get the level of commitment they wanted from me, and that was fine by me. I've put my career as a surgeon above anything else.'

She paused, her eyes gliding away from his face to grab her glass. Her fingers trailed over the rim of it in a wide circle, and he dropped his eyes to watch the movement.

Carlos sensed there was a particular person she was thinking of, but forced himself not to pry. He didn't understand why he wanted to get to know her better, only that there was a need inside of him to uncover more of her.

'With my last boyfriend, Daniel, I'd thought things would be different. He never once complained about me cutting dates short if I was paged, or that we had to figure out plans around my schedule. Turns out he ended up being the worst of them.' Sofia took a sip of her drink, raising her eyes to him as she set the glass back down. The tingling in his fingers where they cradled her head intensified as she looked at him. 'So now I'm ready to try the casual route. That seems the logical way to get my needs met without all the messy attachment.'

Carlos took a sharp inhale when she leaned into his touch, twisting her head so his hand landed on her cheek. Like an automatic reflex, his thumb stroked over her soft skin in a slow arc. This wasn't the direction he'd expected from this conversation. The mention of her latest ex-boyfriend bothered him more than he had expected. The pain still lived within her, bubbling close enough to the surface that he guessed their breakup was recent.

Though that wasn't what was strange. No, what threw Carlos for a loop was the surge of protectiveness zapping through his chest at the thought of the wrongs this man had inflicted on Sofia. The way she spoke about her previous relationships was clinical, like she had long ago processed her feelings. But some rawness had sneaked back into her voice at the mention of Daniel.

He wanted to know how he had turned out to be the worst of them all, but bit back the question. What use would it be to know that about her?

'You sure you want this with me?' he asked instead. The skin of her cheek warmed underneath his hand, sparking a response in his own body. He knew *he* wanted this, yearned to be connected to her in a way he hadn't wanted anyone since Rosa's passing.

Was this the first sign of healing? Carlos wasn't sure he could ever open his heart to another person again, but Sofia reached something within him he'd kept hidden away from everyone. She wasn't afraid to challenge him and, with that simple action, somehow saw beyond the walls he'd raised. It had been enough to bring to life the warmth of attraction.

'As long as we both want the same thing. I might not be experienced in no-strings-attached arrangements, but I know I don't want more than that.' Sofia paused, as if she was listening back to her own words, then extended her hand until it lay splayed on his chest.

The touch sent a current of electricity through him, and her fingers dug into the fabric of his shirt as his chest expanded with a deep breath. His thumb stopped its arc over her cheek, and his hand wandered down to her chin. At the slightest pressure from him, she tilted it upwards, and Carlos's eyes dipped lower, watching her pulse beat against the base of her neck.

He imagined—not for the first time—what she would taste like there, and this time, he didn't fight the urge. He let himself sink into the fantasy and lowered his head to press it against her collarbone.

Above him Sofia gasped, and that small sound was enough to drive his heated blood to the lower half of his body. He paused for a second, composing himself before he whispered onto her skin, 'This is so much better than I imagined.'

Another small sound escaped her mouth when his lips trailed along her jaw. He stopped when he reached her ear and took her earlobe between his teeth as he breathed in. Her scent was intoxicating, filling his head with even more fantasies than he'd been indulging in since their first encounter in the OR.

But before they went any further, he needed to be clear with her. 'I don't get personal with anyone in my life,' he said simply as he drew back to look at her. The glaze over her eyes filled him with regret that they hadn't had the conversation earlier. But if she agreed to come with him now, she needed to know this about him. So he continued, 'The reason I move around a lot is because I don't like to get to know people, and I don't tend to answer personal questions.'

Sofia blinked, slowly, and he wondered if she was struggling with the same restraint he was. Or was what he'd said somehow too much for her? But then she nodded while lifting one shoulder in a shrug. 'Will you still tell me about how you learned to move like that with capoeira?'

He smiled at her words, and his lips closed around her earlobe again before he drew back and angled his mouth over hers. He held her gaze as their noses touched, searching them for a hint of hesitation or second thoughts. All he found in them was a curious spark that lit a flame of hunger he recognised all too well.

Her lashes lowered when he nudged her nose with his, and a shaky breath escaped her throat. Her hand burrowed deeper into his shirt. When she pulled him closer to her, Carlos huffed out a laugh before giving in to his own desire.

Their lips met in a tender, tentative kiss that instantly felt familiar—like he'd been waiting for these exact lips all his life. The silky feel of them engulfed him, washed through his body in a wave of heat and sparks. His hands came up to her face, pulling her closer. He eased her head back to deepen the kiss, and a soft moan drifted to his ear from her throat.

That small sound was enough to drive him over the edge. He rode the rising tide of desire in his body, and forgot that he had ever meant to be cautious around her. All he could think of was how badly he wanted to have her underneath him and wring every drop of pleasure out of her.

Carlos knew he shouldn't. Knew that even if she agreed to go home with him tonight, it would be all about her pleasure. For the last five years, he had not thought about sleeping with anyone and had truly believed that part of his life over. Considered it part of his penance for letting Rosa down. So as far as protection was concerned, he wasn't...prepared. But that wouldn't stop him from getting a taste right now.

If Sofia agreed.

Her tongue swiped over his lips, begging him for entrance that he wanted to grant her. But he forced himself to pull back, leaning his forehead against hers to look at her.

'Instead of telling you how I learned to move like that, how about I show you?' he said, a smile tugging at his lips as he looked at her puffy lips and passion-glazed eyes.

Her throat bobbed, and it took her a moment to catch her breath. His heart skipped a beat when she asked, 'Where do you live?'

CHAPTER SIX

WHEN SOFIA HAD entered the restaurant earlier in the evening, she had not expected to end up at Carlos's place. Then again, when she had left the hospital after her shift, she also hadn't thought she would have dinner with the man she had until fairly recently considered her arch-nemesis.

Despite her question, she knew there was only one reason why Carlos had invited her to his place, and it had precious little to do with explaining capoeira to her. That was clear from the kiss they'd shared. The phantom sensation of his lips on her collarbone still danced over her skin, sending shivers of need through her body down into her core.

As she stepped into the elevator to his flat with his warm hand on the small of her back, she realised—with not a small amount of shock—how much she had wanted this from the moment they met. The tension from their disagreements at work had led to this situation, turning their dislike into a searing-hot attraction that had resulted in the invitation to his place.

Was that what he wanted from her? A quick fling with all the fun and none of the commitment? Judging by the fire in his eyes, he wanted to devour her right here on the spot. And that thought sent more sparks flying through her body in uncontrollable arcs.

Sofia had never considered acting on attraction without emotion and the firm boundaries of a relationship. But maybe that was the way busy surgeons like themselves were supposed to do it?

Would someone as experienced as Carlos be turned off by her lack of knowledge? Though she had been the one to talk about her relationships—and about not wanting one—the way his lips trailing over her skin had her clenching around nothing convinced her of his prowess as a lover.

But then she'd gone ahead and mentioned Daniel. She had only shared a sliver of her experience with him, but she'd seen Carlos's eyes shutter for a moment, as if put off. And a few moments later, Sofia had understood why. He didn't do personal. All he wanted was to come to an agreement and enjoy her companionship without any of her baggage.

That was what she wanted as well, right? It shouldn't bother her that she would never get an answer to the questions about him that were still bubbling up inside of her.

'What's going on? I think I lost you there for a second.' Carlos's words snapped her back to reality, and she looked at the open elevator door. His hand was placed on the sensor of the door, preventing it from closing as he looked at her.

'Sorry, I was just in my head. It's been a while since I've been with anyone…'

A nervous laugh bubbled up in her chest as she stepped into the elevator, and she immediately regretted her words. He didn't want to know anything about her. His interest in her was purely physical, and she needed to remember that. Before long, the fire in her veins would bank until it vanished along with Carlos.

'Tell me about what happened the last time you did,' he said as he followed her into the elevator, his voice still low enough to raise the hairs on the back of her neck.

Carlos took out a key fob from the messenger bag hanging around his shoulder and swiped it over a reader at the bottom of the number panel. The doors closed with a soft thud. Then the elevator moved up. Sofia watched as the numbers went by until they passed twenty and the display changed to *P*.

The doors opened and revealed a panoramic view of Buenos Aires's night-time skyline. The entire wall consisted of tall windows, the moon and starlight the only thing illuminating her surroundings. A modern kitchen opened up to her left, its black marble countertops gleaming in the dying light, and in front of the windows was a couch large enough to seat an entire surgical team.

'You live in a penthouse?' Sofia asked as she stepped closer to the windows to look at the view. 'Damn, I'm going to talk to our boss about getting a raise.'

Carlos stepped up behind her as she peered through the windows and took in the skyline of Buenos Aires. His chest was close enough to her back to touch it, but he deliberately kept a few centimetres of distance between them—or at least she thought it to be deliberate. If she let herself lean back just a little, she would get that touch her insides were screaming for.

'This penthouse is up for sale, and they rent it out for short-term arrangements while they're looking for a buyer,' he said, his voice so close that each word sent a rush of breath over her skin.

'Still has to cost you a pretty penny. And you don't even get to enjoy it because you spend all your time at the hospital.' Sofia dared to shoot him a look over her shoulder. A shiver skittered down her spine as her eyes locked onto his, the hunger she beheld in them stoking the flame in her core to new heights.

'How long is "a while"?' Carlos asked.

'What?' She didn't know what else to say to his question.

'You said you haven't been with anyone *"in a while"*.'

Her heart leapt into her throat as the words dropped into her consciousness like they were weighed down with stones. She spun around to face him, her eyes drawn to his lips, which were curled in a slight smile. The memory of what it felt like to have his mouth pressed against hers sent another surge of heat through her.

Was he suddenly concerned about her level of experience?

'Does it matter? I thought you didn't want to do personal questions.'

Carlos's gaze roamed up and down her body as he stepped closer, causing shivers wherever his eyes went. There was an assessing quality to the sweep of his gaze, but she didn't feel exposed like she thought she would. No, what he awakened inside of her was the raging fury of desire.

'I said *I* don't want to answer personal questions. But you're right to request that rule apply to you as well. So let me ask you something else instead.' Her back hit the cool glass behind her when he took a step forward, his hand coming to rest on the window right next to her head. His head dipped down, finding the hollow of her collarbone. The open-mouthed kiss he pressed onto it shot lightning through her. 'I know what I want from you. But what do *you* want, Sofia?'

Her mouth went dry at the question she'd been asking herself.

There was no denying the attraction heating the surrounding air—and it had been far too long since she and Daniel had broken up. Though their relationship had ended poorly, the sex had always been good. If his kisses were anything to go by, Carlos knew exactly what he was doing. It would be more than *just* good.

'I think we both know you didn't invite me here to show me any capoeira steps. That probably doesn't require as much kissing as we've already done. I liked it, so maybe that's a good place to start and work our way towards...' Her voice trailed off as butterflies bounced in her stomach, throwing her off.

Carlos huffed out a low laugh that skittered across her skin. 'Kissing you hadn't been the plan when I followed you earlier today, but I'm happy to be here with you.'

He paused, his other hand coming down on the glass so that her head was now boxed in between his arms—making her shiver. Her clothes lay heavy on her skin, fraying her nerves wherever they made contact with her, and she was sure if he were to lean in now to eliminate the remaining space between their lips, she would combust.

'So, you want to sleep with me?' He leaned in slightly closer with each word, his lips hovering over hers with a tantalising proximity that made her squirm underneath his gaze.

'Yes.' Sofia let the truth of her intentions shine

through this one word. The cautious part in her wanted to decline—to leave and pretend like nothing had ever happened between them. But it was also the cautious part that had led her into relationships that were doomed to fail. All because she understood the parameters of a romantic relationship, understood her expectations and responsibilities. That was how she had been taught things should be—books, TV shows, her own parents. They all had shown her that there was only one way to have a man in her life.

But what if that concept simply didn't fit into her life, and some closeness here and there when it presented itself was what she was actually looking for? The way Carlos led his life.

Shaking off the last vestiges of hesitation, Sofia let her hands come to rest on his chest, feeling the hardness of his pecs as she dug her fingers into the fabric of his shirt. 'We both know this isn't anything serious. We're simply getting rid of the tension at work in a creative way.'

Sofia already suspected that Carlos wasn't interested in anything romantic either, but she still wasn't prepared for his expression shuttering. It was only for a second, enough to notice, but not enough to understand what was going through his head. A heartbeat passed and then the smile was back, lips curved in an expression of pure seduction.

'I'm leaving Buenos Aires in two weeks. Casual is all I'm looking for,' he said, and Sofia ignored the thing twisting in her chest.

She might have never had a casual encounter before, but that didn't mean she needed to attach needless emotions to what was happening here. It was good that he wasn't looking for anything serious. Neither was she. Her serious relationships, the ones that were by the book, they had all ended in heartbreak. Maybe it was time to paint outside the lines for once.

A surge of renewed confidence emboldened her. She slipped her hands to his back and pulled him closer so his chest lay flush against hers. Then she angled her head up to meet his gaze, putting all her intentions into her eyes, hoping he understood. Carlos did, for the small smile unfurled into something larger and hungrier, and her lids fluttered closed when his mouth finally dipped down to capture her lips.

Her lips were soft against his, the touch filled with more passion and heat than their first kiss at the restaurant. Every single nerve ending in his body was blazing, his skin alight with an invisible fire that burst free from a place he'd long since hidden away from the public. A place Sofia had found and was now standing in front of, trying to figure out how to climb the wall she had encountered.

Or at least that's what the withdrawn part of his brain wanted him to believe—while the part that was starved for touch was ready to let go right this second. Just tonight—and the pleasure would be only hers. Even if he wanted to, he couldn't give more today.

His desire for her wasn't wrong, was it? He wasn't dishonouring Rosa's memory by finally giving in to something he had yearned for? This wasn't about finding a new wife or forgetting what he had done in the past. No, he would carry the scars and the guilt over it with him for the rest of his life. Nobody could erase that.

But Carlos couldn't deny what this kiss was doing to

him—that something inside of him was coming undone. Sofia had found him in a place no one else ever had, and though he had sensed the undercurrent of attraction in all of their interactions, it wasn't until his most vulnerable moment that his view had changed. As though her talking him down from his panic had left a sliver of him open to her. It was the only explanation that made sense to him for why he wanted Sofia as much as he did. How she was the first person to reach him again on any level.

He pressed her further into the glass behind her as their lips moved together, and everything inside him clenched when a muffled moan escaped her throat. He'd forgotten what it was like to be wanted. The ghost of it had visited him during their last encounter, when she had embraced him. The memory was foggy, tainted by the sheer panic he'd been trying to control, but the spark had been there in the moment—trying to break through. His lips had skittered over the sensitive skin of her neck, brushing over her earlobe, and the sound she had made then...

Carlos hardened at the memory. He needed to hear that sound again now.

His hands slipped away from where they rested on the glass, coming down on Sofia's hips and pulling her closer to him. His lips remained fused to hers, their kiss a dance of teeth and tongues as they deepened their connection. All the while, his fingers moved down her sides, finding the hem of her dress and slipping underneath to feel the bare skin of her thighs.

Another muffled moan came from her throat, and Carlos was certain he would shatter if she did it again. His skin was already impossibly tight from the repressed desire surging forward. He had denied himself all this for the last five years, thinking even casual encounters a betrayal of the promises he'd made—and the promises he had broken. What had changed inside him that he was willing to let loose in this moment? Carlos didn't know, but that would be something to explore later.

Sofia demanded all his attention.

His mouth left hers to explore more of her again. A shudder raked through him as he tasted the skin of her neck, the memory of their first kiss in the restaurant radiating through him with a searing heat. She let out a small huff every time his lips connected with her flesh, and her pleasure at his touch brought a primal satisfaction to his chest that he hadn't felt in ages. It only heightened his own desire.

Her enthusiastic response had him eagerly continuing his exploration, his hands moving over her clothed torso and dipping behind, where he found her zipper. He paused there to give Sofia the chance to withdraw or speak up. When she surged forward to press her mouth against his again, he dragged the zipper down.

The fabric fell from her shoulders, revealing centimetre after delicious centimetre of caramel flesh. He bowed his head, feathering kisses onto her skin as he peeled the dress down her body. His hands moved up her sides, relishing the feel of velvety skin. Then he paused, fully enraptured by the sight of her bared to his gaze. Her curves looked as soft as they felt, the gentle slope of her hips narrowing as he traced the line up to her waist and then flaring out again as her torso expanded.

'I see you came here prepared,' he said with a huffed laugh, and watched with way too much male satisfaction as a blush deepened the hue of the skin on her cheeks.

'Bold of you to assume I'm not wearing a bra just

because of you,' she said, pushing her chin out in a now familiar gesture of challenge that he'd observed her throwing at him many times at the hospital.

Carlos decided to play along, looking at her with feigned surprise. 'You're saying this is not for me?'

Before she could answer, he ran his hands back up her body and palmed both her breasts.

The skin was soft and heated against his hand, and when his thumb lightly stroked over her nipple, she arched her back, pushing further into his touch. Renewed desire thundered through him, so strong and savage that he had to take a few steadying breaths. Because he had denied himself the company of a woman for so long, the onslaught of sensation was threatening to overwhelm him. Carlos wasn't allowed to let that happen. He *wanted* this to last as long as possible, taking his time to acquaint himself with every part of her body.

His face dipped below her jawline, his lips brushing over her neck, then wandering lower still. His mouth watered as he hovered in front of her breast. So many things popped into his mind that he wanted to do to her. Tentatively, both to tease and to test the water, he extended his tongue far enough for its tip to just whisper over her nipple.

The response was instant. A soft cry escaped her lips, her muscles under his hands tensing and releasing as pleasure speared through her. He smiled to himself, his own need growing—a fact he knew was apparent by just looking at him. But that wasn't what this night was about. It would only be about her.

When he closed his whole mouth around the tip of her breast and sucked, Sofia's whimper turned into a low moan. Her hands came down on his shoulders, gripping at the fabric there and pulling his shirt up. Whether it was on purpose or because she needed something to hang on to, Carlos didn't know, but he let her pull the buttons apart before flinging the shirt off his shoulders.

He rested his forehead on her sternum as he pulled her closer again, his nose brushing the sensitive skin between her breasts. There he inhaled deeply, her scent sending lightning strikes through his body.

'You smell delicious,' he said, letting the thought out without considering what he was saying. 'I can't wait to find out what you taste like.'

He kissed each breast to underline his words, his tongue briefly swirling around each peaked nipple. Then he shot up, standing tall in front of her, and his eyes narrowed on her with a smile. 'Hold on tight,' he said as he wrapped his arms around her and lifted her off the floor to carry her to the couch behind them.

Sofia yelped as her feet lost contact with the floor. She pushed her hips into his erection as she wrapped her legs around his waist. Carlos hissed at the sudden pressure, his restraint already stretched to near maximum. It would be *very* hard to stop at this point, but he hadn't expected this. He wasn't…prepared. But he couldn't let this end before he knew what she tasted like.

The fabric of the couch was cool against her skin, and Sofia took in a shaky breath. Everything within her was taut and loose at the same time, her body reacting to Carlos's touch in ways she hadn't expected. If she had thought earlier that the sex she'd had in the past was good, she needed to revise that statement.

This was good, and they hadn't even arrived at the

main event. Whatever she had experienced in the past paled in comparison—it wasn't even a contest.

Her mind had completely emptied of everything when Carlos climbed on top of her with a smile that let her see all of his primal intentions for her. Intentions that had her squeezing her thighs together to seek relief in what little friction she could manage like that.

Carlos noticed the tensing of her muscles, for his smile grew into a grin.

'Impatient, are we?' he drawled, and Sofia raised her head to look at him.

Whatever she had intended to retort died in her throat, turning into a low moan when his hands dipped beneath the skirt of her dress and pulled it down, leaving her in nothing but her underwear. When his hands brushed over her wet panties, her head lolled back as a strike of electricity shook her body.

Carlos positioned himself between her legs while kneeling on the floor. Lying flat on the couch, she couldn't see him, but his breath against her skin had her imagination running wild, her body tensing with anticipation—and a dose of fear at the lack of control.

This wasn't a position Sofia was used to. Her entire life was built around the concept of controlling what she could and adapting to the things she couldn't. That was the working principle of trauma surgery, after all. It was how she operated in her relationships as well, taking charge and setting the expectations from the very beginning.

She hadn't done any of that with Carlos, had relinquished so much of her ability to control things to him—trusting him to do that. Where was she taking this trust from? She knew him to be a capable doctor and a surgeon with a level of skill she dreamed about attaining some day. But did she know enough about him to just… let him do things his way?

The thought kept coming back as she tried to push it away and stay in the moment with him. She knew she *wanted* him to continue. Her body's response to his touch was evidence enough. Why was her brain suddenly trying to ruin a good thing for her?

A ripple of pleasure dispelled some of the tension building in her muscles when Carlos brushed his fingers along the hem of her underwear. Then she gasped as his thumb stroked her through the silken fabric, the current of lightning intensifying. She was enjoying his touch way too much, and small bubbles of doubt kept surfacing in her mind when she would rather focus on the moment.

How Carlos had noticed what was going on inside her head she didn't know, but his fingers suddenly stopped their tender caress. He looked up to meet her gaze.

'You're not used to a man pleasuring you?' he asked, his tone curious rather than critical as she had expected.

Sofia swallowed the lump in her throat. A part of her wanted to deny it, yearned to appear as experienced as he clearly was. But the softness in his expression, the complete lack of judgement she saw in his eyes—it coaxed her into a feeling of safety. So she nodded and said, 'I'm usually the person setting the pace.'

Carlos sat up, a thoughtful expression bunching up his brows. His eyes darted around the couch. Then he stood, gathering two large pillows from the opposite ends. Leaning over her with a soft smile, he pulled her into a sitting position by her hands, then placed the cushions behind her before pushing her back down.

He kissed her, and her lips immediately opened for his. A deep moan released from her chest as their tongues tangled, her stomach swooping as if she were weightless. The air between them sparked when he severed their connection, and Carlos wound his way down her body, stopping here and there to kiss, nip and suck at his leisure before settling back down between her thighs, his knees on the floor again.

Her heart squeezed when she realised what he had done. With her head now elevated by the cushions, she could see *everything* he was doing. Not only had he understood where her hesitation was coming from without her having to explain, he had also found a solution for her.

As if he was reading her mind, Carlos said, 'You're in control here. You see something you don't like, just hit me in the back of the head.'

Sofia couldn't help but laugh at that. The image his words conjured in her mind was so different from the situation they were in. 'I think I'll just tell you to stop,' she said with a chuckle, and with each breath, whatever tension she had been carrying flowed out of her body.

'I guess that works, too.' He smirked before he dropped his gaze, and his eyes turned entirely feral again.

His fingers resumed their exploration, finding each spot of sensitive skin with precision. Not only had he known what she needed on an emotional level right now, but apparently he also knew exactly how to touch her in a way she had never experienced before. That she was able to watch him skim his fingers over her, her wetness leaving traces on him even through the silken fabric of her panties, only heightened the delicious torture he was inflicting on her.

When another searing spear of need lanced through her from his slow and deliberate touches, she bucked her hips—to urge him on.

Carlos chuckled. 'You really are incredibly impatient, sweetheart,' he said, his face so close to her flesh that she felt his hot breath grazing her.

'If I can tell you to stop, I can probably also tell you to go ahead?' Sofia asked, knowing the answer even before she saw the eager gleam in his eyes.

'There's nothing hotter than a woman telling me what she wants me to do to her.' His voice was akin to a growl, his tone so low that another wave of need rushed to her core. She moved her hips again, bringing her closer to his face.

Sofia gasped when his lips made contact with the sensitive skin at the top of her leg and then wandered down. He hooked his finger underneath the front of her panties, and his breath hit the flesh underneath as he bent down.

'This is everything I've been thinking about for the last week,' he whispered, each word creating another huff of air that skittered over her skin.

He didn't give Sofia the chance to reply. Instead, Carlos lowered his head and put his mouth to her, his tongue parting her folds in one lazy and smooth stroke that turned her gasps of anticipation into a delighted groan.

Every muscle inside of her loosened at the feel of his lips against her, the intimate caress demanding all of her attention. A ball of tension bounced around in the pit of her stomach—higher and higher with each lick and stroke from Carlos until stars began to drift in front of her eyes. She wanted to watch him, the view of this gorgeous man between her legs adding to the pleasure of what he was doing. But the sensations were too much, and she let her lids close as she gave herself to the sensation mounting within her.

Sofia thought it couldn't get any more intense—until his fingers joined his mouth. He pushed into her. The light of the stars burst alive, blinding her as pure ecstasy flooded her system.

'Right there, right there.' She heard these words over and over, pushing through the haze of bliss enveloping her and grabbing her attention. Then the tension in her stomach crested, firing her down the starlit corridor in a crash landing that turned into a long, drawn-out moan—and had her realising she had been the one urging him on.

Heat flooded her cheeks as the high of her orgasm trickled through her, reality slowly creeping back in. Carlos kissed her thighs gently, the tip of his tongue darting out now and then as he made his way back up her body. His erection settled against her, and her body reacted instantly.

Carlos let out a sound that was half chuckle, half groan as he bent down and pulled her into a kiss. She wrapped her arms around him, her fingers dancing over his back as they found their way down. But when she pushed her fingers below his waistband, he broke the kiss and looked at her.

The fire in his eyes matched the roaring flames underneath her skin, yet there was something else in them. A tiny sliver of regret.

'I have a confession to make, sweetheart,' he said, and the muscles that had been loose from her post-orgasmic bliss tensed up.

Carlos sensed it and immediately bent down to breathe another kiss onto her lips. 'Nothing catastrophic, don't panic. More a selfishness on my part.' His lips trailed over her cheek and down her neck, summoning the fog of lust around her brain. 'I know you can feel how much I want you, but I'm not prepared yet.'

'Prepared?' Sofia asked, trying to focus on his words while the path of his lips caused shivers to rake through her body.

'I don't have any protection to make sure we are both safe going any further than this,' he replied, and the haziness enveloping her dispersed.

'You don't?' The question came out a lot more incredulous than she intended. Carlos seemed to have picked up on that, for he stopped the wandering of his mouth to look at her.

'I'm not in the habit of taking a box of condoms with me whenever I travel for work.' There was an edge to his voice. Sofia knew she hadn't caused him any offence with her question, but she had inevitably poked at something she hadn't meant to.

He didn't travel with condoms? For some reason, that thought was hard for her to reconcile with the image of Carlos she had constructed in her head. Didn't he have a different lover in every single hospital he worked at? Wasn't that what he wanted from her?

'Right… This isn't actually your home. Sorry,' she said, not wanting to spoil the mood further by doubling down on her incredulity.

That seemed to be enough to take him off guard. Carlos shifted his weight off her to lie next to her, his hand splayed on her stomach and drawing gentle circles as he looked at her. 'I had to have a taste—even though I knew that was as far as we could go with things. You are just so…delicious.'

A swarm of butterflies burst alive in the pit of her stomach at his words, and a nervous giggle climbed up her throat. 'You're sweet to say that,' she said, the lack of creativity in her words making her cringe. Was there a more boring person on the planet? If only there was a rulebook on how to speak to a casual lover—that would be her salvation. Because she didn't even know how to be interesting enough to prevent a guy from cheating on her. Things got infinitely more complicated if she considered the dynamic between her and Carlos.

'Just the facts,' he said as he raised one shoulder, his fingers still tracing over her exposed skin, drawing attention to her nakedness.

What was the protocol post-climax? Was she supposed to leave straight away? Was there a certain amount of small talk before they went about their day? God, why was she so bad with men? No wonder Daniel did what he did when she couldn't even navigate this casual interaction with Carlos.

'What's wrong?' Carlos's question pierced through the whirlwind of insecurities rising in her thoughts. He must have sensed her tensing, or how else would he know what was going on in her mind?

Lacking any kind of excuse or experience to fall back on, Sofia decided to go with the truth. 'I've never done this before.'

A line appeared between his brows as he considered her, confusion rippling over his face. He leaned away from her. 'This as in…*this*?' His hand splayed out again, pressing gently down on her stomach to indicate her.

She immediately shook her head as she realised what

he had misunderstood. 'No, I've had sex. I realise I said it before, but I don't really know how to navigate…this kind of casual interaction.'

Carlos relaxed back against her, his fingers resuming their gentle caress as he looked at her. His expression softened, letting her glimpse the man behind the typical surgeon bravado she'd observed in most of her colleagues—herself included. Something lay beneath the surface, something that remained hidden away and might burst into flames if the light of day touched it. A fragile piece of himself that was coming out now as they lay entangled in each other with only half their clothes on.

Sofia had seen the other side of that vulnerability before, when she had grounded him through his panic attack.

His lips parted as if he was going to say something, but then the vulnerable spark died in his eyes. His fingers wandered up her torso, grazing over the underside of her breast. For a fraction of a second, Sofia got the sense that somehow sex with her was an escape for him—though she couldn't even begin to understand what he would be escaping from. Or where that suspicion even came from.

But then his knuckles brushed over her taut nipple, sending a renewed wave of pleasure through her body. 'We make the rules here. Whenever you have a question or a concern, just tell me,' he said, bending down to brush his lips against hers. 'Now I really have to shower. I'm usually one to wash up before doing anything, but you were just so…'

The memory of how everything had started came back to her, and Sofia laughed as Carlos got to his feet.

'You never got to show me what capoeira actually is,' she said, her eyes gliding over his muscled back.

A hum of appreciation escaped her throat, and Carlos looked back at her. 'Next time,' he said, winking.

Then he caught her off guard again when he tucked each thumb under his waistband and pushed his trousers and underwear down, filling in the blanks in her imagination. Before she could say anything, he reached his hand towards her and curled his fingers, beckoning. 'You want to join me in the shower? There are a lot of things we can do that don't require protection.'

CHAPTER SEVEN

CARLOS WATCHED WITH a satisfied nod as the junior surgeons wheeled the patient out of the OR. With his third week beginning today, he now let the trained staff guide the surgery and take the lead on most of it. They had put the surgical plan together on the fly and needed very little guidance on what to do if they encountered obstacles. An observation Carlos was pleased with. He'd spent many hours in the operating room and during rounds teaching his triage technique and had them memorise it, practicing it on made-up scenarios over and over until they could triage a patient in their sleep.

The effort had paid off. They could now fall back on his teachings in emergency surgery, remembering what was critical and what could wait. All the staff had responded well to his guidance, and he knew he would spend the rest of his contract observing and course-correcting.

The lightness of a job well done filled him. Of course, he knew if he looked closer, that wasn't the only thing uplifting his mood—though he didn't dare to think too hard about what else there was. Sofia's draw on him was already overwhelming his senses.

Her taste still clung to his lips days later, the feel of her mouth around him a thrilling sensation that had kept him awake at night with an aching need only she could fulfil. Stepping into the shower to start his day had brought back the memories of their night together, and Carlos had almost grabbed Sofia and pulled her into what he now considered their closet when she gave him a secretive wink earlier today.

Though he had enjoyed the attention of different women over the last five years, he had never let it go anywhere beyond the occasional flirtation. The walls around him were too high to let anyone come close enough, even just for casual sex.

But Sofia had seen him in a vulnerable position, had sensed his panic on her own skin, and had remained there with him until he had calmed down. She'd been willing to do that for someone who didn't rank much higher than a stranger—one she had daily disagreements with at work.

He wondered if that tension had translated into their explosive connection, because he didn't know what else to make of it. No one else had ever managed to interest him. The guilt set in too quickly, not even letting him consider an attachment to any woman—casual or otherwise.

Tendrils of fire licked at his insides, and Carlos did the second most impulsive thing he had done in the last three days—the first one being inviting Sofia to his place. He let the flames burn, relishing the heat they sent coursing through his body.

The guilt was ever-present, and he didn't think it would ever go away. How could he just get over how utterly he had let his late wife down? But it seemed less pressing around Sofia, giving him room to enjoy her company without suffocating.

Pushing through the door of the OR, Carlos glanced at the surgical board on the wall. Two surgeries were currently going on, but Sofia wasn't a part of either of them. He tried to remember if she had told him what she was up to today, but they hadn't spoken since they had slipped into the supply closet yesterday for a make-out session that had left them both catching their breaths—and making plans for when they would go to his place again.

There had only been a short glance exchanged between them when he went to answer a page in the ER earlier. But she had been carrying some snacks and a tablet when he'd walked past her. Chances were that she was catching up on her notes somewhere on the floor. So Carlos went around the trauma department, sticking his head into different rooms and excusing himself when he interrupted someone until he found Sofia in a small staff room, staring at the tablet while popping grapes into her mouth absent-mindedly.

Carlos cleared his throat, and Sofia's eyes only briefly left the screen as if she wasn't worried about someone interrupting her. He grinned when recognition caught up with her and she looked up again, this time with the distinct glow of a blush on her high cheekbones.

'Enjoying yourself?' he asked as he walked over to stand behind her chair. There were several centimetres of space between them, but he still felt the heat radiating from her. Or was he the one setting the air between them on fire? He couldn't tell any more, their mutual attraction taking on a life and shape of its own.

'How much fun can you have doing patient notes?' She glanced down at the notepad lying next to the keyboard, then tilted her head back to look at him.

Carlos bit his lip at that, willing his breath to come out at a steady pace. The way she gazed up at him, he could see the entire column of her throat, the caramel skin looking soft and damn near edible even in the harsh light of the hospital. Then his eyes wandered further, glancing down the front of her scrub top. The neckline gave him a hint of an enticing view.

Without thinking, he leaned forward to see more, his torso coming close enough that it connected with the back of her chair.

'Try writing some silly notes in between the serious ones. It breaks up the monotony,' he said, his voice loaded with a suggestive tone that had nothing to do with his words and everything to do with the feelings she awakened in him.

'Silly notes?' If Sofia realised what the mere sliver of her visible skin was doing to him, she chose to ignore it as she kept her eyes trained on him, one eyebrow raised.

'Yeah, like "Patient demonstrates an uncanny ability to maintain a perfect level of room noise by consistent snoring. Rhythm remains stable. Recommend noise-cancelling headphones for the night shift nurse."'

Sofia blinked at him twice. Then her lips split apart in a wide grin that turned into a laugh. The sound of her laughter filled the small room, enveloping him in a sensation that wasn't part of the flames licking at him from the inside, but it burned just as much.

'Dr Carlos Cabrera, the no-nonsense surgeon who has been hounding us all about proper triage protocols during trauma surgery, writes silly notes into his patient charts?' The amusement twinkling in her eyes had to be one of the most attractive things he'd ever seen. It shot right through him, settling down in the centre of his chest.

'I would never leave the notes in. They're just something fun to do when you feel like the admin work is never-ending—which it is,' he replied, hoping to draw another laugh from her.

But Sofia just smiled and then did something way better. She tilted her head further back so that the top of her head was now pushing against his stomach. Holding eye contact with him, she sunk her teeth into her lower lip, and the sound fighting its way out of his throat could only be described as a growl.

Without thinking, he put his hands on her shoulders. His thumbs brushed over her collarbone before lifting the fabric of her top so his fingers could slip beneath her collar. From there, he let them trail further down, brushing over the tops of her breasts.

'This is so not by the book, Carlos,' Sofia said as she huffed out a breath. Though her words were meant to admonish him, he only heard excitement in them.

'So is sleeping with your co-worker,' he replied. Then he bent down to brush his lips against her neck.

The second he had entered the room and seen her, his mind had emptied out of any other thoughts. The hesitation, the questions over whether what he was doing was appropriate, had gone…along with the heaviness of the guilt sitting on his shoulders.

There was something about Sofia that he couldn't explain, but she brought him a lightness he hadn't felt since that day five years ago. A reprieve of the constant struggle—of *having* to play by the book because going outside of the established lines had brought tragedy to his life in the first place.

In this moment—as well as all the nights spent at his place since the first time—he could just *be* without anything weighing him down. That feeling was one he hadn't felt in so many years. It was intoxicating, and he couldn't resist it. No matter how much he knew it would probably be for the best if he did.

Sofia herself had given him the best reason to pull back. She had said she had never had a casual encounter with anyone. All her experiences had been in relationships. Carlos has almost shared that he wasn't used to casual encounters, either. There had been a few wild years during his early junior years, seeking release from the stress of being a newly minted doctor in different ways. Sex was great for that.

Was it fair of him to pull her into his orbit when he knew he would be leaving in less than two weeks? That he would never be hers? She had said that was what she was looking for. But could he be sure she meant what she said when she had never had a casual affair?

'Yeah, the hospital handbook has a whole chapter dedicated to fraternisation. There are procedures in place to safeguard the hospital from any liability, and we definitely disregarded many of them many nights this week.' Her voice was low and breathy as his lips continued their caress on her neck.

'Are you ready to shed the final vestiges of your aggressively by-the-book vibes?' Carlos had enjoyed that description of her when she had first mentioned it to him, seeing a lot of himself in it. Though people like that definitely didn't come on to their colleagues the way he was doing right now when they were rule-followers.

Hadn't he himself privately criticised Sebastián for living his marriage too openly in front of the staff?

The amount of information he'd heard fluttering around the corridors of the hospital about this man's marriage problems and their reconciliation had him questioning whether he had made a mistake coming to this place.

Now Carlos was the one getting inappropriately close to a co-worker.

Instead of answering him, Sofia turned her head to the side, sliding her lips over his. She moaned into that kiss as his hands dipped lower into her top, slipping under her bra and relishing the skin of her breasts underneath.

Desire roared to life inside of him, and a part of him urged himself towards caution. They were no longer in the privacy of his home, and they couldn't act with impunity—not without risking both of their professional reputations. Sofia was at far greater risk than him for that. He would be on his way in a couple of weeks' time, and she'd be left to clean up the mess they'd both willingly created.

But something about her touch, about the small mewls coming from her closed lips as his tongue clashed with hers, completely enthralled him and almost robbed him of any sense. Almost.

With an amount of self-restraint he didn't realise he was capable of, Carlos stopped kissing her. Sofia let out a huff of surprise when he straightened up, pulling his hands away from her and taking a step back.

'I ran away with myself,' he said when he read the silent question of what had just happened in her eyes. 'We're both new to rule-breaking, so I think we should start small. For example, if we are keen on breaking some more fraternisation rules, why don't we do it where people can't walk in on us?'

Sofia's eyes rounded, and her gaze darted about as if to double-check that no one had been in the room with them when their exchange had started.

His timing couldn't have been more on point, for they both heard the persistent squeak of rubber shoes against the hospital floor that was getting louder by the second—until a woman stepped into the staff room, one hand holding a tablet while the other rested on top of her pregnant belly.

'Bella! I thought Sebastián said you were off today?' Sofia jumped to her feet, the chair she sat on skittering over the floor with a loud screech—as if it had picked up on the nervous energy alive in the room. She was clearly aware of how close they had got to being caught in their heated embrace.

Something that didn't pass by Isabella either. She narrowed her eyes and looked between them. 'He certainly wants me to take more time off, but I'm not stopping work until these babies are ready to pop out.'

A frown appeared on Sofia's lips. 'You are carrying around triplets. That's a high-risk pregnancy, and you definitely shouldn't be working until they are "ready to pop out".' She raised her fingers to mimic air quotes as she repeated the other woman's words.

'You sound like Seb,' Bella said with an eye-roll. 'And don't try to change the subject. What are *you* two doing here?'

Before Carlos could say anything, Sofia opened her mouth. 'W-we were…' Her voice trailed off as her eyes darted around, looking for an excuse. 'We were going over some patient notes for a surgery we did earlier this week.'

Bella levelled a stare at her that said she saw through

the lie—which wasn't all that difficult. Though Sofia had many talents, he realised lying wasn't one of them.

For the second time in a short span, their luck pulled through when both their pagers began sounding at the same time.

'An emergency surgery just came in,' he said to Sofia, then nodded at Isabella before squeezing past her and down the corridor to the operating rooms, with Sofia's steps echoing behind as she followed him.

The heat of their moment in the staff room still clung to her cheeks when Sofia finished scrubbing and stepped into the OR. They had washed in silence, but the tension between them remained in place as neither of them acknowledged what had happened—both between them and with Isabella.

What was strange was that her heart was racing from being caught, but it wasn't fear that had her pulse elevated. No, she had Carlos to thank for that. Though they had spent several hours together the other day, she hadn't expected him to be so forward at work. Not when they were both normally focused on their careers and professional reputations.

In her mind, Sofia knew she should be horrified that one of the senior leaders of the hospital had almost caught her in an inappropriate position with a colleague. She had given up so much to get to this point in her career. Her dedication to her job had been the reason why her relationships had never worked out—including Daniel, who had chosen to punish her for her priorities in the cruellest way.

But there was nothing but excitement dancing in the pit of her stomach. Carlos's touch sent lightning through her body, filling her with a longing unlike anything she'd ever felt. The only regret she had about what they had done in the staff room was that their shift wasn't over yet.

'What are we working on?' Carlos asked as he stepped into the room. If he had any feelings about what had happened between them, he wasn't showing them.

'We have Manny Vargas, a thirty-five-year-old male involved in an accident on his bicycle. Bystanders reported to the paramedics that he was hit by a car and thrown several feet upon impact,' the junior doctor assisting them said, relaying the information from the ER.

Sofia noticed a small crease appearing between Carlos's brows, and she watched him closely as the junior surgeon informed them about the vitals of the patient and the results of the CT scans and X-rays they'd already performed.

The last time they had worked on a car crash victim, Carlos had suffered a panic attack. Since then she had watched him carefully whenever they were in any high-stress situation, noting any differences in his behaviour as they worked. She hadn't seen anything since and wasn't sure that there was anything now, either.

'So we need to have a look at the ruptured spleen and the fracture in his femur,' Carlos said, then glanced at her. 'You run the surgery on the spleen. I'll examine at the leg.'

'Right.' Sofia nodded, pushing the worry about him to the back of her mind. Splitting up surgical responsibilities was one of the techniques Carlos had been teaching everyone—including her. Even though his self-assured air still grated on her, she had to admit that he'd brought everyone on the surgical team to a different level with his teachings.

She stepped up to the patient. The surgical field was already prepped and ready to go. 'Can you bring up the CT scans for me?' Yasmine, the trainee surgeon next to her, nodded, then walked over to the computer and brought up the pictures. That there was damage in that area was obvious the second the scans loaded. The active haemorrhage from the blood pooling around the spleen and other organs stood out in a brighter colour, giving Sofia an idea about the severity of the case.

'There will be internal bleeding, so let's get the sponges ready to soak it all up. Chances are we'll have to remove the spleen if the damage is too severe.' There usually was no other option, and though every surgery was invasive, this was a better outcome than having to remove a kidney or a part of the liver. With high-impact accidents like that, they never knew where the damage would lie.

She received the scalpel from the OR assistant, then opened an incision in the left upper quadrant of the patient's abdomen to expose the way to the spleen. Once she was there, she worked with Yasmine to mobilise the spleen by detaching it from other organs so she could assess it and make her choice about the next steps. 'Put some more sponges in here,' she instructed when blood began pooling in the abdominal cavity again.

Every so often, Sofia glanced over at Carlos, who stood further down the patient at his exposed leg, working with another junior doctor. From the snippets of conversation floating over to her, she could tell they were attempting to set the bone, but the fracture was looking more complex than they'd initially thought. Carlos would ask for help if he needed it, wouldn't he? She didn't know what high-stress situations were triggers for him, and all she had to go by were traffic accidents.

Why had they not spoken about this again? That had been the reason she'd tried to catch up with him in the hospital last week, only for Carlos to dodge her. Then, when she finally had found him again coincidentally, he'd not been wearing a shirt, and all the attraction simmering beneath the surface had just bubbled forward.

Under the bright light of the OR, she could see a film of sweat on his brow, though she knew her own was looking similar. To keep everyone involved safe, they had to wear several layers of protection, and it could get hot in the operating room, especially if you had to set bones, which took a lot more force. Though if they had to move around a lot, they'd wait until the spleen was out.

Sofia pushed those thoughts away. They would have to talk about it after. It was no use if she worried throughout surgeries they did together if he was in distress. They needed to come up with a safe way of dealing with it—like many other surgeons suffering from PTSD had.

'Okay, now that it's secured, we will ligate the spleen and then remove it.' She handed the tool to Yasmine, who took it with an eager nod and stepped closer to the patient. Sofia watched and instructed the junior surgeon as she ligated the smaller arteries and veins before coming to the big one. She paused, adjusting her grip, then went to work while Sofia kept suctioning to keep the surgical area clear.

'We have to wait until we put in the screws.' Carlos's voice drifted to her ear, and she looked up just as he moved closer to her, his eyes narrowing slightly in a smile she couldn't see underneath his surgical mask.

'How is the break looking?' she asked him, her eyes back on the patient.

'Complex, but we can place a rod and screws right now to set the bone, and hopefully we won't need a second surgery.' From the corner of her eye, she could tell his expression was serious. 'He is facing a long road towards recovery, that's for sure.'

Sofia followed the hand of the junior surgeon as she went on to ligate the main artery of the spleen—a task that required the utmost delicacy as it represented the main blood flow.

'Anything we can do to assist?' Carlos asked, and she shook her head.

'We're about ready to remove the spleen. Once that's done, we'll close back up, and you guys can get on drilling away.' She paused, looking over at the leg that was still open but covered with a surgical sheet to keep it secured. 'It must be a complex fracture if you need to set it with a rod. Do we need to page someone from orthopaedics?'

Carlos shook his head. 'I've spent almost a year working with a guy in São Paulo who was the head of the orthopaedics department. His wife runs the hospital they worked at and wanted to free up more of his time to do volunteer work, so they asked me to come in and optimise their processes. Learned a lot about orthopaedic surgery in the process.'

Sofia's eyebrows rose at that piece of information. 'I didn't know that about you.'

'There are probably a lot of things you don't know about me.' The chuckle that underpinned his response was gentle, meant to tease her more than anything else. But it struck at a place of insecurity inside her chest. She really didn't know all that much about him—other than she simply couldn't resist him.

Whenever they spoke, they would mostly have clashing professional opinions, or argue about some triviality in the hospital. Those arguments stopped when they stepped into the OR, where they became one team with one mind as they worked on saving the patients under their care.

She had shared some things about her past, but he hadn't. Not only that, but he had made it a point to mention that he *wouldn't* share anything personal. So the disappointment pooling in the pit of her stomach was out of place.

Would he even tell her what triggered his panic attacks? Sofia had spoken about herself, had even shared with him that she hadn't ever had a casual affair. He'd listened to her and taken the time to understand where her nervous energy had come from so he could find a solution for it. Wasn't it strange that she didn't know anything about his past or what had brought him here?

'All the blood supplies are cut off. We are ready to remove the spleen,' Yasmine said, and Sofia handed over the aspirator as she looked around the surgical field.

'Good job,' she said with a smile, then began across the patient but paused when Carlos held out a plastic bag. She took it from him and fitted it over the spleen, then nodded to the junior surgeon to start cutting.

Her eyes flittered back toward Carlos, who was observing the surgery without making a sound or even moving his face. Nothing about the situation was unusual or should make her feel as nervous as she did. Yet her nerves were frayed, and she wondered not for the first time what she'd got herself into. This whole affair was so far away from 'playing it safe' that she couldn't even see the boundaries. And even though she knew that, Sofia didn't want to quit. With all her failed relationships, this one somehow felt for the first time like she was in control—like Carlos knew exactly what she needed from a man.

She just couldn't get emotionally invested in him. He was leaving Buenos Aires in less than two weeks. They had agreed this was just for fun. Instead of thinking that Carlos was the one she needed, Sofia had to remind herself that what Carlos had *shown* her was what she needed. It had nothing to do with him personally.

There was something oddly calming about postsurgery silence. After they removed the spleen, they had finished up setting the screws and the rod for the broken leg, then checked for other sources of bleeding before closing the patient up. Any follow-up surgeries would be handled by the specialists. A flurry of motion filled the OR as they prepped for patient transport. Then the team exited—leaving the senior surgeons behind as they were having a quiet conversation.

The second the door closed and cut them off from the outside world, something in Carlos's face changed. As if he was dropping some mask he forced himself to keep on in front of junior staff.

'This was a bad break. I can't even imagine what the accident must have been like,' Carlos said as they walked over to the bin to throw away their surgical gowns. Then they entered the scrub room, each of them stepping to a sink and quickly washing potential contamination off their hands and arms.

'All things considered, Manny pulled through. If the broken leg doesn't need any more surgery, then I think he's lucky to just lose his spleen. Orthopaedics will have to see if he needs anything else after some physical therapy,' Sofia replied.

She gave him a sidelong glance, her eyes narrowing as she tried to unravel his expression. The calm exterior he usually projected showed some fine lines—as if the pressure on him was increasing. Was she right to think that traffic accidents bothered him? Had something happened in his past—maybe a bad surgery—that he carried around with him?

Shutting off the water, Sofia turned sideways to face him. She hardly knew anything about Carlos, and even though he'd warned her he didn't do personal questions, she resolved to ask some, anyway. They had already established the casual nature of their affair. What harm could a few questions do?

'You're originally from Brazil, right?' she asked, earning herself a raised eyebrow from him.

'Did you…read my biography somewhere?' His lips twitched in an amused smile that smoothed away the lines of worry. Sofia's heart squeezed at the sight. That was a good reaction to what might be considered a personal question.

'Just curious about what made you leave your country. My whole family is here in the city, and even though I don't see them often because I'm usually too busy working, I can rely on them the same way they know they can rely on me.'

Something intangible fluttered over his expression

as she mentioned her family. A myriad of emotions, as if he wasn't sure what to think or feel. When it settled down, she could see a faint curiosity in his eyes.

'I take it none of them are doctors?' he asked, and Sofia shook her head.

'No, so of course they are very proud of me. I'm the only one in my family, which means any larger family gathering just turns into clinic hours.' Though she liked to complain about it, it didn't bother her all that much. Because she had dedicated her adult life to her career, her parents and her brother had been the only ones to stick it out with her. They didn't complain when they didn't see her for weeks on end because they understood how important this was to her. It was this kind of understanding and patience she thought she had found with Daniel, only to be proved wrong.

'What do they do?' The spark of curiosity in his eyes turned brighter, like he was enjoying himself a bit more than a minute ago. Another hopeful sign that she maybe could also learn a bit more about him.

'They run a horticultural farm mostly focused on local demands. They attend the farmer's markets in their area and sell to smaller *minimercados*,' she said, the fond memories she had of the tiny grocery stores in her old neighbourhood making her smile.

'And your parents run the entire operation by themselves?' he asked, and raised his eyebrows when she nodded.

'Them and my older brother and his wife. They live on the land they cultivate—about an hour's drive from here. Another reason why I don't get to visit often. Their schedules are just as hectic as mine since they grow different vegetables and fruits all throughout the year.'

A stab of guilt poked at her, a familiar sensation at this point. She knew she should make more time for her family, but with her career being in the place it was, she had to put everything into it if she wanted to claim the success she was dreaming of. At least her family understood that she had to give up other things to achieve what she'd set out to do.

Carlos stepped closer, putting a hand on her upper arm and giving it an affectionate squeeze. 'That sounds like a hard life for them.'

'It is,' Sofia said with a nod. 'That's why the thought of leaving Buenos Aires has never crossed my mind. When things are tight, I help them out. Like when they need new equipment, or when they can't afford to repair one of the cars. They supported me throughout med school, and now it's on me to give back.'

He stood close enough that she had to tilt her head back to look up at him. The touch of something ethereal had returned in his gaze, an intangible sensation that skipped the short distance between them and crawled down her spine. 'They're lucky to have you,' he murmured.

'You don't have anyone waiting for you back in Brazil?' she asked cautiously.

'No,' he said. Then his hand came up to her face, cupping her cheek.

'No? No family or friends waiting to hear about your adventures abroad?' How could this man be all alone? Sure, they had clashed during their initial meetings—they still did, their attraction to each other not having changed that. But, despite his sometimes abrasive nature, Carlos was inherently a kind man.

His thumb traced the curve of her cheekbone, sweeping up and down. Its arc slowed ever so slightly when he said, 'No one.'

There was a tremor in his voice. It was faint, barely there and easily missed if they weren't standing so close together, their breaths mingling. Then, before she could ask the next question building in her mind, Carlos bent down and slid his mouth over hers—and like the times before, she melted against him with a sigh.

His tongue darted over her lips, begging for entry, and she more than willingly yielded. With one simple touch, he had her on edge again already, forgetting who she was and what they had been talking about just a minute ago.

Dear God, how was this man so intoxicating? There was nothing in her life she could compare this connection to because they all faded away in comparison. Carlos was like a warm breeze passing through her, leaving her more energised each time he touched her—and also leaving behind a strange sense of emptiness whenever he left.

Control was slipping out of her grasp as Carlos's lips left hers, trailing down her neck. 'Will you have drinks with me tonight?' he whispered against her skin, the gravel in his voice drawing her attention.

'That depends... Did you go shopping?' Their no-strings-attached agreement was about sex, and even though a part of her wanted to have drinks with him simply to enjoy his company, her guarded heart demanded she enforce the boundaries they had set. There had to be a purpose behind their meetings or they would risk getting too close. The lines were already blurring, their attraction burning so fiercely that they couldn't keep their hands off each other at work.

His chuckle rumbled through the room, enveloping her with tendrils of gentle warmth. 'I did.'

'Good. It would have been a bit awkward if we had to explain to the pharmacist here why two trauma surgeons needed some condoms,' she replied, then took a step backwards, peeling herself out of his arms. 'You have a place in mind?'

'I do.' His eyes raked over her, tempting her to step closer again. But something about him caught her attention.

'You're a hard person to get to know, Carlos,' she said, sliding further away from him when he tilted his head, confusion blooming on his face. Throughout this conversation, he hadn't really answered a single thing about himself but had somehow got her to talk about her family.

But why would her words confuse him if his secrecy was by design?

Neither of them got to say anything to follow up her statement. The doors swung open and one of the junior doctors stepped in, freezing in his steps when he noticed two of his superiors just standing in the room looking at each other.

Sofia took that as her queue to leave and made a mental note to no longer get caught up with Carlos when they were at the hospital. This was the second time today that someone had almost walked in on them.

'I'll see you later, Dr Cabrera. Just text me the details,' she said, then squeezed past the other person to leave the scrub room.

CHAPTER EIGHT

YOU'RE A HARD person to get to know, Carlos.

The words wove themselves through his consciousness throughout the rest of the day, popping back up in between seeing patients in the ICU and taking care of some consultations in the ER. Carlos didn't understand what exactly was bringing his attention back to Sofia's statement, but something was, and the more he rolled it around in his head, the less he understood.

It had sounded like an accusation, and the strange thing was that he could understand that—despite him saying that he wouldn't answer any questions about himself. A few days ago, that had seemed like a reasonable boundary, but he could understand what it looked like from Sofia's standpoint. She had learned nothing about him through many of their conversations, while he treasured the morsels of knowledge he had gathered from her.

Carlos wasn't sure he knew how to do casual, and his need to know more about her showed that. Yet when she had turned the questions around to him, the walls had pressed in on him, and he'd shut down, not letting her see anything on the surface and definitely nothing further below.

He would be lying if he said that he hadn't enjoyed

hearing about the farm her parents ran. When she had shared that with him, a thousand more questions had popped up in his head, and he'd shoved them all down.

But then she had asked who was waiting for him in Brazil, and it had taken everything in him not to close down instantly. The defence mechanism inside of him relating to anything connected to Rosa was strong and easily triggered without people even knowing it. That was the reason why he kept people at arm's length since becoming a widower.

How would these people react if they knew he'd been the one responsible for the accident that had killed his wife? Neither the police nor the insurance company could find any fault in his behaviour, but Carlos knew better. He had promised to protect Rosa for the rest of her life on the day of their wedding. He had failed at that, and now she was gone.

With a sigh, Carlos reached for his drink and took a sip before setting it down on the bar again, his eyes flittering to the entrance before looking at the clock on his phone. If he knew anything about Sofia and her preference for rules, she would walk through those doors the moment the minute ticked over to when they had agreed to meet.

He kept his eyes on the phone, staring at the number until it finally moved. Then he looked up. Not a heartbeat later, Sofia walked through the doors. His jaw tightened—along with something further down—when he watched her approach him. The black dress she'd chosen hugged every single curve with such perfection that he had to assume someone had made this dress specifically for her. The neckline dipped down, accentuating the slight swell of her breasts. The skirt of the dress fell down to her feet, but a slit almost all the way up to the top of her hip revealed her thigh with every other step.

She was a vision of femininity, walking towards him as if there were clouds under her feet—almost floating. Effortless.

Her appearance had him staring at her in stunned silence until she came to a stop in front of him, a small smile curling her lips.

'Is this seat taken?' she asked, and the blush glowing beneath her skin told him how much effort she had put into this line—that she was trying to flirt with him.

He stood up, laying his hand on her hip and savouring the feel of the silky fabric underneath his fingertips. His eyes dipped down to her neckline of their own accord, and only when Sofia chuckled did he look back up.

'None of the words in my mind are anywhere near appropriate to say,' he told her with a smirk, and male satisfaction rushed through his veins when the blush on her cheeks intensified.

'Is that a line you found works particularly well with women?' she asked tartly as she took her seat next to his.

'I wouldn't know. You're the first one to hear these words.' Something about the way she raised her eyebrows at him with widened eyes bothered him, though he couldn't quite pin it down. It was the same look she had given him when he'd told her he didn't have any protection with him. Like that idea was somehow ridiculous, because how could he possibly not?

He shook off the thought when the bartender stepped up to the bar. 'What can I get you?'

'Oh.' Sofia looked at Carlos's glass, then let her gaze run along the shelves before stopping at a bottle he couldn't see. 'Could you make me a Clarito?'

The bartender smiled with a nod, then went on to pour gin, vermouth, and some orange bitters into a glass. The clinking of ice mixed with the fast-paced music and the fragments of conversation from other patrons. It was that perfect backdrop of sound that had Carlos coming back here often enough. With so much going on around him, it was easy to let go and just follow his strands of thoughts wherever they might lead him. Even though he wasn't much of a drinker, this space had become a safe haven for him in Buenos Aires.

And now he was staring at Sofia, who he had willingly invited into this space.

'What's a Clarito?' he asked, and followed her gaze to watch as the bartender put a martini glass on the counter and began pouring the liquid into it. When he was happy with how the twist of lemon zest sat inside the glass, he pushed it over to Sofia.

'It's a popular cocktail around here, and one of the few drinks I like,' she said, then raised her glass at him.

Carlos obliged with a smile, clinking their glasses together and then taking a sip of his own drink. 'Don't drink much?'

She shook her head as she put the glass down. 'When would I ever have time to go out? Especially now, with you stealing all my surgeries if I'm not careful.'

'I believe I explained myself about that *and* took appropriate steps to remedy it. I'm hardly in surgery any more.' He leaned into the joke she had started, mounting his mock defence.

Sofia laughed, and something inside his chest loosened at that sound. A soothing warmth bloomed, sending soft shivers down his body. 'Yes, but you replaced surgery with following me around to find opportunities to make out with me. I'm not sure that's more appropriate.'

The smile tugging on his lips was one suffused with the energy he'd been battling all day whenever he'd seen her around the hospital. She wasn't wrong about his intentions for her. But he still shrugged as he said, 'I can stop if you want.'

'No!' The word came from her lips way too fast. As she, too, realised this, the blush that bloomed on her cheeks was exquisite. Carlos almost had to bite his fist to keep himself from hauling her into his arms.

'Eh... I mean... I don't *want* you to stop, but—'

This time, he couldn't hold himself back. He got off the barstool and stepped into the V of her legs, forcing her to look up at him. 'Good. Not touching you costs me more willpower than I can muster. You're all I've been thinking about.'

Carlos observed her throat flutter as she swallowed, her uneven breaths skittering across his face. 'I still don't think it's smart to do these things in the hospital,' she said hoarsely, and he nodded.

'I agree. Not the best look were we to get caught, and I don't want to leave you alone with the fallout when I end up leaving.' Though kissing her had been the highlight of his day at work, filling him with a spark he hadn't sensed inside of him in many years. Work had become his ultimate distraction in life, letting him forget about the things weighing him down. Now he was excited again, and not just to see Sofia and do all the things he dreamt of doing to her. He also appreciated the challenge she brought to each case they worked together, the stubbornness and willingness to fight for what she believed was the right approach. She was drop-dead gorgeous, and she also wasn't afraid to clash with him and draw the best out of him as a result.

'It's been hard not being all over you today,' Carlos said, his hand coming to rest on her thigh.

Sofia smiled at that. 'Well… You kind of were.'

He blinked at her in surprise. Then his smile broadened into a grin as she reinforced the thoughts he'd just had without even knowing about them.

'It's not often I meet someone who is so eager to fight me every step of the way. Whenever I go to a new hospital, there are always people who dislike the change, but they usually get in line when their chief of surgery tells them to. Not you, though.' Affection exploded in the pit of his stomach when he said the last words.

Her face glowed. He wasn't sure if it was due to what he said or because of how close his thumb was to her inner thigh. 'I'm not challenging you because I dislike change. The things you taught everyone are important and good improvements to our overall service quality. You just don't have to be such a jerk about it.'

Her eyes widened, as if she hadn't meant to say that and it had just slipped out. 'What I meant—' she began, but then a laugh burst out of his mouth, deep and jovial.

'I get it. Our first few meetings weren't exactly smooth sailing, and I may have been harder on you that I needed to be.' He remembered the steel in his voice when he had clashed with her in the OR. That much hadn't changed about them, though now he realised their tension might have come from this unexpected place he found himself in with her.

'Who knew this is what was hiding underneath the gruff exterior?' She looked up at him teasingly through her lashes, her golden-flecked brown eyes filled with a twinkle that shot straight through him. This wasn't a tone he was used to from her.

'Are you flirting with me?' he asked, the smile on his lips growing when her eyes widened.

'You can see what I mean now when I said I've never done anything casual. I can't even be subtle about my flirting attempts.' She reached for her glass, taking a sip. When she put it back down, Carlos leaned in and brushed a kiss onto her lips, tasting the leftover Clarito on them.

'We don't have to do anything you don't want, you know?' he said, even though his stomach sank at the thought that they could part ways like this.

The speed with which Sofia shook her head put him at ease. 'I definitely want to be here. It's just that…' She paused, mulling over her words. 'It may sound stupid, but I put so much effort into my career and being the best at it that "being the best" became my standard. So if I'm in situations that are outside of my expertise or don't follow a path I can read up on, then I become hesitant.'

Carlos couldn't help but smile. The hyper-competitiveness of surgeons in general was a reason why it was sometimes much harder for him to teach them. Trying new things led to errors, and they were taught to avoid mistakes or lives could be lost. 'Going outside your comfort zone is the only way to push yourself towards being "the best." Consider this an opportunity to do that,' he said. When the beats of a familiar song hit his ear, an idea struck him.

'Do you know how to dance?' As he asked the question, some patrons sitting at the tables of the bar got to their feet.

A line appeared between Sofia's brows. 'Dance? Like what? Samba?'

'Yes, or more specifically—tango. It's the dance of your people.'

'Maybe as a child, but I don't remember any of it...' There was a hesitation after her words, like she wanted to ask why, but she already knew.

Carlos grinned at that. 'Well, then consider this another way to challenge your comfort zone,' he said, before pulling her up on her feet and leading her to where other patrons were already swaying together.

Of course Carlos knew how to dance. Because apparently there wasn't a single thing on this planet this man didn't excel at. She saw the challenge in his eyes as he grabbed her hand while placing his other one on the small of her back, drawing her closer until their breaths mingled.

'Listen to the music, feel the rhythm of my body and let me guide you,' he said as he looked down at her, the mischievous spark in his eyes only steeling her resolve. She might not know a single thing about tango, but she knew how to approach a challenge.

The first few steps were stiff, wound tight by the concentration she put into every move, trying her best to mirror what Carlos was showing her. His own steps were smooth, flowing from one position to the next while continuing his guidance with soft brushes of his hand against her back or his thigh against hers.

His fluidity didn't surprise her, not after what she'd observed at the capoeira gym. Anticipation for this evening had been slowly building inside of her, but with him close to her now—their movements and glances intimate—it had reached a fever pitch. She couldn't remember the last time she had felt this way, need and desire so tightly coiled in her chest that all she could focus on was where his body connected with hers.

The music flowed through the air, caressing her ear and moving along her body in smooth and sensual beats, and each step became easier to follow until Carlos was swinging her around, his guidance keeping her moving along with him.

'Capoeira and tango. How did you get into dancing?' she asked when she felt confident enough in their rhythm to let some of her focus go into a conversation.

'Capoeira was big in the neighbourhood I grew up in. Every afternoon when I'd get back from school, there would be music filling the streets as people grabbed their drums and guitars to join the *roda*—the circle of people, if you remember.'

Sofia nodded, the memory feeling so far away already. Their attraction to each other really had been brewing underneath the surface if it had boiled over so fast after they'd admitted to it. 'People would just stand in circles on the street and fight each other?'

The chuckle coming from Carlos shot down her spine and settled in an aching pinch in the pit of her stomach. 'We don't fight. The art of capoeira is *avoiding* any direct hits. Sure, we use kicks and punches, but they're meant to form a game, challenging your partner into quick thinking and flexibility,' he explained as he pulled her closer to him. 'It's way more a dance than a fight.'

Sofia's skin heated when his voice dropped low. 'I didn't even know it existed, or that there was a whole gym dedicated to it.'

'You never seen them performing it at Carnival?' he asked, and raised his eyebrows when she shook her head.

'Carnival is prime time for injuries and accidents,

so the most I get to enjoy Carnival is when colourful costumed people come into the OR with light injuries.' Her longest shifts usually happened around that time, as the city let loose for a few days. 'Wait, does that mean you're performing next weekend?'

A smile appeared on her lips when he nodded. 'My contract is wrapping up just before Carnival starts, so I should be able to enjoy it.'

His contract? Even though his eventual departure from Hospital General de Buenos Aires had been one of the primary motivators for her to agree to this affair, she didn't realise she'd been ignoring how close he actually was to leaving. Was there enough time to finally pierce through his shell? Was there even a reason to do it? He had rebuffed any of her attempts to ask even simple questions about his private life. Someone less stubborn than her would take the hint and leave it be. But Sofia hadn't got to where she was now by *not* persisting when things got difficult. Maybe it was all about how she asked him the questions.

'And tango? Did capoeira teach you that you like dancing?'

Carlos hesitated. His step didn't falter, and they were still moving with the beat of the music, his attentive guidance never stopping. But she could see that behind his eyes, where a fire was still burning, there was now a flutter. He was making a decision, only she couldn't even guess what it was. There were much more probing questions clinging to her lips, yet somehow she had uncovered something deep with the question about tango.

He looked at her, the flame in those dark eyes flickering. Then he raised his gaze to look at a point behind her. His throat worked, and then he said, 'My late wife enjoyed dancing.'

The music faded away, and it took Sofia a moment to notice the songs were changing—because the piece of information he'd just dropped in front of her had all her senses occupied. She stared at him wide-eyed. Then her attention was caught by the dancers around them. Some of them were shuffling away as the tempo of the new song was slower. Others pulled each other close, and gentle whispers filled the air with a strange sense of intimacy.

'Oh, Carlos… I'm so—' He shook his head, interrupting her, and when he looked back down, there was a smile on his face. A less bright version of the one she'd seen on him just a few moments ago. But she understood what he was trying to tell her. He'd wanted her to have this information about him—wanted to forge that connection despite his initial insistence that he wouldn't. But he was not open to talking about it any more than he already had.

His arms tightened around her waist, pulling her closer as they swayed to the slow beat of a bossa nova song, and Sofia rested her head on his chest—feeling close to him in this moment. She should not feel as elated about him sharing something personal about him as she was right now. That wasn't part of the plan, and it didn't fit into the rules they had established around their fling. This was supposed to be physical in nature only. But after trying for so long, she'd finally found a way past his walls. How could she step back from him when he had let her in?

'It was some time ago now. I wanted you to know that the womanising version of me you have in your head doesn't actually exist. I haven't…' He stopped himself, and Sofia leaned in more when his flat palms caressed up and down her back. 'What I mean to say is—this is special to me.'

Sofia's heart beat so fast, she was sure if she opened her mouth it would leap right out. Was that his way of saying he didn't usually do casual, either? Or was it that he didn't want this to be *just* casual sex? The meaning of Carlos suddenly opening up to her wasn't clear to her, but the words to ask the important question wouldn't form in her head. This was again a place unfamiliar to her.

His hands reached the top of her back, his fingers grazing over the exposed skin there and leaving a trail of small fires in their wake.

'Does your offer to show me some capoeira moves still stand?' she asked, letting the things he had shared with her sit between them in companionable silence. She didn't know how to talk about it or what to say, but she knew she didn't want to let their personal connection that went beyond the physical disappear just yet. And the first thing popping into her mind when thinking about the things Carlos cared about was capoeira.

His fingers stalled for a fraction of a second before they resumed their caress. 'Sure, but you won't be able to move in this dress. How about we continue this at my place?'

CHAPTER NINE

CARLOS WAITED FOR about a second between stepping out of the elevator and into the penthouse with Sofia and hauling her into his arms, into a deep kiss. The struggle to keep his hands off her all day had been so much more exhausting than he could have imagined. He was drawn to her whenever he saw her, and no matter how much he sated his hunger with her, it kept coming back with an unreal fierceness.

It was all because of this moment that had been in the making for a while. That was what he told himself as his tongue delved into her mouth, meeting her eagerness stroke for stroke. There was something intangible, inexplicable to his burning desire. After such a long absence from his life, the resurgence of it took Carlos aback, and he didn't know what to make of it. If someone had asked him just last month if he had any interest in being with a woman, his answer would have been no. His job was all he cared about, his career what he poured all of his attention into.

Then Sofia had entered his life like the whirlwind she was. Her challenges to his work had thrown him off guard, leaving a tiny gap for her to nestle into. Now she was in his brain, had taken up residence there as if he hadn't guarded himself from such intrusions for the last five years. What threw him off even more than her having got as close to him as she had was his comfort amidst all of it. In his mind he knew he should retreat, that he shouldn't have brought her here in the first place.

He had told her about Rosa. Even tiny morsels of information about his late wife remained under lock and key from everyone, and he wasn't sure what had happened there. It didn't slip out. No, when she'd asked that question, he had reached for his basket of excuses, coming up with one explanation or another why he knew how to dance tango. But something inside of him had insisted on telling her the truth, on giving her this one piece of information in return for all the things she had already shared about herself. For the role she had played in his healing journey—whether she knew it or not.

'Is this how you start your lessons with everyone?' Sofia huffed between heated kisses, drawing a chuckle from him.

'No, this is just for you,' he replied, and sensed in the depth of his chest how much he meant exactly those words. This was not just for her—it was *only* for her. In a life he had designed to be fleeting, she had found a way to make herself far more permanent than anyone else he'd met.

Her lips were swollen already, her breath coming out quickly and sliding over his skin in the sensual promise of what tonight would be.

'What makes me so special to deserve all of your attention?' She tried to hide the edge in her tone, but Carlos picked up on it. He gripped her hips and held her away from him so he could look at her.

'Whoever didn't make you feel special in the past was a fool, Sofia,' he said, delighting as her lips fell open a bit more. 'For the last few weeks, you have been challenging me at every turn, forcing me to up my game and refine my methods.'

He paused as more information about himself threatened to spill out of his mouth. Her words echoed in his mind. He *was* a hard man to get to know, and he had done that on purpose. What if people learned too much about him? What if they realised he was a highly regarded trauma surgeon who found it incredibly traumatic to treat patients involved in a car accident? His reputation was on the line.

But Sofia hadn't hesitated—and she had kept his confidence without him having to ask. She had discovered this one thing about him by mistake. Whatever else she'd learned about him, Carlos wanted it to come from him.

'You saw me at my worst when everyone only knows me as this fixer—coming into hospitals and upping everyone's game. It's disruptive, but in the end everyone walks away better. Stronger. Some would have doubted my abilities after seeing me like that.' Though their conversation grew serious, Carlos didn't let her forget the purpose of her visit to his flat. While he spoke, he traced his hands up and down her sides, brushing over the exposed skin of her arms and raising the hair along them.

Sofia's eyes fluttered closed for a few breaths. When she opened them again, fire lit them, and Carlos's knees almost gave out from underneath him.

'I understand what this line of work can do to you,' was all she said to his confession, and somehow Carlos knew that simple acknowledgement to be enough.

Because if any other doctor had told him that specific surgeries or situations triggered a stress response, he knew he wouldn't think less of them but rather work on whatever had brought it forth.

But his case was different. He was directly responsible for Rosa's death. No matter who else was on the road that night, he had been behind the wheel.

Carlos pushed those thoughts away, willing himself to stay present in the moment. Negotiating his complex feelings around past mistakes was his daily struggle, but it eased when he could distract himself. Work had served him as a faithful diversion, but Sofia… She was something else entirely.

His hands paused on her hips, and he grabbed her, spinning her around so she was with her front against the wall. 'You always want to have your feet grounded before you perform any move,' he said as he squatted down to slide her feet out of her shoes.

When he came back up, his hands slid underneath her dress, caressing her naked skin. 'You want to be as unrestricted as possible,' he continued as he found the zipper of her dress, pulling it down and peeling her dress away.

His mouth went dry. She was naked underneath.

'Unrestricted?' she asked, turning around with a lazy smile that almost brought him to his knees.

Her hand came to rest on his chest. As she traced over him, she undid every button of his shirt until it hung open. He wasn't sure whether he had picked up hesitation or inexperience from her last time. Something had had her tense and unable to let go until they had talked through it.

None of that was present today. No, she looked at him with the sensual smile of a siren, luring him in with the song of her swaying hips as she took a step backwards.

Carlos shrugged off his shirt, then grabbed Sofia with hungry hands, his mouth coming down on hers as he pushed her against the wall. She writhed against him, her legs circling around him and pressing against his erection. The groan loosened from his throat came from an ancient place that he hadn't accessed or even looked at in the last five years.

He wrapped his arms around her waist as he pushed off the wall, carrying her to the bedroom. Sofia let out a yelp when he deposited her on the bed, the sound driving through him like a hot spear.

Carlos kicked off his shoes and hissed when he felt Sofia's hands pull at his waistband, unbuttoning his trousers and pushing them down his legs—along with his underwear. Where they had moved at a leisurely pace last time, today was dictated by urgency, their need running too hot to leave room for delicacy or patience.

Stepping out of his trousers, he turned around and grabbed a condom from the pack he'd bought last night after Sofia had left, safely stashed away in his nightstand. His hand trembled as he rolled it down his shaft—from need as much as from nerves.

Being with Sofia—getting to feel her all around him—had been an obsession in his mind ever since the fantasy had become a real possibility. Once he crossed this boundary, he'd never be able to go back again. The importance of this moment thundered through him, mingling with the need she kindled in him.

'You okay?' she asked, propped up on her elbows and looking at him.

His eyes raked over her, taking in every dip, every curve of her body. Her dark nipples were peaked, her breasts rising and falling with her rapid breathing, and he could already see the anticipation between her legs. But what caught his attention this time was how her hair fanned out behind her in a thick curtain of different shades of dark all mixing.

'I don't think I've ever seen you with your hair down,' he said gruffly, and her eyes widened.

The air between them grew intimate, the spark bouncing back and forth between them as Carlos put one knee on the bed and pushed forward. Sofia moaned when his weight settled between her thighs.

A tremble shook Carlos's body. 'You test my restraint, Sofia,' he rasped against the skin between her breasts.

'You showed supreme restraint last time. Do we really need to exercise it again today?' Her mind was filled with the need for Carlos, and nothing else had space in it. What had happened between them in the bar was gone, their conversations trivial in comparison to the desire rising within her. This moment had been in the making for so long... To feel him now teasing her right where she wanted him more than anything else was too much.

'I'm not a selfish lover, *corazón*.' He dipped his head low, sucked one of her nipples into his mouth, and swirled his tongue around it.

Her back left the bed as she bowed into his touch, a tremble shaking her muscles one by one.

'It's not selfish if I'm asking for it,' she replied in a voice barely above a whisper.

'Mmm...' His voice vibrated onto her skin as he nipped at her other breast. She wasn't sure if the sound was savouring or contemplative—and she didn't have any space in her brain left to think about that when the pressure of his manhood nudged against her entrance.

'You're right. Maybe I am a selfish lover, after all,' he said when he came back up to her face, their noses touching as he looked at her. 'You are such perfection that it's hard to choose where to touch when each spot is so enticing.'

Even though they were naked in each other's arms, and had even been intimate with each other, his words brought heat to her cheeks. No one had ever said anything that made her feel this desirable.

'Carlos…' His name was a plea on her lips. Urgency wound her core tight, and she raised her hips, pressing against where she could feel him.

Above her, Carlos hissed, but then—finally and, oh, so slowly—the pressure at her entrance increased as he sunk into her with a deep groan that rumbled through her. Her muscles tensed, her body adjusting around him until the initial discomfort blurred away into the pleasurable sensation of their bodies combined.

Carlos moved his hips, and she moved with him, never taking her eyes off him. Their breaths mingled, became one, as they got closer to the edge together. When he slipped his hand between them to caress her, the little fires smouldering underneath the surface accelerated into a wildfire across her entire body.

A moan tore from her lips as her hips twitched, her muscles contracting when she reached her climax. Carlos kept moving in her, his pleasure mounting with each shortened breath. A strangled sound left his throat, one that sounded like her name. Then he slid his mouth over hers, drawing her into a long kiss filled with the tension and release they had worked up and found together in this moment.

A warm sensation trickled down her back and roused Sofia from her sleep. Still groggy and half-veiled in slumber, she tried to focus and figure out what woke her—until the memories of the night came back to her.

Carlos ran his fingers up and down her spine, stopping at her shoulder blade now and then before resuming their lazy caress. She sighed when the sensation turned from surprising to pleasant, and she leaned into the gentle touch. A part of her wanted to drift back to sleep, but he might have woken her for a reason. Was it time to leave already?

'I'm sorry I woke you up. Go back to sleep, sweetheart,' he whispered before she could ask—once again anticipating her needs.

'But then I'll miss how good this feels,' she replied as another warm shower of pleasure trickled through her.

'Oh, yeah? You like this?' His voice came closer as he shifted on the bed, and then his breath danced over her skin as he leaned closer. His hand drifted up to her shoulder and his mouth followed, feathering light kisses onto her skin.

She moaned her agreement, her head sinking back into the pillow. Her toes curled at the gentle touch, prompting her muscles to tense in a short stretch before going limp in his arms.

Every stretch of skin he touched came alive under his fingers, as if he could direct liquid flame through her body at his pleasure. The connection was explosive, and Sofia caught herself fantasising more than once about what it would be like to let herself slide down into the feelings he evoked in her. Would it be such a bad thing? She knew they were short-term, but keeping her guard up at every interaction with him was becoming more challenging—his skill at climbing her walls as impressive as everything else about him.

'I was trying to make out your tattoo in the bar last night,' he said against her skin, and Sofia realised why the path of his fingers had felt so familiar. 'The strand of DNA was just visible whenever we spun around, but I had no idea it turned into...this.'

His hands trailed downwards again, sweeping over her lower back. Her tattoo began there. A system of roots, delicately woven together, narrowed into a tree trunk that swept up her spine. Where branches and leaves would normally sprout out were helixes of DNA winding together.

Sofia tensed at the mention of her tattoo—an involuntary reaction from her that revealed far more than she intended. And by the way his hand stopped instantly, she knew he had picked up on it, too.

'You want me to stop?' he asked, and her heart softened at the concern lacing his voice.

'No, it's not that. It's...' She hesitated when the words formed in her head, unsure if she should say them. The warmth of his body drifted towards her, his touch so reassuring that she couldn't remember why she even *wanted* to be guarded.

'My ex didn't like the tattoo. He thought I had ruined my skin by getting it, and... I don't know why, but it just stuck with me.' She tensed again, readying herself to hear more negative feedback about her tattoo. Had Daniel been right? Was it really that ugly?

Warm breath teased her skin as Carlos exhaled behind her. He was quiet for a few heartbeats. Then she gasped as his hand pressed into her lower back.

'The one you mentioned yesterday?' he asked, his fingers tracing each individual root at the base of her spine.

'What?' Sofia wasn't sure if she didn't understand the question or if his caresses had her in a daze.

'Last week, when we were talking about what we wanted, you said you didn't have any experience in casual relationships, and you mentioned Daniel. He said that to you about your tattoo?'

She nodded, fighting the discomfort rising inside her. The second her ex's name had left her lips, she had regretted it. Only for him to come up again. Would she ever be rid of his looming shadow? 'Yes, that was him.'

Behind her, Carlos kept the steady pace of his hand up and down her back, his touch calming while his silence ratcheted up the tension inside of her. He hadn't said if *he* liked the tattoo—not that it mattered. He would only be a fleeting presence in her life, and what she should do was to take the pleasure he offered her and just enjoy it for what it was.

The sheets rustled when Carlos pulled her closer, tangling their legs. 'What else has he done that still lingers with you?'

Sofia paused, both to consider and to soak up the warmth his touch brought her. Should she really talk about Daniel again? Sharing something like that didn't fit into her understanding of a casual relationship. It also violated their rule of no personal questions. A rule that they had already stepped on several times over.

'He…cheated on me. Found himself a new girlfriend while we were still together and posted about it on Instagram. A lot of my relationships failed because they

weren't able to cope with my unpredictable schedule—
which I can understand. But he was very understanding and so encouraging about my career. Never said a
single thing about needing me to be with him more. Not
until...' Sofia closed her eyes as the memories of their
confrontation came back to her. She braced herself for
the hurt they caused, for the nails digging into her heart.
But none of those usual sensations came. 'I confronted
him about his *other* girlfriend, and that's when he said
he wouldn't have cheated on me if I was around more.
That *I* had backed him into a corner where he had no
other choice but to get his needs filled outside our relationship.'

Carlos's hand stopped halfway up her back before he
slipped it around her waist and tightening as he pulled
her closer to him, until her back was flush against his
front. He nestled his face into her hair. Small fires exploded beneath her skin as he took a deep breath and
hummed low.

'Did you believe him?' It was a question Sofia had
heard before, though never in that tone. There wasn't
any pity or bewilderment in his voice. Just an invitation to talk if she wanted it. And for the first time, she
found that she *did* want to.

'For a while. It's much easier to find the fault in myself rather than admit that my partner could say such
hurtful things just out of spite. We had promised to be
truthful with each other, after all.' She shuddered when
Carlos pressed a soft kiss to the back of her neck. 'Now
I understand he acted out of pure selfishness, and that
he did me a kindness with his behaviour. Now I know
serious relationships can't survive the busy life of a
trauma surgeon.'

A twitch went through the hand splayed over her stomach, but when Sofia looked down, it continued to draw circles on her skin as if there hadn't been an interruption. The question formed on her lips, wanting to know what he thought, but his lips against her skin turned the words in her throat into a quiet gasp.

'I'm glad you realised he's an idiot. And not just because your tattoo is gorgeous, but because of everything else on top of that grave insult,' Carlos said with his face still buried in her hair and trailing his lips over her neck.

Sofia didn't have anything to add to that and let herself be engulfed by the sensation his touches raked through her body. Lightness washed over her, one she hadn't sensed in a long time. She had thought herself pathetic for trusting Daniel. Had avoided talking about him because of the fear of being judged.

Sharing that side of her with Carlos was easy. Simple. Like she was *meant* to share herself like that. And it was the yearning bubbling up inside her that urged her to ask the next question—despite them having agreed not to get personal.

'Was it different for you and your wife? She knew what she had signed up for?'

'Mmm…' His hum was low and vibrated through her skin into her body, where it settled in her core. 'My work could be a contentious topic from time to time— like any surgeon married to a non-physician.'

Sofia hadn't expected an answer—or the fireworks going off in the pit of her stomach at his words. Carlos was such a closed-off person, she'd begun combing through his sentences and anecdotes to trace them for any personal information. But he never slipped up, never said anything to hint at the life he'd lived before he left Brazil.

'But you must have found a solution to it?' she asked, though she wasn't sure why. A part of her wanted to know more about his marriage that had ended in his spouse's death.

'Sometimes,' he said, pressing a kiss behind her ear. His breath grazing over her cheek sent a shudder through her.

With each circle his fingers drew on her stomach, they wandered further down, and the closer they got to the apex of her thighs, the tighter the tension wound inside her. The curious part of her wanted him to stop and to talk more. But the part that hungered for him kept her tongue at bay, swallowing whatever questions she had as his hand reached between her thighs.

He had shared *something* with her, and even though Sofia knew she should be cautious, her heart beat faster at the tiny opening she'd spotted in his defences. Maybe with time they could figure something out. Because even though they had both agreed they would never have more than a casual encounter, Sofia didn't know how she could walk away from Carlos at the end of all this.

CHAPTER TEN

WAS IT POSSIBLE for life to feel the exact same way while being completely different? That thought followed Carlos around as he went about his days in the hospital. Because whether he wanted to admit it or not, Sofia had changed things inside of him—and the impact was far greater than he had anticipated.

Their desire for each other hadn't waned after their first night together, to the point where she had now spent most nights since then at his place, tangled up in his sheets. With that prospect to look forward to, it was easier to keep his hands to himself whenever he saw her at work. Easier, but not always possible. The explosiveness of their connection was unexpected and had made the time fly by. Now there were only a few days left on his contract before he would move on to his next assignment.

The affair wasn't supposed to change anything in his life, yet it had. With her gentle touch, her coaxing yet comforting words, and lips he wanted to feel on his skin for the rest of time, Sofia had pried open a door that had remained shut ever since Rosa passed away. But it wasn't the darkness of guilt and failed responsibilities flooding into him from that space. No, what came at him was light and warmth, the touch calm and soothing.

What that was supposed to mean, Carlos didn't know. The desire inside his chest was only growing with each passing day, with each stolen kiss they exchanged hidden away somewhere in the hospital—knowing that their final kiss was just around the corner.

Carlos would have served the length of his contract by the end of this week and was already busy writing up all of his documentation on the protocols he had implemented, as well as finishing some patient notes for a smooth handover. After that, the only other plan he had was a demonstration with the capoeira group during the Carnival days the following weekend.

'Cabrera.' He looked up from the computer screen when he heard his name and watched as Dr Sebastián Lopez approached him with a swift step. Though his gait was unhurried, something about him brought forth the feeling of unending tiredness. The bags underneath his eyes were more pronounced than when he'd last seen him some time ago.

'Chief Lopez,' he said with a nod, and got off his chair. 'Is everything okay?'

'Huh?' Sebastián came to a halt in front of his desk, his brows bunched as if he didn't understand his question.

'You look…tired.' Carlos surprised himself when he realised the concern in his voice was genuine. Had he ever cared about the staff in a hospital outside of what was professional courtesy? Because whatever was causing Sebastián sleepless nights most likely had nothing to do with work, or Carlos would have already heard about it.

'Oh… Yes. Since we're expecting triplets, Bella's pregnancy has been high-risk from the very start,' Se-

bastián said, glancing at his phone somewhat distract-
edly when it made a noise.

'It's been quite a while since my ob-gyn rotation during med school, but I remember triplets having a much
higher chance of preterm birth,' Carlos said in an effort
to sympathise with the man.

He let out another sigh, then put his phone away and
straightened back up. 'I'm trying to reduce her hours
even further, which she's not happy about. I'm not, either, because we're already short-staffed, and Bella is a
menace when she has too much time on her hands and
nothing to do with it.'

There was no harshness in his voice as he spoke of his
wife. Only a quiet joy that shone through his words, and
that sent a stab of guilt right into Carlos's chest. He remembered when he'd been the husband talking about his
wife in the same tone. The accident had taken away his
desire to talk about her. But as Sebastián kept speaking,
a different need bubbled up in his chest now—prompting
him to share something about himself, to keep building
the connection between him and the other man.

Only problem was that what he wanted to share was
about Sofia. About the time they had spent together.
How her rich hair glistened in the moonlight as they had
walked down the beach. That her smile lit the darker
corners of his existence.

He shouldn't want any of this. It wasn't right, and he
hadn't changed, either. He couldn't be the person someone like Sofia needed by her side—even though he knew
the previous men in her life hadn't been deserving of
her, either. Carlos wouldn't become one more on that
list. He refused to drag her down.

'Anyway, that's not what I came here to discuss.' Sebastián paused, a thoughtful expression crossing his face. 'But thank you for asking. I appreciate that. You've integrated well with the staff, and the whole trauma department really came to like you.'

Carlos blinked at that sudden admission, not expecting it in the least. Sure, he had been friendly enough with the staff, but not overly close. His aim was always to instil the knowledge he needed to pass on without trying or wanting to be liked by the staff. Normally, half of them wouldn't be keen on him because he was the harbinger of change, forcing things onto them they weren't ready for. And he didn't get to bond with the other half who did like him because he usually left before he could form any meaningful connections.

Somehow, Sofia had managed to move from one group to the other, but also find a way into his heart to form the connection he usually fought off so vehemently.

'I'm glad to hear that. They have been a pleasure to teach,' he said, and the warmth trickling through his veins signalled to him that he actually meant those words. It was rare that he came to like a place he worked at as much as this—there just wasn't usually enough time to form an opinion. But even if he stepped back from his infatuation with Sofia, he had met people in and around the OR he genuinely enjoyed working with. The junior doctors were eager to learn, the nurses kind and attentive, and the more senior surgeons had all put in the effort to get on board with his plan.

'So...' Sebastián paused, his phone beeping again. He took it out of his pocket, staring at whatever news he had received. 'Shoot, I have to go. With Bella working even less, I'm now doing three people's jobs. What I actually came here for was to make you an offer.'

Carlos raised his eyebrows at his words. Something unspooled in the pit of his stomach, a ribbon of cold that drew itself through the warmth radiating across his body. There was only one offer Sebastián could make him.

'You probably get asked this at every place you go, but I would be mad not to ask you to stay. You've done great things with the team. The average surgery time is measurably down, and morale didn't take a hit with the implemented changes. I've spoken to the chief of surgery, and we have a position open for a senior surgeon. It's yours if you want it.'

'Thank you. I…' He stopped himself before he could go on, sensing that habit was driving him rather than his own intentions. He had received similar offers before at quite a few hospitals over the years, and he had always turned them down. Staying bound to one place wasn't something he had envisioned for his life ever since Rosa passed away. What good was settling down somewhere when all he had to look back on were broken promises?

But he would not automatically refuse this position as well. 'I appreciate the offer. When do you need to know my answer?'

Sebastián was already turning away as he spoke. 'Your contract is up in a few days, so let me know by then if you want to continue. Call my office for the detailed package for this role. You won't regret hearing it,' he said over his shoulder before disappearing into the bustle of the ER and leaving him to his own thoughts.

A role here at Hospital General? His heart had lurched at those words, and within one blink, a world of possibilities had unfolded in front of him. One where he could have the quiet warmth blooming inside of him for good—because Sofia was right there next to him. Meeting her had reintroduced something to his life he hadn't had in so long, and a part of him urged him to grab it with both hands and never let go. Never let *her* go.

But it wasn't that simple—even if Sofia made him want to believe it was. She was the reason his rejection to the job offer hadn't crossed his lips, why he was taking his time to consider it, even though he knew the answer needed to be no at the end. Sofia *couldn't* be the reason why he stayed, because how could he put such a monumental decision on her alone? How could he tell her that she was the reason he was even having to think about the offer? They had agreed whatever happened between them wasn't going to be anything serious.

When they began their affair, she had said she wasn't looking for anything long-term. Sofia had even been the one to make it clear from the very start that she couldn't be more to him than that. He had agreed with her, and wasn't even sure if what was happening deep inside of him was because he was changing. Or if he simply yearned to use her light to cast away the shadows. His mind was clouded, and separating his feelings from the reality of their situation became more of a struggle. Maybe it was for the best that he was leaving soon. That way he would escape even if he had already sunk way too deep into his messy feelings for Sofia.

She didn't want to be with him. That was what he clung to. And she wouldn't in future either, especially not if she knew about his involvement in his wife's death. No one in their right mind would stay with someone like him, so why risk the rejection?

Carlos was a man of principle. He wouldn't go back on his word to her and let her know how he felt—even if the thought of ending it and leaving her shredded his heart into even tinier pieces. It would be for the best. She was looking for far more than his broken self could ever give her.

'All right, thank you for presenting the case, Yasmine. Since we are on day two post-splenectomy, we should start him on prophylactic antibiotics and monitor him for any signs of postoperative complications,' Sofia said as she and the junior doctors in her care finished their rounds on the patients that had been through surgery in the last three days.

'What specific complications do we need to be vigilant about?' Yasmine asked, her pen hovering over the tiny notebook she carried around with her.

'After this surgery and the kind of accident he's been in, watch for anything out of the ordinary, but particularly respiratory distress or any signs of infection,' she replied.

Motion in her peripheral view drew her attention, and a smile spread over her lips when Carlos stepped out of an exam room with his own junior doctors. Snippets of their conversation drifted towards her, too quiet for her to understand any of the words. But the low rumble of his voice was enough to fill her head with memories of last night. And the night before. And all the nights before that.

'Good. Please update the patient charts before going down to the ER. Get your work assignments from the charge nurse there.' The gaggle of junior doctors around her dissolved, and Sofia walked back to the empty nurses' station, her eyes on Carlos, who looked down at the pager clipped to his waistband before moving towards the ORs at a hurried pace. An emergency? Sofia looked down at her own pager, but it remained silent. Probably another surgeon requesting his help.

Their whole entanglement had evolved beyond her expectations in every way. What had been intended as a quick release, a no-strings-attached affair, had become a form of companionship that had sneaked up on Sofia over the last week. Because they hadn't just gone to his place to sleep with each other. No, she had taken him around Buenos Aires, showing him her favourite corners. At times, they would just be quiet together, their fingers intertwined as they enjoyed the moment for what it was.

Was this really how these affairs evolved? Or had they slipped into something else, something more? That thought had bubbled up in her mind whenever they went out, when they held hands or lay in comfortable silence. But she had shut it down each time, not daring to even think about changing the terms of what they had already agreed on.

Still, Sofia had to recognise what had happened during their time together. In the hurt place in her heart that her past relationships had left behind now grew the seed of a new flower, tiny and fragile, hardly daring to poke its head out. But it was there, making her feelings for Carlos as real as their connection was.

How could she have fallen for someone she didn't even know? He'd talked to her about his wife, shared a sliver of the pain he must have felt, but outside of that one glimmer, Carlos had remained closed off to her. Sure, he had shared more of his past, talking about the hospitals he'd been in and what countries he had visited. But did she *really* know anything about him outside of that?

Despite not being able to list lots of things she knew about him, the feeling of deep connection remained. Could knowing a person really be boiled down to how many facts you knew about them? Or was it enough that Sofia knew he preferred orthopaedic work over cardiothoracic during surgery, and that he took a smaller scalpel size even for bigger incisions?

Was that enough to fall in love with someone?

She shook her head to disperse the thoughts, then checked the time before going to the cafeteria. Lulls in her schedule were few and far between, and she took the opportunity of some downtime to feed herself.

When she spotted Isabella sitting by herself, she waved at her and smiled. Then she grabbed some food and sat down next to her friend. 'I haven't seen you around here in some time. Are you getting too big?' Sofia asked, her voice filled with affection for this woman.

Bella looked down at her, her hand patting her round belly. 'Sebastián won't let me do much while I carry these three around with me, and now he's teamed up with my ob-gyn to get me to do even more admin and less of the heavy work.'

Sofia laughed at the genuine indignation in the other woman's voice. 'How mean of them to give you sound medical advice and push you to take it.'

'I know they're right, but that doesn't change that I don't know what to do with myself outside of work.' Bella sighed, looking down at where her hand rested again. 'To be honest, I've not been feeling my best, either. But I would never admit that to Sebastián or he'll lock me up in the house. I'm still scheduled to help run the medical tent at Carnival, but I think I need to let Gabriel handle it. He says one of his childhood friends is a GP who's opening a clinic in the area, and she'll be there as well. But I hate to miss the action.'

'Don't remind me of the Carnival weekend. I already feel run down. The festivities always bring way too much traffic into the ER,' Sofia said, groaning at the thought. Though that wasn't the only thing filling her with unwanted dread. The beginning of Carnival also meant the end of her time with Carlos.

As if Bella read her mind, she narrowed her eyes. 'Are you looking forward to Dr Cabrera's final day?'

'What? No, why would you say that?'

'Sebastián said you didn't like him and that you two were constantly at each other's throats.' Bella shrugged when Sofia let out an indignant scoff.

'"At each other's throats" is overly dramatic, even for your husband. Since Carlos was so involved with teaching the junior doctors, I thought it only appropriate to give some feedback about his behaviour with them. I've known the juniors a lot longer than he has, after all,' she replied, and narrowed her eyes when a grin spread over her friend's lips. 'What?'

'You called him "Carlos",' she said, her eyes twinkling with delight.

Sofia willed her face to remain neutral as she replied, 'So? I call you and Sebastián by your first names.'

'Yeah, after we'd worked together for *two* years. And even then, we had to remind you regularly to be less formal with us. Cabrera has been here for how long? A month?' Isabella shook her head before levelling a more serious stare at her. 'Do you two intend to disclose your relationship to HR?'

This time Sofia couldn't keep her composure. Her eyes rounded at the casual tone Bella had employed. Not that she was wrong to ask the question. Technically they should have filled out a declaration, so the hospital was aware of any liabilities. Expect those rules were for *romantic* relationships, so she hadn't actually broken any rules. At least, that was the shred of truth she clung to.

'I'm not in a—'

'Stop right there, because there is no way you would lie to me like that,' Isabella interrupted her, holding up a hand in front of her.

Sofia bit down on her lower lip, glancing around her to make sure no one was paying too close attention to them, then leaned in to drop her voice to a quiet whisper. 'How could you possibly know that?'

'You two are way less subtle than you think you are. *Dios mío*, I saw him with his hand down your shirt, Fia.'

Flashbacks from that moment in the doctor's lounge came to her. 'I thought he had heard you in time to step away,' she said, then slapped her hand over her mouth when she realised she had just admitted Bella was right.

The satisfied flash in her friend's eyes told her she had noticed, too. 'No, I backed away and made sure to approach the lounge with more…audible steps,' she said. 'Sebastián thought something might be going on between you two as well. And I wouldn't be surprised if other people have noticed the steamy looks you've been giving each other across the ER.'

Steamy looks? Had they really let themselves get wrapped up in their affair so much that it had become obvious to everyone? Sofia hid her face behind her hands, releasing a quiet groan. But despite the embarrassment burning in her cheeks, her breaths came easier than they had in the last few weeks as a weight lifted off her. If Bella knew, then she finally had someone to talk to.

'It's not a relationship. It's a…situationship. He's leaving next week to who knows where, and I'll probably never see him again. Carlos has already been icing me out,' she said as she peeled her hands from her face.

Isabella tilted her head to the side. 'He's withdrawn from you?' she asked, and Sofia nodded.

Though each night still ended with them together, she sensed that his mind sometimes drifted away from the moments they shared, their conversations no longer flowing as freely as they used to. But whenever she asked him if something was the matter, he wouldn't respond—pulling her into a kiss or an embrace instead. Sofia had noticed this pattern in him before, whenever she'd asked him personal questions, and she understood that sometimes it was easier to express one's thoughts with touch and actions—but it was just as easy to avoid them in the same manner.

Was he trying to tell her something or avoiding having to open up to her?

The answer wasn't clear.

'I think it's because he's leaving soon and doesn't want to drag things out. We said this would only be about sex.'

'And is it?'

Sofia paused, the word 'yes' getting stuck in her throat. Bella had caught her earlier lie with such ease, she didn't believe she could get away with another one. One that was far closer to her heart. So she shook her head, her gaze dropping down to where her hands began fiddling with the plastic cup of water to release some of the nervous tension.

'Nope… I've caught feelings for him, and now I'm an emotional mess because I wasn't supposed to fall in love with him.' She resisted the urge to hide behind her hands again as the tension flowed out of her. There they were. The words she'd been dreading saying finally spilled out into the open.

Isabella's expression softened at her words, at the quiet agony she was sure the other woman could hear. Sofia had fallen in love with the one man she'd promised not to, and there was no way out of the web he'd spun around her.

'Obviously, I have no hope of ever being with him, so I just have to…wait for it to pass.' Waiting for that tiny spot of light in her chest to sputter out.

'Why do you have no hope of ever being with him?'

Sofia paused, her brow furrowing. Was that some kind of trick question? 'Because…he's leaving the hospital.'

'Ah yes…' Isabella breathed out, and Sofia almost missed the hint of an expression on her face. But she'd worked with her long enough to understand all her friend's non-verbal cues that were essential for a good working relationship in high-pressure environments like an ER.

Sofia leaned further in. 'Bella… What aren't you telling me?'

The other woman shook her head. 'Nothing that should concern you,' she replied, her mouth thin as she pressed her lips together.

'Spit it out. I told you my secret. You owe me one.'

Her heart beat against her chest in an uneven stutter as her mind came up with all the worst-case scenarios. Was Carlos already gone? Had he told the hospital leadership about their 'situationship'?

Isabella glanced around. 'After talking to the chief of surgery about the results we're seeing in the OR, Sebastián offered Carlos a permanent position here.'

Sofia's eyes rounded. The chief wanted Carlos to stay? Did Carlos want that, too? The lack of knowledge she possessed about this man came rushing back at her when she found herself unable to predict how he would react. She was almost certain that his late wife was the reason he didn't stay in Brazil, but did it mean he had to keep moving?

'What did he say?' Sofia almost didn't dare to ask that question. Because if she learned that he'd declined the offer straight away, that small ray of hope would fade into nonexistence when she had only just now admitted to it. Would he really not talk to her about this before making a decision? Okay, she wasn't his girlfriend, but did she really mean that little to him?

'Apparently he said—'

A shrill beep interrupted Isabella, and Sofia looked down as she unclipped the pager from her waistband. Her blood chilled when she read the message on the small screen.

911-OR 2-Dr CC-pressure.

Pressure? Carlos was under pressure in OR Two? What kind of emergency was he dealing with that he had to...

Sofia jumped from her chair when the meaning of the message clicked into place. Pressure. Carlos was having a panic attack during surgery.

'I have to go,' she said, hurrying to pick up the chair where it had clattered to the floor from her sudden jolt upright.

'Wait, do you not want to know—'

'No time. Carlos needs me in the OR.' The content and direction of their conversation were wiped from Sofia's mind, along with any of her inner turmoil as she sprinted towards the surgical floor—towards Carlos.

CHAPTER ELEVEN

CHAOS ERUPTED AROUND her when Sofia entered the OR, and her eyes widened as she assessed the scene. Carlos had his hand in the chest of the patient, counting evenly under his breath as his arm moved. Was he performing a cardiac massage?

Her silent question was answered when he took his arm out, and the surgeon assisting him inserted the paddles of an internal defibrillator into the chest cavity. Everyone stood back from the patient, who only slightly bowed off the table when the electricity jolted through her.

The monitor continued to emit a flat tone. Sofia stepped closer to the patient as Carlos's hand went back to do the cardiac massage. She could see his chest rising and falling in a faster than normal rhythm. His skin looked pale and sweaty, his eyes focused on whatever his hands were doing. Something during the surgery had triggered him, and this was the result.

'How long has the patient been in asystole?' Sofia asked the anaesthetist sitting at the head of the patient, who wore a look of concern on her face.

'Eleven minutes.'

'What about a pupil response?' She watched as the anaesthetist got up from her chair, slipping a small penlight out of her pocket and lifting the closed lids of the patient. She checked the patient's eyes, then shook her head.

'Palpable pulse anywhere?' Sofia looked at the junior doctor this time, who set the paddles down to check for a pulse at various locations on the body before stepping away with another headshake.

Glancing at the tray to the side of the anaesthetist, she could see they had administered several rounds of epinephrine without getting any results, either. Her heart clenched when she looked towards Carlos, who was still performing a cardiac massage and not willing to give up—even though the patient had.

'Dr Cabrera,' she called out, putting as much steel in her voice as she dared without plunging him deeper into whatever cycle he was descending into. She needed to get him out of this situation. 'We've lost the patient. She's gone. Please call the time of death so we can inform her next of kin.'

Carlos slowed the squeezing of his hand, looking up at Sofia through eyes that were struggling to stay in the moment. But he heard her, which was a good sign. She could get through to him and ground him. 'I will call it,' she said softly, intending the words only for his ears.

When he nodded, she swallowed the sigh of relief and looked at the clock hanging on the wall. 'Time of death is 17:21,' she announced, then looked at the junior doctor. 'Go update the chart and then find out if her next of kin is already here. If so, just tell them that the surgeon will be out to update them shortly. We'll take care to close her up.' She looked at the anaesthetist with her last sentence, who nodded and flipped the switches on the monitor before gathering her things and leaving.

When the doors to the OR swung shut and they were alone, Sofia circled around to Carlos's side. 'You paged me with the word "pressure" because you sensed the panic attack incoming, didn't you?'

Carlos's breath came fast, his hands finally ceasing their attempt at resuscitation, and they fell to his sides. 'She's… I couldn't help her, and she—' His words faded into a mumble she couldn't understand, and Sofia swallowed her mounting concern to focus on calming him. Embracing him was out of the question in their situation or they might risk contaminating each other.

'Okay, let's try to ground you. I have brushed up on PTSD-induced panic attacks since the last time. I know you must be familiar with the five-four-three-two-one technique.' She paused, wrapping her hands around his wrists and pulling him towards her and away from the patient until he could only see Sofia.

'Tell me about five things you can see,' she prompted him.

His eyes darted around, and Sofia strengthened her grip around his wrists to keep him from turning. Whatever had triggered him had to do with the patient. She didn't want him looking anywhere else until she had pulled him out of this panic attack.

'The heart rate monitor, the yellow biohazard waste bin, the OR lights, my hands…your hands.' He said each word slowly and with deliberation, moving from left to right as he named the objects he could see. The rate of his breathing decreased, and Sofia squeezed his wrists again with as much pressure as she could.

'Now look for four things you can touch,' she said to continue the exercise.

His hands curled into fists as his gaze dropped down.

'With your hands around my wrists, I can only touch me and you,' he said, though his voice came through steadier than before.

'I know you're supposed to touch, but there is only so much you can do with gloves. Just observe what you *could* touch if you needed to,' she replied, loosening her grip slightly.

'The heart rate monitor, the instrument tray, myself and you.' Then his hands slackened again, his palms turning upwards. 'Is the family here? I need to…speak to them.'

Her heart squeezed tight at his question. Even through his panic attack, he still tried to think of his patient first.

'You're not in any shape to talk to the family, Carlos. They just lost someone dear to them. Their grief won't help with your panic.' Though she understood his desire to speak to the family, the part inside her that cared way too deeply for his well-being and happiness wanted to shield him from the experience—even if she knew that as a doctor, he had to tell the family what had happened in his OR. 'Now tell me three things you can hear.'

'The ticking of the clock, the rustling of our gowns, your voice.' Sofia paused, her eyes still on his, not sure if she should continue. She worried about the next step— naming two things he could smell. Because as with any long surgery, the sterile scent of the OR had been replaced with the coppery tang of blood. If his senses grabbed onto that, his panic might rise all over again.

'Are you able to move?' She breathed out a sigh of relief when Carlos nodded, and she led him to the bio-hazard bin he had named a few moments ago to discard their gloves and gowns before pushing him out the door into the scrub room.

'I'll page one of the trainees to come and close her up,' Sofia said, and not even a second later, the door swung open as the doctor who'd been assisting Carlos came back in.

'The family is here, Dr Martinez. They're waiting in the meeting room,' he said, and Sofia gave him a grateful nod.

'Please close the patient up and get her transported to a room so they can see her when they're ready. I'll go inform the family.'

Carlos stretched his hand out when she moved to walk past him, grabbing her by the arm. 'She's my patient. I should be the one to tell them,' he said, and even though she knew he was trying hard to calm himself, she could still hear the slight wobble in his voice. Whatever he wanted anyone to think, she *knew* he was not fine.

But she couldn't disagree with him in front of the staff, or she might accidentally reveal his diagnosis. So she nodded, but followed him out the door.

There was only one meeting room on their floor, and it was reserved for the times they needed to talk to families of patients who hadn't made it through surgery. Carlos had never dreaded going into that room to have the tough conversation—until this moment.

He'd received the page to go to OR Two for an emergency surgery. Since all the other surgeons were occupied, he'd had to cut his rounds short to rush to the operating room. A pang of nerves had fluttered in the pit of his stomach as he pushed the doors open, and when he saw the unconscious woman lying on the operating table, the all-too-familiar sound of his blood rushed through his ears.

Unlike many other times when he'd had to work through rising panic while treating a patient who reminded him of Rosa, this time the grounding techniques had failed to keep him from slipping into the blackness of his panic attack. He'd kept it at bay for the majority of the surgery until it became clear that the damage to the patient was too great for them to fix it—and he was once again confronted with his powerlessness.

Another person he couldn't save. How many did that make?

As the blackness had crept in, he'd had the foresight to page Sofia with a code word he hoped she would understand. He'd retreated from her in the last few days as his last shift at Hospital General de Buenos Aires approached, but though he'd kept her at arm's length during the day, his resolve had crumbled whenever he spotted her on the way out—and they'd ended up at his place over and over again.

Twice now had he relied on Sofia to pull him out of a sticky situation, and he wondered why he had such a poor grip on his symptoms when they hadn't been that hard to manage in the past. He took his medication religiously, needing it to function in the high-stress environment of a hospital.

Was it because of his closeness to Sofia? Though it had ebbed and flowed in the years since Rosa's death, the guilt over what had happened remained his steady companion, reminding him to never be that careless again—to keep people out because *he* couldn't be trusted to have them. The pain he had grown so used to had dulled, sometimes even fading away altogether when he was with Sofia—and a small part of him had begun to wonder what would happen if he let her in.

That he would want her as much as he did had not been part of the plan. And that inner turmoil had his nerves stretched so thin, they were close to snapping—and had finally done so during surgery.

Yet Sofia had been the one to fix it…

Nausea roiled in his stomach as he stood in front of the closed door of the meeting room, running the script of what to say in his head. This was just like any other bad outcome, the words exactly the same ones he had said many times over. This was not Rosa, and he wouldn't stand face-to-face with her parents as he told them what happened.

No, behind those doors waited the parents of Valentina Alvarez.

'Are you okay?' Sofia stood behind him, close enough for him to sense the warmth from her body radiating into his back.

He shook his head, inhaling while he counted and then repeating the same on the exhale. He was not okay, and he never would be. These last few weeks had almost convinced him that he might have a normal life again, that he might find it within himself to love again—to let a woman like Sofia love him in return. But he couldn't do it. No matter how much he wished otherwise.

The blackness of his panic came rushing back in with a vengeance that stole all the breath from his lungs. The deep breaths became shallow, and his eyes darted around in search of something to anchor him, but the edges of his vision blurred with each passing second until the world became shapeless and vague around him.

'Carlos, honey…' Sofia must have sensed something, for she put her hand on his shoulder, giving it a reassuring squeeze. A spark travelled down that arm, but fizzled out before he could grasp it. It had been bound to happen. Nothing could take root when faced with the overwhelming guilt inside of him.

'Could…you please speak to the family? I can't do it.' Her grip on him tightened as he admitted to this failure. The words tasted bitter on his tongue, but his muscles were seizing up at the thought of going into that room, his throat almost too tight to speak the words he had just said.

'Of course.' There was nothing but understanding in her voice, and that just threw him further into the pit he found himself in. Would she be this sympathetic towards him if she knew what he had done? That it was his fault his wife had died? He doubted she would find that much compassion in her heart for him if she knew. Maybe she would even regret having met him at all…

'Thanks.' He mumbled the word before shaking her hand off his shoulder to find a place in the hospital where the air wasn't so thick he could choke—like he was choking right now.

Despite only coming in at the end of the surgery, Sofia felt confident in giving the parents of Valentina Alvarez all the information about what had happened to their daughter—and providing as much compassion as she could. It wasn't easy to be the bearer of bad news, and she had never let herself get complacent enough to become used to being the messenger. But emergency medicine produced more bad outcomes than any other discipline, so talking to a distraught family was a regular part of her job.

She'd put the moment with Carlos to the back of her mind, pushing it down into a little compartment where it would sit untouched until she had the time to deal with it. It was a skill she'd learned early in her training as a trauma surgeon. Even in the OR, she needed to compartmentalise different concurrent emergencies to focus on the place that needed most of her attention.

Now that she had left the family to grieve, she could get back to Carlos—and what had happened to him. Something inside her had told her he still wasn't well when they stepped out of the OR, despite his assurances that he was fit to speak to the family. That instinct had her sticking close to him, and the nearer they got to the room where the family waited for them, the more signs of another panic attack looming appeared on his body.

Without thinking, Sofia let her feet carry her to the ER, where she now stood in front of the supply closet in which they had shared several moments. She wasn't sure if he'd ever disclosed his condition to the hospital administration, and she'd figured it was none of her business. Up to this day, it hadn't interfered with patient care. But now that it had, something inside of her cracked. She had to tell Sebastián, didn't she? Sure, Carlos was leaving in a few days, but a lot could happen in that time span. What if he had another panic attack, and she wasn't here to help him?

But before she spoke to the chief, she'd talk to Carlos first. Give him the chance to do it himself.

Taking a deep breath to steel her resolve, Sofia pushed the door handle down, slipped through the open crack of the door, and then locked it behind her. What she found inside wrenched at her heart.

Carlos sat on a box stacked on the floor, his hand bracing his forehead as he stared down at the floor. His breath was steadier than she had expected, showing some signs of calm, but sweat still gleamed on his skin, which lacked its usual vibrancy. The exact hue of his skin had become so ingrained in her memory that any small deviation appeared huge in her mind.

'Carlos…' She sank to the floor in front of him, sitting down cross-legged so her knees were touching his shins. 'Are you doing okay?'

She asked the question, knowing full well he wasn't anywhere near okay, and was wrestling with a lot of different emotions. Asking if he was okay felt wholly inadequate for the situation they were in, but she lacked any other words to express herself…except maybe the truth? 'I'm worried about you.'

Carlos let out a sharp exhale, his eyes squeezing shut for several breaths before he raised his head to look at her. 'It seems to be worse here than in other hospitals I've worked in, and I have asked myself why. Female car crash victims in their twenties are a trigger for me because of Rosa, but I've *always* kept my composure in past situations. Not once did anyone have to rescue me in my own surgery.'

Rosa? Was that his wife? Had they been in a car accident that resulted in her death? A shudder ran through Sofia at the thought, and how often he had to expose himself to the same traumatic event as a surgeon working in emergency medicine.

'Are you in treatment for your panic disorder?' Even though she wanted to know more about Rosa, she swallowed any questions bubbling up. She craved that information, but she wouldn't want to get it when he wasn't at his best.

He gave a terse nod, his gaze dropping back to the floor. 'My psychiatrist is in Brazil. I haven't seen him in a while, but my medication works just fine, so there was no reason to keep seeing him.'

Sofia stretched out a hand, gently wrapping it around his calf. 'Maybe it's not working any more if your panic attacks are increasing. If the severi—'

'My panic attacks are increasing because I *killed* my wife, and now I'm trying to move on with my life like it had never happened. I have let myself think that I can be happy again—that I could be deserving of someone's affection after so long.' The words poured forth with an intensity that rippled through her.

Sofia's blood ran cold as she processed what he had said. The hurt etched into his voice tore at her skin, leaving her breathless for a few moments as the meaning of what he'd just said settled between them. He had done what...?

The rational side of her brain kicked in, and she forced her own anxiety into a box so she could focus on one thing at a time. There was no way he had done anything to his late wife or he wouldn't be sitting across from her right now. Sofia might not know a lot about Carlos or his past, but she knew the person he was deep down inside.

'Your panic attacks are triggered by the victims of motor vehicle accidents. Were you the driver?' she asked as she put her thoughts in order.

Carlos took a deep breath and nodded. 'We were on our way home from...somewhere. I can't remember the details any more, only that it was later than usual. We were having an argument, and then everything just went...dark.'

The brittleness in his voice was a sound Sofia had never heard from him, and it tore at her along with the pain contorting his face. She didn't know what to say, didn't have enough details to comfort him or give him a new perspective—though she still doubted he was truly responsible for what he was describing.

'I woke up at the hospital to the news that a drunk driver had hit the passenger side of the car as we crossed an intersection and that Rosa was killed instantly,' he continued, a deep exhale leaving his body as he said those words.

Her hand remained wrapped around his calf, squeezing it now and then to signal to him that she was still here—still listening. The extent of his trauma hit her, and all the disjointed things she knew about Carlos fused together to reveal the larger picture of who he was. There was no family waiting for him in Brazil because Rosa had been that family, and he spent his time travelling from place to place because he was untethered. Sofia had believed him to be a charming playboy, having a different woman in each city he visited, but she couldn't have been more wrong.

Was she the first person to grab his attention since his wife passed away? The thought sent conflicting waves of heat and cold through her. Sofia didn't want to believe the feeling rising within her, the desperate hope that maybe he felt the same way about her as she did about him.

'A drunk driver hit you from the side and you blame yourself?' The words sounded harsher than she intended, more like a criticism than a genuine question. Carlos's head snapped back up to level a stare at her, and her breath hitched at the steel in his eyes.

'I was distracted, arguing about something I can't even remember. What if there had been any warning signs? Maybe I could have heard the car coming if only...' His voice trailed off as he shook his head.

'If you were treating such a patient in the ER, would you agree with that? Because I think you would point out how powerful survivor's guilt can be in distorting what really happened.' She didn't back down from his gaze.

'So you're just another person telling me what I have seen and felt and experienced isn't true—isn't *valid*.' Sofia took a breath, steadying herself as the words found their mark. She knew what he was doing, knew he was seeking validation for the narrative that kept him from letting people get too close to him.

'What I'm saying is that I understand you have a long way to go until you can forgive yourself. I'm telling you that I see you for who you are—a brilliant and compassionate man, who struggles with his demons like many of us.' Sofia unfolded her legs, twisting them behind her until she was on her knees and close to eye level with him. Her breath shook, but her hands remained steady as she reached out, framing his face with her hands.

Carlos took a sharp breath, but he didn't pull away. Her thumbs stroked over his cheekbones, each sweep sending a tingle down her arms. 'I'm saying that I see both the light and dark in you. I see it all, and I still want you.'

A stuttering sigh left her as the words she'd been longing to say flowed out of her. The truth hung between them, but Sofia wasn't scared of it. She thought she would have been, had believed Daniel had caused so much damage to her heart and soul that she would never recover. But staying away from the man she loved, from a future with him just because she'd been burned before, was exactly the thing she *shouldn't* do. The best revenge would be to lead her best life. And she would always question if that life could have included Carlos if she didn't have enough courage to ask.

She leaned in so that their noses touched, leaving some distance between them to give him a choice. She didn't have to wait long until he closed the gap between them, sliding his mouth over hers. Tranquillity washed over her as his lips moved against hers, as his familiar taste and scent thundered through her. Everything inside of her relaxed as the positive answer sunk into her mind. He was choosing her, too.

Elation carried her away into the clouds—and then her stomach swooped as she fell out of them when Carlos wrenched his mouth away and stood up, putting distance between them. Her heart cracked under the regretful expression on his face as he shook his head. 'I can't be… I'm not free to give myself to you, Sofia.' His throat worked as he looked at her, and each breath he took looked to be as much of a struggle as hers felt.

'There's a reason I don't stay anywhere longer than a few months, including here. It's because…' His voice trailed off, his hand balling into a fist. Sofia could see the mental battle going on, of whether he should trust her with whatever was going on. Was that why they were doomed to fail? Because even now, when she'd seen him broken down, he still hesitated?

'Because you need to keep running away from your problems. I get it.' She couldn't keep the bitterness out of her words—didn't even try. Agreement or not, she had put herself out there for him to hold on to if he wanted. Which, as it turned out, he didn't. She pushed past him and pulled the door open, but then paused to look at him. 'Ever wonder why your problems are already there waiting for you whenever you arrive at a new place?'

Then she turned around and walked away, her heart tearing in two with every step that took her away from the man she loved.

CHAPTER TWELVE

WHY WAS THE ER so quiet? Sofia would never dare to speak these words out loud lest she summoned some catastrophe to their doors. Though she wasn't superstitious, she knew there were important rules for keeping the harmony in the emergency room—and she didn't want to be the person to disrupt it.

The surgical board was empty, the ambulance bay quiet, and even the doctors in the ER didn't need her help. She found herself strolling down the corridor towards the trauma bays once more, poking her head into each one to ask if they needed any assistance. Two were empty, one was being cleaned, and in the last one she found Sebastián in exactly the same position as the previous time she came by twenty-odd minutes ago—hunched over his laptop and staring at the screen.

'Are you haunting my ER?' he asked without looking up, and Sofia chose to interpret his words as an invitation to join him.

She hopped onto the exam table, sitting next to where the chief had his laptop. 'Don't you have an office to work from?'

'With Bella taking it easy, I have to pick up the slack on admin work and actual emergency medicine work, so it's easier to tuck myself away in a corner here and wait to be needed than run across the hospital several times a day,' he said. When Sofia lifted her hands to indicate the empty space around her, he shot her a warning look. 'Don't say it.'

'I wasn't going to! And here I thought I was in a bad mood, but you can have it all to yourself.' The moment she admitted to her bad mood, regret set in, and she prayed Sebastián wouldn't be nosy enough to ask her about it. She was almost certain he knew already. If Bella had noticed what went on between her and Carlos, then she would have told her husband.

'I think the same person put us in a bad mood,' Sebastián replied, and she raised her eyebrows at that.

'Huh? What did Carlos do to you?' Ever since their fight in the supply closet, Sofia hadn't seen much of him at the hospital. They were avoiding each other, which was working rather well. She'd asked the charge nurse to page her instead of him with any motor vehicle accidents coming in, and had left Carlos alone to do whatever he needed to before leaving Buenos Aires. Before forgetting about what had happened between them.

She couldn't forget though—not once she had peered into the Pandora's box that was her wealth of feelings for him. So instead, she had spent the last few days convincing herself that she wasn't capable of a casual *or* serious relationship at this point in her life. Because what was supposed to have been casual had developed into serious far quicker than she'd anticipated—and just like with Daniel, she was now alone again to pick up the pieces.

'He refused the hospital's offer of a permanent position. I'm not surprised he did, but that still leaves us with too few surgeons and ER doctors alike.' He shot her a glance. 'What happened between you two? Just last week, you were glued to each other.'

Sofia let out a groan as the memories of their confrontation came back—along with the feelings inside her chest. Had they really been that obvious with their affection for one another? Everyone had noticed and yet he'd still rejected her?

'It wasn't anything serious. We just got a bit carried away with all the...sex.' Because that was what it had been, right? Nothing more than the two of them enjoying each other's company without any strings attached. Though she didn't quite know how Sebastián had suddenly become her confidant, so she quickly added, 'Not that you want to hear about that.'

To her surprise, he closed the laptop and leaned back to look up at her, his hands folded in front of him. 'You know Bella and I struggled in our marriage. It took us quite a while to find our way back to each other. Why don't you humour me?'

'What's there to say? I'm sure your wife already gave you an update on what happened after I told her all about Carlos. You couldn't have told me that we were being so painfully obvious?' She replayed certain moments in time where she had believed them to be unobserved, but now she wondered how many people had actually seen them together. Not that it mattered. He was gone now.

'You two were *trying* to be discreet. Who am I to burst that bubble for you?' he asked with a shrug.

'The chief of emergency medicine? Shouldn't you be the first one to discourage a secret relationship between two staff members?' Sofia wasn't certain why she was arguing against her own case. Maybe the blatant disregard for the rules was finally catching up with her. Maybe that's why they hadn't worked out…

Sebastián called her out. '*Now* you care about the rules? But while you were having fun, you didn't care all that much? Sofia…' He shook his head. 'I'm not *your* chief, but I do see him every day, and I can assure you that he would have as little of a problem as I do if you two made things official.'

Did she want to be with Carlos? She had told him so, had offered up her heart, only for him to walk away from it—from her. Just like every other man in her life had. Not a single one had stuck through the trouble, stayed with her and figured out how to bridge the gaps. It broke her heart that she had to put Carlos on that list, too. He knew her life as a surgeon, knew her insecurities, and had always—*always*—ensured she was in a comfortable place. Whether that was dancing at the bar or making love back at his flat. He'd shown her how much he treasured her, only to walk away when she wanted to give it all back to him.

'He didn't want that. I…told him that I wanted him, but he said he wasn't interested,' she said after a stretch of quiet, reluctant to dip back into that particular memory.

'Did you tell him you loved him?' Sofia's head whipped around to look at Sebastián at the unexpected question.

'What? No, I didn't.'

Sofia buried her face in her hands, letting out a frustrated groan. 'I do love him, but I shouldn't. I've only known him for a month.'

'I've seen crazier things happen. You two went through several stressful surgeries together, and you've challenged him every time you thought he could do better. I can see why he fell in love with you,' Sebastián said with a casual shrug, but his words sent a trickle of hot and cold sensations racing down her spine.

'He's not in love with me, and he said as much when I poured my heart out to him,' she replied in an immediate defence. Sebastián raised his hands.

'I wasn't there, but Bella and I have both seen you struggle through some pretty bad relationships where you were trying to make yourself fit into a mould when you really should be with someone who appreciates you as you are. Cabrera was the first person to be your equal, where you didn't have to change anything about you to fit perfectly together—because from day one he saw you for who you are.' He paused, his fingers tapping on his closed laptop in a gesture she'd seen many times from him whenever he considered what to say next. 'Daniel really messed you up. We were all there for the fallout, and I think a part of you still believes that you have to choose between work and love. But you don't. The moment you're brave enough to let go of the hurt you're clinging to, you will see that—and then you'll tell him how you feel.'

Let go? Sofia leaned back until she was lying down on the exam table, staring up at the fluorescent lights glaring above her. Had she been carrying the hurt around for so long, never finding a place where she could bury it for once and for all? She knew deep inside that Sebastián was right, or his words wouldn't have shaken her as much as they had. With Daniel, she had believed she'd found someone that could run parallel to her life, who understood enough of her passion as a surgeon to accept the long hours, the abandoned dates and everything else that came with it.

But instead of being honest with her and telling her things weren't working out, he had taken it upon himself to get his needs met elsewhere. Carlos wasn't a dishonest person. In the depths of her heart, she knew that. If she told him how she felt, would his answer remain the same? Or was this the crucial piece of information missing for him to be able to make a decision?

'Am I letting my past experiences interfere with my life this much?' she asked out loud, needing to get the swirling voices out of her head.

'Of course you are. Who doesn't? That's how we learn not to touch the stovetop while it's still hot. We learn from our mistakes. But there's learning how to stand up for yourself better and then there's not even trying because it *might* hurt,' Sebastián replied, and his words shifted something into place that Sofia had already known for a while—yet had not wanted to acknowledge.

Because she was as scared that her involvement with Carlos could end in something spectacular as she was of it going just like any other relationship. She didn't *want* it to be like her previous relationships because that was how much he already meant to her. If Sebastián was right about that, could he also be right about Carlos loving her too?

'Do you know if he already left Argentina?' she asked when a tentative plan formed in her head.

'Sorry, I don't know anything about his future plans. Don't you have his phone number?'

Sofia did, but ever since that final moment in the supply closet, their text chain had remained quiet. Her fingers hovered over the keyboard more often than she cared to admit, but each attempt at a message had resulted in not a single word sent. But even if he was still in Buenos Aires, it was the first day of Carnival, and—

'I know where he is…' she breathed out, bolting upright and jumping off the table with a sudden burst of energy. 'He'll be at Carnival, at least for today. But… I have to stay here.'

This time Sebastián raised his hands—and one eyebrow—to indicate the almost silent ER around them. 'And what exactly are you going to miss here?'

Sofia sucked in a breath. 'But I get into trouble for even suggesting that it might be too qu—'

'You can hint at it, but you can't say the word, Martinez.' He shook his head in mock disapproval. 'Go find him and bring him back. He has transformed our efficiency like nothing else. I *want* him back. If there's an emergency coming in that we aren't able to handle with the junior doctors, I'll page you.'

She stared at him, processing his words, not quite sure if he meant it. Could she really leave, or was that just asking for trouble? Not that there was anything for her to do in the ER. All the injuries coming in were minor scrapes, bruises and a lot of alcohol poisoning. Nothing that needed a surgeon to help.

'Okay,' she said with a nod, her resolve firming. 'I will bring him back.'

Carnival was an explosion of colour and sound that swept Sofia up the second she stepped into the fray. The main procession wound its way down the main street, following the predetermined course from one side of the city to the other. Dancers stood on their floats, their costumes bright and loud as they flowed through their dance steps to the music playing from the speakers. People with drums and maracas stood amidst the spectators, filling the air with a beat that blended seamlessly with the notes the many troupes were playing just a few steps down. Though they were all following their own beat, somehow it blended together into an upbeat sound that embodied the Carnival vibes of Buenos Aires.

How long had it been since Sofia had come here just to enjoy herself? She couldn't answer the question, only remembering how much time she had spent in the OR on these days.

Carlos wouldn't be on one of the floats. He'd told her the capoeira group he belonged to would be performing their usual exhibition *jogos* at the Carnival to drum up some interest in their gym. Apparently most of their new members joined them because of Carnival. But knowing enough about capoeira now, she understood that they wouldn't be able to do their *jogos* on something that moved as much as a motorised float. No, they had to be one of the many dance and entertainment groups spilling over to the side streets.

Would it be hard to spot them? Sofia looked around her as she combed through the streets lined with food stands and collections of furniture people had pulled out of their flats nearby so everyone could sit together.

They would be forming a large circle of white-clad people, so surely this would catch her attention immediately? At least she really hoped it would. Nervous fingers went back to the pager on her waistband, making sure she hadn't missed anything from the ER. Though there were enough junior surgeons still around to consult, she was the senior person they relied on.

Standing at small crossroads, Sofia cast her glance

everywhere. Her step faltered when she saw someone in flowing white linen trousers sitting down on a chair underneath a tented area. A flag hung from the roof of the tent, a white background with a green cross on it. The medical tent.

A smile tugged at her lips when she recognised who was approaching the man sitting on the chair. So Gabriel was in charge of the medical tent? Bella must have asked him to step in for her, like she said she was going to. Then a woman in a wheelchair came into view, looking up at the paramedic before asking the man in the chair a question. Sofia furrowed her brow as she watched them. That must be the GP Bella had mentioned—Gabriel's childhood friend. Sofia wondered what her name was.

She squinted, trying to see the badge clipped to her scrub top, but then the man in the chair lifted his hand and pointed down one of the roads. Sofia perked up. The style of clothes he wore was unmistakable, and she was sure he was part of the capoeira troupe.

She glanced at her phone as she walked in the direction indicated, looking at the hour and checking for any messages from Sebastián. There wasn't much time until she was needed back at the hospital. Determined to find Carlos, she increased her pace, gazing up and down the little alleyways where people were drinking, dancing and celebrating, until she finally spotted the circle of white shirts and trousers along with the now familiar sound of the berimbau and atabaque droning a low and rhythmic beat for the *capoeiristas*.

She stepped closer. Her breath hitched when she saw Carlos leave the *roda* to enter the *jogo*. Luckily for her, he had decided to keep his shirt on, and she smiled when she recognised the logo of the gym emblazoned in dark red on the otherwise white shirt. He moved like he wasn't made out of flesh and bone, but rather a liquid he could form at his will, bending to dodge his opponent and then snapping back.

The control he showed during capoeira extended to the rest of his life, Sofia realised as she watched him. They had been going back and forth in their own *jogo*, each one giving as much as they took, weaving in and out of each other's space without their lives ever truly touching. They had both done it to avoid letting the other one get too close. Her because of Daniel and how he had wrecked her confidence, and him because no one had ever shown him that he was still deserving of love and tenderness in the face of loss.

This would stop now. Sofia would either succeed in laying her heart out for real, making him see everything there was between them—or she would leave here at the very least knowing she had tried to touch his heart. Even if the whole point of their affair had been not to.

Sweat dripped down his brow as Carlos dropped low to avoid a kick, then used the momentum to surge back up and cartwheel to the side as the third *capoeirista* engaged the *jogo*. Then he caught a glimpse of a familiar pair of golden eyes watching him. But before he could process that, he was drawn back into the game, and the cheers around them grew louder.

Was she…? He spun around again, scanning the crowd, but none of them—

His eyes widened when he saw Sofia standing behind the first row of white-clad people, looking at him with an adoration so intense it hit him straight in the stomach—causing him to lose his footing on the next step. He still evaded his opponent's strike, but had to fall backwards and catch himself with his hands. Using the momentum, he pushed himself into a handstand and then flipped backwards to land near the edge of the *roda*, where he tagged someone else in to take his place.

Sofia was here, and the need to know why burned through him. Why would she seek him out again after their last encounter?

Ever since pushing her away, Carlos had tossed and turned in his bed each night, trying to deny to himself how much he missed her. How every day he woke up by himself had been worse for exactly that reason. But he couldn't admit—couldn't accept—how deeply Sofia had dug into his heart, finding the place he had guarded so closely for the last five years, and settling in there with grace and ease. As if she had been born with the key to that door in her hand.

But he couldn't let her wield that key. Not when his heart still bled from the last time, the guilt still gnawing at him whenever he sought it out. He couldn't...yet the last month had brought his soul back to life like nothing—*no one*—else had. Sofia was...everything. Everything he wanted from someone in his life. A person who challenged him, who held him to the same high standards as he had for other people. She was passionate about her work, quick on her feet in the OR, and when their bodies moved against each other—be it on the bed or on the dance floor—he could hear the song of the stars moving through the universe.

Carlos knew he had lost his heart to her the first time they'd danced together in that bar. With her body pressed against his, he could not only see the expression on her face change, but also feel how her muscles relaxed against him with each step. The spark in her eyes that had appeared when she had figured out the right steps had almost undone him there and then. In that moment, he had realised it was over for him—he was in love with this woman.

So pushing her away had been one of the hardest things he'd had to do to save her from himself. Since she had been avoiding him at the hospital, he had thought it had worked. Yet here she stood, gazing at him with unveiled longing that pressed so hard against his chest, he was sure his ribs were about to cave in.

Carlos pushed his way through the crowd, then followed the circle of people until he stood face-to-face with her. His muscles seized up, tension rippling through his body as his mind projected the million different conversations that could happen in this moment. There was only one conversation he *wanted* to have, even though he wasn't allowed to yearn for it. Between now and last week, nothing had changed. He still had too much to atone for to let her into his life.

'What are you doing here?' he said when she stood in front of him with a silent smile curving her lips. All he wanted to do was to wrap his hands around her arms and pull her close to him to feel that smile against his own mouth.

'I came to talk to you,' she replied, her breath a bit unsteady. Had she rushed over here?

He dared to grab her by the arm and savoured the lightning shooting through his body at the touch. They weren't even embracing, yet the heat rising in him was as delicious as it was distracting. He knew he couldn't give in to that.

'Talk to me? Sofia, there is nothing left for us to talk

about,' he said as he pulled her into a small alleyway just past where the capoeira gym members had set up the *roda*. There were a few stands and people mingling around them, but the noise was less—the air more intimate.

'You don't get to decide that all your own. We were in this together, and I have my opinion on what should happen next. You don't have to agree with it, and my biggest fear is that I've simply misread the situation. That my feelings are a lot deeper than yours.'

Her voice wobbled at the last few words, revealing the effort it took her to speak. Carlos couldn't fight the instinct to comfort her. Didn't want to fight it, either. Because when it came to Sofia, he was finding fewer and fewer reasons within himself to fight what was happening between them. Not when she was putting herself out there for him like this. All she had done, and all she was doing—it had all been for him. He knew that in the depth of his heart, yet she stood in front of him right now, questioning how he felt about her.

'Sofia… You're not…' Carlos paused, searching for words that refused to come. How could he tell her about his feelings for her—when he couldn't give himself to her? Feelings and intentions wrestled inside of him, each one struggling to get the upper hand.

Sofia took a deep breath. 'I see you struggling, and I *want* to help. I *want* to be the person that you talk to about your struggles, about your fears, about how guilty you feel on the inside. I want to be this person for you, if you let me. Sure, I haven't been through the trauma you have, but I've seen enough in life to empathise with your hurt.'

His heart lurched when she swallowed so hard he

could hear it even over the surrounding noise. 'You don't know what it's like to live with this heaviness inside of me. I could never burden you with this and watch it dim your light. You mean too *much* to me for that. Not too little.'

He inhaled sharply in unison with Sofia as the words shot out of his mouth, admitting to the thing he was fighting so hard.

'I do know. Maybe not what it's like to lose your spouse, but I *do* know what it's like to carry so much guilt around inside yourself. I *do*. And keeping me at arm's length is not going to help you find a way ahead.' She paused, determination burning in her eyes. 'I'm telling you—I know you. I don't need details to know you. You're not someone that's satisfied with patching over holes.'

Her fists clenched at her sides. She pushed her chin out in that gesture of challenge he'd seen every single day since starting at Hospital General de Buenos Aires. She had never once backed down from a fight, letting him know exactly what she thought of him—even now.

Was that what he had been doing? Patching over holes inside of him rather than putting in the effort to properly fix what was broken? It sounded so unlike him, yet he couldn't explain the choices he'd made since that night because he had simply wanted to leave. To leave every reminder of Rosa behind.

'I don't know what to do about this…' The words left him with a heavy breath, and Carlos took a step back, leaning against the wall of the building behind him while staring at his feet.

'You do know. How else would you have taught all of us how to do it? You look at the entire patient, and then you prioritise where to focus first. Carlos…' His name from her lips caused a shower of sparks to trickle through him. Her feet sounded over the worn-out cobblestone as she stepped closer, and then her hands were on his cheeks, pulling him upward until they were looking at each other.

'You're no longer alone in this, *amor*,' she said, her thumbs sweeping over his cheekbones. 'No matter how much you carry around inside you, how much you beat yourself up, I'm not going to freak out and bail. Not on you. I love you.'

The words sent a jolt through him, waking up all his nerve endings and ordering them to go haywire. Something inside him expanded, and he realised it was the spot where Sofia had already made her nest.

For five years, he'd chosen fear. The fear of admitting he'd caused the tragedy that had happened to him. A fear of opening up to people in case they would leave him—or see the things inside of him and run. Fear that sat so deep inside of him, he had welcomed it as his steadfast companion without realising how much it held him back from living his life.

Because choosing fear was easier than confronting it—like Sofia was doing right now. He had pushed her away, choosing his fear of her eventually fading out of his life over the possibility of a lifetime spent with her. But she had chosen differently, had come here to tell him that. To…fight for him.

'I love you, too,' he whispered. As the words left his lips, a weight lifted—unshackled by the admission. Sofia had seen him at his worst, had helped him through his struggle even before they had agreed to their affair.

Even now, instead of letting him run away again, she had come to find him.

Her eyes rounded, and she breathed out, 'What?' The grip around his face tightened, her fingers grasping at him as if he could float away any second.

'I'm far from perfect, Sofia. You know that better than anyone else has in the last five years. And you're right. Instead of confronting my problems, I chose to patch over them and run away. A part of me still wants to run.' He wasn't proud to admit that, but he needed to show her *everything* if this was to work. 'I…want to get help. I want to be a better man. For you.'

'Carlos…' Her breath caught in her throat in a small hiccup, and he reached out, wrapping his hands around her waist and pulling her against him. One hand slid into her hair, cupping the back of her neck.

'Thank you for finding me. Again.' Because that's what Sofia had done for him time and again. No matter how hard he'd tried to hide, even from himself, she had found him—and hadn't once retreated from what she'd seen.

He leaned back, pulling her face towards his until their lips met in a kiss that went all the way to his bones.

Carlos had chosen fear for so long, it was hard to fight the instinct. But what wasn't hard was giving his all to the woman softly moaning underneath the press of his lips. She, who had seen him for what and who he was after he had spent the last five years building walls so far and wide that no one would ever dare to even approach him.

For Sofia, he would try anything.

* * * * *

COMING SOON!

MILLS & BOON®

Coming next month

HER SUMMER WITH THE BROODING VET
Scarlet Wilson

Eli's hand lifted and rested on Aurora's hip, just as her own palm tightened on his arm, almost like she was willing him even closer.

They moved in unison. Lips brushing together for the briefest of seconds before they locked entirely. Her hands wrapped around his neck, the length of her body pressed up against his.

His lips moved to her face, her ear and her neck and she let out the tiniest groan. He could taste her perfume on his lips, feel it with every inhale.

She let out a breath, and stepped back, nervous laughter filling the air between them. Her pupils were dilated, the green of her eyes nearly invisible.

'Whoa,' he said, trying to catch his breath.

'Whoa,' she repeated, a broad smile across her face.

Continue reading
HER SUMMER WITH THE BROODING VET
Scarlet Wilson

Available next month
millsandboon.co.uk

LET'S TALK
Romance

Follow us:

- **f** Millsandboon
- **𝕏** @MillsandBoon
- **◉** @MillsandBoonUK
- **♪** @MillsandBoonUK

For all the latest titles and special
offers, sign up to our newsletter:

Millsandboon.co.uk

afterglow BOOKS

Afterglow Books is a trend-led, trope-filled list of books with diverse, authentic and relatable characters, a wide array of voices and representations, plus real world trials and tribulations. Featuring all the tropes you could possibly want (think small-town settings, fake relationships, grumpy vs sunshine, enemies to lovers) and all with a generous dose of spice in every story.

♪ @millsandboonuk
⃝ @millsandboonuk
afterglowbooks.co.uk
#AfterglowBooks

For all the latest book news, exclusive content and giveaways scan the QR code below to sign up to the Afterglow newsletter:

SCAN ME

Never Date A Roommate
PBO 9780263322897 £8.99
Ebook 9780008938420 | Audio 9780263324860
For publicity enquiries please contact
millsandboonpressoffice@harpercollins.co.uk

OUT NOW!

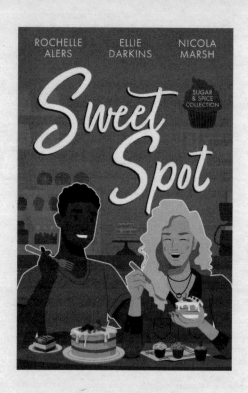

Available at
millsandboon.co.uk

MILLS & BOON

MILLS & BOON

THE HEART OF ROMANCE

A ROMANCE FOR EVERY READER

MODERN

Prepare to be swept off your feet by sophisticated, sexy and seductive heroes, in some of the world's most glamourous and romantic locations, where power and passion collide.

HISTORICAL

Escape with historical heroes from time gone by. Whether your passion is for wicked Regency Rakes, muscled Vikings or rugged Highlanders, awaken the romance of the past.

MEDICAL

Set your pulse racing with dedicated, delectable doctors in the high-pressure world of medicine, where emotions run high and passion, comfort and love are the best medicine.

True Love

Celebrate true love with tender stories of heartfelt romance, from the rush of falling in love to the joy a new baby can bring, and a focus on the emotional heart of a relationship.

HEROES

The excitement of a gripping thriller, with intense romance at its heart. Resourceful, true-to-life women and strong, fearless men face danger and desire - a killer combination!

 afterglow BOOKS

From showing up to glowing up, these characters are on the path to leading their best lives and finding romance along the way – with plenty of sizzling spice!

To see which titles are coming soon, please visit

millsandboon.co.uk/nextmonth